THE BLACK FIRE

Michael Donovan was born in Yorkshire and now lives in Cumbria. A consultant engineer by profession, his first novel *Behind Closed Doors* won the 2012 Northern Crime competition.

By the same author

The P.I. Eddie Flynn series

Behind Closed Doors
The Devil's Snare
Cold Call
Slow Light
The Black Fire

Crime Thrillers

The Watching

Praise for Michael Donovan's writing

'At a time when there seems more competition than ever in the crime-writing genre, Donovan's debut novel is a real winner...'
Lytham St Annes Express

'... a wonderful debut novel in a hugely competitive market ... an enthralling novel ... deliciously complex ... make(s) the readers hair stand on end. Donovan ... succeeds in breathing life into a host of warm, witty and realistic characters.'
Cuckoo Review

'Eddie Flynn is part Philip Marlowe, part Eddie Gumshoe, a likeable wisecracking guy but with a temper when roused ... humour ... violent confrontations ... well recommended.'
eurocrime

'... good old-fashioned detective work. A slick, dynamic mystery...'
Kirkus Reviews Recommended Book

'... one of the best novels I have read this year. Brilliantly absorbing ... escapism at its best.'
Postcard Reviews

'For many thriller fans, one read may not be enough.'
Best Thrillers

www.michaeldonovancrime.com

THE BLACK FIRE

MICHAEL DONOVAN

HOUSE ON THE HILL Publishing

CHAPTER ONE
The explosion would be limited

At nine a.m., two minutes after we'd opened, someone came into the outer office and stood talking to Lucy. I heard a male voice, businesslike but cheery. Something about the weather, which wasn't bad for May. The subject matter tagged the visitor as either a signed-for delivery guy or a tradesman come to fix one of the top floor's problems. Further down the probability scale was the possibility of a cheery client, something I'd never encountered.

I pushed paperwork aside and listened. I'd spent yesterday clearing a backlog of admin and reports but some of it had rolled over into this morning. The life of the real-world private investigator is not all movie material. Car chases and fights to the death accounted for less than one percent of what we did. I shouldn't complain: slow jobs and paperwork are a nice alternative to dying young, though everyone has their opinion. Our associate and veteran investigator Harry Green, for example, was out riding a dentist's chair, which he'd told me he actually preferred to paperwork.

Each to his own, etc.

I couldn't make out the conversation through my closed door so I pushed the keyboard away and ratcheted my Herman Miller executive chair to forty-seven point five degrees recline and got my feet up on the desk where they wouldn't be tempted to rush me out to check if we actually did have a client. If we did, it might appear over-eager.

Over in one of my guest chairs our corporate mascot, a brindle Staffie cross called Herbie who'd partnered up with me last Christmas, lifted his head and listened too, but he couldn't make out anything either. In the end he made do with a low growl. Looked at me to see if it was helping.

'Maybe,' I said. 'Let's see.'

He settled down to wait, ear up, eye open.

Thirty seconds later the voices stopped and I heard the outer door close. A delivery. Or a prospective client who'd taken a look at the place and run for the street.

1

I considered whether it was time to heed Lucy's advice and go for a reception make-over. Something to lure clients with a bright, modern image. By the time they saw our actual offices it would be too late. Up to now I'd resisted. Appearances weren't the thing. What we sold was superiority. We got things done. That's all our clients needed.

Herbie sighed and sank back into his chair. I sighed and wondered whether it was too early for a second coffee. Whether I could legitimately put the paperwork off until tomorrow. Then the door opened and Lucy came in, bright and cheery, with an envelope.

'Special delivery,' she said. 'Personal and private for you. Do you want to open it yourself?'

Normally Lucy opens all personal and private stuff but this was a fat padded envelope that looked out of place, like it was rigged to explode. Lucy was nosy but she wasn't stupid. I reached out. The package was heavy. Solid. I dug through my mind for the list of people who might be happy to see our building demolished. The list was unmanageable. If I started thinking that way we'd need an X-ray scanner.

I got my feet off the desk and racked the chair upright and slit the envelope open. Lucy held her ground. Assumed that any explosion would be limited. Just one casualty. In the event the envelope was non-explosive but its content was just as startling. I up-ended it and two wads of cash and a single sheet of paper dropped onto my desk. The cash had been split to fit inside the envelope and the wads where both an inch thick, which, if the notes were all the same fifties as the ones on the outside, made a stash of about ten thousand quid.

I picked up the sheet of paper. A plain typed note. I read it out to Lucy.

Eddie Flynn, Eagle Eye Limited.

They'd got that wrong. It was unlikely we'd ever pass the standards to register as a limited company but maybe it made the address sound a little more formal. Maybe comforted the sender with the sense that he was not dumping his ten K into the bin. I read on:

Please identify and locate the resident of Room 209
of the BestBreak Hotel, Marylebone.
Information to be texted to the number below.

Our reimbursement for the service is £20 thousand,
half payable on receipt of the information.

Please confirm that you are able to take on this
assignment and will complete it within 48 hours.

Enclosed: 50% reimbursement
Enclosed: key to Room 209.

Foxglove

I reached and tipped the envelope again and a grey plastic keycard dropped out, the old fashioned sort with punched holes. Apparently it would open the door to Room 209 at the BestBreak. I looked at Lucy. Her eyes were popping.

'Wow, Eddie,' she said. 'That's a lot of money for a few days' work.'

I tossed the envelope back onto the desk and laid the note where I could read the contact number. Reached for my phone.

'A hell of a lot,' I agreed. 'Probably intended to dissuade us from asking questions, such as who our client is or why his hotel guest needs identifying and locating, since both should be obvious. Or why he has the key to their room.'

'It's something fishy,' Lucy said.

The firm runs on this kind of expertise. Lucy followed up with a suspicious look. 'You think Foxglove is his real name?'

I grinned at her. The number rang through. Connected. Went straight to voicemail. I waited for the tone then spoke.

'This is Eddie Flynn of the Eagle Eye Agency,' I said. 'Thank you for your request but we do prefer a face-to-face relationship with our clients, and feel perhaps that this is not quite the job for us. Initial consultations are free so if you'd like your cash back just let us know the arrangement.'

I killed the line. Smiled at Lucy. Her eyes were popping even more.

'You've just turned down twenty thousand?' she said. 'Shouldn't we

3

at least talk to him?'

She had her eye on the bottom line, which was the stack of bills waiting on her desk. Maybe even that reception revamp. Twenty K could do a lot.

'If he calls in and shows his face,' I said, 'and explains what he's up to, then we might reconsider.'

Though I doubted it.

~~~~~

Big money, even money you've just turned down, makes you think big. The day was fine and warm, and two hours of paper-pushing demanded the reward of one of Connie's exorbitantly priced sandwiches and a half hour in the sun outside his café two doors down. Lucy had an afternoon job but she accepted the offer of a free lunch fast enough to tell me that she was looking for the opportunity to urge a rethink on Foxglove's offer. It wasn't too late to call him back.

We grabbed a pavement table and Connie came rushing out to urge his latest special on us and talk to Herbie who had learned that private investigators have more tidbits come their way than homeless guys do, though he'd never have dreamed of complaining to his previous owner, an old guy called William whom I'd helped out at the end of last year.

'What ya want?' Connie yelled at Herbie. 'What ya want, boy? Special kofte? Extra thick lamb, all *fatty* part?'

The trick was as dirty as it was obvious. We all knew what Herbie wanted and we also knew the Herbie wasn't paying the bill. On the other hand I wasn't planning on paying myself today so I went along and ordered the kofte with a glass of fizzy water. There'd be more than enough for me even after I'd offloaded half the meat. Lucy went for a salad baguette and diet Coke. Connie brought the drinks straight out and we sat and enjoyed the warmth.

'Why did he choose us?' Lucy asked. She was back on the twenty K thing, building up to her pitch.

'Reputation,' I guessed. We'd had our name in the papers a couple of times in the last year, publicity we hadn't sought but which didn't necessarily do the firm any harm. 'And the new yellow pages ad.

4

stands out with that border and photograph.'

Whether the photograph, which showed a mean-looking guy in a trilby watching a window, actually brought the clients in was questionable but you take what you get with budget art.

'We've got a good record,' Lucy agreed. 'Maybe this guy needs to know he'll get a result.'

Our results over the last twelve months had included two of our clients in jail for manslaughter and conspiracy, and a friend of my ex-girlfriend lying in a grave, but I got Lucy's point. The public impression overall was favourable. The public impression was that we always got our man.

'We need to stick to clients who are prepared to show their faces,' I said, forestalling her pitch. 'We need an idea what we're letting ourselves in for.'

Connie brought the sandwiches and I dug the fat and half the meat off the kofte and passed it to ground level. A businesslike snapping and slurping came up.

'Maybe the guy just wants to be discreet,' Lucy said. 'He might have a legitimate reason for finding his hotel resident.'

I clamped my sandwich between my teeth. Tore.

Legitimate, hell. Lucy's eye was on her reception area. New carpets, pastel colours, unframed oils on the walls, piped music. I guess the music could be tailored, at least – some kind of dirge to let the client know what he was floating towards. I quit chewing. Sipped water. Contemplated the rooftops.

'Twenty K,' I said, 'for maybe two or three days' work. Who's so important that you'd pay that kind of money to track them down?'

'Someone who's a threat,' Lucy said.

'Exactly. And if we found this guy we'd be helping to set up who knows what shenanigans. Twenty K is too good an offer. One we can do without. The guy will get the message from the voicemail.'

I was wrong.

When Herbie and I went back up we found Shaughnessy holding another envelope. Same courier service. Same manila envelope. Same anonymous sender.

Different tactic.

CHAPTER TWO
Maybe he's simply deranged

Shaughnessy knew about the morning's package. Lucy's grapevine. He watched while I tore open the new envelope.

I pulled the contents out. They weren't a return label. They were a folded sheet of paper enclosing three photographs.

The photographs were of three women I didn't know, somewhere out in the streets. One was an elegant blonde in her early thirties, squatting beside a child, maybe tying her laces, maybe after a fall. Behind her were railings and trees and the white facade of a neo Georgian terrace. A London square. The second photo was a different woman: tall; slender; long dark hair; business suit; early forties; walking purposefully towards the camera on a minor street that could have been any of a thousand. A scattering of pedestrians around her but it was clear that she was the subject. Same with the third photo. Another woman in a business suit, this one younger and stockier with a chubby face; short blonde hair; a touch of pink in her lips; eyes averted to something across the road; unaware of the camera. All three snaps had the same flattened perspective of a long telephoto. The photographer had been standing fifty yards away, unobserved.

I handed the photos to Shaughnessy and unfolded the sheet of paper.

Inside was a note.

The note was the same style as the first. But instead of return instructions it requested that we reconsider the job offer:

> *Your agency is right for the job and*
> *the fee is more than fair. Please cooperate.*

> *If you don't, these women will be hurt.*
> *You don't know them but you'll hear about them.*

> *The job must be finished in forty-eight hours*
> *to ensure the women's safety.*

The note was signed off with the same name: "Foxglove". I passed it to Shaughnessy. He looked at me.

'This is a first,' he said. 'We're in such demand that clients will massacre Londoners to catch our attention?'

I went over to watch the street. Herbie snuffled behind me and collapsed onto the floor. The building shook.

'We've caught *someone's* attention,' I said.

'Someone who's wealthy and ruthless enough to throw cash and threats around like they're different shades of the same confetti.'

'The question is whether the threats are real.'

'The photos are random snaps. Not clear how he'd locate the women again.'

'That's my guess,' I said. 'When the guy got my voicemail he just went out into the street and snapped a few faces to provide colour for his threat. But he can't hurt them unless he can find them and that would imply major effort to ID and keep tabs on them.'

'Serious manpower,' Shaughnessy agreed. 'If he's not bluffing this guy must have a hell of an operation going.'

'So,' I said, 'bluff. The women are out of his reach. But the guy's pretty cavalier, throwing threats at us when we've got his money.'

Shaughnessy smiled. 'A surfeit of confidence as well as cash. This guy's either powerful or deranged.'

I watched Chase Street. It's a cul-de-sac but a busy one. Commercial and residential traffic in and out all day. It was a fine spring afternoon. Plenty of walkers up and down. Some of them women. Any of them might have been recently photographed.

I returned from the window. Shaughnessy tossed the note and the photos back onto the desk.

I pulled out my phone. Hit redial.

Voicemail again. I left another message.

'Once again,' I said, 'thanks. But the answer's the same. We know that *you* know that if any of these women get hurt you'll draw more heat than you can survive. If we can assist further we know a couple of good psychiatrists. Meantime our admin fee is now chargeable at five thousand pounds. If you'd like the remaining five returning, together with the hotel key and photographs, just send those instructions along. And good luck with the recruitment.'

I killed the line.

Shaughnessy leered.

'You should be in PR, Eddie,' he said.

'Or psychiatry,' I agreed. 'I get a kick out of helping people.'

'You think he'll give us the return instructions?'

'Hard to say. The guy's put himself in a tricky position throwing threats before he's got his cash back. He's got exposure whichever way he plays it. Getting his cash back and continuing his hotel guest search are both starting to look like risky games.'

'You taking this to the police?'

'Tomorrow. I'll get Lucy to work up an invoice to tuck in with the remaining cash and we'll drop the whole lot off along with any return instructions that Foxglove provides.'

'Five K,' Shaughnessy said. 'That's a nice rate for processing a rejection.'

I grinned at him. 'You think we should up it? There's the drive round to Paddington Green tomorrow, and if the police want a statement from us that could be a good couple of hours billable.'

'I was thinking that the guy might expect more than five K back.'

'He'd have got it all if he'd accepted my original response,' I said. I pushed the stuff back into the envelope. 'And the issue isn't the amount. The issue is whether he's convinced we're not for hire.'

'You think he's not?'

'The way he's pushed this in our faces doesn't suggest a type who backs down easily. And he's revealed the hotel and the target he wants locating, left us with a wad of cash and clear evidence of his intention to harm these women. He's invested too much.'

'So he'll try again?'

'I don't see him quietly backing off.'

'Let's hope he hasn't kept tabs on the women,' Shaughnessy said.

'Or that he's not deranged enough to act.'

Which was the worry. If our judgement was wrong we'd be putting these women in harm's way. The fact that we didn't know them, the fact that even the police wouldn't be able to track them down in time to protect them, didn't reduce that worry. I was staying with bluff but I wondered. Hoped Foxglove's actions were more rational than his job offers.

~~~~~

I shut myself in my room and fought paperwork to keep myself from further speculation about the women. Shaughnessy had gone back out and the top floor was silent bar the rumble and clatter of the personal injuries firm downstairs, occasional Westway horns.

The paperwork was almost done, but as with any good odd-job contractor the last ten percent takes ninety percent of the time. I checked the clock. It's a vintage Time Recorder clocking machine that I'd fixed up on the wall beside my Fred Trueman poster the day we opened. I imagined that with the volume of business coming our we'd way need to keep tabs on each job. Cases would be represented by a card queued in the rack alongside the clock. Eight years later the rack was still empty and the clock's main influence, rather than adding urgency, was to project a sense of time running slow, the same as when you're waiting to clock out at the factory. But it's probably subjective. Whenever I'm looking at the clock it means time is already running slow. Over on my visitors' chair Herbie opened an eye.

'Twenty minutes,' I promised, 'then we're through.'

He kept the eye open, unconvinced. He'd learned the investigator's routine. Things happen when they happen.

Then before I could get back to the keyboard I heard the outer door open, and someone came into reception. I stood, moved fast to catch them before they changed their mind.

When I opened my door our visitor was just turning from Lucy's empty desk, wondering whether anyone was in. I pulled the door wide, ready with a sales pitch.

The pitch was redundant.

Our visitor wasn't here to talk rates.

It was the blonde woman from the first photograph, the one with the child.

The child wasn't with her. She was alone, accompanied only by fear and anger.

9

CHAPTER THREE
We figured he was bluffing

'In a way,' I said, 'I've been expecting you.'

Her face didn't change. She was standing by Lucy's desk, looking at me like I was the Monster From The Deep.

The photo hadn't done her justice. It had hinted at a fine delicacy in her face with its frame of gold blonde hair but had missed the emerald depth of her eyes, the effect of the whole. Up close she was a knockout, even with fear and anger shining in her eyes, even backed up against Lucy's desk and ready to lash out against whatever nightmare Foxglove had unleashed on her. I thought about her child. Toned my smile down. Held the door.

'Come on through,' I said.

She stayed put.

'Do you know who I am?' she said. 'Do you know why I'm here?'

She pushed herself away from the desk. The gleam in here eyes looked like tears.

'Sort of,' I said, 'and sort of.' I worked at holding the remnants of the smile. She returned it with a hard ferocity.

'Is this funny? How about I call the police? Right now.'

I held up a hand. Kept the door wide.

'That might not be a good idea,' I said. 'Let's sit down and see if we can sort this out.'

'You're threatening my child. How do you sort that out?'

Behind me Herbie sensed trouble. He climbed off the chair and sneaked under the desk.

'Believe me,' I said, 'I'm not threatening you. I know as much about this as you do.'

'Liar!'

I stepped back. Waited with the door.

'You ordered me to come here,' she said.

'No, ma'am. That wasn't me.'

'So – a colleague of yours. What the hell do you want?'

I stepped further back. She finally moved and strode into my office.

'Sit down,' I said. 'Tell me what's happened.'

I was still hanging on to the smile. The unflappable detective. But my unflappability seemed to register. She turned and sat on the edge of the nearer club chair. I rolled mine across and swivelled it to face her. Sat and worked the height lever. The seat dropped me with a hiss until we were eye to eye.

'You're claiming you don't know what's going on?' my visitor asked.

'I know something. I know that you received a call an hour ago saying that your daughter was being watched and that if you valued her health you'd better come and talk to me. I know that the caller made it clear that you shouldn't test his word and shouldn't call the police.'

'So you *are* in on it!'

I shook my head. 'I'm just making assumptions.'

'Rather specific assumptions.'

'Deductions. You're here because a guy coerced you into coming. The obvious coercion is a threat against your daughter. The threat needed to be credible and imminent, so a written note or text or email wouldn't do. And face to face wasn't an option. So it was a phone call. And there's no way you'd let your daughter out of your sight after receiving such a call which means you'd already dropped her off somewhere. Probably at nursery class. Your first instinct was to call the class to confirm she was safe. You did and she was. So you were left with a decision: call this guy's bluff and go to the police or come to us to find out what it's all about. You decided to start with us because the police machinery would move slowly and you needed to know now.'

'You're saying you're not connected to this guy?'

'I don't know who he is. He contacted us this morning out of the blue. He had a job offer that we turned down. So he contacted us again. Sent a photo of you and your daughter that he almost certainly took on opportunity a few hours ago. The purpose of the photo was to persuade us to cooperate by threatening to harm you.'

She looked at me.

'That's crazy,' she said. 'Why would you take any notice of a photo?'

I stretched to the desk and pulled the snaps from Foxglove's

11

package. Handed them to her.

'He's threatening to hurt you and them. He assumes we won't ignore that threat.'

She studied the photos. Her eyes opened at the one of herself and her child. There was fury in her eyes when she looked up.

'You bastard.'

'Trust me,' I said, 'This is none of our doing.'

'I don't trust you. Tell me what you want.'

'Really,' I repeated, 'we're not part of it. I'm sorry this guy chose you as a way of pressuring us but we've no control over his actions.'

She shook her head.

'This is insane.'

I smiled. Insanity. Part of our job description. But a good term for the way the world looks when you get a call out of the blue from someone threatening your child.

I took the snaps back.

'The guy doesn't want anything from you,' I said. I explained about our anonymous would-be client and his need to find someone; his refusal to take no for and answer; his threat to hurt innocent people unless we cooperated; my assumption until ten minutes ago that the guy was bluffing.

The executive summary. Simple. Brutal.

Which got a response of hardening eyes. Re-ignited anger.

'In other words,' she said, 'this *is* to do with you and your business.'

She stood. 'You were right about my plans: I just wanted some idea what this was about before I went to the police. Now I know.'

She turned for the door.

'Wait,' I said.

She'd hit the nail on the head: refused client or not, it was *our* refused client who'd come after her, our world that had encroached on hers. We take the dodgy clients and risks with the paycheque, but our affairs shouldn't leak out to mess up other people's lives. A case last year had nail-gunned that lesson into our psyches.

'You're right,' I said. 'This is our world that's caught up with you, even if we never work for people like this. But going to the police might be a bad move.'

She'd opened the door. Hesitated.

'Just hear me out,' I said.

I gestured to the chair again. She stood indecisively for a moment but then made up her mind. Closed the door and stepped back across and sat on the chair arm to make it clear that her listening was a temporary thing.

'We should at least know your name,' I said.

She thought about it. Concluded that there was nothing lost in identifying herself. Gave me two names.

Kim Waters. Daughter Alice.

Handing over the names seemed to dampen her urge to run. Stoked her need to know. She looked at me for further explanation. I rolled my chair away and leaned back against my rolltop to give her space. Herbie stirred, wondering whether it was safe to come out. Nervous scratching came up. People assume it's fleas.

I explained why running straight to the police might not be an option.

'We don't know anything about the guy,' I said. 'Maybe he's dangerous, maybe not. We'd guessed not, even after he sent the photos. We assumed that they were taken on opportunity after we turned down his job offer but that he'd not know who you were or where to find you again. We were wrong. You're here as proof of that.'

'Obviously,' she agreed. 'He knows who I am and he's got my number.'

'Maybe it's all still bluff,' I said, 'but we don't know. The guy seems to have resources. Catching up with you and picking up your phone number is quite a feat, especially if it only started with a spur of the moment photograph a couple of hours ago. Hijacking your phone number is impressive. That takes complex equipment nowadays. Scanners, vans, phoney base transmitters. You don't just intercept a call. So the first question is whether the photo really was spur of the moment. Or had he prepared this up-front?'

'The photo's new. That was Grosvenor Square just after lunch. I stopped to tie Alice's shoelace.'

'May I?' I held out my hand. She pulled out her phone and brought up the call that had come in an hour and seven minutes ago. I recognised the number: Foxglove's. An untraceable PAYG for sure. I handed the phone back and thought things through. Herbie sighed and pushed himself up off the threadbare carpet and shuffled towards our guest, tail semaphoring his good intentions. Kim barely noticed him. He stood a moment then turned to me for guidance.

'Sit,' I said. He obeyed. Leapt into his chair and settled down, eyes tracking between our visitor and me.

'It's fifty-fifty that this guy would actually harm you or the others,' I said. 'On the one hand he'd gain nothing other than a warped sense of retribution for our non-cooperation. Any chance of quietly continuing his search would be dead. On the other, maybe he believes that the search is dead anyway without us. And he's confident that sending you here will persuade us to rethink. Because he knows that neither we nor the police could protect the other women even if we stopped him from getting to you. He perhaps assumes that fact will sway us, that we'll cooperate, help him find his guy. And if we prove his judgement wrong he might just be vindictive enough to strike out.'

Kim kept quiet.

I pushed myself away from the desk. Went to watch the view. A fine spring day. Evening rush hour getting under way on the Westway. Cars streaming right to left. Trains rolling west. The sky blue with fair weather cumulous reflecting the slowly descending sun. The room was quiet behind me save for Herbie's snoring.

I decided.

'Best option,' I said: 'Hold off with the police. My firm will go along with this guy's demands and locate the person he's looking for. If we succeed then he'll have no further need to threaten you. You'll be safe. But after we finish the job we'll follow up and find out who he is. Then his name is with the police.'

Kim was quiet a moment.

'No disrespect, Mr Flynn,' she said, 'but shouldn't the police be searching for this guy from the start?'

I walked back.

'They would search,' I said, 'and they'd try to protect you. But the other women would be at risk. If the guy's determined enough he'll get to them. The only certain way of stopping him is to give the police his name. Keep him happy until then by doing what he asks.'

Kim was shaking her head but the movement slowed as the logic got through. Resistance faltered.

'Is there anywhere your daughter could stay for a couple of days?'

She thought about it.

'Her father could take her,' she said. 'We're divorced. Alice was due to go to him this weekend anyway.'

'Where does he live?'

'Near Lewes.'

'That's good. It's well away from town and this Foxglove guy may be good but I doubt whether even he could have that kind of detail. Alice will be safe there.'

'Hell,' she said. She looked at me. 'I don't know what to do. This has blown up so suddenly. I can't believe it's real.'

'I'm sorry about it,' I said, 'but it is real. You've landed in this guy's crosshairs through simple bad luck. But we'll sort it out. Have your ex-husband hang on to Alice for a few days and keep your own head down. We'll work with this guy and give him what he wants and the threat will be over.'

'Unless he objects to you searching for him afterwards.'

'He won't know we're searching until it's too late,' I said.

She thought about it.

'How long will it take.'

'Two or three days.' I gave her a confident smile.

Kim didn't smile back but her face relaxed a little. Looked nicer for it. A lot nicer. A smile from her would really be something. I sensed she had a smile to break hearts.

I keyed her number into my phone. Called her. Cancelled when her phone rang.

'Store that number,' I said.

She nodded and stood and I walked across to open the door. Herbie stirred and sat up. Beamed a grin at her when she looked down at him. The agency is nothing if not good manners. A half smile flitted across her face in return. PR. That's Herbie.

I walked through and held the outer door and Kim went out then turned at the stairs.

'I suppose this isn't your fault,' she said. 'But I'm having to trust you and I don't know you at all, and I'm not comfortable with that.'

'Got it. Don't worry. We'll not let you down.'

I watched her go down then went back and keyed my phone. Another voicemail for Mr Foxglove.

'Being in demand is flattering,' I said. 'Like a dog with fleas. But

I've talked to the lady, and as you anticipated it's hard to turn down that kind of incentive. So we're on the job. I'll be in touch.'

I killed the line. Opened Foxglove's original envelope and pulled his note out to check the hotel details. Took the keycard for Room 209 and a fistful of twenties.

I whistled to Herbie. He pushed himself off his chair and we went out.

CHAPTER FOUR
Room 209

The Marylebone BestBreak described its tariff as Super Budget, a play on words that suggested cheap but not *so* cheap, targeting the less discerning business client and sales rep rather than the backpacker. I left the car in the alley alongside it with the hood down and Security snoring in the passenger seat. Walked round to the entrance.

The hotel was a converted Georgian on the corner of a busy side street north of Oxford Street. Plate glass and dressed stone at street level but original sash windows on the upper three floors. All in good condition. You sensed a tidy place. The hotel's name hung sideways down the front facade to indicate that Super Budget was trendy.

Inside, behind a street shop and café, was a small but modern reception area with a lift on one side, stairs on the other. The receptionist didn't look up as I walked through to the stairs.

The two-hundred series rooms were on the first floor, immediately above the retail units on a corridor that stretched away in refurbished pastels and new carpeting. When the fire doors closed behind me I was in dead silence. I padded down the carpet and rounded a corner. Room 209 was the second along towards the back. It had a "Do not disturb" card hanging on its door.

I stood and listened. The hotel was late-afternoon empty. If our mystery guy was still in residence he was probably out, though why he'd leave the "Do not disturb" sign wasn't clear. I put my ear to the wood. Nothing.

I knocked on the door. No-one answered.

I peered through the fisheye. People assume you can't see anything when you're looking from the wrong end. They're wrong. What you see is whether anyone's looking out at *you*. No-one was. The lens showed bright light. No-one squinting from the other side.

I pulled out Foxglove's keycard. Pushed it into the slot.

A green light. The door unlocked.

Still valid. The guy hadn't checked out.

I pushed the door open and stepped in. Switched on the lights.

The bathroom was at my shoulder. Tiny. Faux marble flooring; new fittings; phone kiosk shower. Untouched-clean. No towels drying. No toiletries on the worktop. Pristine shower tray. Maybe our mystery resident was a neat freak.

The bedroom was similarly pristine. Its walls were an off-blue pastel hung with generic abstracts, and a king size bed took most of the space. Just room for veneer lockers each side and a wardrobe unit and desk along the window side. A tubular steel armchair and plastic desk chair completed the furniture.

The bed was made up and there was nothing lying around in the room. No clothes or towels, nothing in the wardrobe. The drinks tray on the desk was untouched, and the waste bin was empty.

Sterile. Pristine except for a barely noticeable indentation in the bed cover as if someone had recently sat there. The room might have been waiting for a new guest except that I had a working keycard, which meant that the old guest hadn't checked out.

The sterility shone a light on Foxglove's two-part assignment: *identify* and *locate*. Why he'd have a copy of the key and not know the guest was a puzzle but the other part – the *where* – was beginning to make sense, because the guest wasn't *here* in this perfect room and might never have been here or might never be coming back.

I saw Foxglove's problem. If the occupant had left, the room was a dead end that told him nothing. But he believed our firm could magic something up. We magic lots of things up but we usually start with *something*. Maybe it was time to tone down the Yellow Pages rhetoric. I'd renewed the ad. last year after our heavily publicised success in finding a child who was supposed to be dead, and the mood of the moment had got to me as I'd worked on the wording in the buzz of my jazz club. I should have checked the poetry in the light of day. I didn't recall using the word *miracle* but who knew what had crept in there? *Miracles,* of course, were what our clients routinely expected, but this latest demand came with a forty-eight hour tag. Deliver the miracle fast or Kim and Alice, and maybe some other women, might get hurt.

If Foxglove had the room key then he had the guest name, but apparently the name didn't tell him who the person was or give him direction. I'd pick up same name when I went out but it wasn't going to help me either. So I needed to find the direction right here in the room, even if it wasn't clear that the mystery resident had ever been here.

So start with the one thing awry.

I squatted by the bed and checked out the cover indentation. Someone had sat there since the bed had been made up. Possibly our mystery guest. Possibly Foxglove. But whoever it was they'd sat for a purpose. There was no phone on the bedside locker so they weren't calling the desk. No power point nearby so they weren't plugging in a charger. If they'd been taking a rest they'd have lain full length; if they'd wanted to sit for a while and they'd have used the armchair.

But the top drawer in the bedside unit was open a fraction. Nothing to catch the eye except that the gap jarred with the orderliness elsewhere. I eased it open. It was empty bar the ubiquitous Gideon Bible. But the bible was open too, and skewed as if someone had moved it. Another imperfection.

I lifted it out.

It was open at its cover page. The remaining leaves were printer-pristine. It had never been read. I riffled through and found nothing. Flipped back to the cover page to check a small defacement I'd seen. Someone had inked the number 4169 at the top of the page in characters that were small but no less of a defacement. The writing would have been a pointless vandalism except that there was a purpose to it. The drawer had been opened since the room was serviced and the bible had been left open at that first page and there had to be a reason for it.

The number was relevant. Some kind of code. Maybe a PIN.

I dropped the bible back into the drawer and checked the lower ones. Empty. Checked the unit on the far side of the bed. Same result.

I lifted the stacked pillows and pulled back the bedcovers. Nothing. And no sign of being slept in. Foxglove had sent us the key first thing this morning. Too early for check in. So the room had been taken since at least yesterday but gone unused last night. Our mystery guest had checked in, come up here and parked his backside on the bed for a minute – maybe long enough to open the Gideon Bible – and then left.

I checked the desk. It was bare save for an Anglepoise lamp and the drinks tray. Its three drawers were empty. I opened the wardrobe.

Empty save for hangers and a laundry bag.

And a room safe.

The safe was a surprise. Maybe a perk of the Super Budget tariff. A place for the business traveller to stash his valuables whilst he takes a shower or dines out, in the mistaken belief that his stuff is safe.

Room safes are good against the casual thief but if someone's in a hotel room to rob you then they probably know what they're doing.

But I didn't need to beat the safe. That four figure code in the Gideon was not a coincidence.

Maybe there was something in the safe.

I keyed in the number.

The safe stayed locked.

I cleared the code and walked back to check the bible.

No error. My memory was correct. Maybe the fault was in my fingers.

I went back and tried again.

Same result. No green light. I twisted the knob anyway.

Locked solid.

Another hunch bites the dust. But it had been a good hunch. Too good to shake. A four digit code defacing the bible just an arm's length from the safe, and almost certainly left for either our mystery guest or Foxglove, was not coincidence.

I needed to see what was in the safe,

The code would have saved a minute or two but you work with what you've got.

I pulled my utility key ring from my jacket. It comes on a chain with a tinplate figure of Sherlock Holmes looking disappointed. The ring carries a few small tools that circumvent disappointments. The first of them was an Allen key that fitted the bolts holding the manufacturer's nameplate onto the safe door. I released the bolt on one side and the plate swung down, clear of a keyhole hidden behind.

I selected a key tool and pushed it into the hole and worked my lock pick alongside it. The pick is one of those extra large paperclips. It took ten seconds. The tumblers released and the LED lit up green. I re-attached the nameplate and stashed the tools and pulled the door open to see what our mystery guest had left in there.

The safe was empty.

I grinned. Should have known.

But why would someone key in a code and lock it up empty? When you've finished with a safe you just leave it open for the next guest to set their own code.

I thought about it.

The safe was significant. The Gideon code was significant. I just didn't know how.

I went back to my search. Walked round the walls, feeling along the tops of the wardrobe and pictures. Opened the bathroom cabinets. Unfolded towels and lifted the lavatory cistern lid.

Nothing.

I walked across to check the window. Unlike the front windows the side windows were modern, plain casements hinged at the side to swing back into the room. Double glazed but I could hear the hiss of traffic. I pulled at the handle and the window opened. It had been unlatched. I looked closely and saw that the sill and room wall below it were scuffed. Marks you might get from someone's shoe as they climbed up.

I pulled the window wide. City noise washed in. Euston rush hour. Ventilation fans. A plane climbing. I looked down into the cobbled alley and saw a line of lidded refuse skips. The nearest was almost under the window and was open, its lid propped against the hotel wall. It contained cardboard waste.

Fifteen feet below. Three or four offset from the window.

I stepped away and looked at the scuff marks again.

Leaned back out to gauge distances.

How desperate would you have to be to make that sideways jump?

If you were in a hurry, if your decision was fuelled by adrenaline, then maybe the skip didn't seem so far. Maybe the cardboard looked like a soft touchdown.

There was a good chance you'd take a smack against the edge of the skip but you'd make it. A couple of cuts and bruises, maybe, but I'd attempted worse.

I closed the window and locked the handle. The noise muted. The room was silent. I went out and pulled the door closed behind me with the "Do not disturb" hanging.

CHAPTER FIVE
Private Investigators spend a lot of time there

I went down to the front desk. The clerk was a young guy with a Polish accent.

'Checking out,' I said. I handed the room key over and gave him the number. He ran it through the computer.

'Leave early,' he said.

It was nearly six p.m. I guess he wasn't referring to the time of day.

'Change of plans,' I said. 'It's nice to finish ahead of time for once.'

'Two key.'

I looked at him. He lifted the keycard.

'You take two.'

'Damn,' I said. 'Must have left it in the room.'

So the guest had requested two keys. One of which had ended up in Foxglove's hands.

'No matter,' the clerk said.

He printed an invoice. Pushed it across.

'All paid,' he said. 'No charge.'

I checked the details. Saw that I was checking out three days early on a ten day booking. The invoice was addressed to someone called Simon Andrew Morris with a home address in Potters Bar which was interesting. The drive in from there was thirty minutes outside rush hour. Why book a hotel thirty minutes from home? The pre-payment saved me shelling out some of Foxglove's cash but I shelled some out anyway. Made a thing of sliding a twenty out absently whilst I finished looking over the invoice.

'For room and reception,' I said.

The clerk's frown lightened.

'Very kind. I'll put in pot.'

Sure.

I finished with the invoice. It confirmed that the pre-payment was in cash and that the resident had provided a DL as ID.

DL.

That's Driver's Licence

Which was good if the hotel had made a copy.

'Sorry to trouble you,' I said. 'But could I take a look at my licence details? I lost the damned thing yesterday. If I can get the number it makes the replacement form easier.'

'No problem.' The clerk walked across and pulled Simon Andrew Morris' paperwork from a cabinet. Came back and slid a sheet onto the desk. The sheet was a black and white scan of the licence. The scan was crooked but the quality was good. A UK licence, expiring 2018. Photo of a sour, sagging middle aged face under receding hair. Too ordinary to remember. A face like a million others. Not much like mine but the clerk wasn't paying attention. The address was Potters Bar, the same as on the invoice.

I pulled out my phone and snapped a photo and thanked the guy. He told me no prob. and re-clipped the paperwork. By the time he looked up I was gone.

~~~~~

I hit a Chinese takeaway in Camden two doors up from a late opening pet shop, and Herbie and I ate a rushed tea. Spring rolls and Mongolian beef for me. Chicken and liver dog-mix with Mongolian beef for Herbie. I sloshed water into his travel bowl.

'Last stop,' I promised.

We headed north, picked up the A1 and followed evening traffic out past the Orbital to the address listed on Simon Andrew Morris' invoice. If he was home I'd have covered both of Foxglove's assignments: the who and the where. We'd be through.

And pigs might fly: if Morris was home Foxglove would have already found him.

Still. Formalities.

The formalities didn't take long. The street listed on the hotel invoice was a narrow residential lined with scrappy fifties semis behind flagged-over front gardens. And it was short. Dead-ended against the wall of a parking area servicing a retail unit on the main road. The last house before the wall was number twenty-nine. Simon Andrew Morris' house was number forty-six. I checked my A-Z. Confirmed that the street didn't continue on the far side of the main road. If there'd ever been a number forty-six it had been demolished for the car park thirty years ago.

I sat on the Frogeye's bonnet and looked at the wall. Dead ends. Private Investigators spend a lot of time there. But if it had been this easy Foxglove would have chased his hotel guest himself. He wouldn't have needed to shell out twenty K in a risky gambit involving an agency you didn't know and threats that might come back on you.

I wondered whether Foxglove's forty-eight hours started from our receipt of his initial demand or my late afternoon reconsideration. Not that it mattered. Seven hours wasn't the make or break. We weren't going to find the occupant of Room 209 in forty-eight hours from a zero starting point.

I considered what I had on our mystery guy. I knew he'd booked the hotel room seven days ago for a ten day stay and was now gone. I didn't know whether he knew that Foxglove was after him, nor whether *he'd* given Foxglove the room key. And I didn't know whether he looked like the picture on the driving licence, though I was pretty sure his name wasn't Simon Andrew Morris and certain that he didn't live on the car park in front of me. He'd paid cash, concealed his identity and left by the window when someone – maybe Foxglove – came in the door. In the meantime, he either didn't sleep in the room or he was the neatest freak in the universe.

And he was at least twenty-four hours gone.

Why did he take the room? And what was that code in the Gideon Bible? If it was the safe code what had been in there and why had someone changed the code and re-locked it empty?

Gut feeling said that Morris was local. The fake address here in this dead end street was a little too parochial for someone passing through the city. So Morris might still be somewhere around.

But where to find a pointer?

And the key question: was Foxglove ruthless enough to follow through on his threats against those women? Was Kim in danger if I didn't deliver on schedule?

Lots of questions. No answers.

CHAPTER SIX
Worst case scenario

A call came in at seven a.m.

Kim Waters, Foxglove's threatened woman.

Unexpected. I'd not planned to talk to her for a couple of days.

'Did you find the hotel guest?' she asked.

'He's no longer there.' I described the evidence of his hasty exit. The account sounded like movie action but she didn't pick up on the thrill. Sounded less comfortable than ever at leaving this in my hands. I couldn't fault her instincts.

'You've no idea who he is?' she asked.

'He checked in with a false address and presumably a false name. So no, not yet.'

'So how will you find him?'

'We have means,' I said. P.I.s are vague. We keep our techniques under wraps, at least until we know what they are.

Kim stayed quiet. I heard sub text in the silence.

'Don't worry,' I said. 'We'll find the guy. Foxglove will be out of your hair in no time.'

A nervous laugh.

'I'm looking over my shoulder every second. This is so unreal. I'm still trying to understand why he picked me.'

'Just a random thing. He needed leverage to force us to work for him and just walked out into the street and pointed his camera.'

'But following up? Finding out who I was so he could use me? That feels so creepy.'

I didn't argue, but creepy wasn't the main thing. The main thing was that Foxglove's follow-up proved he was organised. Was more than just a loner. I didn't mention that silver lining.

'He'll do nothing for now,' I reassured her. 'Just stay alert and you'll be fine. Does your ex-husband know what's happened?'

'Of course. I had to tell him. The precious bastard didn't believe me at first. Thought I was in the middle of some kind of boyfriend trouble, that I'd put Alice at risk with some unstable type and needed somewhere to farm her out. And when I convinced him otherwise it took half an hour to dissuade him from calling the police. In the end he gave me two days to tell him everything was sorted out. Threatened to put his solicitor onto me if there was any hint that I was putting Alice at risk.'

I was walking back from the park with Herbie. We crossed the road and went up. Herbie scooted towards food.

'We'll sort this out,' I repeated. 'The threat will be over before you know it.'

She paused. Considered her options for the fiftieth time. Came to the same conclusion.

'Mr Flynn, please keep me updated.'

'Eddie,' I said. 'No need for formality.'

A humourless laugh. 'Sure. Eddie. It's not like I'm your client.'

'In a way you are,' I said. 'It's just someone else paying. But I'm working for your and Alice's safety. Foxglove isn't the client.'

'I suppose that's one way of looking at it...' Kim said. Her words tailed off.

'But you still see it as a mess from my world that's swept in round you. Understandable. The police have the same problem: lumped with the bad guys. They represent a world people don't want to know about.'

'You're right.'

'But we don't make the problems. Foxglove was up to his schemes before he pulled either of us in.'

I went into my apartment. Herbie headed for his water bowl. I crossed to the window. The street was coming alive. People heading out.

'We're on the job, Kim,' I said. 'It will be over before you know it.'

Detectives should be soothsayers. Or run those psychic shows that attract the gullible. We'd make a killing.

~~~~~

I beat the worst of the traffic and made Chase Street by eight fifteen. Shaughnessy's Yamaha was parked behind the building. I backed the Frogeye in beside it, pointing outwards. Sometimes seconds can matter when you drive out. Like Le Mans. I left the hood down and headed upstairs to work out which direction I should go when I stood on the pedal.

I stopped in reception to go through the morning ritual with the filter machine. The ritual rarely produced coffee but it soothed the mind like any lifestyle routine, deferred paperwork at least. Herbie nosed open Shaughnessy's door and I heard the two of them talking. When I went in he was sitting on Shaughnessy's desk watching him work his computer. I planted myself in Harry's chair. Shaughnessy looked up.

'We returned Foxglove's cash?'

'Wishful thinking. He's gone with Option B.'

Shaughnessy quit.

'He's still pushing us to work for him?'

'With a bulldozer. My guess is he's invested too much to back away and look elsewhere.'

I explained about Kim's visit; the empty hotel room; the dead end.

Shaughnessy thought about it.

'He moved damn fast with the woman,' he said. 'And dragging her in is a hell of an investment. We may be looking at a worst case scenario.'

'Which is that he's prepared to hurt people,' I said, 'unless we cooperate. And we can't risk finding out the hard way. We can keep Kim and her daughter safe with his ten K but we can't protect the other women. The police neither.'

I heard coughing sounds from reception. The aroma of Buckaroo came through. I mostly keep the Buckaroo for home. It's a little expensive to risk in the office machine. But the kick is worth the occasional risk. Maybe I'd got lucky this morning.

I headed out to the machine.

'So we need to find his hotel guy,' Shaughnessy said.

'I'm going to complete Foxglove's commission,' I said, 'which should bring in the second ten K instalment. The we use the cash to take a look at him.'

'An empty hotel room and false address. Not much to go on.'

I poured coffee. Dropped in creamer and sugar. 'That's why Foxglove outsourced the search.'

'The mystery guy moved pretty fast to get out of the window in the couple of seconds it took to open the door. That could have been just hotel staff coming in. He must have been on a hair trigger.'

'The "Do not disturb" sign told him it wasn't hotel staff. And he was expecting trouble. He'd identified his escape route as soon as he went into the room.'

Lucy came in as I walked back to the front office. Herbie dropped from Shaughnessy's desk and came sloping towards the prospect of biscuits. I left him to it. Heard Lucy fussing over him, telling him how hungry he looked. She called through to ask if I ever fed him. I heard the thud as Herbie collapsed at her feet, followed by the sound of the biscuit tin.

When they finally came in I gave Lucy the executive briefing. Her eyes opened at the story of our visitor but she confirmed that she'd be ready when I needed extra hands. I got my feet up on the partners desk. Sipped Buckaroo. Made a call and got a break.

The call was picked up directly by Roger Daley. He's our inside man at DVLA. Gets us snippets about vehicles we're looking at. The snippets are return favours for our official help locating vehicles of interest to the authorities in the south east. We try to keep Roger balanced on the legal high wire in respect of the snippets, which is why we never ask for driving licence details. But a forged licence isn't a driving licence. And I only needed confirmation that the Marylebone BestBreak licence was phoney, which was something Roger was happy to assist with. His view on fake licences was that anyone holding or manufacturing one should be looking at a minimum of ten years. Roger's a nice guy but he can be a little focused on certain topics. I gave him the number. He hit a few keys and confirmed my assumption.

'It's not in the system,' he said.

I gave him Simon Andrew Morris' supposed name and age. He ran that search.

'Unlikely,' he said. 'There's only a single UK licence would fit the name. A guy up in the Shetlands. So he's either travelled a long way or the name is false.'

I went with the latter. Thanked Roger. Grinned at Shaughnessy as we considered where this left us.

Where it left us is that we had nothing. The BestBreak mystery guest had taken his leap and was gone.

CHAPTER SEVEN

He took the long way down

The BestBreak receptionist hadn't mentioned any shenanigans when I checked out so my guess was that he knew nothing about guests dropping from windows. But maybe someone outside had spotted something. Maybe there'd be some evidence in the skip.

I drove back to the hotel and parked in the cobbled alley. Looked for possibilities. Beyond the hotel the alley was walled either side with mews houses, tiny windows and doors, garage up-and-overs. All closed up tight. Little prospect of witnesses. More promising was the building opposite the hotel. A restaurant ran down from the corner and a half-open rear service door offered the possibility of staff in and out.

I looked up at the hotel window. Tightly closed. The room had been made up. Our man was gone forever. The skip he'd used as a trampoline was offset from the drop but the guy had made the sideways jump onto its cardboard stack rather than risk the cobblestones. The open lid was a lucky break, though a ten foot drop onto plastic might still have been be the guy's preference over a fifteen foot drop onto stone.

I peered over the skip rim. It was two thirds full of cardboard sheets and boxes. Lower at one side where the content had been crushed. I checked the angle back to the window. The compressed area was about right.

I hoisted myself up and in, and the cardboard subsided under my weight, evened up. The material would have cushioned the guy's fall but he'd still have landed with a thump, maybe bashed a limb on the far rim, or left a button or torn material if he'd contacted the closure flange.

I stood on the uncrushed end and started to dig the card out. Dropped it over the side. Got a few funny looks from passers-by as the mess piled up on the cobbles. My end of the heap became unstable. I started sliding. Shifted down to the excavated end and continued digging. Ten minutes got the skip down level to the last layers. If the guy had left a trace it would be here.

Nothing showed until the impact end of the skip was almost cleared to the base. That's when I saw the glint of metal under the card remnants. I pulled the last of it out and uncovered a scattering of coins. You'll find the odd coin in any rubbish skip but not a pocketful, which meant these had come from the guy as he'd crashed against the side and gone down on his backside. I exposed more of the base and found something else: a scrap of paper curled in a corner. The paper was clean and dry. Hadn't been there long. Maybe as long as the coins. I picked it up. It was a card receipt for a hundred and twelve pounds from a merchant named FoneMart. The receipt might have been tossed in with some cardboard but it might also have fallen down with the coins when our hotel guy landed.

I pocketed it and cleared the remnants of the cardboard until I was standing in an empty skip. Spotted nothing more. I hoisted myself out and dropped back down. My waste heap had spread out and looked three times what it had been. When I looked up a guy in a chef's coat and hat had come out of the restaurant door. A quick fag break before they opened for lunch. I threw him a grin and started lifting the cardboard back into the skip. The agency is nothing if not environmentally friendly. It took a while but I got it all up. Without the benefit of crushing the mound built up above the rim and the last few pieces took some balancing. When I checked behind me the guy in the doorway had gone but the door was still open.

I crossed over and went in. Walked a dim corridor towards noise and light, the sound of knives on boards. Arrived in a kitchen where two guys were chopping and trimming. The fag guy looked up.

'Oy! This is private. You can't come in here.'

'I just need some help.'

'Private, mate. Sorry.' He quit his work and came over with his cleaver. I turned and walked sharpish, back down the corridor.

'Come and talk to me,' I said.

He followed. Either to talk or to plant the cleaver. I got back to the door and stepped out into fresh air. The guy followed me all the way and lifted the cleaver to make his point.

'What the hell you doin' in that skip?' he said. 'You the friggin' police?'

'Why would the police be poking around in a skip?'

'It's where he jumped innit?'

I looked across.

'You saw what happened?'

'I told you: I know nuthin'.'

I turned back.

'You told me? We've never met.'

'Your crazy friend.'

'Someone came to talk to you? Was this right after the guy jumped?'

'Yeah.'

This was good. We had a confirmed exit through the window and this guy had talked to whoever was chasing the fugitive. Either Foxglove or one of his pals.

'So the first guy jumped and then the other guy came looking for him?' I summarised.

Cleaver looked at me. He'd dropped the blade but it glinted at his thigh. A growling started up from along the alley. Herbie was up on the seat, watching.

'Easy boy,' I said. The growling continued.

'The guy who talked to you isn't with me,' I said. 'Care to tell *me* what happened?'

'The man pulled the window open then he came out onto the sill and jumped. Landed with a thump. Then he got himself out and legged it.'

'When was this?'

'Monday. Six-ish. Before the rush.'

'That's it? He just leapt out and headed off?'

'He was limping. Smacked his leg on the skip. Then the other guy pokes his head out and looks up and down and then comes out of the front door after him.'

'What did the jumper look like?'

'Dunno. It was all over in a sec. Just a guy. Old. Sixty.'

'Tall? Short? Big?'

'Average. Podgy build.'

'Hair? Glasses? Jacket?'

'Dunno. Just hair. He wasn't bald. No glasses. Wearing jeans an' a pea coat.'

'Which way did he go?'

The cleaver came up.

'That way.'

I looked down the alley. Pulled out my phone and brought up the fake driving licence photo.

'Is this the guy?'

Cleaver looked. Shrugged. 'Could be. I didn't really see. That picture's lousy.'

I put the phone away.

'What about the other guy? Did he come right down?'

Cleaver lowered the cleaver.

'About sixty seconds later. Fifty-nine seconds too late. He shoulda' jumped after the guy. I told him: what's up, scareda heights?'

'You told him that?'

'Almost. Bit of a scary bastard.'

'What did he look like?'

'Angry.'

That narrowed it down. I grinned.

'Help me here: was he sixty too?'

'Thirties. Forty tops.'

'Tall? Short?'

'Big. Six footer. Tough guy. Maybe Asian, Chinese. Kind of oriental. Mebbe mixed race.'

'What did his face look like?'

'Ordinary. Straight. Smooth. He had tinted lenses. A rude bastard, like you.'

'Like me?'

'You an' your Rottweiler. Came running round with the same attitude. Answer the questions. No please or thank you. A thug.'

'You're the one with the meat cleaver.'

'Yeah.' He lifted it again. 'An' don't forget it. But you're pal didn't look the sort to be intimidated by a cleaver.'

'He's not my pal. You remember anything else?'

'He wore a suit. Dressed up respectable.'

'But he wasn't?'

'He was a thug. A nasty bastard. Like a movie assassin. Bit like you.'

'Take it easy,' I said. It was the first time I'd been likened to a movie character. I'd have to check the mirror. See if I could spot the Willis or Pacino. 'What did the guy say?'

'He's looking up an' down the street and he's asking me where the jumper went. Only he's not askin', he's demanding. I just pointed him right and let him leg it.'

'Anything else?'

'Nuthin'. End of show. Lucky you put that cardboard back, mate. I've got your registration.'

'Littering's not my thing,' I said.

'Sure. Plenty other things are, though.'

'Much appreciated. How's your menu? I'll call in some time.'

'We're Michelin star. But don't bother. We're not that desperate.'

I held the smile. Left him to it and walked up to the car. Herbie wasn't smiling. I patted him on the head. That worked. His eyes closed tight and an ivory accordion spread. He opened his eyes again and licked my hand but stayed up on the seat to give Cleaver the evil eye as we pulled away.

~~~~~

A retail receipt wasn't much, and Cleaver's descriptions of our mystery guy and his pursuer weren't much but they were more than I had an hour ago: our players had just become flesh and blood.

The receipt recorded a card payment at a shop called FoneMart dated mid-day on Monday. I checked Yellow Pages and found a business located in Streatham.

I stopped off at Chase Street and found Harry in. Harry's our tech guy and magician. A whizz at computers and electronics. Good at computer forensics and image processing and what some people would call forgery but he categorises as first-glance copies.

He went to work on the BestBreak licence image. Herbie and I went through to my office. I pulled out my wallet and offloaded most of the junk. Left just a couple of charge cards and re-packed one of the sleeves with a handful of twenties from Foxglove's stash. Lucy brought a coffee and a biscuit for Herbie. Hung around to get an update.

'So what was originally in the safe? Did this Morris guy get it?'

'Not if he was using the code from the Gideon.'

'Maybe he changed the code.'

'Why re-lock an empty safe with a new code?'

'Beats me,' Lucy said. 'You figure it.'

I smiled.

Lucy asked where I was going next and I held up my newly stuffed wallet and told her.

'You think they'll buy it?' she asked.

'Depends how closely they look. And they may buy it and still know nothing.'

The wallet was cash-heavy and held a couple of my real cards plus the FoneMart receipt, and when Harry came in ten minutes later it held a convincing driving licence with the name Simon Andrew Morris on it. Harry's fifteen minute job had produced a simulacrum of the card on heavy gloss photo paper that wouldn't fool DVLA but looked fine to the casual glance. The photo was a colourised version of the BestBreak's photocopy of Morris. Rough but passable. I pushed the wallet with the licence into my pocket and was ready to go.

Traffic was light. We made Streatham in twenty minutes and located the FoneMart business in a line of retailers just down from the station. I eased the Frogeye between an electrical cabinet and bike rack and left it on the pavement clear of red lines. Hopped out and went into the shop.

A basic retail unit. Bare except for a window display of used phones and three rotating stands with PAYG cards and accessories. An Indian guy watched me from behind the counter. Looked meaningfully at the car.

'Bit of a rush,' I explained. I pulled out the wallet and made as if I was handing it over. 'Has someone been looking for this?' I said.

The guy stared without comprehension.

'The owner dropped it as he came out of the shop,' I said. 'My wife spotted it but by the time she ran over he'd disappeared.'

The shop guy shook his head. The thing still had no meaning. He'd not had any customer in looking for a wallet. His eyes widened though when he spotted the small fortune crammed inside. I held it clear in an act of searching through it. The thing was a prop but the cash and my cards were real. I pulled out the FoneMart receipt and the phoney licence. Held the licence up so he could see but not touch. He ignored the licence and took the receipt and recognition came. The hundred and twelve quid transaction was still fresh in his memory.

'Guy over the road,' he said. 'WiFi chip failed. We repair. Good friend of mine.'

He reached for the wallet again, undoubtedly intending to return it to his good friend, but I pulled it away.

'Over the road?'

'Next the kebab. Black door.'

'Got it. I'll head over. My wife will be pleased.'

'Can save you time.' The guy was coming round the counter, suddenly keen to help, but I moved fast. Slotted the wallet away and pulled open the door. Went back out.

I dodged traffic and crossed to a single storey block of flaking shop fronts, tatty awnings, rusting shutters. Way-downmarket retail units. The shop with the black door was jammed between the kebab takeaway and a nail salon. Its small tinted window was obscured by blinds. A business name was stencilled on the glass.

Barker: Investigations & Solutions.

Interesting.

Was our hotel guy a private investigator? It was credible. And even if *solutions* that involve leaping out of windows didn't sound too good I'd done worse myself.

I pushed on the door. Locked. No Open/Closed sign. No way of knowing whether the investigator was in or out. I rapped on the glass. Heard nothing above the traffic. Tried my fist. Same result.

I guess it would have been too easy.

I walked back over the road and backed the Frogeye out. The traffic stopped out of curiosity. I spun the wheel and drove up the road to a supermarket car park. Pulled into a slot and walked Herbie back round to a bench in a bus shelter where we could watch the *Investigations & Solutions* door. The bench was a token, narrow enough to take the weight off your legs without getting comfortable. Herbie flopped beneath it.

It was a little after noon. The pavements were busy. Takeaways gearing up for the lunchtime trade. Traffic was dirty and loud. The shelter kept the sun at bay but not the noise or the dust. I gave it two hours but the *Investigations & Solutions* door stayed shut.

The lunch crowd dispersed. The street stayed noisy and dirty. I looked down at Herbie.

'Break,' I said.

He grinned. Stood. Shook. Ready to roll. Preferably towards food. Food was my idea. Just not here.

We went to retrieve the car.

CHAPTER EIGHT
There Are No Shortcuts

We parked at the top of the Common and grabbed a sandwich and sausage at the café. Sat on a bench by the lake and took the sun. Watched the world go by. Birds flapped out on the water. Walkers pushed buggies and pulled dogs. Kids scooted by on scooters. I ate my sandwich and thought things through.

Barker: Investigations & Solutions was a one man band. The shabby locked door told me that. So *Barker* would be Simon Andrew Morris, our hotel guy, and his would be the name I'd be texting to Foxglove. But I wanted to talk to the guy first. Confirm my assumption and give him a heads-up – the agency's client confidentiality clause doesn't cover coerced jobs. Maybe *Barker* would tell me what this was about and then I'd have a heads-up too.

It all depended on how often the guy showed up at his office.

There'd been no contact number in his window, and Yellow Pages had nothing. *Barker* operated on a low advertising budget. Two-liners in the local rags where his clientele would find him when the need arose.

We finished lunch and drove back to the High Road and this time *Barker's* door blind was up. I left Herbie guarding the Frogeye and went in.

Found a small, mostly empty area lit by yellow fluorescents. Parquet floor, lifting in places. A small counter, bare except for a phone and bell-press. Two grey plastic chairs against the wall in case you arrived at a busy time. The place oozed class.

At the back of the room were two doors. One was unmarked and closed. The other had the words "Meeting Room" up in black adhesive letters and was part open. Someone was shuffling about behind it.

The bell-push seemed overly formal. I walked across to the Meeting Room. Found a space barely eight feet by ten floored in more parquet and furnished with a small table with a leather swivel behind it, two more plastic client chairs in front. A filing cabinet with a shredder atop completed the decor. The whole lot was encased within egg yolk walls that looked like they'd last seen paint in the seventies. Two diplomas hung on the wall behind the leather chair, along with a poster that said *There Are No Shortcuts*. Maybe the slogan was an industry regulation. I didn't know. I'd never seen any regulations. Or diplomas that meant anything. We had none at Chase Street. Our qualifications were our results.

A table, a shredder and walls to make you queasy. Classy as hell.

I quit admiring the decor and took in the occupant, who was standing over the table pushing paperwork into a folder.

A female. Heavyish. Solid rather than fat. Wearing dark grey trousers and a cotton jacket over a knitted tank top. When she heard me she looked up. I saw a broad face framed by slashes of black hair. The black looked natural, though I put her age at early fifties. She smiled.

'Can I help you? We're not strictly open.'

'I'm looking for Mr Barker.'

'He's out.' She put down the paperwork. 'Can I assist?'

'I was hoping to talk to him. Face to face.'

'Okay. Let's set up an appointment. He's in most mornings.'

'I was thinking ASAP. It's a little urgent.'

She held her smile.

'Isn't everything? Give me your number and I'll get him to call.'

I searched and found a card. Handed it over. She read it and her eyes opened.

'Eagle Eye! Well I never. You guys are getting to be the biggest celebs since Sam Spade.' Her smile was still sweet.

I grinned back. Last I'd heard Sam Spade was a fictional character and not a celebrity but I guess the distinction is lost nowadays. And the quip wasn't entirely wide of the mark. My own office has a framed poster over its fireplace of Bogart playing Sam. Sam's holding the Maltese Falcon, which to the untrained eye looks rather like an eagle and makes a nice play on the agency's name. The poster is the kind of stuff we have instead of diplomas, though I liked Barker's slogan. Wondered whether we could adapt it for our own reception area. *There Are No Shortcuts* was catchy. Maybe with a second line to complete the message: ...*Only More Money*.

'It's good to be known,' I said, though it wasn't. The last things a private investigator needs are handshakes and back-slaps when he's on a stakeout. 'I assume Mr Barker doesn't believe all he's heard.'

'He believes enough. He says you make the perfect case for industry regulation. If investigators were licensed he says you'd be out. He's never liked you since you shopped your clients.'

I held the grin. 'Sometimes,' I said, 'complications arise. Mr Barker knows that.'

The woman laughed.

'You got the child back and no-one else was going to do it. I'm on your side, dear.'

Good to know. I felt better right away. I nodded at the card. Repeated that this was urgent business.

'What do I tell him?' she said.

'I'd rather keep that between him and me,' I said.

'No need to be coy, Mr Flynn. I run the office. My brother has no secrets.'

'This is a family firm?'

'His firm. I just help out. Keep things in order. Sometimes he even pays me, though Sam's a stingy bastard.'

Sam. As in Sam Spade. An easy one for the memory.

Sam Barker.

Sam's sister held out her hand. It was beefy but firm.

'Yvonne,' she said.

'Eddie,' I told her. 'Please get Sam to call. Tell him it's about his friend Simon Andrew Morris at the BestBreak.'

I saw her smile finally flicker. If she ran Sam's admin then she knew his aliases so she knew that one of them had just been busted. I wondered what she knew about that leap from the hotel window.

'Is there a problem?' she said. Casual.

I shrugged. 'Hard to know. Are you familiar with Sam's recent activities.'

'Not really. He's busy with all kinds of things. I don't catch up until he bills.'

A straight lie. She knew about the hotel. And knew that it was some kind of fishy business which might be coming unravelled. She'd be talking to Sam the moment I walked out of there.

I asked for Sam's card, just in case. It had a mobile number that Yvonne told me he didn't usually answer when he was working.

I thanked her and left. Called the number anyway. It diverted straight to voicemail. I left a message to supplement the one Yvonne would be leaving.

Simon Andrew Morris.

S.A.M. As in Sam Barker.

Investigators are nothing if not creative.

But there was no doubt now that Barker was the guy who'd checked into the BestBreak for ten nights. He was Foxglove's man.

I had the name and location, as Foxglove demanded. All I needed was a chat with Sam Barker before I delivered the details. If Sam enlightened me I might even hold off on the delivery. If he didn't, I'd give him fair warning that the guy who'd chased him through that window was closing in. At least *Barker: Investigations & Solutions* were on the ground floor. If Foxglove turned up Sam had an easier exit.

I headed home.

CHAPTER NINE

This guy might be paying a call

I was considering options for the evening when Sam Barker called and named a pub in Sydenham. Suggested we meet. He didn't ask questions. Maybe sensed trouble. I drove over.

I went in through the saloon door and spotted a sixtyish guy dressed in jeans and sweater under a pea coat, perched on a stool at the end of the bar where he could drink in isolation. A pint glass and chaser were up in front of him – the organised apparatus of the hobby drinker. Barker's driving licence photo turned out to be real, though the snap hadn't brought out the full florid detail of his face, the dour street-weariness of a life sinking, hadn't brought out the beer on his breath. He looked at me without smiling. Nodded to the stool beside him. I sat and ordered a pint of Pride.

'Urgent,' Barker said. 'What does that mean?'

He was playing me. *He'd* set up the meet double quick. He knew my call was about the hotel caper, and a caper that ends with a dive through a window is one that's out of control. And when he got my message he knew that his one card – anonymity – was blown. Knew that the guy who'd chased him was still on his heels. So things were a little more urgent for him than for me.

'The guy's looking for you,' I said. My beer turned up. I lifted the glass.

'Which guy?'

'The one from your BestBreak job. The one who nearly cornered you.'

Barker shook his head and lifted his own beer. 'What BestBreak?'

I planted my glass. Smiled at Barker's reflection in the mirror. He was staring back.

'Let's not be coy, Sam. The guy's onto you. He's had me track you down and I'm guessing it's not to shake your hand.'

'You've tracked me down?' He took another swallow and lowered his glass. Lifted the whisky and toasted the mirror. 'Well good luck, pal, whoever your employer is. But you've got the wrong guy.'

I pulled out Harry's fake copy of Barker's fake driving licence, which drew his hand instinctively towards the inside of his coat before he checked himself. Realised he was looking at a new fake.

'You saying this isn't you?' I asked.

Barker tossed his drink. Snapped the glass down.

'Spit it out,' he said. 'What do you want?'

'This is just a courtesy. The guy you tangled with at the BestBreak has found you. At least he will have when I call him. I thought you'd appreciate a heads-up.'

Barker's lip lifted.

'So you're double-timing him. Looking for a payoff from me. Is that it?'

'No,' I said. 'I've found you and I'm handing you over tonight. The heads-up is a freebie. I thought you should know that this guy might come calling.'

Barker's face creased into a sneer. 'So you're shafting your client for the *fun* of it. Remind me never to hire you, pal.'

'Noted. But this isn't for fun. The guy gave us no choice when he hired us. This isn't a voluntary assignment. We've done what he asked but we're not letting him home free. And if he's got bad intentions towards you we're happy you know about it.'

'The guy conscripted you? That's a new one. Care to explain?'

'No. But you need to know that I'm calling him tonight.'

Barker paused. Gripped his beer glass.

'Noted. But I still don't believe you're here from the goodness of your heart.'

'Believe what you want. But since I've warned you maybe you can tell me what was going on at the BestBreak. It might help us both. My guess is that we've a shared interest in pushing this guy back.'

'Sorry pal, that information's not for sale.' He took a slow pull at his beer. 'I run my own business along confidential lines. And I deal with anyone who gives me problems. But thanks for the tip. I'll stand your pint for your trouble.'

But he wasn't offering another. Sam Barker was through with me. I couldn't figure whether he really didn't care about the hotel guy or was just hiding his head in the sand. But when Foxglove turned up he could be looking at a bad situation, for all his bravado.

They say free beer tastes better but this one had lost its bouquet. I left the glass half empty beside Sam Barker and went back out.

CHAPTER TEN

Peas and tractor wheels

I drove into Chelsea, told Herbie I'd be back in forty-five with a handout and grabbed a seat in a window alcove in a Chinese restaurant by the Town Hall. The place was a daytime café that switched place mats and cuisine at six p.m. and served the best Huaiyang dishes outside Chinatown. The owner was the brother of a guy we'd once helped, and put out the red carpet whenever I showed. I skipped the menu. Ordered a Yanjing and their gigantic shrimp fried rice. Fast and filling.

The place was busy enough for the buzz to cover my call while I waited.

'Job completed,' I reported to voicemail. 'We've traced your Room 209 resident.' I stated Sam Barker's name and office location. 'Now leave the civilians alone or we'll come for you.'

I was going for him anyway but he didn't need to know it until he felt my hand on his collar. I didn't mention the second instalment of his fee. If it arrived it arrived. The ten K we already had would get us to him. I sat back and sipped beer, and hunger kicked in. I glanced towards the kitchen to see if there was any sign of the fried rice. Nothing, though every time a waiter pushed the doors open a blast of sizzling came out. I put in a second call. Kim Waters' voice answered.

'As I anticipated,' I told her. 'Over before you know it.'

'You've found the guy?'

'We got a lucky break.'

'Who was he? Some kind of criminal?'

I watched the kitchen doors.

'Something like that. He's a private investigator.'

'The same as you.'

'The same as me.'

'Why was Foxglove looking for him?'

'I don't know.'

'Will he go after him?'

'I've warned the guy about that possibility. He didn't seem too worried.'

'So that's it. The threat's over?'

'It served its purpose. Got Foxglove what he wanted. But it may be wise to leave your daughter out of town until the weekend, so we're sure things have settled.'

She sighed. 'I still can't believe this happened. Would he really have hurt us?'

'The main thing is that you're of no interest to him now. Bring your daughter back at the weekend and forget the affair.'

'And we never even knew who he was.'

The kitchen doors swung wide. A waiter approached with a tray holding a plate and serving dishes. I made space.

'I'm going to find out who he is,' I told Kim. 'Then I'll take it to the police. They can decide whether Foxglove was bluffing about hurting people.'

'Why not let it go? If there's no longer a threat.'

'That's not the way we work.'

'But if this guy finds out you're after him it might provoke him.'

'He won't find out until it's too late. I guarantee it.'

'Still...'

'I'll stay in touch,' I said. 'Let you know how it works out.'

'Sure. Please do. And... Eddie?'

I waited.

'Thanks for doing this. You've no reason to be looking out for us.'

'The world's full of bullies and thugs,' I said. 'That's reason enough.'

I told her to take care and ended the call. Tipped the sizzling food onto the plate. There are places in town that serve meals the size of a pea on plates the size of tractor wheels. This one had the tractor wheel plate but with a food mountain. Good marketing strategy. If you cleared the plate you felt smug and were likely to call again to show them you could still do it. So far I was on a winning streak. I took a swig of the Yanjing and set to.

With or without Foxglove's second instalment we'd enough of his cash to spend a week looking for him. And maybe find out what the hotel thing was about. It had been wishful thinking that Barker would tell me why he'd rented that room and who'd put the safe code in the bible and why the code didn't work – or why the safe was re-locked with nothing inside.

I'd have put the hotel room and shared keys down to a simple dodgy business transaction if Barker hadn't made that leap when he heard the door opening, and if Foxglove had known who was inside the room.

But understanding the hotel thing was just icing on the cake. The important job was to introduce Foxglove to the Metropolitan Police. Where they went with it was up to them.

I'd not much to point me Foxglove's way but it was as much as I'd had yesterday when I started after Sam, and finding *him* hadn't taken long. Why should Foxglove be any harder?

Confidence: they should let you bank it.

CHAPTER ELEVEN
It's never stopped us before

Harry and I were out with a client next morning. Follow-up from an investigation of a workplace accident that the insurance underwriter suspected was not accidental, resulting in an injury that might not be as bad as the claimant's tearful solicitor was making out. The claimant had come off a warehouse ladder and injured his back. The injury hadn't produced much visible evidence but the guy had been out of work for a month, confined to his house apart from the weekly hobble to his lawyer's office.

Insurance investigation brings a steady income. We work fixed price and check claimants for evidence of a scam. In the current case Harry had been on the guy for a week and seen nothing. If he was secretly running marathons Harry didn't spot it. But Harry was suspicious. Listened to whispers and dug further. When he turned in his report it was negative but with a caveat.

The insurance company had raised an eyebrow. Listened to Harry's proposal and sent a letter to the guy's solicitor citing new internal guidelines that dictated a settlement offer of a straight million, subject to satisfactory agreement on both sides. The offer was ten times what the guy's lawyer had been demanding.

If the injured guy had suspected that the insurance company was watching him – which he had – his caution was thrown to the wind when his solicitor phoned the offer through. Which is why he failed to spot, as he headed for a celebratory night out with two brothers and some pals, a green Mondeo creeping after them.

Harry had Lucy with him to go places he couldn't. She followed the celebrants into a rave. Found that the guy was a pretty decent dancer. Lucy snapped a gigabyte's worth of action on her phone camera as he got down and dirty with the ladies, and neither his exertions nor his injury stymied his ability to get into a brief fist fight when the club closed nor to climb a street sign to jam a celebratory traffic cone up top.

When the guy hobbled into his solicitor's two days later for the lottery sign-up he found himself across the table from an insurance rep's stony stare. Apparently his solicitor's tears were real.

Harry's caveat had been the thing. It concerned the claimant's two brothers who, on closer inspection, also turned out to be disabled following claims with their own insurance companies. Which of the three brothers was the best dancer Lucy couldn't say but the insurance company didn't care. They just pushed her nightclub snaps across the table and sent copies to the other underwriters who'd footed the bill for the brothers' work-free lifestyle.

On the back of the job the company had pulled us in this morning to discuss a regular consultation role. They planned to implement extended background checks for any major claimants who roused their suspicions, using in-house staff under our supervision. We named a price and shook hands on a contract good for five hundred hours and headed back to the office. A productive morning.

When we finished commending Lucy on her photography skills she pushed a package across her desk. Another courier delivery. Addressed to me again.

Foxglove.

We came back to earth.

Shaughnessy was in the front room. We went through and Harry flopped into his chair and Lucy and Herbie perched themselves on the desk while I tore open the package. It was another fat one. I up-ended it beside Lucy and a wad of banknotes dropped out. The second instalment of Foxglove's twenty K.

The guy was as good as his word.

A nice fee for twenty-four hours on the job.

'You closed it?' Shaughnessy asked.

'Foxglove got his ID last night. The hotel guy was a P.I. working over in Streatham.'

'The guy needs to be sharper at hiding his trail,' Shaughnessy said.

'He got unlucky. Was caught out and had to make a quick getaway. Left things behind in the excitement of the moment.'

I described the guy limping away from a ten foot jump. The big, Asian featured guy seen going after him. The trail to Streatham.

'You talk to the P.I.?'

'He wasn't interested in talking. If he feels threatened by Foxglove he was hiding it.'

'So what was the hotel thing?'

'Beats me,' I said. 'Not our problem.' I picked up the wads of cash. 'But this will get us to Foxglove. When we find him we'll decide whether he's still a threat to these women and whether the hotel thing is relevant.'

'Any pointers?'

I tossed the cash back onto the desk. Went to watch the street.

'None I can see,' I said. 'But we'll find something.'

'At least the guy pays on time,' Lucy said.

'Bank it,' I said. 'Clear some bills. And if we find this guy without spending the rest of it we'll be in profit. Maybe the office can use it.'

Lucy grabbed the cash, visualising makeovers and fancy computers, potted plants. The money was ours. The rest of the stuff, though – Foxglove's notes and the photos – would be in the hands of the police once we identified the guy.

I left them to it. Headed out with Herbie on two routine jobs, mulling over the question of pointers. The search for Foxglove would be a filler for any gaps in my schedule.

I got back mid-afternoon. Found the office empty.

Herbie and I kicked around for a while. I watched the sky over the Westway and looked for inspiration, ideas that would get me to Foxglove. Eventually the clock said it was time to fight the rush hour. I locked up and was turning for the stairs when I saw a woman's figure coming up, tall, lithe, easy. Kim Waters' face came out of the shadows. She stopped. Checked herself as if she was surprised at finding me here or finding herself here. Then for the first time since I'd met her her face broke into a smile.

Which almost knocked me over.

I held the handrail. The stairs go a long way down. When I was steady I returned her smile.

'This is a surprise,' I said.

There are websites nowadays that give you chat-up lines by the thousand. I keep meaning to visit them.

Kim's smile broke into a laugh.

'I'm sorry. I should have called. I don't know what I'm doing here but I was just down the road and...'

'You thought you'd check the detective's roost.'

'Something like that. But I wanted to thank you.'

'No thanks required. We did what the guy forced us to do. And we're happy to help if there's any further trouble.'

'The thing is...' She searched for what had really brought her here. 'I was a bit short two days ago. The shock of what was happening. I saw you as part of it. I want to apologise. And to thank you.'

'Just doing our job,' I repeated. 'We wanted to close this thing just as much as you.'

'Yes...'

We stood a moment, awkward. Doors banged downstairs. Voices called. The legal firm, shutting up shop. Kim looked down, uncertain.

'It's a nice evening,' I said. 'How about a walk?'

~~~~~

The walk was over in Battersea. Herbie and I do a round of the park most evenings before we eat. When I clarified the location it didn't faze Kim. She said that Battersea sounded fine. Tailed me over the river in an Aston Martin of all things. Apparently Kim's line of work was paying.

We stopped by my place and I fed Herbie and left Kim browsing my jazz collection whilst I showered and changed. Then we went out and crossed to the park. I didn't know why we were doing this. I didn't know whether Kim knew. But spontaneity is the spice of life and it was a nice evening for a stroll with a beautiful woman.

'That looked like a fortune hanging on your walls,' Kim said. 'Assuming they're originals.'

I grinned. 'They're originals. But the fortune is smaller than you think. The acrylics are mine.'

'You're a painter? That's interesting for a private detective.'

'We're arty types. Sherlock Holmes played the violin.'

'Do you also smoke heroin?'

'The law has caught up in some areas.'

'Do you play an instrument?'

'Listener only. Jazz. As you noticed. How about you? What do you like to do? I don't even know what you do for a living, except that it's nothing mundane.'

She smiled. 'Do you fancy dinner?'

~~~~~

There was a restaurant called Kiki's in a glass complex just off the far side of the park. Prices were through the roof but their food was spot on and they allowed customers with dogs.

We ordered drinks and Kim told me about herself.

I'd guessed right. Her occupation was not mundane. What it was was lucrative. Aston Martin lucrative. Kim was a lawyer-turned-human, an entrepreneur who'd set up her own legal recruitment and head-hunting company in her twenties and was now working part-time drawing a high six figure income from the business whilst she devoted her remaining time to a hands-on legal practice that assisted people with housing problems, which mainly translated into helping tenants fight ruthless landlords. The marriage that came along soon after Kim started her recruitment company had burned brightly and faded quickly, but left a daughter Alice who burned brighter every day and was the single point of harmony between Kim and her ex.

'He a solicitor too?' I asked.

She shook her head. 'Landlord. Property developer. You see the conflict? Opposites attract but they don't always stay attracted. Oliver always had this thing that he was the ethical type and fundamentally he was but there were too many times when ethics took second place to his business interests. Eventually I couldn't avoid seeing the flip side of every coin. It ended up that we couldn't talk about his business without fighting, and in the end we couldn't talk about anything.'

'Can't be a great income stream, protecting tenants' rights.'

'The agency brings in all I need,' Kim said. 'I've got a Mayfair house a Saudi princess would envy and a dream car. I can afford the low-paid day job. How about you? Does private investigating make you rich?'

She'd already seen my apartment, and my apartment was stylish and snug and quintessential London but it wasn't Mayfair and I wasn't driving an Aston Martin. I realised that the dig was a reminder of the impressive fee Foxglove had stumped up for two days' work. Or maybe it was just a dig for the sake of digging. Maybe she didn't care about my wealth, was just fine at this dinner table with a Staffie cross warming her feet – it wasn't me playing footsie – and the prospect of good food, unusual company and two hours away from career and family.

'The only way to get rich in this game,' I informed her, 'is to start richer. Not many clients send us twenty K in an envelope.'

Not many young lawyers live in Mayfair either. But this young lawyer was a savvy businesswoman. This one had me reading the menu backwards. When the waiter reappeared I still hadn't got a clue what was on offer. Plumped for the pepper steak I'd eaten last time. Kim plumped for some kind of duck dish. I took a sip of beer and pulled myself together. Kim sipped wine.

'I love it too,' she said. 'Jazz. But the modern stuff. You know? Sax. Candy Dulfer. Rob Stewart.'

I knew. Could even tolerate some of Dulfer's stuff. Funk fusion. Beat a little too pacy for me but the woman has some of the lightest fingers in the business. My own taste went harder and deeper, the frantic mystery tours of Parker and Davis, but Dulfer's Chilled Out had seen me right through a late night stakeout back in January.

The food turned up. I watched Kim as she started on the duck. Watching her face could become a hobby. Her clear, unlined complexion could pass for mid twenties but I fitted mid thirties to her potted history. Asking would be impolite. And age didn't matter. The woman had a timeless allure that transcended detail.

A beautiful woman. Tasty food. Jazz talk. My idea of a perfect evening, even if I was pushing aside the fact that Kim was only sitting opposite me because some crazy bastard had invaded her world and tossed her my way as a pawn.

The more I liked Kim the more I disliked Foxglove.

Kim read my mind.

'I've been thinking about what you said,' she said.

I quit sawing my steak.

'This guy isn't interested in me now. He's got what he wanted.'

I concurred. 'His only interest was in using you as leverage to get me to do his dirty work.'

'So I'm history. I'm still thinking of reporting it to the police but I'm half tempted just to let it go.'

'Your decision. But I think you're safe now.'

'Why was he so intent on hiring your firm?'

'Beats me. There are plenty of agencies in this town. Maybe we had a little too much publicity last year. Maybe the rags made us out as unbeatable, the firm that works miracles. And maybe time was critical. So Foxglove selected us and went in heavy handed with the up-front cash and didn't want to expand his exposure by shopping around elsewhere when we turned him down. Maybe didn't want to lose time. But if he'd done his research he'd have found that we were the wrong firm. That we wouldn't want the job, nor let his coercion go afterwards.'

'So you're going to track him down?'

'As long as his twenty K lasts. I want to know how dangerous he is. And I want to be sure he's forgotten you.'

'But won't that provoke him? Especially if you hand him to the police.'

'We'll only bring the police in if we find out that he's an ongoing threat or has hurt people in the past. And only when we've got the evidence to guarantee that he's heading for time inside. He'll have more important things to worry about than you.'

She hesitated. Forked her salad and duck breast. Dropped another piece of meat down to her feet where her attempt at discretion was spoiled by the furious snuffling and panting that ensued. She looked across. Reignited her smile.

'So you always get your man,' she said.

'I don't always know when to stop,' I said. 'Maybe that amounts to the same thing.'

She leaned forwards. 'Please don't take any risks on my behalf,' she said. 'You've already helped me. You don't need to save the world from this guy. Maybe you're better off just banking the money.'

'If we think he's not findable then that's what we'll do.'

'And don't get yourself hurt.'

I grinned. Went back to my steak.

'Hazard of the trade,' I said.

I looked up. Her face was serious. I shrugged to make light of it.

'I try to keep out of trouble,' I said.

~~~~~

Dinner had to end sometime. Just a few days sooner than I'd have liked. When we came out onto the street it was almost dark. We walked back across the park to Kim's car and I was wondering whether to invite her up when she beat me to it and said it would be great to meet again, that maybe I could show her my jazz club. I promised to give her a call next time I had an evening lined up.

We stood by the car for a moment. Then she leaned forward and touched her lips to my cheek and wiggled her fingers at Herbie.

Herbie swooned and rolled over.

Those duck handouts.

We watched her drive off and went in. I refreshed Herbie's water bowl and went to sit with my feet up watching the street, with Dexter Gordon blowing softly in the shadows. When my eyes opened it was after midnight and Herbie was snoring on the sofa. I crept past him and hit the sack. Sank like a stone into a vision of flowing gold hair and shining emerald eyes.

Then my phone woke me.

The screen said it was two a.m.

I picked up. Half recognised the voice, but my brain had to work overtime to place it whilst I listened to the message.

'Flynn: you need to get down here. They've killed him.'

Computing...

'Killed who? What the hell time is it?'

'They've put him in a lake. And you're part of it. Your name's going to be up in lights, Flynn.'

Still computing...

'Slow down. Who's in a lake?'

'Jesus, Flynn. Who do you think? Sam. His car's in the water and he's strapped inside and you've got some damn explaining to do.'

Sam Barker.

Yvonne.

The voice clicked into place. I was up and out of my bed in a flash.

'Where are you?'

'Chislehurst. The north side of the common. Follow the police lights. Come and see what you've done.'

53

CHAPTER TWELVE
Probably inebriated

I dodged a patrol car blocking the road by walking down under the cover of trees. Emerged at a cluster of vehicles parked by a small lake right by the road. More of a pond, though it was deep enough twenty yards out to swallow the BMW 3 Series that had rolled down the earth bank into the water. Police lighting and recovery vehicle strobes illuminated the ridge of the boot and the rear window, part of the roof, all that showed above the black surface.

The driver was still inside.

The uniformed patrol officer who'd been first on the scene had waded in and ducked under to shine his torch into the vehicle. The door was locked and the interior flooded. No-one saveable. He'd left the body where it was.

A line disappeared into the water and a diver was stripping out of a wetsuit. I kept a low profile and watched the tow guy heave on the line, check the clevis.

Yvonne Barker was standing in a cluster of onlookers. She turned and clocked me and a uniformed sergeant walked across to confirm my identity and ask if I was the guy who'd been following the victim. I doubted whether they had a positive ID on the victim yet but I went with the odds and repeated what Yvonne had just told him, which was what Sam had told her after our chat the other night. The sergeant asked whom I'd been working for and I said I didn't know. He asked if I knew what had happened and I said that it looked like Sam had drowned. He asked if I'd like to spend the night in a police cell and I said no. When we'd finished our exchange we walked back towards Yvonne. The recovery guy climbed into his cab.

'Probably inebriated,' the sergeant concluded, contradicting the implications of his questioning. How he came up with his theory with the victim still under the water I wasn't sure but then Yvonne noticed me again. Explained.

'He was at the pub,' she said. 'Probably for a few hours.'

But she knew this wasn't a drink-drive accident. The First Rule of the investigation business says there's no such thing as coincidence.

Someone had wanted the identity of the BestBreak guest sufficiently urgently to go for overkill in recruiting me. And twenty four hours after I'd handed over a name the subject was in his car under this lake. I hadn't mentioned the overkill to the sergeant. Details of the twenty K fee and threats to innocent people would only complicate things. I'd bring Kim Waters' name into the affair only when we'd enough information to nail Foxglove. I didn't want her in his crosshairs before he'd been taken off the street.

I pulled Yvonne aside.

'Sam talk to you last night?'

'Yes.' Her eyes were on the recovery vehicle. 'He phoned about some business for tomorrow. Mentioned you. He sounded fine, though he was in the pub when he called. But Sam knows his limit. He doesn't get too drunk to drive.'

'Would Sam normally drive past here?'

The recovery guy threw a lever and the gears began to whine. Yvonne was watching it. Pulled her attention away for a second to give me a look. Her face was a patchwork of shadow and light, reflected sheen from the amber strobes.

'He'd pass about half a mile away on his way home,' she said.

'He say anything about meeting someone?'

'No.'

I let it go. Watched the operation. The cable came taut and the BMW came slowly out of the water. When it was clear and on level ground the winch guy applied the brakes and a policeman walked down and smashed the driver's window. Stepped clear of the flood. All the windows had been open six inches which would allow the car to fill inside a minute as it settled under the water. But that was plenty of time for a driver to get out. And the car had taken no obvious damage. No airbags deployed. Just a slow roll down into the lake. I wondered how drunk you had to be to stay unresponsive as the water rose up your chest.

With the window out we could see Sam behind the wheel, head drooped forwards, hands down at his side. Yvonne walked across and stooped to confirm it was him then walked away out of the light.

I stayed put and watched the sergeant greet a guy in plain clothes who'd just driven up. The guy came across to me and held up a warrant card. Introduced himself as DS Keith Prior from Bromley

CID. I gave him my name and profession.

'I'm hearing stories,' he said. 'What do you know about this?'

'Only the fact that someone had me looking for the victim. It may not be relevant but I'm assuming it is.'

'You mean someone put him in there?'

'It's a possibility. Someone was keen to find him and we delivered his ID. That's all I know.'

'Sure it is. Who's the woman?'

Yvonne had drifted back to watch the police open the BMW's door and start to manipulate the body. I confirmed that she was the victim's sister.

'She knows as much as I do,' I said.

Prior waited for her to come away from the car then introduced himself. Asked questions. Just a formality. He'd need a longer chat with both of us.

Yvonne answered his questions but provided little information.

'Okay,' Prior said. 'I need statements from you both.'

'We already talked to the sergeant,' Yvonne said.

The DS looked at her.

'Just a formality. I need to talk to you in more detail, ma'am. Is first thing tomorrow convenient? I could be a while here.'

We both agreed that first thing was convenient. Kicking our heels in the local nick waiting for this guy to roll back in didn't appeal. He checked our ID's again, wrote down our details and told us to be there at nine.

I walked Yvonne back to her car. She was breathing heavily now. She stopped and turned to me.

'I hope to god,' she said, 'that you really do know nothing about this. Because right now I could tear you apart. And if it does turn out that you were involved then that's what I'll do.'

The road was dark and her face was shadowed but enough came through to say that she meant it. Could maybe do it. The lady was a bulldozer.

'Let's talk at Bromley,' I said.

Tomorrow there'd be time to think. And policemen nearby if she went for the tearing apart option.

She nodded at me and walked to her car without saying anything more. I walked up to the Frogeye and drove back into London with the windows open.

Three a.m. Deserted streets. The faint hiss of the city reflecting off the buildings. Something uneasy in my stomach.

CHAPTER THIRTEEN
He's my lawyer

I lost half the morning at Bromley nick before Prior showed his face. It was a face exhibiting all the good humour you get from a night's lost sleep and a mutinous breakfast. Yvonne had got in first and had kept him for two hours. She came out with him and nodded to me. Sat down a few chairs away to wait. Prior invited me through.

Herbie slid off the adjacent chair and followed me across. He'd killed the two hours by checking out uniformed police and civilians as they passed. Growling at a selected few. One in three got the treatment. I'd watched closely but hadn't discerned his system. Some passed. Some failed. Simple as that. When we approached Prior Herbie growled for both of us.

'Not the dog,' Prior said.

I stopped.

'He's my lawyer,' I said.

'Funny. Do you think you need a lawyer?'

'Who knows. You might trick me with your clever questions.'

'Then you'll need a human lawyer. The dog can't come in. Regulations.'

I stopped.

'The way I see it,' I said, 'this thing – the fact that someone was tracking down Mr Barker – is complicating what you believe to be a simple road traffic accident. So all you want to do is get the paperwork done and get back to your real case load. Which will happen sooner if we get this over now rather than wait for me to find a dog sitter and come back. So why don't we forget the bullshit and get on with it. My dog's sworn to confidentiality. What we discuss stays between us.'

'Clever Dick,' Prior said. 'Go on then: piss off and come back when you've got rid of the pooch. Waste everyone's time.'

I turned and started back towards the front doors. My confidential colleague followed.

We were halfway across before Prior blinked.

'Okay,' he yelled. 'For cryin' out loud! Get through here.'

We about-turned. I considered saluting but the look on Prior's face dissuaded me. He held the door and took us up two flights of stairs to a ten by six interview room with one table and two chairs. Herbie settled beneath the table and kept his growl going so the interrogator wouldn't get too comfortable.

Prior dropped a pad and pen onto the table. Ready for shorthand notes. This wasn't a formal interview. No caution. And he wasn't going to spend the rest of the day listening to an audio.

'Tell me again,' he said. 'What's your involvement with the person who was looking for Mr Barker?'

I took him through it a second time. There was nothing he hadn't already heard but repetition and the pen and paper cemented the memory. I stuck to the basics. The anonymous cash payment, the hotel mystery guest, the trail that lead to Sam Barker, and Sam's nonchalance when I tipped him off. I left out the oddities of the safe and the Gideon code and the threat to Kim Waters. Kim wasn't going to be reassured by a call from the police. And a search for the other women in Foxglove's photos wasn't going to help us find him. I didn't need Foxglove looking over his shoulder or going to ground. Not that Bromley CID were about to invest any hours. The slant of Prior's questions made that clear. He couldn't ignore the potential connection between Sam's accident and Foxglove but it didn't excite him.

'So Mr Barker was up to some dodgy business at the hotel,' Prior summarised. 'Facilitating some kind of exchange that wouldn't bear scrutiny. And who knows what kind of people he was dealing with? But Barker was a habitual drink-driver. He'd been in the pub for four hours last night. Maybe he didn't need anyone's help to find that lake.'

I assumed that Prior's dodgy business theory and Sam's drinking habit had come from Yvonne. I wondered how much she'd told him. How much she knew. Not enough to convince Prior that Barker had been murdered. And I wasn't about to take up the campaign.

Prior was a heavyset guy in his late fifties. An honest face behind his wire frame glasses. Competent rather than imaginative. Buried under mountain of unsolved petty crime. There was nothing for him in Sam's accident unless evidence came in to show that there'd been foul play. When I came up with that evidence I'd bring it in.

Four hours' boozing wasn't a good preparation for a late night drive, and Prior's information didn't contradict my impression of Barker as a lush. The flabby, florid face, weary eyes, chasers lined up beside his pints, painted a picture of a guy not long for this world. But his drive into that lake wasn't coincidence. For some things you don't need forensics.

We were in there just forty minutes. Prior got what he wanted, told me he'd be in touch and kicked us out.

Yvonne Barker was still waiting.

She hadn't slept since she was called out last night and didn't look better for it. The big woman's face was creased with inner turmoil. Her eyes were dry but blotchy as we walked across.

'They killed him,' she said. 'You know it.'

'It's hard to ignore the circumstances,' I said. 'How are you holding up?'

'I'm holding up fine. Fine enough to want to know who the killer was.'

'Me too,' I said.

She stood.

'So where do we start?'

'Have you got the keys to his office?'

'Of course.'

'Let's start there.'

CHAPTER FOURTEEN
Maybe he just got sloppy

Yvonne opened up at *Barker: Investigations & Solutions* and stood looking round the empty room as realisation hit home that she no longer belonged in the place. The business had died with its owner and the room was just a vacant space waiting for the next tenant. In a month it would be a nail salon or charity shop. Whatever had tied Yvonne Barker to the place had gone. Whatever she had shared with her brother, any fondness and history or regrets and irritations, were obsolete. She stood a moment, unsure how to proceed.

I closed the door and pulled one of the plastic chairs out. Spun it round to sit saddle-wise. Propped my arms on the back. Herbie wandered around, checking things out.

'Hell,' I said.

Yvonne snapped out of her reverie and looked at me with mixed sorrow and anger. Clamped her lips to keep her thoughts under lock and key whilst she walked round to perch herself on the chair behind the counter. She rested her arms on the surface and almost lowered her head down. Caught herself.

'Hell,' she said. 'You're spot on there, Flynn. Sam didn't deserve that.' She glared at me and the glare made it clear that if I wasn't the actual guy who'd put Sam into that lake I was pretty close. And right then I felt pretty close.

'How long have you worked for him?'

'Since the start. Twenty years ago. Sam was just out of the police on a disability pension. He'd smashed his leg up in a stolen car incident and was full of plans to go it alone. He needed someone to look after the office and I was divorced and skint so I took the job. But within twelve months Sam was drinking most of his profit and he's done as much of that as investigation ever since.'

'Looks like the investigating paid its way,' I said. I was thinking of the BMW, not these premises. I suspected that Sam Barker had a nice house somewhere.

'It's easy money if you've got the touch. But he could have made a lot more of it.'

The story of most investigators. It should go on our headstones.

'How often was he drinking?'

'Every night. He only had one hobby after hours. He called it socialising but he was sour when he was in his cups. He's my own brother but I won't deny he was sour.'

'Did he habitually drive when he'd had a few?'

'Yes. But he could hold his drink, drive and talk better after five pints than most people sober.'

Five pints and *chasers*, to be precise. And no-one drives as well as they think with that level of lubricant in their bloodstream.

'So it's not beyond the bounds of possibility that this was an accident?'

'Get off that horse, Flynn. Neither of us believes it.'

'Eddie,' I said. 'No need for formalities. And I'm just considering possibilities. I believe Sam was killed. I'm just sorry I played any part.'

'Your choice, Flynn.'

I clenched and unclenched my fists. Leaned forward on the chair. 'There were compelling factors,' I said. 'We weren't tracking Sam down voluntarily.'

'Really? What compelling factors were there other than a fat pay packet?'

'The pay packet *was* hefty,' I conceded. I named the amount and Yvonne's eyes opened wide. She pursed her lips to whistle.

'Well, that damn well settles it,' she said. 'Someone pays twenty grand to find Sam. Then a day after they get his name he's dead. Did you tell Sergeant Prior how much you'd charged?'

'The charge wasn't ours. We turned the job down. But we were put in a position where we were forced to reconsider.'

I explained. Her eyes opened.

'Being in demand is good,' she said, 'but that's a little extreme.'

'Extreme and misjudged. The guy assumed that the sheer weight of money would guarantee our cooperation. And reverted to threats when we declined his dirty work.'

'But you took his money anyway.'

'The money is funding an investigation into who he is. I don't like people who threaten women and kids. Nor ones who kill people. And I've no doubt it was Foxglove who caught up with Sam last night. My guess is he squeezed him for information about the hotel affair then set up the accident. Maybe upped Sam's alcohol level then tapped him on the head. Something to incapacitate him when they rolled his car into the water.'

'And you say you're going to find him?'

'We were already looking. Sam has just added incentive.'

She watched me, juggling facts and probabilities to decide where I was on the bad guy scale. Maybe spending Foxglove's cash to track him down upped my rating a little because she sat up behind the counter and her gaze seemed to favour me a little more.

'Tell me about the BestBreak job,' I said.

'It was an exchange. Sam was hired to deliver four packages without leaving a trail.'

'What kind of packages? Money? Drugs?'

'Documents. In four sealed envelopes. Four sequential exchanges. Sam was told to set it up so that the recipient couldn't trace the deliveries back to either him or his client.'

'What were the documents?'

'Sam didn't say.'

'Who was the client?'

'He didn't know.'

I grinned. Herbie was sniffing at one of the counter drawers. Yvonne stretched and opened it. Pulled out a tin and handed Herbie a biscuit. He crunched. Sprayed crumbs.

So Sam had been working for a secretive client. The thing had a resonance. Sam delivering packages for someone he didn't know, tracked down by me working for someone *I* didn't know. So was *my* anonymous client the packages recipient, chasing the source?

'How did Sam's client contact him?'

'He arranged a meet. A week last Tuesday. He didn't give Sam a name.'

'Was Sam okay with that?'

'More or less. Sam understood the guy's desire not to be traced and Sam had no need to know the name. They met at The Red Dragon in Sydenham and the guy handed Sam the packages and fee.'

The same pub in which I'd talked to Sam.

'Did Sam describe the client?'

'I didn't ask.'

'How was the exchange set up?'

'The client wanted four deliveries made over several days. Each one after he'd given Sam the go-ahead. Sam used a two-drop chain. He rented separate hotel rooms with safes for each delivery. Requested two keycards for each room and left a package in each safe waiting for the go-ahead. As each came through he left the relevant keycard in a drop round town – places where there was minimal risk of anyone finding it by chance – and texted the location and hotel detail to his client, including where to find the safe code. The client passed the information to the recipient and the recipient retrieved the hotel address and key and then picked up the package. It was simple and foolproof. Sam was long gone before the recipient knew either the key drop or hotel for each delivery. There was no way the recipient could catch up with him.'

Though Sam would have known there were ways. Which made it odder that he got caught.

'Do you think the recipient was buying the packages?' Yvonne asked.

'That would explain the staged delivery. Part-payment, part-delivery. Even if there were four recipients all the effort put into the exchange suggests a profit motive. But I'm seeing just one recipient. Four payment instalments and four part-deliveries, reducing the risk for both sides.'

'That sounds right,' Yvonne said. 'Especially if the sum being paid was large. But why did the recipient come chasing after Sam once it was over?'

'Because he didn't consider it over: either he wanted his money back or felt threatened by Sam's client. Maybe the documents were damaging to him and he needed to make sure there were no other copies out there.'

Yvonne leaned forwards on the counter and looked round the room. Eyes trying to comprehend just how *empty* this place suddenly was. I gave her a moment.

'Sam always said that drop exchanges were a foolproof way of avoiding contact between the parties,' she said eventually.

'They're not far off if they're done correctly,' I said. 'And in this case Foxglove was always two locations behind Sam. When did Sam complete the deliveries?'

'Monday afternoon. The BestBreak was the last package. The

document had been in the safe there since last week. On Monday Sam got the final go-ahead and texted the keycard location and hotel details for his client to pass on.'

'What time was this?'

'Late afternoon. Fourish.

And Sam had taken his dive into that skip around six that evening, two hours later. But he should never have been near the hotel once he'd texted the location. Going back was his fatal error.

'Did Sam mention any problems with that delivery?' I asked.

Yvonne shook her head. 'The only thing he mentioned was that his client was dealing with dangerous people. That was the morning after the BestBreak. He told me the job was finished, but something was bugging him. He came in late and looked like hell and he was limping more than usual. I put it down to a rough night at the Dragon, his old injury.'

I explained that what was bugging Sam was the skip stunt. For some reason Sam had gone back to the BestBreak. We didn't know why but he knew he was breaking the cardinal rule of a safe drop. And he'd almost been caught. His concern on Tuesday was that they were looking for him.

'That's when they came to you,' Yvonne said.

'They were moving fast. Foxglove had contacted us by nine a.m.'

Yvonne thought about it. Pushed her hand through her hair.

'And we don't know,' she said, 'who any of the players are.'

'Sam's client set it all up so no-one would know anyone. Foxglove might be the package recipient or not.'

'But he's Sam's killer.'

'Hard to see it any other way.'

'Is he still looking for Sam's client?'

'Yes. Unless Sam gave him the name. If he ever knew it. '

'And now you're looking for Foxglove?'

'Yes.'

'How can I help?' Yvonne said.

I stood. Lifted the chair back to where I'd found it.

'Is that Sam's office?' I nodded towards the unmarked door alongside the Meeting Room.

'Yes.'

'You can show me that,' I said.

CHAPTER FIFTEEN
Retro pin-up

Yvonne unlocked the door and flicked on fluorescents to illuminate a windowless office with the soul of a store cupboard. An untidy teak veneer desk centre stage with a Herman Miller carbon-back chair behind it that was the twin of the one in my own office apart from having both armrests. The chair delivered a jolt of recognition for a fellow traveller: Sam Barker perched on his seat wasn't so different from me perched in my own back at Chase Street. I had a vision of my own chair, empty one day after a case had turned bad.

The epiphany didn't last. Most of our cases tended to go bad. If I worried about it I'd never leave my bed.

And here I was and here Sam wasn't, and the difference was something Sam had done wrong. The difference was his going back to that hotel room when the cardinal rule of the dead drop is that you *never* go back. The difference, shouting from every corner of this ordinary room, was that the BestBreak had just been an ordinary job to a world-weary, heavy-drinking investigator. And ordinary doesn't keep your guard up.

Sam's desk was cluttered with junk and paper and a PC screen. The wall behind the desk had a cork board cluttered with more junk — fast-food menus, a retro pin-up calendar, a postcard of the London Eye, another of somewhere abroad and a photo of a guy in police uniform who might have been Sam. Next to the cork board was a whiteboard with scribbled notes covering what looked like fifty jobs: abbreviated place names, times, names. Nothing meaningful.

The decor was completed by two filing cabinets and a plastic chair and a tangle of electrical cords and computer cables. The office had all the character of an accountant's back room.

Class.

The thing Sam Barker had been lacking.

An ordinary job grown mundane.

He was probably offered a hefty fee for the exchange job. Took it without a second's thought. The guy who owned this desk hadn't been working for the love of the job.

'Most of what Sam needed for the package exchange would be in his head,' I said, 'but there might be something here. Did he use the computer much?'

'Online research. Case notes. Reports. I cover the admin.' Yvonne huffed round and sank into Sam's chair. 'You want me to go through it?'

'Yeah. I'll cover the paperwork. Has Sam got stuff in the cabinet?'

'Nothing relevant. The package exchange was just action. No research, no report. There'll be nothing in there.'

Made sense. Which left us with jottings and notes.

We got busy. I started with the cork- and whiteboards because they were the most palatable. Yvonne fired up Sam's computer. She'd be familiar with some of the stuff there from her admin work. What she was looking for were new files from the last ten days.

The corkboard yielded nothing. The retro pin-up calendar turned out to be unrelated. The London Eye postcard had been posted in Croydon and had a cryptic comment "Usual. Car Five" but Yvonne dated it as five years old. The foreign postcard was undated but had been there forever. And the guy in police uniform was a three-decade-old version of Sam that had long since vanished.

The whiteboard scribblings were meaningless at best, illegible at worst. The single jotting that made sense was the FoneMart name circled with a price next to it that matched the charge listed on Sam's repair receipt. Yvonne explained that the WiFi on his backup phone had packed in two weeks ago. She was unaware that he'd had the repair done.

I moved to the desk. Sifted the mess using a technique recognisable to archaeologists. Looked for papers and folders that showed signs of having been disturbed recently. A dust covering counted as a negative, likewise anything buried in a low stratum. Loose stuff and papers with signs of recent movement got checked. Most of it was commercial paperwork with nothing of Sam's added. The single hit was a Post-it pad whose top four sheets had been scribbled on.

Unlike archaeological remains, the top layer of Post-its is the oldest. In this case there was a note saying "Call Harrow" which Yvonne dated as the day Sam was approached about the package job but which was unrelated. She'd written the note herself.

Next down was more interesting.

Sam had written the note after taking on the package exchange job. It was a cryptic message with a name and address. The note said:

Package 4...
J. Coates.

"Package 4" was circled with a marker, and the name was followed by a question:

Who are YOU?

Below this was a Caterham address.

Something had stirred up a little extracurricular interest as Sam organised the exchanges. I wondered where he'd dug up the name J. Coates. Was Coates the client or the package recipient?

Yvonne didn't know. She hadn't seen the note.

The next note down gave us a time stamp. The note said

Phone – ready after 12

which was a reference to Sam picking up his repaired phone at midday on Monday. So Sam had dug up the *J. Coates* name sometime between taking on the job and noon of the day he collected his phone, which was the day of his final package delivery.

I turned to the final marked Post-it. It said:

Flynn.
Met.
Out '04.
Kosher

which was a summary he'd produced from a phone-around yesterday after he got the message to contact me. It had to be a phone-around because the internet didn't have my history – certainly not an opinion that I was *kosher*. And even the blower wasn't guaranteed to get you that opinion. I wondered whom Sam had spoken to.

That was all I got, but Yvonne picked up one more snippet from the computer. It was a photo file dated last Friday, slap in the middle of the package operation. Barker had transferred the file yesterday, probably from his main phone camera, which had not turned up at the accident scene.

The photo featured a guy squatting beside an ornamental bird in a park. His fingers were poking at a wide crack in the stonework.

'It's him,' I said

'You think?'

'He's picking up the hotel address and keycard. Sam hung around to catch sight of him. That was dangerous, since the pick-up guy might have had someone watching too. Maybe that's part of how Sam got caught.'

'This is the person receiving the packages?'

'Almost certainly. His appearance matches the description of the guy who chased Sam from the BestBreak on Monday. Tall. Hint of Middle East in the face. Tinted lenses. It's the same guy.'

'Coates?'

'I don't know.'

I rooted round and found a cable, copied the photo onto my phone.

'Okay,' I said, 'here's where we go next. You carry on digging through Sam's stuff in case we've missed something. Check his house. Call in at The Red Dragon. See who saw him or spoke to him last night. Look for anything out of the ordinary. And find what time he left. We need to know the window between the pub and that lake.'

'Okay.'

'I'll continue looking for Foxglove. Maybe this is him in the photo. And I'll take a look at J. Coates, see whether he's the same guy or whether he's Sam's client.'

Yvonne was sitting back in Sam's vacated chair, looking at me. There was moisture in her eyes.

'Don't worry,' I said. 'We'll find him.'

'Yes,' she said. 'We will.'

But finding Sam's killer wasn't going to bring him back. In a week this office would be cleared out. Case closed.

CHAPTER SIXTEEN
Jeep watch

An unknown party had hired Sam Barker to deliver the packages and an unknown party had hired me to find Sam, and with Sam dead all I had was a name. J. Coates might have been either party or neither, though there was no doubt he was involved in the affair.

Sam had set eyes on the people on both sides of the exchange: he met his client when they set things up and he snapped the guy who turned up to take the deliveries. Did he follow one of them back to the Caterham address he'd annotated against Coates' name? I headed there to take a look.

Traffic was light and the weather warm. I stashed the hood and breathed fresh air. Drove to a gastro-pub just outside Caterham whose landlord, Louis, I knew from when Lucy and I were together. The guy was her second cousin's brother-in-law. And he ran a good eating house. I still called in for lunch when I was on that stretch of the Orbital and Louis still gave me a head-shake when I tried to pay for my drink. The guy's food prices clawed back the lost profit but it seemed like a good deal. Herbie and I sat in the beer garden and waited for our orders. Herbie was new to the place but had already spotted a sucker. Grinned and looked thin when I introduced him to Louis. Duly received a free sausage when my order came out. The routine was noted for future reference. I demolished my duck ciabatta in five minutes and we headed back through the town and out along the shopping drag until it transitioned to a residential road with Edwardian semis perched up on a rise either side. Front doors were accessed via steps that climbed past parking areas and garages that had replaced the original sloping gardens. J. Coates' address was a sixties fill-in jammed between the older buildings, a plain two storey semi in red brick, mundane enough to have me double-checking the address. If a killer or criminal mastermind lived here his cover was good. But killers *are* good. It's not their front doors you look at it's what's planted under their gardens.

The house number checked out. J. Coates' address.

I parked fifty yards down, facing back into the town with an unimpeded view of Coates' door and the steps down to the street. I re-rigged the hood. Slotted in some Charlie Parker and settled in to wait. Herbie snored beside me.

Two p.m.

If J. Coates was at work I'd be here a while. But I didn't know his routine or his work. He might be in the house right now. The simple tactic was to wait and see.

Traffic blasted past. I kept my window shut and the Bird turned up loud. Watched pedestrians walk up from the centre. None climbed the steps to J. Coates' house and no vehicle turned into the garage. In two hours nothing happened.

Then a black Jeep Cherokee stopped just beyond the steps.

The driver made no move to get out. Maybe making a phone call or picking someone up. But no pick-up appeared. Ten minutes passed. Then twenty. Thirty. The Jeep was just another parked vehicle except that there was no reason for it to be there.

The guy behind the tinted screen was watching the house.

The Bird blew out and I slotted in a Gil Evans compilation I'd recorded from a stack of old vinyls. The playlist was good for six hours. I stretched my hands. Tapped my fingers on the dash. Waited to see what the Cherokee was up to.

Another sixty minutes passed.

Rush hour peaked. Endless traffic noise and lorry gusts. I turned up the Evans. Herbie's snore accompanied the synth. By six thirty the traffic was thinning and Herbie lifted his head.

'One more hour,' I promised.

Then the Jeep's door opened and the guy stepped out. I grabbed my Leica and snapped a telephoto as he waited to cross the road. A big guy with a flat face. Clipper-cut tan hair. Dark grey chinos. Ski jacket. Phone grasped in his hand like he'd just finished a call.

The traffic thinned and he jogged over the road and up the steps. Pressed J. Coates' front door bell. Got nothing. He turned and walked round the building and was out of sight for two minutes. Just long enough to peer through windows. Then he reappeared and went back to the Jeep. Fired up the engine and executed a three-point turn and disappeared back wherever he'd come from.

Six thirty-five. Still early. J. Coates might be on his way home from work right now but the Jeep guy hadn't thought it worth waiting. The successful investigator cultivates tenacity. Fifty stakeouts have turned up results an hour after I'd given up hope. A hundred more have turned up nothing, of course, but that's the game.

I held on until seven before deciding that tenacity is trumped by action.

I killed the music and pulled my shooting jacket from the boot. Its vest has stuff that comes in handy for house calls. I stepped out and shrugged it on. Climbed the steps to Coates' house. Rang the doorbell.

Same result as Jeep.

The road below me was busy and it was still daylight but the porch gave privacy. No-one spotted me working at the Yale. In thirty seconds I had the door open.

I stepped inside.

CHAPTER SEVENTEEN
A nice dose of red-eye

I closed the door and picked up the mail scattered behind it. Twenty envelopes, junk and otherwise. The oldest postmarks showed that the house had been empty for ten days.

J. Coates was away.

I flicked on lights and worked through the house.

A guy's pad. Plain. Functional. Neutral colours. No ornaments or flowers or pot pourri or scented candles. No woman's stuff in the bathroom. No woman's shoes or clothes. No hair bobbles dropped in sofa corners, no trinkets lying about. No toys or games or kids' bedrooms.

Plain and functional.

I started with the lounge. The room was decorated with a few stylised landscape prints and architectural engravings. A small bookcase held books on architecture and chess, and half a dozen paperback thrillers, leaning at one end like the remnants of vacation travel. Beside the bookcase a decent hifi system fed Bluetooth speakers mounted around the room. Other than that the room was sterile. No photographs, no drawers or cupboards holding paperwork

I went through to the kitchen. The refrigerator was empty apart from some rotting veg. and apples, a tub of margarine and carton of out of date milk. The freezer was stocked with ready meals for one.

A guy living alone.

Mr Ordinary.

So why was his name scribbled in a dead private investigator's Post-it block?

I culled part of the answer from a small office room where J. Coates – that's J. for Jeremy, DOB 7th July 1960 – stored his admin documents. The paperwork told me that Jeremy Coates, RIBA, was a chartered architect employed by an international property development firm called Diamond Covault which I knew from an out-of-town shopping mall they'd put up near Guildford ten years ago and a new HQ they'd built on Bow Creek, just downstream from

Canary Wharf. I wasn't familiar with their overseas interests but I sensed they were substantial. The owner was one of the richest guys in the UK, if my memory was correct. According to the paperwork J. Coates had been with them for twenty-three years and took home fifty-four thousand plus pension credits, and the evidence around me suggested that he lived within his means. No sign of loans or expensive habits or hobbies. A DVLA logbook for a newish Toyota Avensis placed him right in mid-market land.

The admin. revealed little else. The only clue to Coates' interests outside work was a membership card for the Sevenoaks Chess Society.

Professional architect and chess player. I was still missing the ruthless killer aspect.

A set of passport snaps showed a fiftyish guy you'd never notice on the street. Soft, flabby face, plastic frame specs hiding startled eyes, weak mouth with a lower lip droop that made you think of tantrums. But appearances are unreliable. The guy was probably respected in his profession, knew what he was talking about if you gave him your attention. What he wasn't was the killer type. But he was up to something. He'd come up on Sam's radar for a reason.

I was looking for a link to Room 209 at the BestBreak and a pointer to where Coates was now. Found neither. The only travel-related item was a printed itinerary for a trip to Singapore the weekend before last. A Qantas business ticket. Out Saturday evening, return Monday. Thirteen plus hours each way. That was a nice dose of red-eye for a single day's business in the city. But the timing was interesting: Coates had arrived back in London ten days ago and his house had been empty since. If he'd been involved in the package exchange it was not from here.

I kept searching. Found paperwork for previous business trips – occasional flights to the USA and Middle East – though none shorter than four days and nothing to say where Coates was now. I went back out into the hallway and inspected architectural prints. Thought about things. Whatever I'd expected for Sam Barker's *Who are YOU?* guy it wasn't Jeremy Coates.

The only theory that made sense was that Coates was involved in a white collar crime, maybe commercial espionage. Did Sam's packages contain company secrets? Or was Coates on the receiving end of the deal? But how many industrial secrets are there in the architectural business? The idea didn't convince me. So maybe not industrial espionage.

I checked the rest of the house and found nothing else. Went back out and rang the neighbouring doorbell. The woman who answered didn't know where Coates was. She hadn't known he was away. I sensed that she never did. Stranger-neighbours who nodded to each other twice a year but never spoke. I tried the house on the other side and got the same result. The neighbour was a guy in his seventies with bad hair and liver spots who didn't even know Coates' first name. Coates had moved in ten years ago and kept himself to himself.

Neighbours as fixtures in the environment.

I thanked the guy and trotted back down to the road. Coates' home had told me nothing about where he was or *who* he really was. But the nuggets of info I'd picked up might get me some answers. I had an ID and home location, a workplace and a hint of how Coates spent his leisure time. It was a start.

~~~~~

I drove back to Battersea and took Herbie for a spin on the park whilst a leftover hotpot heated up. When we got back I set the window table and brought a glass of beer over with a mountain of hotpot and granary bread. Herbie finished his own tea and came to hang out under the table and wait for the mountain to defeat me. I sprinkled pepper. Made a call.

'Eddie – anything?'

First names now. Yvonne Barker, showing signs of thaw.

I told her what I had on Jeremy Coates. Sam had probably had the same but maybe that was it. We were no nearer knowing why Sam was interested in the guy. All we knew was that Coates was connected to the package exchange. The timing of the Singapore trip and his absence from home coincided too neatly with the package exchange. Maybe Diamond Covault had something on in Singapore. Maybe Coates was their technical guy out there. Maybe he'd brought something back.

Yvonne filled in my knowledge gaps about the company.

Explained that they were one of the biggest privately owned property developers in the UK. Built shopping malls and towers across the globe. She recalled the Singapore development, one of the tallest buildings out there, apparently. The company's global operation implied a team of architects chasing round the world and we speculated that Coates was one of that team, though the Caterham house and fifty-four K salary said he was just one of the grunts. We speculated too on what might have been in the packages but came up with nothing. You could build all kinds of scenarios, all equally credible, but we were going to have to approach this the old fashioned way and find things out.

On this subject Yvonne said she'd take a look at Coates' trip to Singapore. She had a contact in the city, an old friend of hers and Sam's who worked at a security company there. If there was anything off about Diamond Covault's business there her friend might have caught whispers. I read Yvonne the itinerary for Coates' dash out there and she said she'd follow up.

Meantime she'd already done some footwork.

She'd been in The Red Dragon talking to people who'd seen Sam on Thursday night. Didn't get much other than some confirmed timings but the times were interesting. Sam had been in the pub until eleven p.m., gabbing with a few people but mostly sitting alone with his beers and chasers. The landlord remembered pulling five or six beers, which is a lot if you're driving. The police had estimated the time of Sam's drive into the lake at one in the morning, which left a two hour gap from the time he left the pub. If we allowed time for the drive we had an hour and a half unaccounted for. Had Sam been intercepted after he left the pub?

Maybe. Because by then Foxglove had Sam's details from me.

The thought ended our discussion on a downer. I sensed Yvonne Barker's anger resurface, maybe anger towards me. Anger in her voice as she told me she'd keep sifting through Sam's stuff and get moving on the Singapore thing.

My hotpot was cooling. I planted the phone and picked up a grinder. Added more pepper. Sneezed and ate.

CHAPTER EIGHTEEN
Armageddon Quickfire

I woke to street noise. Herbie snoring in the corner.

Seven a.m. Saturday.

I still woke sometimes with the face of Arabel Mackie in my thoughts. Arabel was my former girlfriend who'd seemed like a permanent part of me barely eight months ago before the risks associated with a private investigator's profession came home to roost and tore us apart. Today, for no good reason, I surfaced to another image, a porcelain face framed in blonde hair. I let my mind drift for ten seconds then shook my head and planted my feet on the floor. Kim's image faded, leaving something like emptiness.

Herbie woke and sensed emptiness too but his was gastronomic. He worked up a grin and licked my hand and went to wait at the top of the stairs. I donned my running gear and we headed out to the park.

I was showered and shovelling down an omelette on stone baked rye bread fifty minutes later when Yvonne Barker rang with an update. It was barely twelve hours since we'd spoken and most of those hours were night time but the woman didn't seem to sleep. And her night shift had produced a mixed bag.

Non-productive was the completion of her brother's office search which had yielded nothing new. It was more or less what we'd expected: the package exchange job had been a quick in-out, no background work required, no notes or observations or report-writing. The computer photo and Jeremy Coates' name in the Post-it block had been our only breaks. Everything else Sam Barker had known had been in his head.

On the productive side was another chat with The Red Dragon's landlord whom she'd prodded into thinking back to a week last Tuesday when Sam had met his client and taken possession of the packages. The same landlord had struggled with timings and details from two nights ago when Sam had left his pub for his last drive but he remembered something from further back that sounded like a jackpot. He couldn't name the specific day but he did recall that Sam had been in one lunch time talking to a guy, and recalled a stack of envelopes beside him on the bar. It was that image that had brought back the additional recollection. He'd gone through to empty broken glassware into the bin behind the pub and seen a vehicle driving out which had stuck in his memory: it was an Isuzu pickup in gleaming gold paint, pimped up with lights and mirrors. The bizarre colour had fixed his memory. When he went back in, Sam was alone at the bar with his envelopes.

The landlord recalled nothing about the guy who'd been with Sam except for those fancy wheels. But there weren't many gold Isuzus on the street and the sighting told us that Sam's client wasn't Avensis-driving Jeremy Coates.

The productive side continued with Yvonne's chat with her Singapore contact. Singapore was seven hours ahead and it seemed that Yvonne Barker had enough clout with their old pal that he'd already done some serious digging.

He was familiar with Jeremy Coates' company: Diamond Covault had built a skyscraper called the Covault Tower in Singapore in '06. It was the third highest structure in the city, eighty-seven floors of business space above a shopping and hotel complex. Two thirds of the building had been continuously occupied since the Tower opened its doors. Seemed the development was paying its way. And the top floors were used by Diamond Covault themselves as their Far East HQ. They also ran the shopping complex and hotel.

The friend had no inside information on visitors to the HQ but he was intrigued by one thing: Jeremy Coates' lightning itinerary had him staying overnight in a hotel located in the Changi Business Park near the airport. The hotel was a modern budget chain used primarily by tourists. A twenty minute taxi ride if Coates was visiting company HQ. But if he was visiting the company why didn't they put him up at their Covault Tower Hotel in the HQ building?

What the airport location did bring to mind was an engineering consultancy company NQQ, located on the business park. NQQ were a major contractor for Diamond Covault and their offices were two minutes walk from Coates' hotel. So maybe Coates' business was there, though it still seemed odd that he'd overnight at a third party hotel when Diamond Covault had three hundred rooms going spare down the road.

Everything about Coates was coming up odd. But he was coming into focus as a central player in this thing. Sam's Post-it reference to *Package 4* with Coates' name beneath it had hinted at that. And the timing of Coates' Singapore trip, his absence from home since he'd got back, pointed the same way. And the Jeep Cherokee surveillance at his home pretty much confirmed it.

Yvonne promised to keep digging. Didn't say exactly where she'd be digging. I asked how she was holding up. She said she was fine, contradicting the weariness I heard in her voice, and killed the line. I wasn't exactly sure of my own plans but my anticipated morning in the attic indulging my painting hobby had lost its attraction. The light was perfect but my mood didn't match. Maybe later. I decided to kill the time by finding out more about Jeremy Coates.

~~~~~

I called the number I'd copied from Coates' chess society card. Maybe someone at the club would know his whereabouts. A voicemail message promised to get back to me and meantime if I was looking for information on the Tournament the first round started at nine sharp. Details were up in the Reform Club annex.

I drove to Sevenoaks.

The Reform was a social club in the centre of the town. I went in and found the annex and a notice board. The board listed the opening pairs in the Monthly Armageddon Quickfire. The tournament title was startling. You think of chess as this quiet pastime. Maybe I should have brought my bulletproof vest and a cricket visor. The notice pointed upstairs. I went up.

The function room door was open and the sound of the Armageddon Quickfire spilled out.

Inside the room eight tables were active with live matches and the rest of the space was occupied by people milling around, spectating or waiting their turn to play. An air of stress was on the place. I guessed the Quickfire tag was a reference to limited time between moves. I hear there are matches played nowadays with just ten seconds a move. Usually it takes me at least five minutes to comprehend the dirty trick my opponent has just played. That's why I rarely play.

I asked a couple whether the membership secretary was around and they pointed me to a guy marking up the results board. With eight matches on the sizzle the guy was working to keep up but he turned with a smile and held out his hand.

'Paul Hughes,' he said. 'Visiting? Or interested in joining?'

I told him neither. Said I was a pal of Jeremy's. I left off the surname. If Coates was known here I'd blend in better with a taken-for-granted. The assumption that everyone knew Jeremy.

Hunch correct: no surname needed. Apparently Jeremy Coates was a celebrity. More significantly, he was already on the Membership Sec's mind.

'Where the hell is he?' Hughes asked. 'We got wiped out last weekend.'

'I'm looking for him myself,' I said. 'You say he didn't show up last weekend?'

'He called me on the Friday. Said he'd a business trip, but it was damn short notice. And if he misses more than a couple of matches we can kiss the championship goodbye.'

'Did he say where he was going?'

'No. Just a trip. But he usually lets us know well ahead of time.'

'What about the previous weekend?' This was Coates' Singapore weekend.

'That wasn't a league weekend. We wouldn't have seen him.'

'How often is he away?'

'Once or twice a month. Doesn't he tell you?'

I smiled. Mixed in a little wistfulness. 'We're *old* friends. I'm just passing through. Thought I'd catch up. But I can't find him. Not home and not answering his phone. I thought someone here would know.'

Hughes shook his head. 'Jeremy's not the social type. He just comes in and wins the league and tournaments for us. That's all we see of him.'

I held the wry smile. 'Chess and work. Sounds just like Jeremy!'

'I doubt he's time for anything else. His job's pretty demanding.'

'Yeah,' I said. 'You don't know the half of it.'

'I know he keeps Peter Covault's empire propped up. Puts up new skyscrapers for him like they're going out of fashion. Covault's the money but Jeremy's the brains. I heard he's an even more talented architect than chess player.'

I grinned. The name-dropping had just climbed to stratospheric. Sam's *Who are you?* guy was suddenly hobnobbing with the billionaire who owned Diamond Covault. 'Jeremy never blows his own trumpet,' I said, 'but Peter Covault knows how to find talent. And Jeremy's good at building things.'

'One of the top five architects in the world, I once heard.'

Probably from Jeremy.

I kept the cold reading flowing.

'The thing about Jeremy,' I effused, 'you can always talk to him. His job hasn't gone to his head.'

Hughes looked unsure about that assertion. The crash of a clock and a stifled curse drew his attention. We turned. A woman was standing from a table, holding up a hand.

'Got it, Anne,' Hughes said. 'Well done, my dear.' He turned back to me.

'He has an important job, no doubt. Those skyscrapers and malls are huge risks. You need people like Jeremy to make sure the risks don't go bad. I hear everything Covault does goes across Jeremy's desk. If Jeremy doesn't give the nod it doesn't happen. And now he's running around with this floatation thing. Up to his eyeballs.'

'Floatation?'

'The company are on the stock market in a week or two. Five quid a share, they're saying. And Jeremy has to convince the investors that the business is solid. There's all kinds of problems he has to sort out so the company can show a good face.'

I nodded. 'Yeah,' I said, 'that's Jeremy. One busy guy.'

'I just hope he gets back for next weekend.' Hughes got back to the point. 'I don't give a toss about property development. I care about chess. We've got Tunbridge coming up and Jeremy needs to be here.'

'Next weekend's a little late for me,' I said. 'I'm going to miss him if I'm not careful. Is there anyone here who keeps in closer contact?'

Hughes thought about it.

'Martin, I'd say.'

'Martin! Yeah! He's the...'

'History teacher.'

'That's him. So Martin's a member here?'

'Of course. He'll know where Jeremy is.'

'Have you a contact number?'

'It's in the book but I'm not sure I can give it out. Maybe you're better just trying to get hold of Jeremy.'

'I just have that feeling I'm going to miss him.'

'Martin wouldn't be able to help anyway. He's away on holiday. Back mid next week if I recall.'

'I guess he'll have taken his phone with him...'

'Probably. But I can't give you the number. Confidentiality and all that.'

'Of course. But how about putting in a call to him yourself? Just a message to get back to me.' I took out a card. Hughes read it and his face changed.

'Private investigator? What's this about?'

'Jeremy never mentioned me?'

'Never.'

'Well,' I said, 'that's my job. Ask Jeremy. He's got a few stories.'

Hughes looked more dubious than ever. I backed off. Pointed to the card.

'Just get a message to Martin,' I said. 'Say it's urgent. If he knows anything about Jeremy's whereabouts I'd appreciate a call. If I miss him it could be years...'

Hughes gave me an uncertain nod and something that sounded like okay.

'Today,' I said. 'If you get a chance. Appreciate it!'

I moved fast before the nod could change to a shake. Whether Hughes would find time, or whether he'd put the call off or just forget it, I didn't know. The Armageddon Quickfire seemed to be heating up. As I walked out a fist came down on a clock and a chessboard flipped and scattered pieces. The crowd stepped back. Voices called. The final would be something.

But Jeremy Coates had just got a little more intriguing.

I'd been searching for him because of his connection with Sam Barker's document exchange, which might be extortion or espionage or just about anything except legitimate. And what I'd found wasn't fitting the bill. If Hughes's information was correct then Jeremy Coates was a big shot in Diamond Covault, up with the boss himself, controlling projects far and wide, and now smoothing the way for an upcoming company floatation.

So why would you find a guy like that in a Caterham semi living a church mouse lifestyle?

The more I saw of Coates the odder he looked, and oddity is listed in the investigator's bible right after coincidence. Oddity is the shady relative of coincidence. Oddity is the thing that makes you look twice. And where you need to look twice you need to look three times.

I needed to find out more about Jeremy Coates and the people he worked for.

CHAPTER NINETEEN
Some kind of survival thing

I took a walk in the park. Time to think, if I could drag my thoughts away from their persistent drift towards Kim Waters' emerald eyes, the touch of her lips. Kim wasn't a client but becoming involved with her was no more advisable than if she was. If Foxglove's game heated up our involvement would tie me and endanger her. The risks were clear. I told myself to get a grip. Then pulled out my phone and called her.

She picked up on the street. The roar of traffic; car horns; a newspaper vendor. I half expected disapproval, reflecting my own apprehension, but her voice was bright when she agreed that tonight was as good a night as any to follow up on her jazz evening suggestion. She gave me her Mayfair address and a time and I cut the line and asked myself what the hell I was doing. So much for getting a grip. It felt like I was standing on the edge.

Meantime, the anticipation of the evening left the drag of a long afternoon ahead of me. I reverted to my original plan. Went up to the loft and pushed acrylics around for a few hours. I was working on a cityscape set over in Silvertown. The hobby's my version of Holmes' violin as I'd told Kim. But whilst Holmes never cashed in on his musical talent the painting was pulling in two grand a year. Small beer, but it got me into a couple of restaurants a month. And the real benefits weren't financial. Painting worked when I needed time out. Working under the skylights could either focus the mind or calm it. Right now the calming influence would be good. Right now it didn't work: my concentration kept drifting to the image of Kim's face until progress ground to a halt. I quit. Took Herbie for another spin then dropped him off downstairs with my neighbour Henrietta Hutt. Henrietta worked at the dogs' home and had offered free sitting services in consideration of my rescuing Herbie when his homeless owner was offered a roof on condition of ditching his dog. Henrietta's offer was one that Herbie and I exploited shamelessly, Herbie being partial to sofas and hand-outs. When Henrietta opened her door he disappeared in a flash. I said I'd be back and headed out to pick Kim up.

Seemed legal recruitment was a paying business. Kim's address turned out to be a three storey double fronted bijou jammed into a narrow street off Park Lane. I parked outside and pressed the doorbell and got chimes to outdo Big Ben. When the peals faded Kim Waters was standing in her doorway. I played it cool, pretended that the sight of her hadn't just hit me like a defib. going off. It had been barely a day and a half since I'd seen her but my brain had suppressed the full memory of her face. A survival thing, protection against a stroke. But you can't protect yourself when the real thing appears and the real Kim Waters with her real emerald eyes and cascade of straw-blonde hair had me fighting a dizzy spell. She was wearing jeans and a denim jacket, which jazz clubs permit, and looking cute as hell. She smelt as fresh as a dawn forest. She smiled and I grinned and concentrated on not tripping up as I walked her to the car.

'Nice neighbourhood,' I said.

I've lots of lines like that.

Kim smiled sweetly. 'This is Mayfair. We don't have neighbours.'

I stooped to open the car door, waited whilst she figured how to get herself into the seat. With practice it's simple. When she was done I walked round and folded myself into the driver's seat like a pro. Pressed the button. We rolled towards Park Lane and turned into the flow.

'Is Alice still away?'

'I asked my ex to give it the whole weekend so I could talk to you, make sure nothing's happening.'

I angled the Frogeye across the lanes and swung round Hyde Park Corner. Reversed direction. Thought about all the nothings that weren't happening. Decided that she needed to know that the thing hadn't gone away yet, that the guy I'd tracked down had taken a drive into a lake just hours after she and I ate dinner two nights ago. So I told her. Concentrated on traffic while she digested the news. When I risked a quick glance she was watching me, hand to her mouth.

'Foxglove killed him?' Her voice was quiet.

'Looks like it. A guy called Sam Barker.'

She dropped her hand. Clenched it in her lap and looked ahead. I looked ahead too. Road noise diluted our silence. We were almost in

Paddington before she uttered soft swear words.

I looked across.

'Don't worry,' I said. 'We're going to find him. Hand the evidence to the police to put with their forensics.'

'Will there be evidence?'

'Depends how he did it, whether Barker was breathing when he rolled into the water.'

'But if this guy's a killer he'll not hesitate to hurt us.'

'He's no reason to. You're out of it. You were just leverage to get my cooperation. And we've cooperated.'

I sensed her watching me. The argument hadn't convinced her.

We hit the Podium, and Barney took a tenner from each of us and let us in to grab one of the last tables. The Podium fills up fast at weekends. They get the touring bands in, though sometimes it's just the bands gigging round town, the same as weekdays but with a fiver-a-head premium. The board had a quartet up for the first set who rotated through about once a month. An act strong on sax and electric guitar that reminded me of Larry Coryell's style from the 70's. Lively. Perfect for Saturday night if you're in the mood.

Juke was on the ball and a pint of Pride came over with an enquiry about what the lady was drinking. Kim requested a daiquiri and the girl went away to get him mixing. I looked across and caught his eye and he grinned and ringed his thumb and forefinger. I grinned back and raised my glass and Kim saw it and grinned too and we both relaxed a little. But as the quartet warmed up Kim leaned forward and came back to the bad thing following us, still looking for reassurance that I could track Foxglove down fast. I told her we would do exactly that. Described the leads: Sam Barker's interest in a guy called Jeremy Coates who was mixed up in the affair even if he was an oddity. I described the global business high flyer who lived a dour private life behind his front door until it was time to come out and play Master Of The Universe with his chess buddies.

Kim recognised the Covault company name but was short on detail. I didn't know much myself so my spiel was limited to a few snippets about billionaires and global property projects. If anything we dug up pointed towards the firm we'd educate ourselves.

I diverted the discussion onto Alice, and Kim made a decision that it wasn't time to bring her home yet. Despite my reassurances the thing scared her. This guy was killing people. He'd shown he could cross the line. I tried to reassure her but couldn't spin that simple fact any other way.

'I'm sorry,' I said, fighting the music. 'You don't deserve this.'

She pulled herself together. Smiled.

'I'm not blaming you, Eddie,' she said.

Which was progress relative to her first trip to my office. But there was still a shadow there. Bad news and I had arrived in the same taxi.

I pushed the conversation back to Alice and Kim relaxed finally as she got effusive on her favourite topic. I said I'd like to meet her which got an assurance that it would be soon. It was an assurance I liked. Our fingers touched and our heads stayed close as we communicated across the music. The evening settled. Three more daiquiris materialised at intervals without summons. My beer stayed unreplenished. Juke, assuming I'd be doing the chauffeuring after the late set.

I did do the chauffeuring. Drove an empty Park Lane to Kim's street which was little more than a narrow alley of shadows and lighted windows. I hopped out but Kim was a fast learner. She'd got herself unfolded and out before I got round. Her slight unsteadiness probably helped. When I walked her to her door her golden hair floated, and her presence radiated like summer sun. I resisted the urge to grab her. Sometimes patience is the thing, especially when you've come into a woman's life through a dose of bad news. We reached the door. Stopped. Then Kim reached round my neck and planted a long warm kiss.

'See you tomorrow,' she said.

We hadn't discussed tomorrow. I didn't know what Kim did on Sundays and she hadn't a clue what I had on but her words were the only ones she could have uttered. Like a statement of the obvious, a simple truth.

The truth shone brightly.

CHAPTER TWENTY
Jack The Ripper hike

I did see Kim next day. Earlier than either of us expected.

She called at seven thirty whilst Herbie and I were on the park.

Up bright and early, I guessed. Planning her day.

I was wrong.

Her voice wasn't bright. Just frightened.

'He's been here,' she said.

'Who?'

'Your Foxglove guy.'

I was already turning, retracing my steps from the river. Herbie picked up the vibes. Sprinted to catch up. I stooped and clipped his leash. We moved faster.

'When? What did he do?'

The thing had come out of nowhere. Foxglove had no gripe with Kim Waters. She was leverage only to coerce me, and the coercion had been successful. Our business was closed and Foxglove and Kim should never have met. Pursuing her now didn't make sense, unless I had the wrong picture. I'd seen Foxglove as a ruthless criminal. But was that the whole picture? How about Foxglove as a nutcase, an unstable guy, going with his urges? Maybe the package exchange affair and Sam Barker's killing were just his day job. Maybe he had weekends to kill. All kinds of pictures and speculations and guesswork sprang up at Kim's frightened voice.

'Just come and see,' she said.

A chilling thought: 'Is he there now?'

'No. I'm okay. But I'm scared. I'm shaking, Eddie.'

'Give me fifteen minutes,' I said. I broke into a jog.

~~~~~

It only took eight. Three of those were the sprint back to my apartment. I came back out with the car keys and was across the river sixty seconds after I pressed the starter. Covered the Kings Road in another sixty. Cleared the Palace Gardens with Herbie up on the seat like a Dakar co-driver scanning for trouble. If the Hyde Park lights had been on red he'd have got it. I kept my foot down and skirted the park in the outside lane. Swung into Mayfair and left the Frogeye straddling the yellow lines as I ran in through the opening door. Herbie scooted past to check for intruders whilst Kim snared me in a death grip. Her body was rigid. It took effort to untangle her.

'Show me,' I said.

She led me across an annex floored in marble and backed by French windows that opened onto an inner entrance hall with a marble staircase climbing out. The stairs were carpeted in a lush green that matched the vegetation growing in the bright daylight of the recessed street windows and glass vault. We trotted up past varnished wood, cream speckled marble, pastels. My subconscious upped my estimate of Kim Waters' worth as we climbed. The building and location had looked good for five to ten million but someone had spent at least that much inside.

But I wasn't here to dream of lottery wins. I was here to see how Foxglove had confronted Kim. More importantly: to understand *why* he'd come.

I planted my hand in the small of Kim's back as we went up. Felt the tension.

'He came up here?'

'Yes.'

'Did you talk to him?'

'I didn't see him. I didn't know he'd been in until a few minutes ago.'

'But it was him?'

We were walking a gallery floored in varnished oak that ran round three sides of the upper space opposite the street windows. Kim took us along the rear length, past framed artwork that looked like Dora Carrington reproductions but was probably the real thing. We stopped at the centre door. The master bedroom.

Some new artwork.

Bold marker-pen lettering ran across one of the door panels. Red ink against the pale varnished oak.

I looked at Kim.

'Your room?'

She nodded.

'And the message wasn't here when you came in last night?'

'No.'

Her voice was small. Uncertain. I was starting to tense up myself but my tension was all anger. Because this was Foxglove. No doubt.

'He was right here while I slept,' Kim said.

Herbie had followed us up and was checking out the fragrances of polish on varnished wood. I looked at the door. The writing looked deceptively mundane until you considered its implication, which was that a killer had been standing here whilst Kim slept inside.

And the words were not mundane. The message left no doubt about who the caller had been.

We're through, Flynn.
So BACK OFF.

This is your only warning.

Next time I'll go in.

Say hello to Alice, Kim.

I thought about it, adjusting my assessment of Foxglove.

'Has he been watching us?' Kim asked.

'That's the only explanation,' I said. 'But he's damn good. I hadn't a clue.'

Kim was still fixed on the message.

'This really scares me,' she said.

'Understandable,' I said.

But my thoughts were still on Foxglove. "Back off" from what? How did the guy know I was looking for him? And what kind of resources was the guy throwing at this to keep tabs on me and break into houses.

'I'm sorry to be a cry-baby,' Kim said. 'I ought to be standing up to the bastard. But the thought of him getting near Alice terrifies me. How much does he know about me? About her?'

I had no answers. I pulled her to me and assured her we'd keep them both safe. Which we would. Protecting Kim and Alice wouldn't be a problem. But it might mean her stepping out of sight. And hiding would be a problem for a busy businesswoman.

I'd planned on a quiet investigation to dig out Foxglove's ID but the guy had been watching me. How he did it, how he'd stayed out of sight, beat me. But his actions told me that I'd become a major issue. The graffiti on Kim's door was his clumsy attempt at damage control.

Kim walked me round the house, looking for the place Foxglove had got in. We discovered a damaged sash window at the back. He'd come through the back yard and forced it. I looked at Kim.

'I saw an alarm panel.'

'State of the art. Rings through to a central control room. They call me back if there's any suspicious activity. Unfortunately I forgot to set it last night. But Foxglove couldn't have known that. Unless he planned to disable it.'

Which was not so easy. You have to be quick to stop the phone ringing at a control room. So Foxglove had got lucky. And Kim needed to be more careful in future, even in the delirium of arriving home from a night out with London's coolest detective.

But for now we were through. Foxglove had left nothing except the note and the damaged window.

'How about breakfast?' I said.

~~~~~

We secured the window and Kim called her handyman then we drove over to Covent Garden where we ate a light breakfast and drank strong coffee under an awning. Herbie skipped the coffee but polished off a couple of sausages and flopped down to watch the world go by. Six months ago his patronage had been limited to eatery back doors. He'd made a fast adjustment.

'The good thing,' I said, 'is that Foxglove has paid up-front to keep you safe. We'll push a couple of jobs aside and free up some time. I've people I'd like you to meet.'

'You mean like bodyguards? Isn't that a little over the top?'

'That message on your door says it's not over the top. We need to keep this guy away from you.'

'Do you have bodyguards for Alice too?'

'If you were together it would be easier.'

'We're never together during the day. Alice has a nanny and her nursery. And my job isn't the most flexible.'

'Okay. We'll cover you separately if need be. Maybe Alice should stay away for a few more days. We can put someone with your ex-husband.'

I was thinking about my old school pal Bernie Locke, the Jamaican mountain we pulled in when we needed extra hands. Bernie ran a business leadership school but he had minions who could look after things for a while and even if his time would cost and arm and a leg it would be Foxglove's arm and leg. If Bernie covered Alice the rest of us could take shifts with Kim.

Kim watched the street. Snapped back with a humourless laugh.

'Shit! Five days ago I was just living my life.'

'Weren't we all. But the bad stuff is always there. Every day in every street. Foxglove's operation is a little off the norm but he's one of the bad guys you never see but who are always watching. Like wolves round sheep. They'll leave you undisturbed until the time is right.'

My lecture threw a cloud across Kim's face. It's an ability I have. I grinned to lighten the message.

'We'll keep you safe,' I promised, 'and we'll find Foxglove. Then it's over.'

Kim finished her coffee. Managed a smile.

'Sheep in wolf country,' she said. 'That's a different picture from the world I imagined I was living in.'

'You'll go back to that world,' I said. 'It's the real one.'

'But not for you. You live on the edge. You deal with these people.'

I shrugged. 'Sometimes. Most of the time private investigation is nearer to insurance sales or legal work.'

Her smile held.

'I don't see you as an insurance salesman or lawyer.'

'We have skills in common. The main difference is pay.'

Kim held her smile but then drifted back to her new reality.

'I can't believe that I've had to hide Alice,' she said. 'That there was a guy in my house.' She struggled to find the next words. 'Eddie: why not leave this guy alone? Let him disappear. If he knows you're off his case he'll forget me. I don't want him in my house again.'

'Get the window fixed,' I said,' and keep your alarm on. We'll put someone with you and we'll catch Foxglove. We'll get back to normal.'

She thought about it. It took a while but her smile returned, a little uncertain, like the sun cutting through clouds. 'I suppose the other side of the coin is that I met you,' she said. The sun gained strength.

I smiled back. Liked the progress. Five days ago she'd had me on the same side as Foxglove.

'I'll make some calls,' I said.

She reached across. Planted her hand on mine.

'Can I think about it? I'm still not sure how my ex will take it if we tell him that Alice and he need protection. He's not the most rational person. If he senses a threat to her he'll move to have her removed from me. And he'll bring the police in. Maybe that's what *we* should be doing.'

'They'll be in it soon enough,' I said. 'The problem is that right now they couldn't watch your back twenty-four hours. And they'd slow us down getting to Foxglove.'

'I believe you. But my ex won't take it well if we tell him he needs a bodyguard. But as long as Foxglove doesn't know where they are they should be safe without one.'

'What about you?'

She smiled again.

'I've got you, Eddie. What could happen to me?'

I returned her smile. Switched subject.

'What are you doing today?' I said.

~~~~~

It turned out that Kim was doing nothing much beyond trying to stay safe. But the sun was shining and the world went on and I didn't feel like leaving Kim alone with her fears. We decided we'd do something together.

We thought it through and came up with a game of "I've never been there" which had us touring the nooks and crannies around town that we'd both passed a thousand times without a second thought. We started at the London Dungeon, which took our minds off Foxglove's antics with its display of gory history that made the real-world look tame, though I'd seen worse in my old job. Then we crossed the river and joined a Jack The Ripper hike, continuing the black humour approach to middle-fingering the bad guys. We lightened up early afternoon. Grabbed giant burritos from a Camden food stall and took a canal cruise. Regained dry land and circled Primrose Hill following Herbie's nose. Called it a day at six and drove across to a canine-friendly Knightsbridge restaurant.

After we ordered food Kim rang her ex and asked him to hold on to Alice for a few more days. Made no mention of bodyguards. Explained the change with a reference to the anticipated imminent arrest of the guy who'd threatened them; her preference that Alice stay clear until he was in custody. I saw the effort it took to prioritise my assurances over the memory of the graffiti.

I called Yvonne Barker who had nothing new above her growing conviction that Jeremy Coates and the firm he worked for were central to the affair, that we were looking at some kind of industrial espionage. Then I called Bernie Locke to confirm his availability. I wanted someone ready to step in if there was any sign of things heating up further. Bernie bent my ear with a few bawdy anecdotes and said something could be worked out if needs arose and the cash flowed. I said I'd get back and cut the line. Our food arrived and we tucked in. The lunch burritos were still heavy on our stomachs and dinner comprised salads, with wine for her, fizzy water for me. No starters or desserts. Coffees to finish. By the time our tourist binge was through it was nine o'clock.

'So, do I get my protection tonight?' Kim asked.

'That could be arranged,' I said. 'Experienced operative with canine assistant.'

She smiled. 'I feel safe already.'

The power of marketing.

We drove over to Battersea for a change of clothes. Herbie rushed ahead into the apartment. We'd developed a routine of a bed-time bowl of milk and he's a stickler for schedule. I don't know whether milk is good for the canine digestion but Herbie liked to live dangerously. I poured it out and told Kim I'd be ready to go in five minutes.

'Or we could save the journey,' Kim said. 'I'm not sure I'm ready to face that message on my bedroom door. Even with protection.'

I grinned. Full service protection, breakfast thrown in. It's the kind of deal that makes us different.

'I'll fix up the sofa bed,' I said.

Kim's hair flamed. Her eyes were pools.

'Don't bother,' she said. She reached up and slid her arms round my neck and I grabbed for her hair. It was gossamer fine in my fingers. Her lips were firmer.

CHAPTER TWENTY-ONE
Expensive ghosts

I dropped Kim off at eight a.m., both of us a little weary from the strenuous ending to the weekend. Herbie scrambled from his perch between the seats and settled into her place as Kim stooped to close the door.

'Thank you for everything,' she said.

'You sure you're all right in there?'

'John's fixed the window. And my security guy will be in the cottage from six p.m.'

The cottage was her name for a back annex used by staff when they were needed for late night functions. She didn't expand on what the late night functions entailed but I guess you don't get a ten mill. house by being a hermit.

The security guy she referred to would be from her home security service who offered on-site presence when needed. Maybe when those late night functions got out of hand. Kim's security company wasn't going to cut it if Foxglove followed up on his rhetoric but a guy on site and the house alarm wired to their control centre should provide early warning of another intrusion. If things heated up we'd look after her ourselves, twenty-four hours.

Meantime I told her to steer clear of quiet places, set her alarm and make sure the security guy was awake at night. And contact me if anything happened.

She promised she would and blew a last kiss. I floored the pedal and accelerated towards Park Lane. Drove across to Paddington.

Connie's was Monday morning busy with cross-city commuters out from the Hammersmith and City, snatching a croissant and coffee in the spring sunshine as they waited for office doors to open. I grabbed a place at the counter and ordered a bacon roll and coffee. Called Yvonne Barker.

She was in Sam's office, digging for information on the phone and internet, searching for ID on the gold Isuzu, though how she'd get that without a DVLA contact wasn't clear. I said I'd talk to mine later today. Yvonne was also waiting for another call from Singapore and was trawling for Jeremy Coates' name in connection with the architectural world or Diamond Covault. She'd already confirmed that he worked in the company's Architectural Oversight and Project Management department but had nothing on his current activities or job position. His LinkedIn profile was spartan. She also reported that Sam's autopsy had been performed on Saturday morning but that DS Prior was staying tight-lipped about the result. Without an inside contact she was going to struggle to get more. I said I'd take a run at that one too, not being too constrained by lack of contacts. But my first job was a trip to Jeremy Coates' firm. If I could catch him there he could clear up a few unknowns.

I rang off and called Prior's nick. He was out. I left a message implying information of interest.

Next call was to Diamond Covault's London number. The switchboard informed me that their Oversight and Project Management Department had their own personnel who handled messages and appointments. They'd be available at nine a.m., which was precisely four minutes away but four minutes too far for the switchboard to try to put me through. I ended the call. Finished my breakfast and left Connie with a wave and a promise. Went to open up. Rook and Lye's, the personal injury solicitors on the floors below us, were already in full swing as early litigants swarmed their doorway. I went up past the chaos.

Our own door was open too, figuratively. The sign was turned behind the glass, welcoming visitors, though no office hours were published. We liked to stay on solid ground.

Lucy jumped up to pour coffee, which was her way of intelligence gathering. I'd already had coffee and told Lucy to relax. Sean and Harry came out. I leaned back against the reception desk to bring them up to date. Started with the bottom line that it wasn't clear exactly how much of our twenty K windfall would be left once we'd chased down Foxglove. Maybe enough for a new doormat, which we needed.

'You still chasing the guy?' Shaughnessy asked. 'We got his hotel guest. You can't un-inform him.'

'I'm still chasing him,' I confirmed. 'He made us part of it.'

'Maybe these people can sort it out amongst themselves.'

Shaughnessy was a few days behind. The sorting out had already started. I brought them up to date. Told them about Sam Barker, dead under that lake.

'Foxglove?' Shaughnessy said.

'The police theory was that Barker went on a binge and put his car in the lake himself. A simple drink-drive. But they're going to find it's not. Maybe already have.'

Lucy was wide eyed.

'Wow,' she said. 'Twenty four hours after you ID'd the guy he's dead.'

'And it's related to whatever was going on at that hotel.'

'But you'd no choice to do what Foxglove asked if he was threatening that woman.'

I grinned. That woman. Aka Kim of the emerald eyes and knockout beauty, the irresistible lips. A weekend can make a difference. I brought them fully up to date, gave them tentative theories about what Foxglove and Barker had been up to, told them about the guy called Coates whom Barker had been interested in but didn't fit the affair. And Foxglove's renewed threat against Kim, which was odd since I hadn't yet caused ripples in my search for him. Seemed the guy was proactive.

'He's watching you,' Harry concluded. 'He's seen enough to know you're a threat.'

'That's my guess,' I said. 'But his people are good. They're ghosts.'

'So what's so interesting about this guy Coates? He doesn't sound like he fits into this thing.'

'He fits,' Shaughnessy said. 'And when we find out how we'll probably know everything.'

'Wow, Eddie,' Lucy said. 'You've another can of worms opening up.

I grinned. Cans of worms. Our speciality. We should get it etched in the door glass.

'This guy Foxglove needs stopping,' Shaughnessy said.

I agreed. Said I might need a little help once I knew what was happening. And we might need to make good on my offer to protect Kim. I mentioned Bernie Locke in this respect which got their attention. Bernie hadn't been in since we took a commission to protect celebrity child killers a year back, which had ended spectacularly.

Shaughnessy and Harry sensed another one warming up. Agreed they could clear their desks when the call came.

'Bring Kim to see us,' Lucy said. 'We want to meet her.'

I looked at her.

'Come on, Eddie,' Lucy said. 'You're all over her.'

I gave her perplexed. 'You're reading too much into this,' I said.

'No way. Even Herbie likes her. He perks up every time he hears her name.' She squatted down.

'You're infatuated with Kim aren't you, baby?' Lucy said. 'Your new friend Kimmy?'

Herbie had been listening seriously. But Kim's name perked him up with a grin wide enough to plough snow. His tail worked like a wind up toy. He looked at me for approval.

'Tittle-tattle,' I said.

CHAPTER TWENTY-TWO
Stratosphere

I drove across town and caught my first glimpse, between the buildings along East India Dock Road, of the skyscraper that was Jeremy Coates' workplace. The Covault Complex was a thirty-six storey edifice, the latest in the London vogue for big and crooked, with a side elevation that shouted unfinished construction or drunkenness. The complex was the first skyscraper to go up down river from Canary Warf as commerce overflowed onto Bow Creek, and the building's curved glasswork bounced the late morning sun in a blinding laser as I rolled down the extended slip from the Crossing. I circled and the tower straightened up into a five hundred foot glass obelisk with low-level walkways and an adjacent low-rise complex. The skyscraper's planning application must have been interesting. Or maybe they just moved the London City climbout path. I left Herbie guarding the Frogeye on a one-hour spot by a newly planted park and walked to the entrance.

The atrium was dazzling even with the tint in the glass. Mezzanine panoramic windows ricocheted light like tracer from the marble entrance floor. A reception desk was wrapped round the building's inner core and shone like the check-in to heaven. I bypassed it. Scanned a board that listed restaurants and retailers on the mezzanine and seventeen companies in the building above, capped by a sky complex of restaurants and gardens. Diamond Covault were listed as the top three working floors.

I rode glass escalators to the mezzanine where the lifts took off for the stratosphere. Security turnstiles protected the lifts but the gates were open. Crowds drifted without restraint. I boarded a lift and piloted it up to Thirty-Three which was the lowest of the Diamond Covault floors and the only one not accessed via a keypad. I stepped out into a reception area slightly smaller than the ground floor atrium but with the same marbling and thirty feet of head space. The extravagance had to be taking a chunk out of the floor upstairs but first impressions etc...

Wall planking inset with the company name and logo hung over a fifty foot reception desk. I crossed to the nearest receptionist who was called Julia. She flashed a smile.

'Flynn,' I said. 'For Mr Coates.'

Julia tapped her keyboard and frowned at her computer screen and asked if that would be OPM.

Oversight and Project Management.

'Project meeting,' I said. 'Eleven thirty.'

Julia held the frown and picked up a phone. Mentioned my name. The frown stayed. She mentioned eleven thirty. The frown deepened. She glanced up and checked me out as if there was some uncertainty. I didn't know whether my cord shirt and folded linen jacket was a plus or a minus on her checklist. How formal are architects? Casual is cool nowadays, especially in boardrooms, though it's usually the guy who owns the company who's sporting the tee-shirt.

Julia ended the call and invited me to sit. I checked my watch but went over. The seat was comfy as hell and had a view out over the Millennium Dome. When I came out of my trance a guy in shirt and tie was standing over me. He checked my name and apologised and said they weren't expecting me, which tallied, and asked when the appointment had been made. I said something vague about a previous meeting and he took me back to the lifts and punched keys for a floor up. The glass stairs at the far end of reception would have got us there in half the time but when the ride's there I guess you use it.

Upstairs we hit a bright but smaller mezzanine feeding work spaces visible through semi-frosted glass doors. My escort took me through into one and we walked across a low ceilinged open plan office with a maze of partitions bounding two-place work pods. The expanse of window kept the place bright but after the wide open spaces on the way in it felt like anti climax. End of the day, the most impressive towers are only there to hold as many worker ants as possible. Receptions and atriums don't make the profits. The guy took me to a door and knocked and showed me through. Said Mr Rush would take care of me.

The office was small but the view of the river was nice. The three walls had prints of skyscrapers and glass complexes. Half the buildings were under construction, eagle's eye views over cityscapes. A dome behind one of the constructions identified the subject as the building I was in, half built. I pulled my attention back to my host, a tired looking guy in navy suit and gold tie standing up from his mid-size executive desk. He waved me to a chair at a small conference table. I held out my hand but didn't sit so he didn't either. The guy's name was Don Rush. He threw me a cautious look through his round wire frames which stretched across the heavily mottled skin of a face caught between a spiky, streaked beard and a bed head top whose soft spikes were twenty years too young. His voice was British upper class.

'I'm a little confused,' he said. 'We don't have a visitor in the book for Jeremy. Which project is this for?'

The book reference was rhetorical. Don Rush's desk was clean of such things. I put his confusion to rest.

'There's no appointment,' I said. 'This was an off-chance. Jeremy doesn't know me.'

If that clarified things it didn't show. Rush folded his arms across his chest and gave me a perplexed head tilt.

'Who do you work for?' he said.

'This is a personal matter. We're trying to catch up with Jeremy. We're wondering whether he's away on business.'

'Personal but you don't know him? I don't understand.'

'I don't know him personally. But I need to talk to him.'

Don shook off the perplexity.

'Jeremy isn't on business,' he said. 'And we can't talk to people coming in off the street. This is a workplace, you understand.'

'Got it. I wouldn't have come if it wasn't urgent. I only know that Jeremy works here. Thought I'd catch him.'

'Not any longer.'

I stopped. 'He doesn't work here?'

'He was let go.'

'As in fired?'

'As in nothing I'm afraid. We don't discuss personnel matters with outsiders. Jeremy no longer works for the company and that's all I can say.'

'Since when?'

'I'm not at liberty to say.' He started to move towards the door. 'If that's all...'

'But he did work here? For you?'

Rush didn't answer. He pulled open the door and gestured to the guy who'd brought me up. I walked over.

'You mustn't come back up here,' Rush said. 'These are not public floors.'

'Were you his boss?' I said.

'I was. Steve: show Mr Flynn out.'

I grinned at Steve. Turned in the doorway to take a last look at the river. A nice view. A nice office. But not *so* nice. And if Jeremy Coates worked for this guy then he wasn't quite the big shot I'd heard. If he worked for this guy then he didn't have an office. I looked across the floor, wondering which of the cubby-holes had been Coates'. Then I thanked Don Rush and followed Steve back out to reception.

'A misunderstanding,' I told him by way of conversation. 'Jeremy's gone missing. We thought he might have stayed in touch with someone here.'

Steve was young, formal but not yet starched. Not looking for traps in everything you said. He shook his head.

'Once someone's left that's it,' he said. 'We wouldn't stay in touch.'

'It was just a thought. His friends are concerned.'

Steve nodded. Concerned, but not much.

'He's probably on vacation,' he said. 'Time to think. Plan his next move.'

We stopped at the lifts and Steve pressed a button.

'I guess you're right,' I said 'What day was Jeremy last in?'

I turned to stare at Steve as I threw in the question, a little psychological pressure whilst the guy was deciding whether he should answer. The lift arrived and the doors clicked and my imminent departure notched up the pressure.

'Friday. Three weeks back,' he said.

'Why was he sacked?'

But that was more than Steve could tell me. He clammed up and waited for me to step into the lift. I grinned and left him to it.

Fired.

The hotshot who'd been putting up Diamond Covault's skyscrapers almost single-handedly, driving the company's expansion operations and steering its billionaire owner clear of risk, the hotshot who was currently up to his eyeballs with the company floatation, had been found surplus to requirements. He'd been dismissed. Downsized. Kicked out.

Fired.

The hotshot who'd beavered away in one of the worker-pens on Thirty-Four whilst his frazzle haired boss Don Rush watched the river. Fired. Gone.

But the hotshot had taken the Singapore trip *after* he'd been thrown out.

Which was odd.

~~~~~

I pressed the up button. Took the lift to the roof to get a view. Crossed a garden between restaurants and a gym to a pedestrian promenade that put the whole city in front of you – at least the part not blocked by the Canary Wharf and City towers. A blue spring sky hung over the river but the haze hadn't burned off and my view was limited to five miles. But what was visible danced and glittered. It was the view the people who'd built this tower had seen as they drew up their blueprints. More likely, they were looking further, gazing out over the horizon to distant icons of their company empire. To Asia and America.

I leaned against the rail and watched. Listened. London breathed softly below the haze. Car horns and distant traffic were barely audible. High up here the city was just light and form. A river flowing peacefully.

I thought about what I'd learned, which wasn't much beyond the fact that Coates hadn't been the one in charge of Oversight and Project Management on Thirty-Four. That he'd maybe shone his chess cronies on a little. And that he was now history.

History his ex employer wasn't about to discuss.

Which left me struggling for direction. Coates wasn't Foxglove but he was the one player in the affair I knew anything about. He was involved and could probably explain it all, including who Foxglove was. But I'd need to find him.

I quit my sightseeing and walked back to the lifts.

The lift panel showed three underground parking levels. No locks on the buttons. I descended below ground to the first of the levels. Walked out into an oppressive space of concrete pillars and made a circuit. A row of executive parking places right by the lift doors had Diamond Covault plates up on the walls, Jags and Mercs gleaming in the dim light. The company had reserved the prime spots when they handed the building over to the management contractor. I continued round. More company spots but narrower with longer walks to the lifts and a mis-mash of vehicles parked on them. Employees with prized permits. Most workers would come in by train or bus. I kept walking, looking for Jeremy Coates' Avensis. If he'd been fired it shouldn't be here but I wanted to be sure.

I completed the circle. Came back towards the lifts where the extra wide company spaces started again. Nothing. Until I spotted something I hadn't expected.

Six spaces from the lift doors, slotted in beside the Jags and Mercs, was a gold Isuzu pickup with an array of lights and mirrors.

I stopped and stared.

The vehicle was way out of place. Except that the company sticker in the windscreen said otherwise. I looked and grinned. I'd hit figurative and literal gold.

Because the guy who hired Sam Barker drove a pimped up gold Isuzu.

Well, well.

Had Sam been hired by someone linked to this company – someone who parked in an executive spot – to organise the document exchange? That put a new slant on Sam's interest in Jeremy Coates, who was also linked to the company.

My trip down here hadn't got me nearer to Coates but it had opened up new directions. Whoever drove the gold Isuzu was central to the affair.

The pickup's cab had heavily tinted glass. I tunnelled my hands and peered in. Saw only seats and a wheel. I stood back and walked round the vehicle. It was in pristine condition, someone's pride and joy even if the someone was exhibiting a surfeit of dubious taste. There are people whose hobby is vehicles like this. Just not many who park in the executive slots at the London HQ of a global-reach company.

The vehicle gleamed like new. Even the tyres had been shined up. The only imperfections I spotted were a dent on the back of the cab roof and a dusting of white on the tyre walls and in the treads, as if the vehicle was waiting for its Sunday wash. I pulled out my phone and snapped pictures. Then walked back up the ramp.

CHAPTER TWENTY-THREE
Not a people person

Herbie and I took a break. Walked across the tiny park to the river. Returned and found an open air table at a bistro opposite the Covault building. The fine weather was drawing workers from the tower to eat lunch in the real world, and the buzz infected the waiters. They upped their flair to pure Italian, and even if their accents were Polish and Estonian their smiles were genuine. Favourable meteorology sends tips skyward.

I ordered a sandwich and fizzy water, and a nod and wink got a black market sausage delivered gratis under the table. I ate quickly with the curved glasswork of the Covault Complex shimmering above me like a magnesium flame. Global power radiating. I squinted high. Wondered why this building was suddenly the centre of things.

Something that was not normal business was going on up there, something that had reached down into a silent hotel room and a P.I.'s office and onto a London street where a young mother was walking her child.

It came back to this building because the package exchange had been organised by a guy whose gold Isuzu was parked in an executive spot right under the tower. The guy had hired Sam to run a delivery operation. Sam had run it and completed it but then Foxglove came after Sam and killed him. One of my theories was that Foxglove was the receiving party in the exchange, but why come after Sam afterwards? And why had Sam been interested in a guy called Jeremy Coates who had been fired from his job in this same building just before the exchange?

Then I quit my speculations. Came alert.

Don Rush, Coates' ex-boss, had just planted himself at a table at the far end of the bistro's paddock. The table had two chairs but barely space for one. You'd get maybe a plate and a laptop on there. Good for a solo working lunch. I finished my sandwich and watched Rush place his order and get back to tapping away at his notebook. I waited until his food arrived and he'd got everything nicely balanced on the table then wandered over and sat opposite him. Rush opened his mouth and looked at me. Looked down at Herbie. Herbie grinned.

'What is this?' he said.

I grinned too. 'Seemed a nice spot to eat lunch. Expensive but cheaper than the restaurants up there.'

Rush switched to a frown. 'If you're still chasing Jeremy Coates you're wasting your time. I've nothing to say.'

'Maybe I can do the talking,' I said. 'You must be interested in the circumstances of Jeremy's disappearance.'

Rush shook his head. 'I'm not. Jeremy doesn't work here any more. Who are you exactly?'

I handed him an agency card. It helped as it always did.

'A private detective? Holy hell, what is this?'

'Perhaps I should have been clearer: Jeremy seems to have disappeared.'

Rush shrugged. Tried to stare me out. But his face was being tugged by a sudden anxiety. I didn't know whether he knew something or was just not good with stress. Guessed the latter. Rush wasn't the confrontational kind. I waited until the stress opened his mouth again.

'Why are you looking for him?'

'That should be obvious. People who disappear without warning are often in trouble. Someone was concerned about him and our agency became involved.'

I didn't mention that the person who'd been concerned about Coates wasn't concerned about anything any more, or that our purpose in chasing Coates wasn't his safety.

I waited whilst Rush's face did a few more callisthenics.

'This is utterly irregular,' he said. 'Jeremy doesn't work here. You've no right to come badgering company personnel.'

'Might his sacking have affected him? People are sometimes knocked back when their job disappears. I hear Jeremy was with you over twenty years.'

Rush sat back finally. Distancing himself. Attempting to project authority. What came over was mostly exasperation.

'I repeat: I'm not talking about Coates. Nor is the company.'

His face was all over the place and his jaundiced skin was gaining colour that hinted at internal pressure, and his delivery lacked conviction. Exasperation and fear were messing it up. And his beard couldn't hide the weakness of his mouth. Don Rush wasn't a people person. He was running an important department in Diamond Covault but he operated from behind the barrier of his desk, hid behind formality, company-endowed toughness. Don let others keep the workers happy. My guess was that he'd barely known Coates as a person. But he'd known the guy's place in the company.

'I'm puzzled about the sacking,' I said. 'Jeremy was one of your main people, right?'

'Please, go away.'

'In fact, I heard he was your key project guy. Made things happen. Kept developments on track. I got the impression he was pretty much running things.' I smiled. 'How long have you been in charge of the department, Don? Just a couple of weeks?'

Rush finally showed spirit and spat out a swearword that brought his flush on nicely. His face tightened up.

'I've been running the department for ten *years*,' he said. 'Get the hell out of here.'

'Okay, ten years. But Coates was the real mover and shaker, right? He was your expertise. He was your eyes on company projects all over the world. So why would you let a guy like that go?'

Rush's mouth opened. Twitched around for the right words.

'The company has experts all over the place. Jeremy wasn't in charge of anything. He worked for me. The buck stops with me.'

'But he had the real knowledge. That's what I'm saying.'

'He was an experienced architect. The company employs hundreds of talented people.'

'But Jeremy was your guy. Kept things running smoothly in Architectural Oversight. Your job is more a figurehead position, I'm guessing.'

But it wasn't guesswork. The fact was written all over Don Rush's face. Don was a manager, not an architect. And not a good manager. And his primary project was his own career. When you're focusing on that you don't always have time for the nitty gritty of getting the job done. You need someone who'll do it for you without being seen. But Don didn't grab the bait. His mouth clamped and he reached to snap his notebook shut. Lunch terminated. His fingers danced briefly on the computer before he killed the tremor with an overcompensating grip. The guy was good with throwing his authority around on Thirty-Four, not so hot on the skirmishes. When the latest Third World enterprise was skidding off track it would be Jeremy Coates wearing the hard-hat down in the foundations.

I stood. Don had to squint against the light.

'What I'm trying to see,' I said, 'is why Jeremy took that business trip to Singapore *after* you fired him. Singapore's your Far East HQ, am I right?'

Don stood too, getting ready to shift, but my words stopped him.

'What are you talking about?'

'Or was it just a twenty-four hour vacation that Jeremy took right after you handed him his cards? I guess Singapore's a nice spot.'

Don held his laptop like a shield.

'You're insane,' he said.

Didn't mean I was wrong.

'Are you denying that Jeremy had business in Singapore at the time he was fired?'

'Goodbye, Mr Flynn.'

'...Because I suspect that your company was involved in something dodgy there and that Jeremy was right in the middle of it.'

Rush was looking for a way through the nearby tables. Found his way blocked. He turned back, seeking another route.

'Were you in on it, Don? Does Diamond Covault have a problem that's landed in your department? Or did Jeremy go renegade? Was it all *his* game?'

Rush face me. Waited with clamped lips for me to step aside and let him pass.

'We're going to dig it out,' I said, 'whatever it is. And I'm wondering whether we'll find your name mixed in there. If there's anything you'd prefer us to know now maybe it will count as a plus when the indictments are read out.'

Rush lost patience. Pushed past. A chair went toppling. Heads turned. I watched him go then righted the chair and headed back to the car.

CHAPTER TWENTY-FOUR
Just the guy's taste

My phone rang.

DS Keith Prior, the detective looking at Sam Barker's accident.

'I got your message. What's your new information?'

The information I had – at least the part I was willing to share – was patchy. My call to Prior had been simple fishing, a chance to talk so I could get a sense of whether he was becoming more interested in Sam's death, of which way the autopsy had gone. It wasn't beyond the bounds of possibility that Sam *had* just got drunk and put himself into that lake. If he had, it wouldn't affect my decision to go after Foxglove but it's always good to know your opponent's capabilities.

I gave Prior a few embellishments on the theories I'd given him on Friday. Held the new stuff back. I didn't know what the new stuff meant.

Prior saw straight through it.

'Marvellous,' he said. 'That was worth the call-back.'

But he still wasn't dismissing my theories about Foxglove's involvement in Sam's death. And despite his annoyance he did concede that the foul play explanation might not be without basis.

'The autopsy picked up something?'

'Yes. We're treating the death as suspicious.'

'What killed Sam?'

'He drowned whilst he was under the influence.'

'How's that suspicious?'

'Barker had point eight percent blood alcohol. Max estimate of his consumption at the Red Dragon that night was four to six pints plus whiskey chasers. That would put him five times the limit but it wouldn't account for the point eight. Barker sunk the equivalent of an additional half bottle of spirits between the pub and the lake.'

'Any booze in the car?'

'None.'

'And if he'd had the habit of drinking that quantity of alcohol before driving home he'd have been in the lake years ago.'

'Yes. Something broke the pattern last Thursday.'

The something was clear.

'Someone forced the drink down him,' I said, 'then maybe tapped him on the head to stun him and rolled the car into the lake. Any pointers?'

'None I'm sharing. I've already told you more than I should.'

'Noted.'

'And in return you're keeping me in the dark.'

'I'm giving you what I can, Sergeant. When I've something concrete I'll bring it in.'

'I'd rather you gave me everything right now, Flynn. How about I bring you in and sit you at a table until you've done just that?'

'Waste of time. I'd have nothing worthwhile. Best leave us to run with this for a day or two. We'll either dig out something useful or hand the whole thing over.'

'Not good enough. I'm scraping around here for a reason not to bring you in.'

'Got it. If you find one give me a call.'

My phone had a call coming in. I killed the line before Prior could respond. Picked up.

Yvonne Barker.

I told her what Prior had just told me. Asked if there'd ever been any suggestion that Sam was that serious a drinker.

'No. He did his drinking at the bar. He wasn't the type to open a bottle at home or in the car.'

'He left the pub at eleven. Ended up in the lake around one. So someone jumped him and had him for a couple of hours. Time to prod him for what he knew about whoever had hired him to deliver the packages. They probably slapped him around a little. Not enough to leave signs but enough to make it clear that he was on a one-way trip unless he cooperated. But Sam probably knew he had a one-way ticket anyway.'

Yvonne was quiet for a moment.

'Bastards,' she said. 'He was just doing his job.'

Same as all of us. But when you work with or against the bad guys you take the risks.

I brought Yvonne up to date on Sam's mystery man, Jeremy Coates. The fact that Coates' ex-boss didn't share the guy's own picture of himself as a key player in Diamond Covault, overseeing their global projects. To Don Rush, Coates was just another body in his department. And Rush's view had the ring of truth: it was hard to see a top company guy living quietly in that Caterham semi on fifty-four K.

I also told her about the gold Isuzu sitting in an exec. parking slot at the Covault building. It sounded like the vehicle Sam's exchange client had been driving. So I'd be talking to my DVLA contact again and we'd know who the driver was. Sam's client would be ID'd.

But Yvonne butted in and stopped me.

'I know who the client is,' she said.

'The Isuzu driver?'

'You've just confirmed it,' she said. 'And now I'm really wondering where this is going.'

I sat back on the Sprite's wing.

'Who?'

'Barclay damn Brent, that's who!'

I grinned at Herbie. Waited for astonishment to kick in, which it would once I knew who Barclay damn Brent was. Yvonne picked up on my silence.

'Jane Brent's son,' she clarified. 'She's Peter Covault's wife. The guy who built the skyscraper you've just come out of.'

Astonishment duly kicked in. I'm not up on high society but I was about to learn. All I'd known was Peter Covault's name, that he was the fourth richest man in the UK or something, or maybe the world. I winked at Herbie.

'Told you,' I said.

Herbie grinned back. We'd both known this would go funny. A twenty K fee doesn't bring the quiet life. I looked up at the wall of glass in front of me. Craned my neck. So Sam Barker's client had descended from the very top of this building to run his caper and now we were dealing with one of the richest families in the world.

'How did you ID Brent?'

'I was checking out the company to see if Jeremy Coates' name came up, which it didn't, but I was curious about the firm and Peter Covault. I scanned the social media sites and spotted a photo of Covault and Barclay Brent at a bird shoot last November. And one of the pictures had a gold Isuzu parked in view. I searched further and found a puff piece on Barclay, some crap about new blood transforming our cityscapes. The piece had picture of him standing next to the Isuzu in front of the Covault Complex when it opened two years ago. Apparently Barclay was brought into the firm when his mother married Peter. But I guess he didn't shed his boy racer instincts when he climbed aboard.'

'What was his background?'

'Privileged. Jane Brent is wealthy in her own right from an earlier marriage. Barclay had a cosseted upbringing. Eton educated but no higher. Has never worked beyond dabbling in two failed start-ups. Spent most of his time on the social and club scene. Drove flash cars as well as the Isuzu. There's an old photograph of him driving a Bugatti, a couple of newer ones with a Porsche Cayman. He had a nice pad on the South Bank even before he moved into a penthouse on Jermyn Street. I'd say the move into the Covault family was more a sideways step than a climb.'

'A dodgy business transaction sounds a little downmarket for someone in that position,' I said.

'Unless he was acting for the company. Maybe we're talking espionage or blackmail against the firm.'

'I don't see it. Barclay is on the wrong end of the transaction. If Diamond Covault were being sold commercial secrets or were being blackmailed they'd be *receiving* packages, not delivering.'

'You think Barclay was acting for himself?'

'That's how it looks, but that scenario leaves us with the "downmarket" issue. What kind of crooked business would return a worthwhile payoff to someone in a billionaire's clan? If Brent's living on Jermyn Street he can afford to throw away half a million a year just for his roof.'

I was still watching the Covault tower. Caught vague movements in the rooftop public areas. The floors below reflected sky.

'It's a puzzle but it's all coming back here,' I said.

'So where do we go?'

'I've a few ideas. But let's get more on Jeremy Coates. His chess buddy Martin has a message to ring me but I'm not sure he will. If you get the chance dig around at the club. Try to get Martin's full name and contact details so we can talk to him directly.'

'Leave it to me,' Yvonne said.

We ended the call. I drove back across town.

I was at Chase Street just before four. Shaughnessy and Harry were out and Lucy didn't work on Monday afternoons, so our door was locked, leaving the two men in suits standing frustrated out on the landing.

CHAPTER TWENTY-FIVE
Legalese

The first guy was sixtyish, tall and well built, in a sharp charcoal check suit and navy tie. The second used the same tailor but was twenty years younger and twenty pounds lighter, though he had the same frown on his face. I had their measure in two seconds. Jabbed a thumb.

'The legal firm's downstairs,' I said. 'They're expecting you.'

Herbie growled to clarify things.

The two looked at him but didn't move for the stairs. The older one pulled out a card.

'Flynn?' he said. 'Eagle Eye?'

So, my mistake. Maybe they were *from* downstairs, here to throw us out of the building. Rook and Lye usually handled the attempts themselves but maybe they were outsourcing now.

I took the card. Read it. It was impressive, faced with some kind of holographic texturing that scattered light round a company logo. Alongside the logo the words said:

Diamond Covault Ltd
James Coleridge Devonshire, MA, LLB

When I looked up the second guy was holding out his card. I read that one too. It said :

Diamond Covault Ltd
Adam Hane, MA, LLB

I wondered how many lawyers worked for Diamond Covault and whether they all had hologram cards and whether our budget would stretch to a set. Cards like this could double our turnover.

By the time I'd finished being impressed I was asking myself what the hell James and Adam were doing at our door barely three hours after my visit to the thirty-fourth floor of the Covault Complex. We get legal visits, but this one had just set the new record for speed of response. I pictured Don Rush *rushing* back into the building and grabbing the hotline. Pictured his boss informing *his* boss who called a meeting with Legal and Kickass Dept to discuss the threat of me crashing back through the plate glass windows any moment.

I looked up. The two were watching me.

'How are you, Mr Flynn?' Devonshire said.

'I'm fine.'

'Mind if we step inside?'

I saw no reason to refuse. Sensed that I might be about to learn something.

I unlocked the door and ushered them through. Turned the sign to *Open*. Adam Hane stifled a snort but Devonshire threw a look that shut him up. We went through into my office.

Herbie pushed past to grab one of the guest chairs.

First come, first served, suckers!

I crossed to my desk, and the Miller creaked and leaned sideways as I sat and waited for the two lawyers to decide who got the remaining chair. They reached the conclusion that it would show weakness for either of them to sit and leave the other stranded, which meant they both had to stand. If we'd had just a single cup I'd have offered them coffee.

Not that they'd have accepted. You drank coffee with big-shots in company boardrooms. Not with the small fry you'd come to roast.

I grinned. Waited for them to open the show. Devonshire finally did.

'This is just a friendly visit,' he said.

The same as when Freddy Krueger calls. I racked the Miller back and lifted my feet onto the desk and clasped my hands behind my head to show how friendly I was feeling.

'We represent Diamond Covault,' Devonshire said, 'and the company owner, Mr Peter Covault.'

I held the grin and kept my hands clasped. Enlightenment comes to those who wait, etc.

'We're here,' Devonshire said, 'to request that you stay away from the business.'

I dropped the grin and pursed my lips to show that I was digesting the request whilst I waited for specifics. The room was quiet except for Herbie's growl and the hiss of the Westway. This time James and

117

Adam outwaited me.

In the end I said: 'I don't understand.'

'Yes you do,' Adam said. He stared at me like he'd like to punch my lights out but Devonshire stopped him. Turned back to me.

'Your visit this morning,' he explained. 'Your discussion with one of our staff. It was rather irregular. Unsettling, even, for the person in question. Our premises are not open to casual visitors, Mr Flynn.'

'I just popped in to ask about one of your employees,' I said. 'He's missing. We're a little concerned. We thought perhaps someone in the firm would know his whereabouts.'

'You're referring to Mr Coates. He's no longer with us.'

'Well I didn't know that when I called. Mr Rush enlightened me.'

Devonshire smiled and cast his eyes down to think it through. Looked up again.

'Understandable,' he said. 'Mr Coates was with us until very recently. Do you have any particular concerns? I hope he's not in any trouble.'

I unclasped my hands and slid my feet back off the desk. Stood and went to the window to look down on the Great Western.

'I don't know anything,' I said, 'except that we can't get hold of him. I wondered whether he might be away on company business.'

Devonshire smiled: 'And now that his employment status is clarified you have your answer. You'll have no further need to contact us. Is that our position?'

I turned.

'It may be yours,' I said, 'and it may even be mine if nothing else crops up. But I'm going to find Mr Coates and if I need to talk to his work colleagues again I assume I can expect your full cooperation.'

'Absolutely,' Devonshire said. 'We'll do everything to help. All we'd ask is that you make an appointment through our HR people.'

'Sometimes the direct approach saves everyone time,' I said. 'Mr Rush was very helpful this morning.'

'Doubtless. But you need to understand, Mr Flynn: first of all Mr Rush – any company employee – is not available for meetings with casual visitors; and secondly we can't discuss employee affairs with anyone outside the company. We also have a concern that you pursued Mr Rush outside the building and approached him in a somewhat aggressive manner. It's important that this doesn't recur.'

I jabbed my hands into my pockets.

'Help me out,' I said. 'The thing that's puzzling me is how you legal people got onto this so fast. I came in for a quick chat with one of your staff and I'm hardly out of the door before you're at my heels. I always imagined legal issues demanded briefings and discussions and board meetings, maybe a few special-delivery letters. Say a few weeks between me treading on toes and receiving a face-to-face legal sermon. But what is it: barely three hours and the legal heavies are already in my office? I assume you *are* the heavies, James – or are there people with even flashier cards?'

Devonshire smiled.

'Our discussion has indeed been expedited,' he said, 'and yes, we are the heavies. I run Mr Covault's legal department. But sometimes it's better to nip problems in the bud rather than wait until we've a litigation on our hands. Diamond Covault are focused on a complex commercial venture at the moment: preparing a public floatation, as you perhaps know. We're maxed out with all kinds of legal work without having our people diverted into affairs of no relevance.'

'I don't know whether Jeremy Coates is still relevant to you or not,' I said. 'Though I suspect he is. What are your own thoughts?'

Devonshire's smile faltered.

'I really don't know,' he said. 'My thoughts wouldn't help.'

'I thought so,' I said. 'In fact, James, you don't even know why you're here. You're thinking the same as me: that when someone pokes their nose into company affairs a snotty letter and first class stamp should suffice to send them packing. That would have saved you the drive, at least. The traffic's hell across town. Worse than before the Congestion Charge.' I pulled my hands from my pockets. 'How are we going to sort that one out? There's no more room on the trains and the damn town is choked half the day.'

Devonshire rebuilt his smile.

'I commute from the other direction,' he said, 'so I'm spared the worst. But when Mr Covault instructs us then duty pushes us out into the jams and pollution and we suffer like everyone else, although Adam is driving so I don't find the ordeal too challenging.'

'That's good,' I said. 'And I'm sorry I can't help you with whatever the hell you're here for but at least you can tell Mr Covault that you've delivered his message. You can also tell him that whatever interest I had in his company has just tripled.'

Devonshire held me with his genial eyes, like he was trying to figure me out, though he was still trying to figure out why he was here. Adam just stuck with hostile.

'Good,' Devonshire said. 'I'll tell Mt Covault that. But please be clear about our position. Our legal department has the resources to take vigorous action if your firm persists in interfering with our business. If there were any legal skirmishes between us, Mr Flynn, I think you'd be out-gunned. That could prove costly.'

'Well,' I said, 'depending on how things work out I'm thinking that the skirmishing may be between you and the authorities. Your resources would be matched.'

'You've lost me, Mr Flynn.'

I grinned. Moved towards the door. Herbie turned up his growl, his version of the same hint.

'This isn't just a puzzle over an ex-employee,' I said. 'I'm trying to find out how a guy who had business linked to your firm ended up dead. And I want to trace a guy who's been threatening me over the same affair. There's some funny business going on and I suspect your company is involved. When we catch up with Coates we'll find out what the funny business is. And we *will* catch up with him. Please convey that message too.'

Devonshire and Adam both looked blank. But they came towards the door, finally. Adam jabbed a thumb at Herbie.

'Are these pit bulls legal?' he said.

I held the door. 'Staffordshire,' I said. 'He's legal and friendly, though not always friendly to legal.'

Devonshire held up a hand, cutting off our discussion.

'That was a strange assertion,' he said. 'People threatened and killed. I'd have to say it doesn't sound like anything related to Diamond Covault.'

'Perhaps,' I said. 'But I'll find out.'

'If Mr Coates has some kind of problem then it's not related to the company. You have my assurance on that.'

I smiled. Walked over to open the outer door. I didn't doubt Devonshire's sincerity. Maybe the Jeremy Coates' puzzle and Sam's death *were* nothing to do with Diamond Covault. But an assurance from a guy who'd just admitted that he didn't know why he was here wasn't going to convince me.

The two of them went out. Herbie came and stood at the door and watched. He looked up. Grinned.

'When we get those hologram cards made,' I said, 'we'll put your picture on them. Style *and* ferocity.'

The grin stretched wider. We'd need big cards.

~~~~~

I was walking back to the Sun Gate after our round of the park when Kim called.

'Thank you again,' she said.

'I usually have more in for breakfast. I like omelettes stuffed.'

'I meant for last night. For yesterday. The omelette was fine.'

'Maybe a repeat's in order. I excel at security stuff.'

She laughed, though it wasn't much of a laugh. She wasn't forgetting what this was about.

'I'm calling to say I'm out of town – an unplanned business trip. I'm just getting into Manchester. Back Wednesday. I don't think I'll be in any danger in the meantime.'

Her words popped the bubble that had been forming. The bubble of anticipation of an evening on the town, getting to know a little more about Kim Waters.

'That's fine,' I said. 'Maybe Wednesday...'

'For sure. I just wanted you to know that I'm safe for tonight.'

'I agree,' I said. 'I don't see Foxglove following you out of town. But keep your eyes open.'

'I will. Anything new happening?'

Plenty was happening but nothing that made sense. I was tempted to tell her that the thing was getting bigger, maybe had links to the company Jeremy Coates worked for – to the very top of that company. But feeding Kim the information without any explanation of what was behind it or when it would end wasn't going to help her sleep so I let it go. I'd bring her up to date in a couple of days. Maybe by then I'd know what I was updating her on. For the moment I stayed vague. Told her we were on this full time. That we'd have the full picture before the end of the week.

For once I was right.

CHAPTER TWENTY-SIX
He didn't take unsolicited calls

I kick-started the day with five laps of the park. Exited at the Albert Gate and walked out over the river. I leaned on the rail and watched the ebb tide sluicing east. Squinted towards the silhouettes of Canary Wharf six miles away. Caught the flash of the Covault Complex building beyond them.

The needle in the Foxglove affair had swung resolutely to point at that tower. The guy Foxglove was chasing – the one who'd hired Sam for the package exchange – belonged to the family who'd put it up. And Sam's mystery guy, Jeremy Coates, had worked on its top floors.

And the lawyers' visit yesterday had turned up the spotlight. Whatever was going on was sensitive enough to bounce my chat with Coates' boss straight up the chain to the top guy himself. And Peter Covault had lost no time ordering his legal troops across town.

But for a guy running a global business Covault had come up short on tactics. All the visit had done was focus my interest.

Covault had never heard of me before yesterday. Didn't know what I was up to when I came asking about Jeremy Coates. But he sensed danger quickly enough to send Devonshire scrambling, which meant he knew who Coates was and that his name represented danger.

My guess: my visit was part of a bigger problem, an ongoing defensive action. One that involved the Marylebone BestBreak and a guy who pointed cameras at innocent women and silenced investigators who knew too much.

I let my thoughts ebb with the tide. Concluded that I needed to talk to three people: Jeremy Coates, who could tell me what was going on; Barclay Brent, who was unlikely to; and Peter Covault who just needed me to go away.

~~~~~

When I got to Chase Street Shaughnessy and Harry were in their room discussing strategy for a notice serving on behalf of a council weary of seeing their people lining up in A&E over a dispute with an uncooperative landlord. Sean and Harry could avoid the A&E but the tricky job was getting eyes on the guy. The council had likened the task to sighting the Surrey Puma. Sean and Harry would get their beast but there might be a long slow trail before the fireworks started.

They broke off their discussion to get an update on the Foxglove affair.

Lucy came in, fresh from a tangle with her hair therapist. Yesterday her crop had been crimson with green highlights. Today it was a soft white cascade that reminded me of our early days. The sight stoked nostalgia. Lucy was still a woman to turn heads. Then a newer picture pushed into my head: Kim Waters. As different from Lucy as a soprano from a hip-hopper, but I sensed that I'd been snared just as deftly. The thought of Kim distracted me for a moment. Having her out of town for a day or two was no bad thing if I could just stay sane until she returned.

I pushed the distraction aside, along with the question of whether I was giving Foxglove leverage if the heat turned up.

From tomorrow we'd be keeping an eye on Kim twenty-four hours. That would negate any leverage.

'Wow Eddie,' Lucy said. 'Beautiful!'

I snapped back.

She was toying with one of the lawyers' cards. I'd just been showing it to Sean and Harry.

'With quality like that you're going places,' Harry enthused. Not that Harry's ever been one for flash. Men dressed in herringbone and driving ten year old Mondeos aren't partial to vogues. Harry's interest was in the forgery side. He saw the cards as a challenge. We got back to topic.

'What kind of lawsuit can they bring?' Shaughnessy asked. 'Have we done anything illegal?'

'These guys have unlimited means. If they put their minds to it they'll make breathing illegal.'

'When you take on a billionaire you're going to get push-back.'

I agreed. 'We've poked the stick into a gold plated nest this time. And there's something big going on if Peter Covault's sending calling cards.'

'So what's next?' Lucy perched herself on Shaughnessy's desk and kicked her heels. Her shoes were white, matching her hair. Everything in between was black.

'I'm going to look at Covault's stepson, Barclay Brent. He was the guy selling those document packages. If we can find out what the documents were about we'll understand things. Same if we talk to Jeremy Coates. But my main target is Foxglove. You got some time, Luce?'

'Sure. I've cleared all our bills from Foxglove's twenty thousand. I could use a new purpose in life.' She shook her hair. 'You need some sleuthing?'

'Go and sweet-talk the courier people,' I suggested. 'Find out which depot took the packages Foxglove sent us. Any name he gave them will be false but maybe there's a real contact number'

'Wilco.'

Shaughnessy and Harry got ready to leave.

'Give us a shout if you need extra hands,' Shaughnessy said. 'We'll be sitting in a car.'

He and Harry went out. Lucy went to fire up her computer. Herbie and I went through to my office to shuffle priorities. Decided that the first would be a quick tip of the hat to the Diamond Covault top guy. Maybe he'd be keen for a chat.

I pulled up the company's corporate number. Asked their switchboard to transfer me to Peter Covault's office. They put me through to someone called Corporate Scheduling who informed me that Mr Covault didn't take unsolicited calls. They suggested I make an appointment with Communications and Public Affairs. I asked if I could leave a direct message. Corporate Scheduling said sure, they'd see that it was delivered straight to Communications and Public Affairs. I left my name and number and the message, which was that Covault and I needed a chat about the company's termination procedures. Corporate Scheduling assured me that the message would reach C&PA as soon as possible, at the latest by next week or next year. They asked if there was any other way they could help but I'd already cut the line.

I got my feet onto the desk. The call had been whimsy. I might as well have called the Queen or the US President. They've all got ten layers of people between them and the outside world. But I'd not been aiming for a natter. I just wanted Covault to know that I was still poking around. If the message got through it would be a nice irritant. He'd know I was not backing down.

I left Lucy working her phone and went out and unclipped the Frogeye's hood. The sky was blue. Temperatures were heading up towards twenty degrees. Fresh air would be good. The only downside of an open top was that it encouraged Herbie to vault the door, which was producing scratch marks. By the time I stowed the hood he was already in his seat, focusing through the windscreen. I jumped in.

'Watch the paintwork,' I said.

Herbie grinned. Concentrated. The engine fired. We backed out and pulled round to the street. Crossed the river and left town.

CHAPTER TWENTY-SEVEN
Alive or dead was hard to say

At Tunbridge Wells I took a minor road west to a hamlet called Chester Wood which was a cluster of fifty houses under a low wooded hill on the Weald. Pristine gardens flowering with spring bloom fronted former farm workers' cottages and staff homes built for the nearby estate. The farm workers were long gone and the estate's staff drove in nowadays from cheaper locations in Tunbridge or Crowborough. City commuters had claimed the cottages. I followed the lane out until it intercepted an eight foot stone wall protecting Peter Covault's country retreat.

I followed the wall.

After a quarter of a mile it was broken by the entrance to an old stable yard and then by the main gates where the wall curved in to meet twelve foot gateposts. The gates were closed, protecting a two storey gatehouse and cameras watching from a twelve foot pole. I coasted past. Followed the wall for two miles as it curved round the estate's far reaches, curved again and finally turned sharply back towards the hamlet. I drove a final mile and arrived back at the cottages. My clock showed four miles. Quite a wall.

I'd known Peter Covault's name for years, had a vague awareness of the estate along with hazy images of a castle just outside Monaco – or was it St Moritz? – and a superyacht named *Global Mistress,* which had stuck in my memory through the sheer crassness of the moniker. I'd always sensed that that name said something about the guy.

Whatever the guy's character, it's the money that counts, and a four mile wall in the heart of the home counties shouts wealth as loud as any Swiss castle. The question was how the walls tied in with Sam Barker under that lake, to threats against innocent women.

I rolled through the hamlet and started a second circuit. This time I pulled up at the gates. Hopped out and looked for a bell plate. Saw none. There was a pedestrian side gate but it was locked. If there was a way in it wasn't obvious. Maybe the postman climbed over.

'Good morning, sir.'

The voice came from behind the gateposts. Hidden speakers. I assumed they had a mike there too.

'Visitor for Mr Covault,' I said.

'I'm sorry,' the gateposts said. 'He doesn't accept visitors.'

I guess they meant *unknown* visitors. A polite way of saying get lost.

'The name's Flynn. Peter's expecting me. I talked to his people recently.'

The gateposts were silent. Checking their diary. The diary returned a blank.

'We've no record of an appointment.'

'Call the house,' I said. 'Peter knows who I am.'

'We'll let him know you stopped by.'

'Is he home right now?'

'We don't give out that kind of information.'

'How about Barclay? Is he around?'

'Sir, could you move away from the gates?'

I stayed put. Gripped the metal bars to peer right and left inside the walls. Trees and bushes. Curving driveway that hid the way on. I looked at the gatehouse. Its door opened and a uniformed guy came out and walked over. He was young and tough looking and his uniform was like a policeman's without the helmet or insignia but with some useful looking implements strapped to his belt that might or might not be legal in public. He was wearing a pair of wrap-round shades that also might or might not have been legal and which the regular police are missing. The guy stopped on the other side of the gate.

'I'm sorry, sir. Your name's not in the book. Perhaps if you tried Mr Covault's office number.'

His head was pointed in my direction. Maybe he was looking at me. But all I was picking up from his demeanour was disinterest. A guy doing his job. Keeping the gate closed.

'If Barclay's here he'll want to talk to me,' I said.

He shook his head. 'Not without an appointment, sir.'

'Just give him a bell. Is he up at the house?'

But the guy just stood and waited. He had time to kill. It was probably a slow day.

'Okay,' I said. 'See you later.'

'Have a fine day, sir.'

I grinned. Flicked a salute. The day was already fine.

And about to get finer.

~~~~~

I hadn't expected to meet Peter Covault or his stepson. Hadn't expected to learn much from a tour round his estate. I'd driven down here for orientation, to get a sense of the guy. Time to think. But in the event I *had* picked up something. Maybe nothing relevant but I didn't know that yet.

I drove round to the far side of the estate. Got to a corner I'd spotted where a track went off into the woods. I pulled over and parked on the verge.

The track had been surfaced in chalk aggregate. When I kicked at it I got a dust cloud. I looked up it. A chained five-bar gate blocked the way on. A notice said "Strictly Private. No Trespassing". Another said "Shooting In Progress".

I listened. Heard nothing. Seemed the shooting notice had been left from the weekend, or the one before. The notices made me wonder if this was Covault's land too, somewhere he invited people for a weekend's sport. But it was the chalk track that interested me. The tyre walls of Barclay Brent's Isuzu had been covered in chalk dust and there probably aren't too many places you'd get that. Maybe just coincidence, but standing across the road from the walls of Covault's estate it was hard to dismiss it. My guess was that Barclay had driven up this track recently. According to Yvonne's social media he was a shooter, and if that was the reason for his visit then the place was of no interest. But call it idle curiosity: I was here and it looked like Brent had been here recently and it felt like I should take a look.

Herbie had vaulted the car door. I picked him up and dropped him on the other side of the gate then climbed over and we walked up into the woods. The evergreens dimmed the light; brought a hush.

The path climbed gradually. We followed it up, looking for anything other than shooting that might have brought Barclay here. Five hundred yards up, after a couple of bends, the track ended in a turning area. On shooting days the area would be cluttered with four-by-fours. Today it was empty. Nothing here except an oddity: a ten foot high stone edifice off to one side. A wall, cylindrical, twenty feet across without windows or doors, capped along the top but without any roof visible. I thought of mine shafts. Didn't recall any industry in the area. I'd seen no sign of abandoned facilities on my drive round the estate. A narrower track continued past the turning area. I walked it to where the trees opened and gave a view of undulating farm land. No sign of mine workings. My recollections from the back of my Geography class said that Kent once produced coal but weren't the fields over by the coast? Did they get something else out of the ground here? I walked back and circled the stonework. Spotted crushed shrubs at the base on the turning circle side. I lifted stems that had been snapped at ground level. Stood back and stared at the wall and worked out heights and angles. What was over that wall? A grille cover? Nothing? And how high was Barclay's pickup? Call the bed three feet and the cab roof a touch under six. I thought of the dent in the Isuzu's roof. I'd assumed something heavy had toppled from the bed but the bed had been pristine, never used for transporting loads. So could the dent have been someone climbing onto the roof? Why would you do that, and how heavy would you need to be to crease the metal? I pictured the Isuzu parked here. The cylindrical edifice would be only chest high once you were up on the roof. Low enough to heave something over.

Speculation, but it was hard to dismiss the picture of Barclay Brent's vehicle parked here with chalk dust dulling its shiny tyres.

I looked for a way to climb up the stonework. Spotted nothing. I'm no rock climber. And if this was a mining shaft it would go a long way down. There'd be nothing to see in the blackness.

File under "Possible".

I whistled to Herbie.

'Let's go,' I said.

We went back out and over the gate and Herbie jumped into his seat whilst I rooted for my Kent A-Z.

The maps are large scale and often contain more precise information than Ordnance Surveys. If there were old mine workings in the area they'd be marked. I saw none. But when I zeroed in on our location, traced the chalk path, I spotted what the stone building was. The construction wasn't shown on the map but a dashed line ran right through the spot. The dashes were annotated *Lime Wood*

Tunnel and exited the low hill as the solid black marks of a railway. The tunnel was half a mile in length which put the stone cylinder at its mid point.

It was a ventilation shaft.

I turned the car and backtracked the lane for a couple of hundred yards to where the woods ended and a field of spring barley ran alongside the road. Another hundred yards brought the railway cutting into view. I parked up and jumped a fence, pushed through undergrowth to get a better sight. The cutting was twenty feet deep, dull grey ballast and rusty rails smothered in high weeds. The line looked disused.

I went back and grabbed my tactical flashlight and lifted Herbie over the fence and we went down to check.

It was a single track, rusting, rotting, half buried by vegetation. The smell of hot pitch came up from the sleepers as we moved towards the woods. I walked between the rails, matching my stride to the sleepers. Easier than trudging through the gravel and weeds. Herbie muddled along behind, keeping to whichever side had the more interesting smells. Then the trees closed in and the cutting deepened into rock walls and a tunnel mouth expanded up ahead. In two minutes we were there, standing thirty feet below the woods at a stone-lined portal covered in moss and ivy. The mouth was barricaded by a rough timber frame with wire mesh stretched across, barbed wire along the top timber. A notice pinned to the centre post said "Danger. Keep Out."

I'd not brought any cutting tools but local kids had already kicked at one of the boards down at ground level and the netting was loose. I eased it away and crawled in. Looked back at Herbie. Herbie was sitting on the track in a way that said he was fine where he was. I grinned.

'Good boy,' I said. 'If I'm not out in a couple of days go and find a policeman.'

I stood and flicked on the tac. light and walked into the dark. The flashlight was two-thirty lumens but I was blind anyway after the daylight. I walked slowly, feeling my way. The temperature had dropped ten degrees and I could sense clammy walls though my eyes could barely see them. The warm pitch smell had gone, replaced by the stink of mould and soot.

The tunnel curved. I turned and looked back. I was a hundred yards in and the entrance was a dim glow, all warmth and life gone. But my eyes were adjusting. I could see rails and brickwork ahead of me. I picked up my pace. Went deeper in. The chill intensified and water dripped into trackside pools. Shadows danced in the tac. light.

Then the bend eased and revealed the silver illumination of the airshaft a hundred yards ahead and a minute later I was there. The shaft's light wasn't much but it was enough with the tac. to show me what had come down from up in the woods.

What had come down was a person.

The sixty-foot drop had broken him. He was sprawled on his back across the rails and his split head stained the ballast. Whether he'd been alive or dead when he came down was impossible to say. Whether he'd been wearing his glasses was hard to say. He wasn't wearing them now.

I was looking at the face of Sam's mystery guy, Jeremy Coates.

CHAPTER TWENTY-EIGHT
Rats, I guess

The body was still fresh, though something had gnawed at his left cheek and at both hands. Rats, I guess. He'd been dead maybe a couple of days. It was hard to say in the light. I squatted and pushed the tac. light under his right forearm and lifted. It rotated easily from the elbow, just a hint of resistance. Rigor mortis mostly gone. So two days at least, given the temperature.

I switched to the left arm and inspected Coates' wristwatch. Its glass was smashed and its face dented. The damage had killed the movement. The trapped hands stood at twelve thirty-one. The date window said that Coates had taken his plunge two days ago. Either shortly after midnight or early afternoon.

I stood again. Listened to the darkness. The sepulchral walls returned faint echoes and a timeless chill. If I hadn't come along Coates might have lain here for decades undiscovered. When they tore up the tracks outside they'd probably breeze-block the entrances without coming in. Cap the airshaft.

I looked up. The opening was a bright circle that I could obscure with a lifted hand. No sign of a protective grille. Barclay had got lucky when he climbed up on his cab.

The discovery balanced things. Now we had dead bodies on both sides of the affair.

The question was how was Coates involved? And why was a billionaire playboy heaving people down airshafts? Maybe the answers to those questions would tell me who Foxglove was and why it was so important that he catch up with Sam Barker and whoever had handed over packages. And the answer to that would tell me why Peter Covault, the billionaire big shot, was taking a personal interest in the affair.

My breath misted. I watched it rise. Looked back at Jeremy Coates who'd probably known all the answers but hadn't seen what was coming. The real puzzle with Coates was that he still didn't fit on either side of the affair. If he was on Barclay Brent's side, delivering documents, why had Brent killed him? If he was on the opposite side why would Brent, and presumably the firm, be delivering documents *to* him? Was Brent playing a game of his own?

I had a fistful of jigsaw pieces, none of which fitted.

I stepped back and looked at the body. A nice crime scene for some lucky crew. They were going to love that trek up the tunnel.

That was after I'd reported my discovery, which had to be soon but not too soon. If the police swarmed all over this then Barclay Brent and Foxglove and maybe Peter Covault and his whole organisation would skitter away and take cover behind their legal armies. Foxglove wouldn't need to skitter far, of course, since no-one knew who he was. But the others would close up tight and the police would be facing months, maybe years, of pick and shovel work.

Better if Coates stayed out of it for a day or two, until I had something to give to the police along with the body.

I aimed my flashlight back into the darkness and commenced the long walk out. It took a while but eventually the curve opened up and light expanded ahead of me. I reached daylight and crawled under the wire. Heat enveloped me.

~~~~~

I parked behind Chase Street and walked round to where Shaughnessy, Harry and Lucy were sitting at one of Connie's tables. Either the firm was prospering more than I'd realised or the sun had brought a fit of extravagance. Connie had a special up on the board that Harry and Lucy urged on me on the basis that having ordered it was the same thing as having tasted it. But Connie's a reliable chef. His home-baked breads are the best in town, even if the bill has you grabbing for the indigestion tablets. I yelled in and added one to the order, plus a coffee, extra cream.

'Any luck with the big guy?' Shaughnessy said.

'I'm waiting a call back.'

Shaughnessy smiled. 'Pigs might fly,' he said.

'Something's been flying,' I said. I told them about Jeremy Coates. About my theory that Barclay Brent had driven him into the woods by the Covault estate and dropped him sixty feet into the tunnel.

Lucy made an "O" with her mouth. I sensed her appetite waning.

'This thing's beginning to notch up collateral damage,' Shaughnessy said, 'which means it's out of control.'

I agreed.

'The odd thing is that the business at its centre – the package exchange – was finished. The job was done. So why have both sides gone on the offensive?'

'Maybe there's more than two sides,' Harry said. He was thinking about Coates. The guy who didn't fit.

'My feeling too. Unless he was working with Foxglove. You get anywhere with the courier people, Luce?'

'Glad you asked, Eddie,' she said. 'I called at their Barnes office. That's the walk-in where Foxglove dropped off his packages for you. And they have this really cute branch manager.'

I grinned. This was Lucy-speak for a guy she'd wrapped round her finger to advance her flirt-based investigation. Seemed the courier company recruited staff who liked cute girls with snowstorm hair. But being a pretty face is not enough in this business. You've got to know how to use it. Lucy knew how to use it.

'The guy's name is Terry,' she said.

'Foxglove's?'

'The branch manager's. Foxglove's name isn't readable on the form.'

I'd known it. But readable or not, any name Foxglove had left would be meaningless.

Connie and his girl came out with our orders. Three specials. One salmon salad. One sausage. Connie planted my plate and delivered the sausage. Herbie grinned wide and swallowed it in one gulp.

'Bad boy,' Connie said. I didn't know how much the sausages were costing, since we hadn't paid the tab for a while, but my guess was that when the figures came out we'd be putting Herbie on a diet.

'What did Terry know?' I said.

'He let me see his CCTV for the days in question and we spotted the same guy handing over all three of your deliveries.'

She pulled out her phone and swiped a picture. Not a great picture since it was a snap of a fourteen inch monitor but the courier company's cameras were high res. It was good enough. I looked at the face of a fortyish guy with a long dome of forehead bounded by crisp, receding hair. His nose was strong, lips fleshy, cheeks stubbled. His eyes were indistinct behind tinted glasses. The whole had a hint of Middle East. And the face matched the guy Sam had snapped picking up the hotel key and matched the description from the chef by the BestBreak. We were looking at the guy who'd chased Sam out of the window. I asked Harry to print a few copies when he got back in.

'There's more,' Lucy said.

We looked at her.

'The manager talked to one of his clerks who was just going off shift when Foxglove brought our last package in. The clerk had passed him in the doorway and they kind of bumped which is why the clerk checked him out. He remembers a car right outside and a guy standing by it. The guy had an Asian face and had tattoos across his fingers, hieroglyphics at the knuckles and a snake running right across. Both hands, he thinks.'

I filed the information. We'd known Foxglove wasn't operating alone but this was our first supporting evidence.

Lucy mailed a copy of Foxglove's CCTV snap to me and Harry. I forwarded the pic. to Yvonne. Followed up with a call. She picked up and we confirmed what this gave us: which was that Foxglove, the guy who'd recruited me to chase Sam and probably killed him, was the person who'd received the documents from him. So we had Sam working for Barclay Brent, the billionaire playboy, delivering his documents. And Foxglove receiving them and then coming after Sam.

And Jeremy Coates on no-one's side.

I updated Yvonne on my discovery of Coates' body. She swore and asked what the hell he'd been up to to end up at the bottom of that shaft.

I knew as much as she did.

But we were moving.

'Need extra eyes?' Shaughnessy said.

I grabbed my baguette and went on the attack.

'Tomorrow,' I said. 'Let's see if we can close this off.'

'We'll clear our desk,' Shaughnessy said.

Meantime there was today.

I looked at Foxglove's photo. The guy looked right for the part. Young, professional, predatory.

So far we'd communicated through text messages. But messages weren't going to get me to the guy.

I still didn't know who or where he was but he knew who and where I was.

That's what I'd work with.

CHAPTER TWENTY-NINE
I guess I got carried away

I got my feet onto the desk and keyed Foxglove's number. The call went through to voicemail.

'This is your friendly private investigation agency,' I said. 'All problems solved and all wrongs righted. In this case the problem is you and the wrong is the writing. Specifically the graffiti on Ms Waters' bedroom door. I do get your message, of course, but you've seen our record. Backing off isn't our thing. And we both know that sticks and stones aren't going to work for either of us. So how about an alternative? A win-win. How about our agency pulls its nose out and forgets the whole thing and you rustle up a golden handshake to express your gratitude. Sound good? I've given it some thought and it seemed to me that doubling the original fee would be about right. But then I gave it some more thought and wondered whether we should factor in our position of now holding information that would be problematic for your operations and might interest the authorities investigating Mr Barker's accident. I'll spare you the detail but we basically know everything and have proof to back things up. And a good business never sells itself short, as you'll agree. So let's set the non-disclosure fee at a hundred K. If we discount your earlier instalments that leaves barely eighty to pay. Eighty K and we're out of your hair forever. How does that sound? Get back to me and we'll arrange the transaction. But let's move fast. This offer ends at close of business tomorrow. After that it will be between you and the authorities and that sounds like nothing but trouble to me.'

I killed the line. Grinned at Shaughnessy. He was leaning against the wall by my barometer.

'I thought you said forty K,' he commented.

'I got carried away. And once it's said you can't change the recording. You think I should call again, drop the price?'

Shaughnessy smiled.

'Might sound weak.'

'Or maybe up it. Would he swallow two hundred K?'

'What if he paid? We'd have an ethical decision on our hands.'

'He might pay the hundred. That's still going to be tricky.'

Shaughnessy held the smile.

'We're worrying about nothing,' he said. 'The guy's not going to pay a penny.'

'It's just nice to dream...'

Shaughnessy twisted and leaned to get a view out into reception.

'Lucy's on the blower,' he said. 'She didn't hear. She'd have been lecturing us on the ethics whilst she ran for the furniture catalogues.'

I leaned back. Clasped my hands behind my head. Watched the sky. A beautiful spring day. Barely a wisp of cloud. A day when your spirits soar. Maybe too high.

'A hundred K is pushing it,' I admitted. 'But it's still credible. The guy needs to believe we're serious, which means the extortion has to be something he might actually pay if he wasn't a psychopath.'

I looked back.

'Give him two hours,' Shaughnessy said. 'He'll have made up his mind by then.'

'My phone is on charge,' I said.

~~~~~

In the event, my phone rang sixty minutes later.

'You're being very stupid,' Foxglove said.

Finally: his voice. A deep, thick delivery. Not natural English but no specific accent. Someone who'd grown into the language.

'I can live with that,' I said. 'But unless you're stupid too you'll sort out the payment. Then we can close this affair and go home.'

'You think I'm going to hand over another eighty thousand pounds on the basis of a vague threat?'

'Well you're calling me on the basis of the vague threat. Which means you know I'm serious.'

'I don't believe you have anything. So this is your final warning, Flynn: walk away.'

'Not without the eighty K.'

A couple of seconds' pause. Then:

'We're watching you, and we're watching the women, including Ms Waters.'

I grinned.

'Don't mess with me, Mr Foxglove. I have photographic proof that you were with Sam Barker the night he was killed. When the police see it they're going to come knocking on your door.'

'Bluff.'

'And we've photos of you picking up the hotel keys and entering that room plus witnesses to you delivering the cash and threat notes to me. So try us. Then explain it all to the police along with your connection to Jeremy Coates. We've located Jeremy, by the way.'

Nuggets of truth in a mash of speculation. Enough to tell Foxglove that we really did know stuff, to get him understanding just how dangerous we were. Enough to confirm a decision he'd already taken.

'You're playing with fire,' he said. 'I *will* hurt those women, including your new girlfriend. You knew we've been watching the two of you?'

I hadn't, until that graffiti on her door, and the reminder hit me like a kick. But Kim wasn't relevant to this conversation. Hurting Kim wouldn't make Foxglove's problem go away. He knew he needed to handle me directly. I'd offered him a way to close this off and he was going to run with it.

The line was silent for a moment before he spoke.

'Okay,' he said. 'We'll pay. You can have your little extortion. But then it's over. If I ever see you again I'll kill you and hurt your lady friend, just for the fun of it.'

I was silent a moment myself.

'Just stump up the cash,' I said. 'And if you ever go near Kim afterwards the whole deal is off. I know who you are and where you are and I'll come for you. Are we both clear?'

'Where do we meet?'

'My office. This evening. Just follow the stairs up.'

'I'll be there at eight,' he said.

I cut the line.

~~~~~

I sat in the car fifty yards up from our building and watched the sunset paint the rooftops. Miles Davis played softly through the Frogeye's sound system. I checked the time. Five to eight. Chase Street was dimming but distinct. Eighty yards away, opposite

Connie's, Harry's jalopy was pointing towards the main road. The dark green Mondeo blended in nicely with the parked vehicles. You'd never notice his eyes in the rear view because you'd never notice the car.

Number Twenty-Six, our building, was deserted. Even the lawyers had to sleep sometimes, though their lines were open twenty-four hours.

I checked the time again. Eight dead.

Then the black Jeep Cherokee I'd seen outside Jeremy Coates' house rolled up from the main road looking for a place to park. It passed our building and stopped and reversed into an access way on the opposite side. Didn't come back out. Vehicles blocked it from my view.

I pressed and spoke.

'Get it?'

'Watching it now,' Harry responded. 'I can just see the bonnet. He's waiting to go.'

I picked up my Leica and readied the zoom.

Nothing happened for sixty seconds whilst the Jeep occupants watched the building, wondering why there were no lights. Maybe double-checking numbers and postcodes. Making up their minds. Then two figures stepped out from between the parked cars and walked across the road. One of them was the guy who'd knocked on Coates' door in Caterham. Six feet plus, well built, clipped hair, same ski jacket. The other guy was shorter but muscled from long sessions in the gym. Jeans and tee shirt. No jacket.

Both were carrying baseball bats.

'It's them,' I reported. Harry double-clicked an acknowledgement.

I snapped a couple of pics as they crossed the street. Watched the big guy stand on our step and ring the bell. The shorter guy was bouncing around in a display of impatience. He stepped back to look up at the windows and his bat drifted away from his side. He swung it back. Smacked his leg. The first guy pressed the bell again. Got nothing.

The short guy jigged around some more until the tall one turned and said something sharp which calmed him down. The big guy pulled out a phone. Made a call. Turned back to the building, gesticulating. Listened. Took the hit for our door not opening.

Ended the call and looked up at the building again then up and down the street. I snapped a few more face shots to add to my Caterham collection. Then my phone rang. Foxglove's name on the screen. I didn't pick up. After twenty seconds the line disconnected. Ten seconds after that another call came through to the bat guys and they were told to stand down. The tall guy looked angry. Disappointed he'd not got to use the bat.

They crossed back over and I watched the Jeep pull out and turn at the bottom of the road. Harry moved out behind them, lights off. I fired up and joined the procession.

'Bayswater,' Harry reported. I turned at the end of Chase Street and put my foot down to close the gap, ready to skip past Harry if tactics demanded.

'Behind you,' I said. I cranked up the Davis.

'Stupid,' Harry said.

'Very,' I said, above the trumpet squeal.

CHAPTER THIRTY
That won't work twice

The Cherokee drove across town to a three storey apartment block near the centre of Mitcham. Harry pulled into a side street and was out lounging against a wall, watching the building. I picked up his commentary from a hundred yards back.

'They're on the blower. The big guy's taking instructions.'

'He's being told to stand down,' I said.

I'd logged two more missed calls from Foxglove. No voicemail messages. There was nothing to say unless we talked directly. He knew that the payoff meeting was a ruse. He'd just told his guys that. Told them to stay sharp.

'The smaller one's heading in,' Harry said. 'I think he's home for the night.'

'Keep an eye on him. Check he doesn't come back out.'

I already had the Frogeye rolling when the Jeep moved off. I followed it towards Lewisham with just my side lights on.

Twenty minutes later it parked behind a club in the centre of the town. I stopped short and killed the lights. The guy came out and walked up to the club door and disappeared inside. I rolled again. Turned into the same parking area and backed into a corner where I could see the Jeep. Transferred the Chase Street photos to my phone and messaged them through to an old pal of mine, Zach Finch. Followed up with a call. He was waiting.

'They didn't play ball?' he said.

'They arrived with bats. Some kind of cost-saving measure.'

'I'm keen to hear about it, Eddie, but meantime I'll put in a search. The good news is that I can tell you about the guy in the ski jacket right now.'

This was the lead guy, the one taking orders from Foxglove. The guy who'd just gone into the club.

Zach Finch had worked for me back in the job. He was my DS, the copper who got things done and watched my back, and the only person in the Met I ever trusted a hundred percent. After my move to the private sector we gave each other an unofficial hand now and again.

'His name's Marco Rossi,' Zach said. 'A freelance. Born to the life. In and out of the system since he was fourteen. Served juvie on peewits then progressed to muscle for hire and armed robbery. He's been fingered for six jobs in town and a couple elsewhere. Sent down in '05 for the G4S Rochester job. Out on licence six months ago. Looks like he's already been down the Job Centre.'

'We got an address?'

'It's in the system. I'll have it tomorrow.'

'I'll call if I need it. I'm on the guy right now. Maybe he'll take me there.'

'Got it. And something I forgot earlier: we had a query from Bromley. A DS called Prior. Asking about a DODI you were stirring up. Is this it?'

'Yes. But Prior already knows his RTA was no DODI. It was a homicide. The victim was a P.I. called Sam Barker who was being chased by the guy who sent this pair out tonight. Prior's starting to see his RTA morph into something from the depths.'

'I'll watch out for that one,' Zach said. 'Meantime we put in a good word. My guv'nor told Prior he should listen to you.'

'He's already listening. He thinks we're holding out on him.'

'Which you are.'

I pictured the body in the railway tunnel.

'More than he imagines. But I need a couple of days before I can put something meaningful in front of him.'

'Let's meet soon,' Zach said. 'I want to hear the whole story.'

'Soon as it's over. We'll have an evening. Regards to the missus.'

I heard a laugh like tipped gravel and killed the line. Sat back to wait. An hour passed. Rossi's car stayed where it was. I called Harry. He confirmed that Rossi's pal hadn't reappeared. I suggested he stand down. I was with the main guy and I wasn't leaving him until I knew who'd sent him out with the bat. I ended the call and sat back to wait. After another hour I gave Kim Waters a late call.

'I was just thinking about you,' she said. 'You at home?'

'Still out. Looking for Foxglove.'

'Poor you. Are you any nearer to finding him?'

'In a way,' I said. 'The guy's getting nervous. He's coming after me.'

'Why's that?'

'I've stirred things up. Let him feel my breath on his neck.'

'Is that wise?'

'Very little of what we do is wise. But I want to shake the guy loose. I've threatened him with the story that we've found things that will blow his cover.'

'And have you?'

'Not as much as I hinted. But enough to get him worrying.'

Kim didn't need the detail, the solidifying connections to Diamond Covault's global business or the bodies in tunnels. The thought that we might be up against people with unlimited resource wouldn't ease her mind. Not that it was easy anyway.

'Is there a chance Foxglove will panic? Will he come after one of us?'

'That's his last resort. Once he hurts someone there's no going back. But we'll be keeping an eye on you once you're back in town. We'll have people outside your house. You won't see them but they'll be there. And I'll be five minutes away if you call.'

'Then I'll be safe. My alarm will be on and a security service guy is staying in the cottage.'

'That's good.'

'Better if you were there, of course. Or here in Manchester...'

I couldn't argue with that. The rear of a Lewisham club has limited attraction. But I was here until Marco Rossi came out and Manchester was a hell of a drive so I told Kim I'd see her tomorrow. She started to say something in reply then cut herself off. Wished me goodnight.

I decided to stretch my legs. Left the car and walked onto the street. Found a doorway across from the club. If Rossi was drinking he might take a taxi home whilst I baby-sat his Cherokee, and I didn't want to lose him so easily. So I stood in the shadows and watched the club door. People and groups went in and out. Two a.m. passed and there were more people coming out than going in. I kept watching.

Freezing in the shadows on a dark street, waiting for something that might not happen, isn't everyone's idea of a job but you learn patience in this game. I can listen to Miles Davis and six hours go by. That's when I'm in the car. Standing outside is never as comfortable. I could use buds but I prefer to hear the night. Traffic and talk.

Sirens and screams. Car doors banging.

And empty doorways are good places to think. I was wired, buzzing with the internal energy of motion. I was closing on Foxglove. Marco Rossi was going to take me there. What's a few hours' waiting?

Three a.m. A steady stream of punters coming out.

Then Rossi emerged in a group of four: a girl on his arm and two guys behind. But after a natter they split up and Marco and the girl walked round to the car park and Marco did the chivalry thing and held the Jeep's door. Didn't see me as I walked across to the Sprite.

I was ready to follow them out but the Jeep didn't move. The two of them sat inside it and seemed in no hurry. The interior light extinguished, leaving only shadowy figures behind the glass. A light flared. A shared joint. Then movements that suggested they were sharing more than the smoke. We hit three fifteen and I realised we might be here all night.

I decided to move things forward.

I left the car. Walked across and opened the Cherokee's door. Rossi was angled away from me, his lips on the girl's as she held the joint away, but the door caught his attention in a flash, and I guess ambushes must be part of his job because he whipped round and launched himself out over me before he'd any time to see who or what was coming. Great reflexes. Just not smart. If I'd had a knife it would have been in his stomach. His dive out also left him unsteady, grasping the car door to keep himself from going down, which limited his options in the critical first half second which was when I hit him hard in the abdomen.

The girl screamed.

Credit to Rossi, he stayed in the game and I had to dodge a nasty right to land my second punch and kick his knee. The kick toppled him sideways away from the vehicle and I slammed the door to mute the screaming. The interior light was back on, illuminating the thrashing girl. Her panic was mostly for the reefer she'd dropped at her feet.

I didn't pay her further attention. Marco Rossi was coming back with another right fist. I jumped away and he smashed the wing mirror off the Jeep, which must have hurt. Almost as much as the power drive I landed in his ribs and the right fist on his temple. A follow-up damaged his nose and finally got through. Rossi grunted and backed off in a defensive crouch, balled his fists and focused. Finally saw who'd jumped him.

'You,' he said. 'Well, fuck me.'

The girl was still screaming inside the cab. The light had gone out and she was a noisy silhouette.

'You know me?'

Rossi grinned through the pain. Straightened a little. Composed himself. His fists stayed tight.

'The freakin' detective,' he said. 'You had a lucky escape tonight, pal.'

'Luck was never part of it,' I said. 'I saw you coming a mile off. Do you have another bat handy or are we on a level field now?'

'I don't need a bat, pal.'

'Got it. That explains the cracked ribs and the blood all over your face.'

Rossi grinned. 'You jumped me you bastard. But that won't work twice.'

Which was true. Meting more punishment was going to be an uphill struggle. And it wasn't why I was here. Even Rossi realised that.

'What's your game? You want us to get the bats back out? Because we're happy to oblige.'

'I'm happy if I never see you or your bats again,' I said. 'And that trick won't work twice either.'

'So what are we doing here?'

'What we're doing is that you're going to tell me who sent you out tonight.'

'In your dreams.'

I grinned. Pushed my hands into my pockets. My right knuckles were hurting.

'No,' I said. 'In reality. I'm not giving you a choice, Marco.'

The name stopped him. His face digested the news that he'd been ID'd. Then he shrugged it off. Pulled a tissue from his pocket and dabbed at his nose.

'You probably believe in the tooth fairy,' he said.

'I never believed in the tooth fairy.' I pulled out my phone and brought up a picture. Held it so he could see without snatching.

His eyes focused. The photo was of him and his pal on Chase Street with their bats.

'Not a good snap to fall into police hands,' I said. 'Correct me if I'm wrong but those bats will land you back in court for reconsideration of your parole. What are we looking at then? Another six?'

'Try it and you're a dead man, Flynn.'

'I'll take the chance.' I stashed the phone. 'I want the name of the guy who sent you. Then maybe we can forget the pictures.'

'No deal. I've got a brief who'll shred any review. Who says it's even me in the picture?'

'I've got fifteen or twenty more. Your face is clearer in most of them.'

'No deal. I wouldn't give you a name to avoid a life sentence.'

I grinned. 'Call me persistent,' I said, 'but "no" is not a good answer. How about we continue the discussion when you get home. Maybe start a late night altercation. That should bring the cops running. My guess is they'll be interested in what they find inside your house. Because there's stuff there for sure.'

Rossi shook his head. 'Do your worst. All that's going to happen is you'll get another visit. Are we through?'

I dropped the grin. It's amazing how stubborn these criminal types are. It's a point of honour to avoid cooperating with anyone. If I pulled the guy's fingernails he wouldn't tell me who'd won the cup final. I shrugged and opened the Jeep door for him. The mirror clattered against the metalwork, hanging by its electrical wires.

'Go ahead,' I said. 'I'll tag along. We'll finish the chat at your place.'

'You think?' Rossi said. He climbed into the vehicle and slammed the door. The mirror clattered again. He needed to sort that out before he had some serious touching up to do.

The Jeep's interior light was on again. The woman had calmed down. Abandoned the joint. Maybe there were a few carpet burns down there. Rossi made no move to start the car. What he did was pull out his phone to call his pal back on duty. Probably with a few others. I watched him key the numbers then yanked the door open and grabbed the phone before he could react. He cursed and tried to get out but I slammed the door and leaned back against it. When he saw what I was doing his efforts intensified. Then he changed tactics.

Scrabbled across the woman to get out of the far side.

We keep all kinds of stuff on our phones, protected by the security code. Trouble is, the code is good for shit once the phone's live. I killed the call he was making and brought up history. Three down the list was the call he'd made at Chase Street outside our front door. Second down the list was the same number.

The number was tagged: LAD MBL.

Short, sweet and meaningless. I noted the number.

Rossi was climbing out of the far door. I walked away from the Jeep and flicked through the contacts list. Found another LAD. This one was LAD OFFICE. I noted that number too and hit call. The number dialled through. Rossi was coming after me fast but I'd twenty yards' start. The call connected to an answering machine. The answering machine said: "This is Lad Associates. Our office hours...'

I didn't need the rest. I killed the call and turned as Rossi charged. Hurled the phone high over his head. Smartphones weigh about the same as cricket balls but are not as aerodynamic so I wasn't going to get the seventy yards I threw in a league match last season but the phone managed a good fifty before it hit the tarmac. Instinct had already turned Rossi, barely a second from piling into me, and he was sprinting back across the parking area in a futile chase after plastic shards and printed circuits. By the time he was scrabbling for the pieces I was rolling onto the street.

Smart phone. Dumb user.

CHAPTER THIRTY-ONE
Things always get tangled

I searched the internet over breakfast next morning and found that Lad Associates was a limited company with an address in West Ham and a single named director, John Lad. The business was described as "Security Services". I shut down the computer and called Yvonne Barker to tell her that Foxglove was out in the open. She swore with unconcealed glee. Came back to earth and agreed to dig out what she could on the company whilst I went to take a direct look, maybe spot John Lad himself.

At six forty I went down and pressed Henrietta's doorbell. A barrage of barking confirmed that someone was up. Luckily Henrietta's an early starter. She opened the door and Herbie barged out like an escapee from Colditz. Planted his paws on my thighs.

'He's been perfect,' Henrietta said. 'We watched TV and he helped with dinner leftovers. He's already had breakfast.'

Some Colditz.

'Always grateful,' I said. 'The job doesn't always accommodate four-legged escorts.'

'He's welcome any time,' Henrietta said. 'I know about the job.'

Henrietta had heard a few of my anecdotes but still imagined that private investigation was glamorous. All shoot-ups and car chases, every investigation a triumph. Most of my stories described disasters but she was convinced that I was being coy.

'I may need another favour later this week,' I said.

'Any time,' she repeated. 'Big job?'

'Getting bigger.'

'Just knock on my door.'

'I'll do that.'

Herbie and I went out. Twenty minutes on the park then we drove against the morning flow to West Ham. Lad Associates' office was located in a run-down eighties' block by Green Street. A frosted glass door with the company name in gold lettering, adjacent to a mobility scooter shop. I parked in a restricted zone and walked to a spot where we could watch. Maybe someone would show up. Maybe the place was just a registration address.

Eight a.m. People hurrying to bus stops and Tube stations. Shattering traffic din. We settled in for an unpleasant wait but at twenty past eight a woman unlocked the Lad Associates door and five minutes later three more people – two men and a woman – went in. First floor blinds were adjusted. Coffee brewing; emails being checked. So the place was a working office, though you'd not get a sense of Foxglove's activities from the mundane facade. I wondered how much the people up there knew about threats to women, bodies in lakes.

I waited.

Just before nine a white Audi R8 pulled onto the pavement outside the door. The engine barked and died, the brake ratcheted and the driver got out. I brought up my camera and snapped telephotos of the guy at the centre of everything. The guy who'd hired me, the one Sam Barker had photographed picking up the hotel keycard. The smooth bland face and dome forehead, the crisp hair, were unmistakable.

The Audi flashed and chirped and Foxglove disappeared into his business premises.

Foxglove was finally ID'd: John Lad, the firm's owner. Because if the guy driving a supercar wasn't the owner then the agency must be one hell of a place to work.

I grinned down at Herbie.

'Got him,' I said.

Lad had looked relaxed but this thing had to be hanging over him. He had to be just a little tense. He'd have been a lot more tense if he'd known that Marco Rossi's phone had been compromised. But he didn't know, because Rossi's debriefing on our early-hours encounter would have been limited to the fact of his tough guy refusal to give me anything. What Rossi wouldn't have mentioned was that I'd had his phone in my hands, that I'd picked up Lad's number. If Lad had had any inkling of that he'd have been looking up and down the street. He'd have known I was here.

I waited some more.

At nine fifteen a couple of tough guys in jeans and tee-shirts went into the building and came out ten minutes later. Lad's operatives, I guessed, but none I'd seen before. There was no sign of Marco Rossi or his sidekick. I wondered whether Lad had sent them back to Chase Street.

At half past nine Lad himself came back out. I skipped round the corner and hopped into the Frogeye, pulled out and followed the Audi towards the river. The Frogeye is a distinctive car if you're watching for a tail but it's also small enough to be invisible in modern traffic, especially if your rear-view is all engine. I held well back and followed Lad down onto the Lea Crossing and into the Bow Creek development where Lad circled the Covault Complex and turned onto the basement parking ramp.

Interesting.

Seemed all roads were leading to this building.

I put the Frogeye's wheels on the kerb and trotted down the ramp. Spotted the Audi backing into an executive spot on the first level.

So John Lad – Foxglove – probable P.I. killer and key actor in the document exchange had business with Diamond Covault. And not routine business. It looked like the executive parking spot was his norm.

I went back out and recovered the car. Rejoined the rush hour tail end. I knew who Foxglove was and where he was based and that he was connected to Diamond Covault. New possibilities were opening wide.

A call came in. I took it, hands-free.

Yvonne.

'Couple of things,' she reported. 'John Lad is also named as the registered owner of an overseas company – Lad Associates (Pte) Ltd in Singapore. My contact says that they provide security and investigation services which apparently are cover terms for all kinds of chicanery. It seems that "Johnny" Lad is a known figure in Singapore and Malaysia. His firm gets things done for people and companies who don't want to get their own hands dirty. And get this: my contact threw in the Covault name without me having to ask. Apparently Lad has close ties to the company. He's worked for them in Singapore and other countries and word is that the work looks a hell of a lot like bribery and extortion and "enforcement", all in the cause of oiling the company's plans. Lad opened the London office two years ago when the Covault Complex went up. My guess is that they're the favoured security contractor here too. But they didn't take

151

offices in the building. Makes me think that Diamond Covault aren't too keen to have their relationship with Lad Associates up in lights.'

I grinned.

'We're tripping over each other's feet,' I said. 'I just followed the guy to the Covault Complex.'

'My oh my. If this isn't getting bigger and dirtier. That gives us two lines in to the company: one from Sam's killer, one from Coates' killer.'

'Security guy and stepson,' I agreed. 'Both on opposite sides of the exchange and both killing people. The big question is which side was Coates on?'

'Coates was stuck in the middle,' Yvonne said.

Which was my own guess. I suggested that Yvonne come in to Chase Street to talk about where we went next. The explanation for the affair was almost at our fingertips. She said she'd drive straight over.

I turned away from the river at Tower Bridge. Another call came in.

'Mr Flynn. I need to talk to you again.'

DS Keith Prior.

'Something new?'

'There doesn't have to be anything new. When can you come in?'

'I'm kind of dashing around right now. How about we set something up later?'

'Dashing round on the Sam Barker case?'

'We've picked up a few things. We don't know how they tie in to Sam but we're getting there. Our methods are unofficial but they're fast.'

'This is a police investigation, not a private party. I want you here at Bromley soonest.'

'I'll be there, Sergeant. This all ends up on your desk.'

'Not good enough. I want what you have right now. We'll take it from there.'

'You've checked the records, Sergeant. You know I'm no amateur. I can get results whilst you're still doing the paperwork.'

'I've heard plenty about you from your old pals. Most of it barely credible. Rose tinted spectacles and all that. And I also read the papers last year. So you can stop blowing the trumpet. I want you in here and it's not negotiable.'

'As soon as I can. Let's talk this afternoon. We'll arrange a sit-down.'

'I want you *in*, Flynn, not discussing diaries. Do I have to come and get you?'

'That won't be necessary. Just give me a few hours. We'll set something up. I'll have some information that will interest you.'

Prior paused a moment. I heard exasperation.

'Call me this afternoon,' he said. 'Or I'll drive over and knock on your door.'

He cut the line.

Impatient. His instincts were telling him that we were well down the road to explaining Sam Barker's drive into that lake, though he probably didn't imagine just *how* far. But we'd soon be further. Things were starting to tie up. We didn't know what we were tying but Johnny Lad and Barclay Brent knew everything. That's why they were killing people.

~~~~~

I stood at the window, back to the street. Shaughnessy was in his chair. Harry was in his on the far side of their shared desk. Lucy was perched between them along with Herbie. And Yvonne Barker was sitting in one of Shaughnessy's chrome and leather guest chairs. The chairs are more comfortable than mine but Yvonne didn't look comfortable. She looked like she'd rather be pacing up and down chewing a phone book. Sam's body had been released and she was now responsible for getting their few relatives and acquaintances in the same place at the same time to give him some kind of send off. But she also wanted to find out who killed him, or rather, since we'd already established that, to produce the motive and hard evidence.

The superficial reason Sam was killed was that he was collateral in Johnny Lad's search for the guy delivering the documents.

And we'd found that guy. He was Barclay Brent, who was a member of the billionaire clan who owned the global development company that Lad coincidentally worked for in the guise of enforcer and chief thug. And Barclay Brent had done a little thuggery of his own when he pushed a nobody by the name of Jeremy Coates down an airshaft in the woods near the Covault estate. Coates wasn't quite a nobody, of course, because it turned out that he'd recently worked for the same company and had travelled out to their Far East HQ right after being fired by them, though it was not on their business. A disgruntled ex-employee might be good for some kind of extortion if he had something to extort with, maybe something brought back from Singapore, but if that's what the exchange had been about – say the handing back of sensitive documents in exchange for cash – then we had the oddity of Coates working with clan member Barclay Brent, which only worked if Brent was scamming his own family and company. We also had the oddity of Brent throwing Coates down that airshaft, which implied that if they had been working together it had gone sour. Did Brent simply double-cross his co-extorter?

But it all came back to the credibility of Brent, a privileged member of the Covault clan, extorting the company. So maybe the document delivery wasn't extortion. Maybe it was delivery of information gleaned from commercial espionage. But then another question arose: why would Barclay Brent be delivering goods to his own company? And why would a fired ex-employee be helping him?

'Maybe Lad wasn't working for the company,' Shaughnessy said.

I lifted the blinds to watch the street.

'We'll have a better idea when we know what Barclay was delivering,' I said. 'And how Coates' Singapore trip fit in. Coates had been fired. He'd be locked out of the company and any that worked with them, including their Singapore consultants NQQ.'

'Maybe an NQQ employee got something out to him,' Yvonne said. 'I'll keep my contact digging on it.'

'Wow,' Lucy said. 'Things always go in funny directions. But this has climbed right up the beanstalk.'

I turned from the window. Lucy kicked her heels and pressed her palms into the desk top.

'Those lawyers were acting for Peter Covault,' she said. 'So he's involved. The question is who is it working with him? Is it his stepson or his security guy?'

Tangles and knots. Our speciality. I didn't recall many cases where knots didn't materialise sooner or later. But we needed to start untangling things. We needed to close this off before Prior jumped all over me.

We planned it out. Agreed the split. Shaughnessy and Harry would travel across town and get on Johnny Lad's tail. Maybe pick up a pointer to what he was up to. And keep him away from Kim Waters at the same time. If they didn't catch up with him then Harry would switch to watching Kim. Stay with her once she arrived back in town. I'd take Barclay Brent, look for any sign of the strain he should be showing from having just murdered Jeremy Coates. I didn't see Brent as a hardened killer. If he was running scared we'd exploit it.

Yvonne would talk to her Singapore contact again and pull out more information on the Covault family and company. She was also waiting to follow up with Jeremy Coates' chess club, see whether she could get in touch with Coates' pal Martin who'd still not got in touch with me.

Lucy was off to her afternoon job but she agreed to detour through Mayfair, see whether she could find anyone who'd spotted Lad as he snapped the photo of Kim and her daughter a week ago. The photo had been taken on the south side of Grosvenor Square where South Audley Street went out. She'd talk to people there.

'That's the plan,' I said. 'Let's give it twenty-four hours. My guess is we'll know what's happening by then.'

Why do I say that stuff?

CHAPTER THIRTY-TWO
You don't do that unless you're a psychopath

I waited for Shaughnessy's call from the Covault skyscraper. When it came he confirmed a sighting of Johnny Lad's Audi parked in the basement. He and Harry had their quarry but Barclay Brent's gold Isuzu was not in sight, leaving me with a search.

Yvonne had described a penthouse apartment on Jermyn Street. I started there.

The address was a mid-century post art deco block with a white stone facade, street-level retail units and four floors of apartments. And above those, invisible behind a parapet, a fifth floor penthouse. The street door numbering listed just a single dwelling up top, which left plenty of room for a roof garden and maybe a swimming pool and cricket pitch.

Nowadays you're not allowed to build parking spaces into new residential blocks in central London. Residents must use the Tube or have their chauffeurs pick them up. In the decades after the War most buildings went up with basement garages. I spotted the entry ramp to Brent's building beside a tailor's on a side street. The ramp was unguarded. I walked down into a low space running fifty yards under the building. Found Brent's vehicle parked by the central stairwell. It was the premium spot right by the lift. The pickup's tyres were still dusted in chalk and its cab roof was still dented and it looked as out of place here as a shopping trolley on the Palace forecourt. How the vehicle got down here with its cab lights and mirrors I didn't know. Brent must have eased it down with a tape measure the first time.

The yellow Porsche Cayman on the adjacent spot was Brent's too, according to Yvonne Barker's research. Alternative wheels for whenever a refined image was called for. Good for reminding the neighbours who turned up their lips at the Isuzu whenever they came down that the redneck was loaded *way* beyond their level.

It was mid morning on a working day. Either Brent had another vehicle or he was taking the day off.

I went back to the street and moved the Frogeye and its sleeping passenger onto a pay-by-phone spot where I could watch the exit ramp. Got lucky after just ten minutes. A flash of gold burst onto the street and the Isuzu turned out towards Piccadilly. I eased into the traffic and followed it south out of town.

Brent drove steadily, barely over the speed limits as they opened up south of the river. We hit the Orbital and Brent accelerated to eighty but minutes later rolled off onto the A21 and drove towards the coast. We skirted Hastings and drove across into Bexhill where he parked the Isuzu behind an odd assortment of cottages backing onto the beach. The destination was odd. Well out of billionaire playboy territory, though the Isuzu might fit in. I pulled over and got my first sight of the guy as he climbed out of the vehicle. He was in his mid twenties, a few inches under six feet and either well muscled or carrying a little fat. Hard to say under his sports jacket. His clothes were pressed sharp, a neat guy with short tidy hair and a smooth handsome face. The face was casual, friendly, but you sensed that the friendliness was for the select. Dissenters and can't do's could keep clear. If you were a waiter you made damn sure you shovelled the caviar from the left. Brent walked up the pavement and passed me without noticing the vintage car that had tailed him from London. Up close, if you ignored the location, he was the archetypal billionaire playboy. Maybe I'd got Bexhill wrong. I peered past the cottages but still didn't see any superyachts. Maybe not wrong.

I hopped out and followed Brent back across the Parade to a white painted five storey Victorian apartment block with street level fast food shops. He went to a bright blue door between two of the shops and pressed the top bell. I looked up. The top floor was a line of ornate dormers that would give nice views of the Channel but looked a little limited in headroom. Small rooms and a long hike up, balanced against a great view.

The blue door stayed shut. Brent pressed the bell again and stood back. When he looked round I saw something like annoyance in his face. The annoyance you'd feel after travelling an hour and a half, wishing you'd called first. Maybe he had called. But something had tightened his smooth face.

He gave up. Crossed back over to retrieve his pickup. Climbed into the cab and made a call short enough to suggest that it was unanswered. He tucked the phone away and started the engine and I jogged back to the car and followed him back through Hastings. Five minutes out of the town the Isuzu took a country lane then turned in through the impressive gateway of an up-market golf club.

I followed Brent through pristine grounds to a line up of Mercs and Bentleys parked below the imposing portico of an Edwardian country house. I didn't recognise the club's name but then I'm not a golfer. Though it was pretty clear that if golf *was* my sport I'd be teeing-off elsewhere. The gate sign had said members-only and I pictured a lengthy waiting list.

Brent backed in right by the portico. The gold Isuzu looked impressively out of place, which was what he wanted, a gross enough aberration to mark its owner as a bigwig amongst the bigwigs. The elite needn't pay too much attention to taste and propriety. The elite break the rules. It's why they're elite.

I watched Brent hump a bag of clubs up the steps under the portico. The stress had gone from his face. Maybe it had been simple frustration back there in Bexhill rather than, say, the jitters you might get if you've just killed someone. If Barclay was feeling like a would-be fugitive it didn't show.

I gave him five minutes then followed him in.

I'd anticipated something akin to a sports club foyer behind the grand entrance but this wasn't a sports club. Inside the doors was a high entrance hall with duck egg plasterwork hung with paintings in gilded frames. The hall ran back towards Doric columns that guarded the way into the main house. In lieu of a front desk a handful of armchairs was scattered round rugs on a polished parquet floor. Two of the chairs were occupied by women, chatting as they waited for their husbands to appear. Early starters. On the green by eight, aperitifs going down before one.

I walked across and through the far doorway which brought me into a lounge bar with impressive floor to ceiling windows overlooking the course. The windows were framed in curtain hangings thicker than my carpets, which muted the room sounds. Not that there was much sound. Just a couple of tables taken, whispered conversations. Another doorway led on into a conservatory with a bit more buzz. That's where the life was.

'Good afternoon, sir.'

The uniformed guy had materialised from nowhere. Front desk

service, millionaire style.

I threw a relaxed smile.

'Hi. Okay if I go through?'

The fact that I had to ask gave the game away. Said it *wasn't* okay. There'd be no bluffing the staff here.

The guy feigned ignorance and asked if I was a member.

'I'm here with Barclay,' I said.

Simple name-dropping wasn't going to do it either, but the name was just a prop as I pulled out my real ticket which was a fan of fifties from Foxglove-Lad's stack. Club members here would spend cash like confetti but the uniformed help took home minimum wage. Tips mattered. And the fan in my fist was large. Five hundred quid large. I pushed it towards the guy like it was a fiver and was past him before his fingers had grabbed the notes and tidied them into a more discrete package.

Confetti.

Scatter it and move on. You're still not a member but you *belong*.

I walked into the conservatory and pushed a little more confetti across the bar to clock up a new world record for the price of a fizzy water. Even Connie would give change from a fifty.

The room was busy. People coming in, going out, people waiting for their luncheon table. Animated buzz. Polite society. The first sauvignons and brandies were hitting the throat. I sipped water and watched.

Then a group of three men and two women became a little more animated and Barclay Brent appeared from wherever he'd stashed his golfing gear. His momentum carried the group into the centre of the room where Barclay and one of the men pointed fingers for orders. Seemed there was time before the first tee.

I leaned on the bar and watched. Barclay was talking and the group was listening and chuckling and giggling, and people in the room were looking up and smiling across. The women anyway. The men, who were mostly an older crowd, kept straight faces. They knew the gold pickup.

The sun was shining beyond the conservatory windows. Colourful golfers and buggies moved silently across the backdrop of a green park landscape. A sense of the world at right came in. A sense of peace, a world away from the thirty-fifth floor at Bow Creek. But it wasn't a world away. It was exactly the same world. It was the world money made.

Which left the same question of why *Money* would get involved in a dodgy document delivery at a Marylebone hotel; why *Money* would be up on the roof of a pickup hefting a guy over a wall into a sixty foot drop. What *Money* had been doing half an hour ago in Bexhill. If I was super rich I'd be on a beach watching the cricket.

I was watching Barclay for signs but he was carrying on as if nothing was happening and I began to sense that I wasn't going to learn anything here. I wasn't going to spot Brent talking to a furtive type in a raincoat and hat in this conservatory. The only furtive type here was me. The only one in a leather jacket, at least.

Then Barclay and his buddy came over and the barman sharpened up even faster than when my fifty had slid his way. He didn't need to move this time since he was already standing at the spot where he'd computed Barclay would arrive, but his posture quivered straight. Barclay was oblivious of the attention, though he knew the guy's name and was ready with a *Hiya, Man* as he threw in his order. His buddy was dressed in similar gear, a dark grey wool three-piece, red shirt and blue tie. But his long face had wary eyes, a hesitant smile developed from past uncertainties and new fears. He was a guy who'd always be afraid of falling off the perch. A recent property millionaire waiting for the bubble to pop. The negative vibes were there in his eyes and body language but they bounced off Barclay. Brent had been born to privilege and didn't know fear. I guess the move up into the Covault stratosphere hadn't been much of a change. But there had to be something going on behind Barclay's smooth facade. He'd just killed a man and if you do that you're either a psychopath or afraid.

But I still saw nothing. Just the confident, casual playboy everyone in the room knew and half probably hated.

The barman pulled beers and left them to settle and Barclay leaned casually my way to grab mats. His eyes caught mine but didn't see me. He counted out the mats and continued an anecdote for his pal about a guy who'd had his Lamborghini towed three times from outside their building because he couldn't be arsed to use the basement slot. Greysuit twitched his mouth into a knowing chuckle and his shoulders shook but you knew he always fed the coins into the meter wherever he left his own Lamborghini.

The drinks got sorted and Barclay nodded to the bar guy to slate them and went back to deliver the goods. He was held up a moment by a silvery old guy in tweed with a thicket of eyebrows and stubbled jaw who came over to pat his arm and give him a message for his step dad. They batted back and forth for a few seconds before the guy gripped Barclay's arm firmly and continued on his way.

The group chatted for a while. Barclay looked at his watch. Tee off in thirty. Meantime he was the focus of the buzz and fizz as he chatted about whatever you chat about when the world is your footstool. I didn't catch the words but the conversation wasn't about extortion or commercial espionage or dead bodies in railway tunnels. Not unless we had a whole different level of sinister going on.

And how about bodies in lakes? Was that on Barclay's mind too? He must know that the P.I. he'd hired to organise his package delivery was dead. Did that shake him just a little bit?

I thought about it. Concluded that this was Barclay's safe place. The place he could park his fears and pretend the world was fine. I wondered how much the world ever saw behind his facade. Which Barclay Brent had Coates seen as they struggled towards that airshaft?

I finished my drink and went out.

The same uniformed guy nodded a curt goodbye. No smile or suggestion I'd be welcome if I came back. If I ever did reappear I'd better have another damn sackful of cash, whoever's pal I claimed to be.

I drove out of the gates and back to Bexhill.

CHAPTER THIRTY-THREE
He wasn't coming back

I parked the car and donned my shooting jacket. Walked Herbie back across the Parade to the white Victorian with the blue door. Just as we got there it opened and an elderly couple exited and smiled down at Herbie. We both smiled back and I grabbed the door before it re-latched. Nice timing.

We took the stairs up to see who lived on the top floor. It was hard to imagine a connection between a Bexhill apartment and a billionaire playboy but he'd driven here and rung this bell and that meant there was something up there that mattered.

The stairs climbed high. Ended at small landing and a door.

I rapped on the wood. No-one answered. I pulled a key tool from the jacket and worked on the Yale. The lock clicked. I pushed open the door and walked in.

It was an attic apartment, baking under the roof. A stifling hallway gave access to a lounge-diner and bedroom under the front dormers and a kitchen, bathroom and second bedroom at the back. I checked the lounge. Saw minimal sign of anyone living in the place, just a couple of newspapers, a used coffee mug, a phone charger. Over by the window a low table was littered with pamphlets and a ring binder. The pamphlets were tourist information about Bexhill. The ring binder contained information about the apartment's services and the contact details for an estate agent called Whatley Jones.

A holiday let.

But I wasn't the first unauthorised visitor. Against the back wall a sideboard's drawers had been left open as if someone had searched them.

Interesting. I went and checked the bedroom.

That had been searched too and was a little messier since some of the drawers had contained clothing which was now on the floor. A man's stuff, sufficient for a short stay. The bedsheets and pillowcases were on the floor too and the mattress was half off the bed but undamaged.

Someone giving the place a quick search. Looking for something out in the open or pushed discretely away. Not purposely hidden. No need to rip open sofas and mattresses.

I was sweating. Herbie was panting. I took a moment. Opened front and back windows to get ventilation. Checked the kitchen and poured water for Herbie. The kitchen was neat and tidy but all the drawers were open, though the searcher hadn't seen the need to empty them onto the floor. This was strictly a skim-search.

The fridge contained milk cartons and packaged food that was still in date. Purchases a few days old.

I checked the bathroom. Found used towels, scattered toiletries. A cabinet and storage cupboard, open but empty.

The second bedroom hadn't been in use but the mattress had been pulled from the bed and the drawers and wardrobe were open. Searched quickly, the same as the other rooms.

I returned to the lounge. A sea breeze flowed under the sash and had dropped the temperature ten degrees. Herbie padded in and flopped on a rug. I checked the view. Watched water glittering out on the Channel.

A holiday let. Tenanted. At least up to a few days ago. Disturbed by someone looking for something left casually or pushed discreetly out of sight. Not tidied since. I'd seen nothing to ID the tenant but the tenant was someone Barclay Brent had wanted to talk to which meant the tenant was someone of interest.

I closed the windows. Locked up and went down. Asked directions to the estate agents and found their shop in the centre of the town. We went in and were greeted by a woman with bright blue plastic glasses and a layered bob hairstyle. She pushed the spectacles up into her hair to attend to me.

I identified the apartment and asked if there was any chance of extending my booking. I didn't know how long the place had been booked for or how may properties this office serviced or whether the woman had a sharp memory for faces but my query passed muster. She flicked the glasses back down and checked her computer.

'I'm sorry, Mr Coates,' she said. 'It's booked from next weekend, right after you leave.'

She offered to check other properties in the area but I told her to hold off. I'd think about it.

'We're busy until the end of September,' she warned. She flicked

163

her glasses up. 'Would it be just the week?'

I gave it some thought.

'Probably the same again,' I said.

'Another three? In that case we'd struggle before October.'

I threw a smile and said I'd get back as soon as possible. Left her to it.

Walked back to the car, thinking.

Jeremy Coates.

I'd already guessed it. The clothing on the bedroom floor had matched the drab, conservative stuff I'd seen at Coates' Caterham house. And Coates had been out of sight somewhere. Bexhill was as good a place as any.

But it didn't quite make sense.

Had Coates come down to Bexhill for a break? If so, the timing was interesting. But his connection with Barclay Brent was way off. I'd put Brent and Coates either on opposite sides of the affair or on the same side until something went wrong. But if Brent had killed Coates why was he ringing his doorbell? Did he think Coates had come back from the dead?

I drove back to town, turning over what I'd got. Called Shaughnessy. He reported his day with Johnny Lad. Lad had come out from the Covault Complex late morning and driven to Covault's estate which was busy with contractors' service vans going in and out. One van had the name and logo of a marquee hire company. Some kind of event in preparation. Lad was still in there.

I tried Lucy. She was at her uncle's music shop up in Bethnal Green.

'The photographer was Lad,' she reported.

Bingo!

'I found a woman named Jane Dewar. She's an assistant at a fashion boutique at the Grosvenor Square end of Audley. She remembered the guy. She'd stepped out for a smoke that morning and saw him walk out to the middle of the zebra crossing and stop to take the photograph. He used a proper camera. Big lens. The crossing's in the right place, about fifty yards from where Kim and her daughter were snapped.'

'Did you show her Lad's picture?'

'Yeah. It's him. So we've got a witness to his threats against those women.'

'Good work.'

'What's happening with Barclay?'

'The guy's going about his life as if he's not a care in the world. But he's up to something.' I explained about the Bexhill rental.

'You checked Barclay's apartment yet?'

'It's on the list.'

'I'll see if I can get more background on the guy,' Lucy said.

'Do that. We'll talk tomorrow.'

I decided to call it a day. Drove back to Battersea before the rush hour geared up. Fed Herbie and went out. We walked across the park and watched the river whilst I planned the next step, but the only plan that came to mind was to collar Barclay Brent and pressure him hard, see if his facade cracked. If it cracked I'd have my next direction.

When I'd hatched that devious plan we headed back.

We crossed the road and walked up to the building.

Found Kim Waters sitting on the step.

CHAPTER THIRTY-FOUR
Yowling and chopsticks

She was wearing skinny jeans and a denim jacket over a white tee-shirt, sitting there like she lived in the building. Herbie scuttled up and got in first lick. She tickled his ear. He collapsed and rolled over.

'I was back in town,' she said. 'Hope you don't mind.'

She stood and reached out. I skipped up the steps to show her how much I didn't mind. When we broke for air she stepped back and reached into her pocket. Her cheeks were flushed.

'Actually these were the reason,' she said. 'If I must be on my own I'm not going to sit around moping. As long as Alice is safe I'll take the good with the bad.'

She held up two tickets.

'My Manchester client. Do you like opera?'

'I'm open to new experiences.'

'Then get yourself spruced up. The show starts at eight. We'll eat afterwards and you can convince me that this Foxglove thing is under control.'

I grinned down at Herbie.

'How about a night out?' I said. I wasn't talking about the opera. Herbie knew it. He touched his nose to the front door and when we went in he diverted to Henrietta's. I rang her bell. No answer. We'd catch her later.

We went upstairs and I took a shower. When I came out I found Kim in my bed. Her denims were on the floor along with other things.

'We've got time,' she said. 'The curtain doesn't go up until eight.'

Her smile lit the room. I smiled myself. Moved towards the bed. I've never been a clock watcher.

~~~~~

We made the first act of her opera with seconds to spare. It was an oddity called The Lighthouse which comprised three guys yowling at the orchestra in the first half followed by three guys yowling at each

166

other in the second. The show's main attraction was that it lasted less than ninety minutes. I spent the second forty-five trying to figure whether the three guys trading shots round the table were the same three from the first act. Didn't reach a conclusion until I checked the programme when the lights came up. Only three names for the bass, tenor and baritone credits. The same guys. It should have been obvious but I'm not much of an opera buff. Kim was no help. Her defence over dinner was that the tickets were a gift. I chalked the evening up as a lucky escape. If her benefactor had got his hands on tickets for *The Ring* we'd have needed sleeping bags.

We were eating Chinese in Covent Garden. I dodged the Foxglove topic and nudged Kim onto lighter topics, and the evening settled and stretched. I spent most of it watching her. She caught me a couple of times and blushed and told me my food was going cold. But good things never last. An innocent question about Alice snapped her back to reality. Apprehension came back into her face.

She fought it, concentrated on the positive, effused about her daughter in a way that suggested that trying to paint her in words was hopeless. But the moment was spoiled. When her words dried up the fear came back. This nightmare world wasn't hers. Meaning my world. I looked at her and felt bad for every evening I'd taken off in the last few days, including this one. I should be working twenty hour days until I found Foxglove.

I tried to vindicate myself with a positive slant as I brought Kim selectively up to date on our search. I left out the fact that the dead body count had doubled. That we'd found Coates. Concentrated on the name-dropping part. Told her that the guy Foxglove was chasing – the guy who'd organised the document exchange – was Barclay Brent, a name she might know as the bad boy of the billionaire Covault dynasty.

She did know. Dropped a prawn from her chopsticks then dropped the chopsticks. They cartwheel to the floor. Her eyes were wide.

'You can't be serious,' she said.

She stared at me. Saw that I was. I guess it was like hearing that the Prince of Wales was in on the scheme. I signalled a waiter and he brought new eating implements. Kim was still looking for sense in what I'd told her. Gave up. Forced something like a grin and picked up her replacement chopsticks.

'Tell me you're joking, Eddie,' she said.

'No joke,' I said. 'Your food's going cold.'

But she waited for a good ten seconds before she pulled herself together and extracted her chopsticks.

As she started eating I gave her a second snippet: that we'd ID'd Foxglove. He was a security consultant called Johnny Lad, working for the Covault family firm.

The new information impressed her too.

'You're saying that one of the richest families in the world are involved in this?'

'There's precedent,' I said. 'They say the foulest material floats to the top.'

She flinched at the image then shook it off and revived her smile, though it wasn't so bright now.

'I can hardly believe it,' she said. 'Those are powerful people.'

'We're powerful investigators. Whatever Barclay Brent or his family is up to we'll find out.'

'So Barclay was delivering documents to a security guy involved with the family business?'

'Yes.'

'Was the security guy stealing company information?'

'My guess is the opposite. I think he recovered the documents for the company. Was working to find their source.'

'But either case means that Brent was working against the company. The guy's worth a fortune. He's got yachts, cars, private jets. Everything. Why would he do something to hurt the family business?'

'I don't know.'

But she'd put her finger on it. I didn't know how many yachts and planes Barclay actually owned but toys like that were certainly part of his life. I'd seen the pictures. Membership of his golf club had to be running at a quarter of a million a year even before the bar tab.

'What we do know for sure,' I said, 'is that you were threatened by a security consultant working for Diamond Covault. And freelancing or working for the company he's a ruthless guy. He killed the investigator Barclay Brent hired to organise the document exchange. I assume he was trying to get to Brent. I don't know why but we'll find out and when we do we'll put this guy is off the street. He won't come after you again.'

Kim poked at her food.

'When will it be safe for Alice to come home?' she said.

'A few days. We're moving on this.'

But she didn't look convinced. She caught a prawn and lifted it to her lips. 'I'll keep our security service on night watch,' she said.

'A few days, max.,' I told her. 'Count on it.'

A P.I. likes to project confidence. He rarely has cause but it's an image thing. But my need to close this off was also a Kim Waters thing. Just one short week since we'd met and the idea of anyone harming her had shifted from repugnant to unthinkable.

'How about we watch out for you twenty-four hours,' I said. 'The guy won't get near you then.'

She thought about it. Shook her head.

'I'll be safe enough around town and my service will be watching the house. And Foxglove – Lad – doesn't know where Alice is. I don't want bodyguards following me round, Eddie. Not even you.'

'Let's review it tomorrow night.'

'Sure.'

'Meantime, how do we keep you safe for tonight?'

I grinned to lighten the message, bring her back to other important stuff.

Her face brightened again, but not much. When Johnny Lad was off the street, which would be soon, we'd put fear behind us. Tonight all I could do was keep Kim close.

'You're saying I get a personal bodyguard tonight?'

'Saves me a taxi ride.'

Kim's smile finally came natural. Eating accelerated. Clearing our plates had an urgency.

We got to my place at one a.m. Crept past Henrietta's door and hit the sack and forgot about Johnny Lad and rogue billionaires and bodies in lakes. If Kim was still afraid later she didn't show it. She was asleep within sixty seconds of my turning off the lights. I cradled her and took a little longer, still wondering if my attachment to her was presenting Lad with a weakness to exploit. I wondered whether his thugs had called back at Chase Street or knocked on this door whilst I was out.

169

Fact was, now I'd provoked Lad, shown I wasn't backing off, he'd be moving into full defensive mode, and collateral damage would be incurred wherever it worked for him. Maybe Lad would see Kim as a soft target to push me back. So I needed to move faster. Find out what that package operation had been about and dig out the links to tie Lad to Sam Barker's killing. I needed to hand enough to Keith Prior and his Bromley CID to get Lad out of our hair for good, and I needed to do it soon.

The question was whether Lad would see it coming.

For the moment I was a step ahead which gave me the advantage. The thought finally dropped me into sleep, even though it was entirely misplaced.

CHAPTER THIRTY-FIVE
Clients who get spooked

We ate an early breakfast then Kim pulled me into a clinch and asked what we were doing tonight. I didn't know what we were doing tonight, though I now had the day to let my imagination work on it. I held Kim away and suggested she reconsider the offer of us putting someone at her side. I was thinking of Bernie Locke. Bernie's presence at Kim's shoulder would lack the discreet element but she'd be safe from anything short of a nuclear strike.

But she was adamant.

'I really don't want that,' she said. 'I'll be safe around town. I'm with people all day. And my security service will be in tonight.'

'We don't want to underestimate this guy,' I said. 'I've smoked him out of his burrow and he knows that simply sending idiots with bats isn't going to work. So he'll be looking for new leverage. You might come into his sights.'

Kim pulled away.

'If you protect me won't he just switch to one of the other women? It might be his second-best option but you wouldn't ignore a risk to them either.'

I grinned. She'd spotted the weakness in my proposal. I couldn't keep the others safe. But bottom line: I didn't know the other women and I hadn't started this thing. My actions had produced responsibilities only towards Kim. If Kim stayed safe I could live with other consequences.

'We're talking about a couple of days,' I said. 'It'll be over by then.'

Kim stepped forward. Planted a kiss.

'Let's talk about it tonight. The whole thing scares me, Eddie, but I don't want bodyguards following me round. I've colleagues and clients who'd get spooked if I'm looking over my shoulder all the time.'

She grabbed her stuff. I went to open the door.

'Look over you shoulder anyway,' I said.

She stepped out and was gone and the place darkened a little and I knew that the world would darken a hell of a lot if anything happened to her. Bernie was coming into this tomorrow whether Kim liked it or not.

I put in the call. Caught Bernie. He agreed to clear his diary. Bernie ran an executive leadership school in Hampshire, applying his experience as a decorated Marine captain to tutor captains of industry in how to outmanoeuvre the world of commerce. He had a seminar finishing tomorrow but his people would cover the last day. Classroom stuff.

'The lady need me tonight?' he said.

'Tomorrow morning should be okay.'

I sensed Bernie's eyes opening.

'I *see*,' he said.

'What the hell do you see?'

'I see a bonny lass in my crystal ball. I see you taking the night shift.' A chesty laugh. The sound you'd hear when one of his fee-paying execs falls on his arse in a muddy ditch. All that from a half second's silence.

'She's a nice girl,' I said. 'We hit it off.'

'I'll bet you did. I'll come in tomorrow. Your place or hers?'

'The office will be fine.'

'Eight a.m.' The line disconnected.

I stashed the phone and went down to retrieve Herbie. Found a note on Henrietta's door saying "Working early. H with me for day."

Seemed Herbie would be doing his own tutoring over at the dogs' home. Henrietta had recognised the benefit of having a calm Staffie as an assistant and wasn't above co-opting him for some of her therapy sessions. But solo was good today. I was going to be running about.

I called in at Chase Street and updated Shaughnessy and Harry.

Harry agreed to take the bodyguard detail with Bernie. From tomorrow we'd watch Kim twenty-four seven until this was over.

Shaughnessy had nothing new from following Johnny Lad round yesterday. Lad had flitted between the Covault HQ, Peter Covault's estate and his own firm. Hadn't gone near Kim. Hadn't killed anyone. Sean would stay with him today. Same objectives. I brought Yvonne Barker in on a conference call and she promised to get hold of Jeremy Coates' friend and keep digging into Lad's background.

Lucy showed up and agreed to trawl for more background on

Barclay Brent. Meantime I'd take the direct approach and take a look at Brent's Jermyn Street penthouse once he was clear. Maybe there'd be something there to give us a pointer to what Brent was up to. Names, contacts, bank accounts, maybe emails. Harry would come along. There'd be a decent security system protecting the place but Harry had a decent set of kit to handle it.

Harry would also take a drive over to the Greenwich apartment Shaughnessy had identified as Johnny Lad's place. Lad would have pretty decent security too but Harry would take a look. Once he'd checked out the system we could go in any time we wanted.

With luck we'd find a few things in the apartments, something that would give us ammunition to pressurise Brent and Lad, draw them out until they made mistakes.

'You think they'll screw up?' Shaughnessy asked.

'Lad already has. Sending people after me who are in the system wasn't smart. When we hand Marco Rossi to the police he'll talk. The baseball bat photos are enough to send him back down and that's going to trump protecting Lad despite his attitude. And once Barclay Brent knows we've uncovered his connection to Jeremy Coates and that we know about Coates' dive down that airshaft, he'll panic. Maybe try to retrieve Coates' body before the police got there. That would mean involving people, spreading money around, piling up more evidence in the process.'

'When does this go to Prior?'

'Twenty-four to forty-eight. The wires need to be connected by then.'

'As long as they don't get crossed and explode the whole thing,' Lucy said. She smiled brightly to give the words meaning. We'd seen explosions before. Not all of them helpful. She jumped off the desk and headed out to work her computer. Shaughnessy headed off to pick up Johnny Lad. Harry said he'd hang back at the office until I confirmed that Barclay Brent's pad was vacant.

I went to find out.

CHAPTER THIRTY-SIX
Express ticket

I walked up Jermyn Street and descended the parking ramp beneath Barclay Brent's building. Brent's Cayman was in its spot but the Isuzu was gone. I called the lift and checked the panel. The top floor was key only. I pulled out my phone to call Harry. Got no signal. Exited the lift to regain the street.

Then tyres squealed on the ramp and a black Merc rolled onto the polished concrete and glided towards me. It was a Maybach, with a radiator grille like the cow catcher on a Wild West loco. The German answer to a Rolls Royce. I stopped to let it pass. Admired the nerve of a driver navigating the monster down here. Brent's pickup was probably an easier drive.

The Maybach slowed.

Stopped in front of me.

I got a sudden feeling. The feeling intensified when the rear doors opened and two guys stepped out. Both wore suits. One of them had shades and leather gloves. The other had neither but had hieroglyphics on his knuckles, a snake running across. It was the guy who'd accompanied Lad to the courier drop-off, though I doubted he was here to hand me more cash. I scanned the parking level for alternative routes to the street and saw that there weren't any because three more men had just come out from the stairwell to block me. Leather jackets in lieu of suits. Dusters and coshes in lieu of gloves.

I turned back to the Maybach crew. If I was leaving it would be that way. The vehicle pretty much blocked the route but a hop over parked cars would get me to the ramp. I can be athletic when needs arise.

Then the Maybach's front passenger door opened and Johnny Lad stepped out.

He came round the grille and stopped and I was reminded of the lawyers' visit. Not because of his suit but because of the Maybach. The Maybach announced that Lad was here on Covault business the same as the lawyers. It was the sort of wheels only billionaires have on call, and there was only one billionaire I knew linked to Johnny

Lad.

But if Lad was planning something messy then bringing the works limo down here didn't make sense. It would have featured on too many CCTVs across town. On the building cams. Things would get right back to the company. I put my acrobatics on hold whilst I waited for Lad to open the discussion.

He stood a moment beside the cow-catcher. Clasped his hands in front of him and raised his chin. He was wearing the same tinted lenses as in Lucy's snap. The parking basement lights flashed off them and his long forehead.

He gestured.

'Please...' he said.

His guy on the near side stepped back to give me a clear run to the rear door.

'My own car's round the corner,' I said. 'Thanks anyway.'

The light continued to bounce off Lad's head. He didn't move but his crew were closing the gap behind me.

'Please,' Lad repeated. 'Get in.'

I still had two seconds to make the bonnet of the nearest Jag. I spent them checking calculations and presumptions for flaws and downsides and what-ifs. But the answer stayed the same.

I relaxed and stepped towards the Maybach. Lad watched me get in then walked round.

Gloves stepped forward and slammed my door. Lad ducked in from the other side and slammed his door. Snake Knuckle slid into the front passenger seat and slammed that door too.

Clunkety-clunk.

Snake Knuckle pulled on a seatbelt. Lad and I didn't bother. If we got into a prang we'd bash our noses on the plate glass screen separating the rear cabin, maybe bounce around on the leatherwork, but we'd be safe.

The car slid silently forward. Circled and climbed back to daylight, though not much came in through the tint. The interior was lit by its own soft lighting that brought the leatherwork up nicely. If there was an engine running somewhere I didn't hear it. We rotated onto Piccadilly and glided towards the river. Accelerated along the north bank. The outside world floated past.

'Okay,' I said. 'You've got my attention. Is this a mystery tour or do we have a destination in mind?'

Lad continued looking out of his window. He was separated from me by a leather and gold centre console kitted out for serving food and drinks and entertainment. There were probably dancing girls in there if you knew which button to press.

'Relax,' Lad said. He didn't look at me. The guy would be a crowd-puller at parties.

I sank back into the soft leather. Lifted my feet onto the console and clasped my hands across my stomach to show how relaxed I was.

Then my phone rang.

I pulled it out. Checked the screen.

'Sergeant!' I said.

'Where are you, Flynn?'

DS Prior.

Lad tensed and turned towards me but the console and my angle kept the phone clear of his grasp.

'I should apologise, Sergeant,' I said.

'Don't bother. We're through with niceties. I'm at your office. We're going to drive down to Bromley together. That can be voluntarily or under arrest on a charge of obstruction. How soon can you be here?'

I looked at Lad. He'd relaxed again but he was calculating. My hobnobbing with the police was one more problem to add to all the other problems piling up around him. But he ran the scenario. Decide it was a problem that could wait. I wasn't going to scream for help. The Maybach ride wasn't a threat. He knew I knew it. If he'd been planning to whisk me off for a Sam Barker style of negotiation he'd have done it differently.

How soon I'd be back at Chase Street though wasn't clear. I covered the phone.

'Is this a long trip? I've a policeman waiting.'

Lad's specs glinted. Maybe his eyes too. I couldn't see. He looked away. Said nothing. I uncovered the phone.

'Detective,' I said, 'I'm caught up in something that may take a while.'

'Stop playing games, Flynn. You've had your leeway. Do I need to put out an Anper?'

'Wouldn't work. I'm not in my own car.'

'Are you still chasing around after the Sam Barker incident?'

'Yes. And I believe I'm close to the guy who killed him.'

'What do you mean?'

I grinned. Sometimes the simplest interpretation is the best.

'Close,' I repeated. 'Meaning I'll have something very soon.'

'I want whatever you know right now.'

Buildings parted alongside. Light flared from the river. The silhouettes of Canary Wharf came and went. I still couldn't hear the engine.

'Right now is tricky,' I said. 'How about I call you? Earliest opportunity.'

Prior swore. 'You've got two hours, Flynn, then it's the Anper.' The guy wasn't being fobbed off. His simple RTA had gone bad and I was his chief witness. I cut the line. Grinned at Johnny Lad.

'They're smelling a rat,' I said. 'Sam Barker's drive into that lake was a little obvious. Professional-to-professional.'

Lad watched the view. Said nothing.

'In fact, the whole thing's looking a little shaky, Johnny. We know who you are and who you work for. And we know what you're up to.'

The last statement was stretching things but there was no harm in turning up the heat on Lad and whoever in the Diamond Covault organisation had sent him out. If I'd any doubts about the company's involvement the dull shimmer of the Covault Complex's glass cliff expanding in front of us clarified things.

Watch and learn.

I was about to be shown the pages of the golden book.

We turned down the Covault parking ramp. The light died. The Maybach burrowed.

'Your biggest mistake,' I said, 'was bringing civilians into this. Threatening Kim Waters and making me believe you really would hurt her. That left me no choice. And I'm going to put you out of business, Johnny. Send you somewhere you won't be threatening civilians for a couple of decades. Do you believe that?'

Lad sighed.

'Please,' he said. He was still looking through his window, though there was nothing to see. 'If I had my way,' he said, 'or, rather, when

I get it, you'll be a dead man. Worry about that.'

I stared at him. Gave a half second's thought to leaping over the console. Decided against it. Whatever was waiting for me at the top of this building was more important than putting out Lad's lights.

Then the Maybach pulled up and the locks thudded open. We got out and Lad and his pal walked me to the lifts. Lad pushed a key into the slot for Thirty-Five. Covault HQ, executive level. Express ticket.

CHAPTER THIRTY-SEVEN
The saintliness of Mr Lad

The dramatics had been first class but Johnny Lad wasn't the man I was here to see. As soon as we hit Thirty-Five he melted away and I was taken through by an assistant straight off the Paris catwalk. She showed me into an empty conference room with a view of the Millennium Dome and an oval table guarded by twenty leather seats. The table's mirror-shine surface reflected the sky in a blinding glare. If you were facing the river I guess you wore shades. Made you look meaner. Ms Catwalk asked if I'd like coffee. I said I was fine. She told me that Mr Covault would be with me momentarily and disappeared.

I circumnavigated the table to get the view. It was as good as last time, though the haze still hid the East Sussex horizon. I looked east but the London City runway wasn't visible from the angle. No line of sight on the planes climbing towards you. I guess when you're chasing signatures on trillion dollar contracts you don't want your clients ducking for cover.

When I turned, five people had filed in.

Two of them were the lawyers who'd called at Chase Street. James Coleridge Devonshire looked just as imposing as he had then. Today's tie was red. His sidekick, Adam, looked just as kick-ass, though today's expression was a little more reverent. Two other twenty-something guys were in support. Their razor sharp suits and eagerness marked them as high fliers, though their leather document holders said they were here mainly as props.

The final guy was Peter Covault.

I recognised him from his pictures. He was a big guy in his mid sixties with a broad swarthy face slashed by cold steel eyes and fleshy lips that reminded you of Kerry Packer. When he caught my eye his face creased into a wide smile. He stretched across the table to offer a paw and call out my name like we were old buddies but the handshake was as brief and as artificial as the smile. He told me to sit down which I did, grabbing the chance to hog the river side, which left them squinting at a silhouette. The suits all stretched to grab my hand before they sat, which was no mean feat since the table was six feet across and my comfy chair left me with little incentive to stretch. When the sham was through we were all sitting and ready to go.

Peter Covault reached and jabbed a teleconference console in the centre of the table and the room's light diffused as external blinds dropped behind me, killing the glare. As I came into focus Covault sized me up with his smile. I stayed relaxed. Waited for him to speak. The leather chair had almost swallowed me. It was just missing a recline function. I adapted. Kept my feet under the table.

'Thank you for coming,' Covault said.

I smiled. God bless those coshes and knuckle-dusters.

'It seems,' he continued, 'that there's a bone of contention between us.'

I watched him.

'My associates inform me...' – Covault tilted his head towards his guys – 'that we didn't quite reach an agreement the other day.'

'I wasn't sure what the agreement was,' I said. 'Neither were they.'

Covault thought about it. James Coleridge Devonshire and Adam Hane, MA, LLB, held their stares. Devonshire's stare still had its hint of benevolence, or maybe amusement. Adam's stuck with hostile. The wannabes on Covault's other side weren't sure of the etiquette so they kept their faces neutral.

'You've been enquiring about a former employee Mr Coates,' Covault said. 'That's our subject of interest. In principle your investigations are none of our affair but you seem to have rattled the cage somewhat.'

'You've got that correct,' I said, 'judging by the speed of response on Monday afternoon. I assume that Mr Devonshire's marching orders came directly from you.'

'Yes they did,' Covault said. The switch from informed bystander to instigator was seamless, as if the pretence had never happened. 'I understand,' he continued, 'that Mr Devonshire explained to you why we were keen to avoid any disruption to our company business just now.'

'He told me. Explained nothing. For example: how a simple enquiry about an ex-employee could affect your floatation.'

Covault clasped his hands on the table. Leaned in. 'Believe me,' he said, 'it can. We're about to take the most important step in this company's history. Launching an IPO that will see majority control transfer to public shareholders. The purpose is a capital acquisition essential to our future. And achieving our target depends on investor confidence in the share price.'

Covault strained further: 'Confidence, Mr Flynn! Such an ephemeral thing. So dependent on whim and wind direction.'

He stopped. Sat back. 'Which is why any hint of adverse publicity, any noise or rumour, can topple the whole house of cards. Investors are a nervous bunch. If you were to camp on our front steps campaigning to save the whale or to bring back corporal punishment they'd all take fright. You don't believe in Save The Whale do you, Mr Flynn?'

'I believe you're blowing smoke,' I said. 'I believe that Mr Coates' affairs, whatever they are, worry your company a hell of a lot more than saving the whale. And everything you're doing to push me back strengthens my impression that you're scared of what I might uncover. That's why you've brought me here.'

Covault pinned me with his eyes while he thought about it. The soft light flattened his face and tightened the flesh but I spotted a slight tension in his cheeks. His eyes flicked inside their slits.

'Mr Flynn–' Devonshire said.

Covault lifted a hand. Leaned forward.

'Is this a personal crusade, Mr Flynn?'

I thought about it. Nodded.

'Good point. I think it is, to the extent that I don't take kindly to thugs like Mr Lad coercing me into helping them do their dirty work. And to the extent that I'm now attempting to clean up that dirty work and expose Lad as the killer of a private investigator called Sam Barker. But there's also simple curiosity. I'd like to know why Mr Barker was killed and what's happened to Mr Coates. And both these things are connected to this company. Can you explain them?'

Covault didn't react. Took a moment. I guess he'd sat through a few corporate argy-bargys in his time. You don't get to head a global company by reacting before you think. When he spoke it was calm and considered.

'James mentioned your private investigator. Some kind of accident, apparently, although you undoubtedly know more. But to be honest with you I don't see the connection to Mr Lad. He's a trusted consultant. Has worked with us for years. He's a hard man but he doesn't go round killing people. And I don't know what's happened to Mr Coates. Perhaps nothing. Maybe he's flown off on a short holiday. Frankly, we're not keeping tabs.'

He sat back and looked sideways for any explanation that might be incoming from his legal people. Nothing was. And if Covault had any inkling of just how short Jeremy Coates' recent flight had been he wasn't showing it. But I wasn't swallowing his story that he didn't know that his man Lad played dirty. The question was whether he knew what had happened to Sam, or knew what his stepson had been up to. Maybe he didn't know it all but there was no way Peter Covault was ignorant of everything. He'd known enough to send Devonshire and Adam sprinting to my office door after I'd poked my nose in here.

'What's all this about?' Covault asked. 'You've obviously come up with some kind of theory about this company.'

'Hell if I know what it's about. But your pal Johnny Lad does. Did he mention to you about handling some documents recently? Was that on your behalf?'

Covault hardly paused.

'Yes, Mr Flynn. We recovered some confidential documents that had been stolen from us. A little commercial blackmail. We paid the extorter and recovered the material.'

'The extortion has interesting timing. Was it to do with your floatation?'

'I can't tell you that.'

'The problem is, you're not a tech company, or pharmaceutical or defence. So I don't see the documents being technical stuff that might interest a competitor. That leaves me with the hypothesis that they were something that might damage your share floatation. What's your target for the floatation?'

'One point two.'

'Million?'

'Billion.'

I pushed out a low whistle. Looked left to right along the suits. Their faces were all impassive except for Covault's which was holding its smile.

'So,' I said, 'hypothetically: something that might embarrass the company would not be welcome right now.'

'Exactly the point I just made,' Covault said. 'But, Mr Flynn, well-intentioned and thorough as your investigations might be, if they stir things up it won't matter whether what comes out has any basis of truth. Rumour and fantasy can hurt us as much as truth.'

'We tend to stick with the truth. Will that hurt?'

'*Anything* might hurt us,' Covault said. 'Look: we're not doubting your professional integrity or the fact that you may have uncovered some unusual happenings but I can assure you that all that has just happened is the recovery of commercially sensitive documents. Our problem is that the market isn't geared to react rationally if unfounded speculation gets out. We're just a company trying to do business. What we do is all above board. Rest assured of that.'

'But the content of the documents would hurt your floatation if they got out. And you're trying to hide them. Is that above board?' I grinned at the line of faces. It was like shooting ducks in a gallery except that I was getting no visible hits.

'Every company that ever went public has had some facet of their operations that could be misconstrued,' Covault said. 'That's the nature of confidential information. We've got fights, we've got wrangles, we've got legal actions left and right. But none of it is relevant to the valuation of our core business. We're selling shares that will be great value down the line. But we need to keep the waters calm right now or those shares won't bring in the cash we need to deliver our plans and deliver value to the investors.'

'Got it,' I said. 'I'm almost thinking of buying stock myself. But I don't believe that your recovered documents were routine stuff. And if your man Lad was the guy who got them back for you then he was working for you when he killed Sam Barker. Which makes you complicit.'

Covault spread his palms.

'Let's not go round and round. You're mistaken about Mr Lad. We don't know how Barker had his accident but nothing irregular has been sanctioned by this company.'

'But you know Barker's name?'

'We looked into it after James and Adam spoke to you. He wasn't previously known to us. My suspicion is that you've misinterpreted the circumstances of his death. Or that if there *was* foul play it was unrelated to this company.'

'Could be, but it's not. Johnny Lad killed Sam Barker and Johnny works for you. You see my reasoning?'

'Yes. You're wrong.'

'Then there's our other connection to the company. Barclay Brent.'

Covault pulled back just a fraction too fast this time.

'What about Barclay?' he said.

'He's mixed up with Jeremy Coates and with the extortion thing – the documents you've recovered. Our information is that Barclay was the source of the documents. It's hard to see the rationale for him extorting you, being the well-off guy he is, but the explanations will come.'

Covault turned to Devonshire. A look passed between them. Devonshire shook his head and Covault looked back at me.

'This is sounding more fantastical by the moment,' he said. 'Barclay is a close family member and a valued company executive. The idea that he's involved in any kind of skulduggery is absurd.'

'I know Barclay well,' Devonshire added. 'He worked with us to recover those documents. You're misinterpreting things, Mr Flynn. You've pulled some facts and figures together and drawn the wrong conclusion.'

'But wrong or not,' Covault said, 'this is the kind of rumour we don't need right now. Take it from me: Barclay is a fine company man. Forget him. And I won't extol the saintliness of Mr Lad but I assure you he doesn't go round killing people.'

He turned to look at Devonshire. Devonshire pulled things back in.

'Let's stop this before it gets out of hand,' he said. 'Because if something got out that penalised our capital acquisition we'd have no option but to pursue the matter through the courts.' He looked at me. The benevolence had dropped from his face.

'We'd be forced,' he said, 'to clear our name and initiate recoveries. And we'd do it with maximum prejudice.' He paused a second to work the benevolence back up. 'We'd much rather,' he said, 'take the proactive approach.'

I waited. Wondered whether the approach was the one with suits or with baseball bats. Then Covault came back in.

'I'm offering you fifty thousand pounds to close the matter,' he said. 'That's a generous recompense. More than covers your time and costs.'

I said nothing. Eased myself out of my seat and turned to the windows but the panorama had gone. The blinds gave only a slant view five hundred feet down. I watched the ground, the ants running round.

'That's a nice offer,' I said, 'but I think I'll leave it. Professional integrity and all that. We'll be off this in a couple of days and your friend Mr Lad has already paid us more than enough for the work done. And I'm confident that whatever we dig up will hold up in court.'

I turned back to the room.

'And it won't be me upsetting your share floatation,' I said. 'What we find will go to the police. They'll decide what's in the public interest.'

'Fifty thousand, Mr Flynn! Think about it. We just want what's best all round.'

'I want only what's best for the investigator your man Lad killed. The guy has a sister. She's working with me on this. Also, I want what's best for Jeremy Coates. And most of all I want Lad off the street for both the murder of the investigator and for his threats against a friend of mine. And if Lad is working for you in all of this then I want your head too, Peter. Fifty K just doesn't cut it.'

Covault was watching me. His eyes narrowed.

'Okay,' he said. 'I'm sorry we couldn't reach an agreement. Do what you must do. Police enquiries won't find evidence of a crime. No murders or disappearances. And nothing illegal in our actions to recover company documents. If the police want to go after the party who extorted us they're welcome. Fifty thousand, Mr Flynn.' He threw it in one last time, eyebrow raised, the face of a reasonable guy trying to make things run smoothly. But it was also the face of wealth measured in billions. The face of power. And if there was ever a face for hiding secrets this was it. I didn't know how much Peter Covault knew but it was *his* people who'd turned up with bats and coshes at Chase Street. *His* people who'd threatened Kim Waters and killed Sam Barker. And *his* family who'd killed Jeremy Coates.

And I didn't know which was worse: Covault knowing it all or Covault knowing nothing. Like the engine of his Maybach: the thing purred away so quietly you never knew it was there and as long as it got you where you wanted you never needed to know how it worked.

Regret crossed Covault's face for half a second, then he stood and reached across the table and I shook his hand with a firm, long grip that delivered my message. I ignored Devonshire's and Adam's hands. The two other wannabes saw which way things were going and kept their hands tight round their document holders.

All five waited for me.

I walked round the table and Covault stepped across to open the door for me. He smiled brightly and thanked me for coming. Devonshire and Adam didn't smile, though Devonshire nodded politely. The wannabes played safe. Stayed hostile.

I walked out.

CHAPTER THIRTY-EIGHT
I think they're hiding something

The same supermodel assistant walked me back to the lifts. She asked if I needed a taxi. I said I was fine and stepped into the lift. Hit the button. The doors closed on her smiling face.

The lift took me down to the parking level. I walked out to take a look at the Diamond Covault spaces. Found Barclay Brent's gold pickup there, which is what I was looking for. It had been through a wash and scrub. Restored to a golden sheen. No chalk dust on the tyres, though the dent in the roof hadn't rinsed out.

I went out and sat on the steps in front of the building. Watched people come and go whilst I called Harry. He said he'd see me in twenty.

I was facing away from the building but I could sense the immensity of the monolith behind me, the creepy feeling in my neck that anything could come down. I pushed the thought aside and watched clouds over the river. Enjoyed the sun until Harry's Mondeo rolled up. After the Maybach the ride was a let down. I wondered whether Peter Covault had sat in an ordinary car in his life, if you called Harry's wheels ordinary. The Mondeo would curl most lips but had the attraction of being invisible, which an investigator likes. We circled the building and headed out.

'So it's the company,' Harry said.

'Peter Covault denies everything except the extortion but I don't believe him. His buy-off attempt was about more than that.'

'Lucy's gonna love his fifty K offer,' Harry said. 'With the cash everyone's throwing at us we could move into the Covault Complex ourselves.'

'You think our clients would climb thirty floors?'

'There's the lifts,' Harry said.

'Wouldn't work for our image. When you're climbing stairs you've a different set of expectations.'

'So we'd get a sign pointing that way.'

'Think of your legs, Harry. You're not getting any younger.'

'Yeah,' Harry agreed. 'Scratch the river view. Maybe the fifty K could put in a lift in Chase Street.'

The dreaming got us across town and back into St James's. We walked up Jermyn and stopped at the entrance to Barclay Brent's building. No point breaking in if someone was home.

Turned out someone was. A female voice answered the bell. Young. Breathy. A little uncertain, as if visitors had caught her out.

I apologised. Wrong button. The breathy voice said no problem and the intercom cut out.

I grinned at Harry. It would have been too easy...

We walked back up Jermyn and drove to the office.

~~~~~

I'd just briefed Lucy on my visit to the stratosphere and returned to my office to figure out my next move when my phone rang.

Kim.

'If you're in the area we can have lunch,' she said. 'I'm at a café on Westbourne Grove.'

Her voice was bright, slightly breathless. She explained that she'd just finished with a client. Had forty minutes. She named a trattoria. I asked her to skim-read the lunch menu. When she hit a gnocchi dish I told her to put in the order and headed out. Lucy was packing for her afternoon gig.

'Hey,' she called, 'we want to meet her.'

'You will, Luce. As soon as this is sorted. We're running round like fugitives in a mad chase at the moment.'

'Sounds like the fugitive has been caught.' Lucy gave me a look with meaning.

'I'm a catchable guy when the right girl shows up.'

'I know it. Is she the right girl?'

'You'll meet her,' I said. 'You can let me know.'

'What if I don't like her?'

'You will,' I said.

I headed out.

Kim had a window table and water for each of us. She was wearing a tailored navy suit that accentuated her light complexion and blonde hair. She lifted her head and I planted a hand on her neck and a kiss on her lips.

'How's your day so far?' I said. 'Mine's been interesting.'

I sat to explain.

I sensed that she didn't want to talk about interesting mornings and Johnny Lad but she put on a game face.

'It's all still unreal,' she said. 'And I just want it to go away. I was watching the street just now, in the middle of the day, wondering whether this guy's going to pop out of nowhere.'

I'd have told her that the idea was far fetched if Johnny Lad and his pals hadn't popped out of nowhere and whisked *me* away two hours ago. I gave her a sanitised account of the incident and my trip to see Peter Covault. Kim's eyes opened wide.

'What did he want?' she said.

'He wanted to buy me off. Drop the search for Sam Barker's killer. I told him I already knew the killer: he was the guy who'd just chauffeured me across town on Covault's orders. The bastard denied everything but he knows. You don't buy people off when you've nothing to hide. And what he's afraid of is more than just a concern about their floatation plans.'

Kim looked at me. Lost for words at this escalation of the affair. She opened her mouth but the waiter turned up just then and planted our food and we set to. At least I did. I forked gnocchi. When I looked up, Kim hadn't started. Then my phone rang. I picked up.

Yvonne.

'Jeremy Coates' friend is back,' she said. 'His name is Martin Langlois. Lives near Uckfield. And he's got something.'

This was Coates' chess club pal who'd been sent a message to get back to me. When or whether he'd do that wasn't clear, so Yvonne had short-circuited things. Taken a trip to Sevenoaks and sweet-talked another club member into handing over the guy's name and number, then left a persuasive message of her own, which had delivered.

'He got back from holiday yesterday,' Yvonne told me, 'and picked up a signed-for package that was waiting. It was from Coates. Contained a document and a note that was odd enough to persuade him to return my call.'

'What did the note say?'

'Coates asked Langlois to see that the document was delivered to the authorities if anything happened to him. Langlois tried to ring

Coates yesterday evening but couldn't get through. By this morning he'd decided that I might know something. I told him that his friend was being chased by some dangerous people. I didn't mention that we'd already found him.'

'What was the document?'

'Some kind of technical report. Its front abstract talks about structural defects in the Covault Tower in Singapore. It was gobbledegook to me but it sounded pretty fundamental – meaning expensive to fix. Something about an inadequate bracing skeleton and substandard material in shear wall edge joints, whatever they are, and the fact that repairing the problem will, quote "entail external re-stabilisation and partial deconstruction, blah-blah-blah". They use the word "radical" and conclude that "viability must be reviewed", all of which sounds like engineering-speak for *major* problems. I'm assuming this was the report that Sam delivered to Lad.'

'Who wrote the report?'

'You remember Coates stayed in that hotel in Singapore near a consultancy firm who've worked for Diamond Covault? It's their report. Maybe Coates' trip out there was to pick up a paper copy, though it's hard to see why they'd hand it to him if he was no longer working for Covault.'

'I wonder how expensive we're talking for the repairs?'

'Who knows, Eddie? Maybe hundreds of millions. That phrase about reviewing viability sounds ominous. Maybe the whole building has to come down. So the high hundreds. I hear these skyscrapers cost several billion to put up. Maybe when you start from having to salvage a disaster it's worse. And if you take into account the compensations for all the temporarily displaced tenants maybe we're talking two or three *billion* liability.'

Guesswork, but someone knew the figure. Someone had done the maths.

Theory confirmed: the extortion document was a very big deal for the company's floatation, despite Peter Covault's denial. If the news that the company was about to take a massive hit went public then Covault could kiss his target share price goodbye. He'd be lucky to raise ten bob in the sale.

Yvonne's information left us with the likely scenario that Coates was involved in the extortion, had posted a copy of the report for safekeeping whilst he ran the scheme, possibly working with Barclay Brent. And Peter Covault's insistence that the extortion was related to simple confidential information, of no interest to the wider world, was a straight lie. Covault's company had been blackmailed over an existential threat.

Yvonne had offered to meet Langlois to take a look at the document but he was out for the day. I told her I'd meet him myself. If he was reluctant to hand the document over then photos would do. We agreed to talk later and I killed the line. Grinned at Kim.

'We've got the motive,' I said.

She looked at me.

'The exchanged packages were parts of a report used to blackmail Diamond Covault. A report that could crash their floatation.'

I explained my theory. Held back the news that despite his precautions Coates was dead. Kim would take that information a little more easily when the bad guys were off the street. Which might be soon: the report copy should be enough for Keith Prior to take this thing forward, might bring us to the end of the affair. I picked up my fork and returned to my gnocchi. Kim still didn't make any move towards her own food.

'These are powerful people,' she said. 'You need to be careful.'

'Caution is my middle name.'

'And you're sure this Lad character really is a killer?'

'Yes.'

'What do they want from you?'

'They want me to stop. They suspect that the report copy is out there and they're focused on finding it. But Sam Barker died over the report and I want Johnny Lad's head for that. And whether or not Covault knew about Sam's killing he's still party to it. So I'm going to bring the whole house down.'

Kim looked at me. 'This scares me,' she said. 'If these people get to Alice...'

I planted my fork.

'They won't. It's almost over,' I said. 'And we're going to put people with you from tomorrow until it is. It's time to retire your security service. I'm bringing in a guy who could stop a platoon.'

'What about Alice?'

'She'll be safest with you. It's easier to watch you both. It won't be discreet – the guy I'm talking about doesn't pay much attention to the niceties – but it will be safe. And in twenty-four to forty-eight hours the police will have everything.'

Kim looked unconvinced.

'I trust you, Eddie,' she said. 'But if there was any way I could persuade you just to leave the whole damn thing, just walk away, I'd try. I'd hate you to get hurt on my behalf. If the thing just went away I'd be happy.'

'It's not going away,' I said. 'If we dropped the investigation then Yvonne Barker would continue alone, digging for hard evidence, and Lad would stop her. I opened the door for Lad to reach Sam and her. I can't walk away.'

She said nothing. Lifted her fork and pushed at her food. Then her eyes found mine again and she forced a smile.

'Life can be shit,' she said, though she said it with affection.

I grinned back. 'We take it as it's served,' I said. 'But we'll keep you safe.'

She thought about it some more. 'Do you know,' she said, 'I never knew people like you existed.'

'This town's full of people you never knew existed,' I said. 'Both ends of the spectrum. Eat up.'

She looked at her food, surprised. Looked at her watch.

'Damn,' she said, 'I should have ordered a sandwich.'

She grabbed her things, signalled for the waiter.

'I'll get it,' I said. 'At least I've eaten.'

We both stood.

'How about tonight,' I suggested. 'We'll try again. Maybe manage three courses.'

She smiled. A little forced.

'Sure. Maybe I'll have my appetite back.'

I grinned. I knew about her appetite.

'We'll all be fine,' I said. 'Just a couple of days.'

Kim's smile wavered but she leaned in and we touched lips and then she was gone. I waved the waiter away and sat back down to finish my gnocchi. Found time for a double espresso. Wondered whether Barclay Brent's lady friend had stepped out to take air. Because there might be something in that penthouse to give me leverage, to get him to talk about his own involvement in the affair, maybe about Lad's.

The two were on opposite sides of this thing and in twenty-four hours this was going to be all about survival of the fast-talker.

~~~~~

Barclay's friend wasn't out. The same voice answered when I pressed the bell, though there was a hint of suspicion this time when I repeated my wrong bell excuse. I walked back out. Found a spot twenty yards down the street. Waited.

My current theory was that Coates acquired the Singapore document for Barclay Brent and that Barclay was scamming his own firm. What I didn't know was why. Nor why he'd killed Coates, which was the start of a losing game. You don't get away with killing people unless you're a professional. Amateurs don't see the flaws, the mess they're leaving. And somewhere up in that penthouse was a tiny scrap of mess. Something Brent had overlooked.

I stood on Jermyn for an hour and watched for an exceptionally good looking woman to appear from the building but none did. By four thirty it was too late. Either Barclay's friend wasn't coming out or she'd driven out without me seeing her. And I was out of time. Brent could turn up at any moment. I called Harry and told him I wouldn't need him. He'd already taken a shufty at Johnny Lad's place, checked his security system so we were ready for a quick in-out whenever we decided to check the place. Which would be soon. Next I called Shaughnessy. He reported an exciting day following Lad between his office and the Covault Complex. Long waits in between.

Last call: Bernie. He agreed to come in first thing tomorrow to look after Kim.

I drove home. Picked up Herbie and changed into running gear and completed five park circuits. We'd just got back when Kim called and cancelled our date, which rounded things off with a negative.

'Alice has been upset,' she said. 'She wants to know why I've not come for her. And Oliver's throwing a fit. Says he won't keep her a prisoner any longer. He was about to call the police. I dissuaded him. Said the police are about to be informed and I'd have twenty-four hour protection from tomorrow. I said I'd come over and spend the night, then bring Alice home. It was touch and go but he agreed. He's finding life as a single parent a little harder than he anticipated.'

'Want me to tag along?'

'No. I'm fine. I assume these people don't know where Oliver lives and I'll make sure no-one's following me out. If your guy Bernie is with us from tomorrow we'll be okay. But I need this to be finished.'

'It will be. By the weekend,' I said.

I got that one right.

CHAPTER THIRTY-NINE
Consequences

I dropped Herbie off with Henrietta at seven. Seemed his calming influence was helping at the dogs' home. Some of Henrietta's more behaviourally-challenged charges were losing their fear or aggression faster when Herbie was in the training compound, though I suspected they were also getting fatter. Maybe Battersea would soon be re-homing dogs with mile-wide grins and a propensity for collapsing on their backs at the mention of food.

I called Martin Langlois. Introduced myself.

'Ms Barker explained,' he said. 'But Jeremy wants the document handed to the police if anything happens to him and I don't know what the hell *that* means or where he is, and I'm not letting anyone take the document until I do.'

'No problem. How about I just photograph a few pages?'

'I'm more concerned about Jeremy.'

'We're concerned too. He's become mixed up with some dangerous people over that document. They're implicated in the killing of a private investigator. So the police will be in this soon. But a sight of the document would help me.'

'Holy cow! I didn't expect to come home to a spy movie.'

'This is no movie. Can I call round?'

He thought about it.

'I'm in work late morning. I'll hang on here until ten thirty. If you're here by then you can take a look. And you know more about Jeremy than you're saying.'

I did, but he wasn't ready to hear the bad news. Until the thing was with DS Prior the fewer who knew the details the better. I told Langlois I'd be there by mid morning and cut the call.

My phone lit up with another incoming.

Kim.

I asked how Alice was.

'She's fine. We're just setting off.'

'Come straight to the office. Harry and Bernie will take you home. and Bernie will be staying with you. This is almost over.' I explained that we'd have a copy of the report in our hands by mid morning.

She said she hoped to God that would be enough. I heard stress in her voice. Told her to be careful and rang off.

~~~~~

Shaughnessy's room was full. Mostly due to Bernie being in there. He was up on the desk telling a story about a company exec. who paid two hundred K to fund six of his people on a trekking jaunt in Kenya only to find that he had to fund immediate return air fares when the trekking outfit turned out to be bogus.

'I'd have taken 'em to Brecon for half the price,' Bernie was saying, 'and if they weren't good company people afterwards they never would be. They'd work wonders for the guy to avoid being sent back. Peer pressure and fear. Fuels all successful companies.'

Shaughnessy was behind the desk. Harry was sipping tea. Lucy was leaning against the fireplace, grinning like a Cheshire cat. That's Bernie and the ladies.

He looked round as I came in and his face split into a grin. The same grin he probably used when he pushed his business clients into the mud.

'Eddie,' he said. He held out a paw. I shook it and grinned through the pain. The hand crush was a tradition, Bernie's test of character. He was waiting for the day I'd burst into tears. I was waiting for the day he decided that I really *couldn't* feel anything and quit the charade.

When we were through I flopped into one of Shaughnessy's guest chairs to explain where we were. Told them about Peter Covault's admission that the report was a problem. Our own findings that it was a *big* problem. An existential problem.

'You're saying the company could go under?' Shaughnessy said.

'It's got to be possible. Even Covault acknowledged that the thing could hit their floatation. And from the detail we know I'd say it's more likely to kill it outright. Covault might be pushed to raise tuppence next week. And the Singapore problem might demand cash that wouldn't be there.'

'He'd call off the floatation,' Shaughnessy said. 'No cash, no point.'

'But that's not his biggest problem,' Bernie said. 'If Covault's been keeping the report under wraps whilst he's running his floatation then that's big time fraud. That's jail time.'

I agreed. 'That's why they paid off the extorter, who I'm assuming was Barclay Brent working with Jeremy Coates. It just doesn't explain what happened after. The thing should have ended with the last exchange. Everyone gone home happy. But somehow the wires got touched and the thing exploded in their faces and Johnny Lad's job switched from working the exchange to putting out the fire.'

'Only it's getting bigger,' Shaughnessy said. 'And here you are running round with the petrol can. My guess...' He stood and went to watch the street: '...they're going to move fast. They need to stamp this thing out.'

Lucy had gone out and came back with coffee. Handed me a cup. Strong, sweet, extra creamer. I sipped.

'They're going to come after us,' I agreed. 'So we need to close this off. Bernie: we need you to keep an eye on Kim and her daughter. That will give us the breathing space for a *blitzkrieg*.'

Unless Prior pushed his own schedule. If he was as good as his word he already had Met patrol vehicles out looking for my car. I'd half expected blue lights as I drove across town this morning. And I'd be dealing with a seriously annoyed policeman when he did collar me. Another promise of rabbits from hats wasn't going to cut it.

I grinned at Lucy.

'Has the buggy got fuel in the tank?'

Lucy drove an orange and black Smart Fortwo round town when she needed personal transport. The car's about the smallest production vehicle you can buy but it's still roomier than the Frogeye. I'd spotted it parked alongside Shaughnessy's bike at the back.

'Sure. But I might need to get around myself,' Lucy said.

I grinned. Tossed her the Frogeye's keys.

'Don't scratch it,' I said.

I didn't mention Prior's Anper on the vehicle. That's Automatic Number Plate Recognition, which is how patrol cars pick you up without their crew even knowing they're looking. But God help the cops who pulled Lucy over. They'd have their work cut out trying to figure whether her hair was legal.

The plan for the morning was intel-gathering. I'd take Barclay Brent's penthouse. If Brent's woman was there I'd handle her.

Shaughnessy would take Lad's place. Harry would get us into both places and make sure any cameras were blind. We'd turn the places over and find what we found.

The plan for the afternoon, if we found enough, was to put a pack together for Prior. Whatever came out of the apartments plus the rest of the circumstantial stuff and the photos of the Covault report. Prior would be round in a flash when we called him. Probably with a platoon of coppers. But he'd cheer up when we showed him what we had.

I'd not be cheering up much myself. We'd be handing Prior enough to take a serious look at Johnny Lad and Barclay Brent but when you hand over the reins there's always the risk that the horse will bolt in the wrong direction. We knew the big picture – the dirty game Covault was playing to protect company plans – but we didn't know the small stuff. We didn't know how or why Barclay Brent had been working with Jeremy Coates, why Barclay was scamming his own company or why he'd killed Coates. We were still missing something at the core of this thing, and if Prior messed up then the things we didn't know might be the escape routes for the bad guys. And if Johnny Lad stayed on the street we'd have a problem. Despite what I'd told Kim, we might be looking after her for a while.

So right after any chinwag with Prior I'd be back on the streets with Sean, looking for the knots that would tie Lad and Brent securely.

I checked the time. Nine forty-five. Kim would be up the stairs any moment. Once she appeared I'd head out to meet Martin Langlois then move on to Brent's apartment. Meantime, we stood down. Harry took a moment for a little admin. Lucy went out to continue digging at her computer. Sean, Bernie and I killed time with chit-chat that interested none of us.

Ten o'clock.

I called Kim. No answer. I left a pointless message. Pictured the route from Lewes. The traffic would have been hell once she got past Croydon. So maybe another ten or fifteen minutes. I went out for a refill. Took it through to my room. Set the blinds and straightened the chair. Went back through to the front and asked Bernie for the sixth time how business was going. Tried to ignore a growing unease at Kim's non-appearance. But after fifteen more minutes I was getting bad vibes. I kept telling myself that there was no way Johnny Lad could know where Kim stayed last night, and if he had known he'd have acted before this morning. My concerns were paranoia. Kim was stuck in traffic.

At ten twenty I called her again. This time the call went to voicemail. She'd switched her phone off.

Shaughnessy, Harry and Bernie looked at me.

My unease grew. We should have had Bernie down at Lewes this morning to bring Kim in. Obvious with hindsight.

I walked across and lifted the blinds.

Roadworks or an accident blockage could add an hour onto Kim's trip but why hadn't she rung? I was down to the only innocent explanation which was that her battery had died. Innocent but not credible. I turned from the window.

'Something's happened,' I said.

Lucy came through. The mood chilled. We'd been through something like this before.

I was about to call Kim's number again when my phone rang and her ID finally came up on the screen.

I picked up, fast.

'Hello Eddie,' the voice said. It wasn't Kim. I pushed the phone hard against my ear.

'You!' I said. 'Lad.'

'A courtesy call. You had your chance to walk away, Flynn. Now it's time for consequences.'

The line went dead.

I cursed and called back but there was no tone. The phone had been switched back off. I looked round the room.

'They've got her,' I said.

CHAPTER FORTY
Just a little situation

'We're going to get instructions,' I said.

Kim was Lad's leverage just as he'd intended but my blind stumble into a romantic liaison had amplified its effect. If I'd put someone with Kim yesterday she'd have been safe. But I hadn't. All my promises and not even the most basic protection.

'He's going to ask us to stamp out the flames,' Shaughnessy said. He was watching the street. 'The question is whether he believes we can.'

'He's going through it now,' I said. 'If he's talked to Kim he knows there's another copy of the document out there. He needs to get that back. Then he needs all of us – including Yvonne – to step back. He's going to demand cooperation in return for Kim. Demand we stay silent for good or he comes back for Kim or her daughter. We can't protect them for the rest of their lives.'

Harry stood. Rapped his knuckles on the desk. 'My worry,' he said, 'is he might hurt Kim to reinforce his message.'

The same thought was running through my head.

'Up to now,' I said, 'he's not seen much cooperation from us.'

'That's the problem,' Harry said. 'He might feel the need to convince us that he's serious. Kim and her girl will come back but they might be hurt.'

'Is Peter Covault behind all this?' Lucy asked.

'Directly or indirectly,' I said. 'This whole mess is his.'

'Why not go after him?' she said. 'If you scare the top man he'll look for the best way out. And the small fry won't matter. Maybe Johnny Lad is expendable.'

'You may be right,' I said, 'but it's not a cert. The small fry may have issues Covault doesn't know about. He keeps clear of the details so he can hide behind deniability but we don't know how much control he has. If Lad suspects that he's about to be sacrificed he'll take measures. Outmanoeuvre Covault and protect himself.'

'So Lad's the priority,' Bernie concluded.

I agreed. Called Yvonne Barker. Switched my phone to speaker and explained that we had a major problem. She listened in silence. Then:

'We need to go after *him*,' she said. 'Strike first.'

'That's our plan,' I said.

Shaughnessy grabbed his helmet.

'Action,' he said.

'I'll take Lad,' I said. 'Fancy a ride, Bernie?'

'Right behind you.'

'Sean: two birds. Call on Martin Langlois. We need to get that report safely out of his hands before Lad gets to him. The report will give us a little leverage. And Langlois' address would put you right by Kim's drive in from Lewes. It's a long shot but let's follow her route back, see if there's any sign of where she was intercepted.

'Luce: drive over to Mayfair and check Kim's house. Lad needs somewhere to keep Kim and it might just be there. Look for her car or his, anything suspicious. If it seems clear, ring the bell. If anyone answers stay on the street and let us know.'

'Wilco.'

'Harry, let's take a look at Barclay Brent. If he and his lady friend are home you can pick him up when he goes out, see what he's up to right now. We may need to talk to him at short notice. If he's already out then take a look in his apartment.

'Yvonne...' I spoke towards the phone: 'how about taking a drive out to Covault's estate? See if anything's happening, anyone turning up.'

'I'm on my way,' Yvonne said. 'We'll get these bastards, Eddie.'

Reassurance. Or just rhetoric. But you take what you can get. I cut the conference call and gave Shaughnessy Martin Langlois' address.

Bernie slid off the desk.

'He's still deciding his best play,' he said. 'But he knows we're not sitting at home.'

Harry heaved himself up.

'Second that,' he said. 'He'll anticipate us coming.'

'But we'll come anyway,' I said. I left them to it. Went out with Bernie and jogged down the stairs like this was just another situation but inside I felt sick.

And angry. Mostly at myself.

CHAPTER FORTY-ONE
It's like following a firework

I drove across town to the Lad Associates office. Bernie's Land Rover stuck with me at every lane change and jumped light and parked behind me on the pavement outside the firm's door. I signalled to him to wait. Went in alone. If Bernie heard any thumps and bangs he'd come in after me.

I climbed stairs. Arrived at a reception area with counter and cute receptionist. The girl was early twenties with long blonde hair and gloss crimson lipstick. She smiled brightly and grabbed for her book when I asked if Mr Lad was in.

'He's out today,' she said. 'Would you like to make an appointment?'

'I need to talk to him now.'

She apologised. Said that everyone was out. 'We've a busy day on,' she said.

I'll bet.

'Is there no-one else here?'

'Everyone's out,' she repeated.

I grinned and said okay and walked through to the back room. She jumped from her stool. Too late.

The room behind the reception had been knocked through to give a decent office space. Sufficient for eight desks with computer screens and a line of cabinets. There were just two guys at the desks. Admin or IT staff who'd know nothing. Two doors off the back of the room serviced a bathroom and kitchen. A third had a frosted glass window. Lad's office. The glass was dark.

The guys working the keyboards looked up as the receptionist came running in. I turned and pushed her back out.

'Okay,' I said. 'No-one home.'

The girl had lost her smile.

'You're not allowed in there,' she said.

'Got it.'

I went back out. Turned back to her

'Thing is, I really need to speak to Johnny.' I threw a smile meant to charm.

Charm crashed.

'I'll pass on a message,' she said. 'Mr Lad will call you tomorrow.'

'Not good enough. I need to catch him today.'

There was no pretence at charm in Blondie's own face.

'He just can't do it. We've got a major event on. Mr Lad won't be contactable until it's finished.'

Seemed Lad still had his regular commitments to take care of whilst he was running round abducting people.

'What's the event?'

'I can't tell you that.'

'But he's got all his people there? A big do?'

'Yes. We've no staff at all. If you give me your name and number–'

'I'll call back,' I said. I left her to it and went out. Gave Bernie a wash-out wave and jumped into the Fortwo.

Bow Creek was just down the road. Worth a gander. Lad's people might be on a job but there was always the chance that he was in the Covault building. I needed to catch him or I'd have no choice but to go back to his office and things would get messy. Things would get broken. If I did catch Lad things would get messy anyway because I'd throttle him until he gave me Kim's whereabouts. That was my plan. Everyone out looking for threads, me going for the short-circuit. Bernie my backup: if I caught up with Lad he could drag me off.

As I passed Canary Wharf Lucy called.

'She's not at the house,' she reported.

No surprise, but it felt like another nail being banged home.

I accelerated down the slip into Bow Creek. Skimmed behind the Covault edifice. The rear glass wall was shadow, lacking the blinding cataract of the river face. The building was almost ordinary from this side, just big. Then the road swung round and I was out in the light, braking by the parking ramp. Bernie stopped behind me. I signalled to him and jogged down the ramp to see who was home.

No-one was.

Which was a surprise.

Eight of the ten exec. spots by the lifts were empty. Lad's R8 wasn't there and Barclay Brent's gold pickup wasn't there and most of the Mercs and Jags I'd seen previously weren't there. Which was odd. Company execs could be in and out all the time but eight empty spaces on a workday morning just wasn't right. It was as if the bosses were on strike.

I cancelled thoughts of a ride up to Thirty-Three and went back out. Bernie was leaning against his Land Rover, arms folded. We both looked up at the tower.

'Something's going on here,' I said. 'The big shots are all out. And Lad's firm has something on.' I explained. The big job might be unrelated to Diamond Covault but those empty spots made me wonder.

'Company away-day?' Bernie said.

We watched the top floors. Clouds scudded across the glass.

My phone chirped. Shaughnessy.

'I've just left Martin Langlois' place. He's not home. Not answering his phone. Probably got tired of waiting. I'm just picking up the A22 to follow Kim's route in.'

'Got it. Talk later.'

I disconnected. The screen lit again. Harry.

'Barclay came out half an hour ago with his woman. Both dressed to the nines. Tailcoat and topper. LBD. They took the Isuzu though. That gold tack is going to turn the atmosphere somewhere today. It's like following an explosion.'

'Where are you?'

'Just through Croydon. I'm thinking the family estate. You mentioned preps the other day.'

'Could be.' I recalled the contractor vehicles, the marquee van. Maybe Covault had a bash on. I told Harry to stick with Barclay, see where he ended up. Harry grunted.

I called Yvonne and she confirmed that something *was* going on at the estate.

'It's a wedding,' she said. 'You can't move for Daimlers and Rollses. The pub tells me it's Peter Covault's niece. Marrying some Italian aristocrat.'

'Anyone we know showed up?'

'I've seen no-one, but I'm sure Covault's in there. And the gate security is pretty heavy. I'm thinking those are Lad's people. In which case he's in there.'

I concurred. This was the big job Blondie had mentioned. If Lad was on Covault's estate surrounded by his army he'd take a bit of getting to.

'Keep watching,' I said. 'Barclay Brent is on his way. Harry will be on his tail.'

'Tell Harry he can ditch Barclay at the village. No need to come right down. I'm back in the trees with a sight of the gates so we've got things covered.'

'I'll tell him.'

I called Harry and passed on the information. He agreed to hang back in the village until we knew our next move.

Which wasn't clear. If Lad's people were tied up at the Covault estate we'd have little chance of picking up anyone who'd lead us to Kim and Alice. And the estate celebrations could go on late. We were looking at a long shift before Lad came out.

I was still watching the tower.

'Where would he stash her?' Bernie asked.

'That's the question.'

Then my phone rang again and Shaughnessy told me he'd found Kim's car.

CHAPTER FORTY-TWO
Neon arrow

Bernie drove a Land Rover for its off-road qualities, not its speed. I'd lost him before I got off the Crossing. Skimmed the East India Dock traffic and put my foot down on the tunnel approach. Came out south of the river with the Dome shrinking fast in my mirror.

The early afternoon traffic was capricious but light. An hour and fifteen with my foot to the floor got me to a lay-by off the main road south of East Grimstead. I spotted Shaughnessy's figure on a wide grassy area separating the parking area from the road. The parking was empty but Kim's Aston Martin was abandoned on the grass.

I jogged across.

The car's offside wing and bumper had been pushed in and the headlight was smashed.

'It's unlocked,' Shaughnessy said.

I opened the driver's door and took a look. The interior was tidy. Door pockets clear except for a pair of sunglasses. Leather seats pristine, unmarked, undamaged. No sign of the blood you might get if someone had been hurt during a struggle. And no child seat. If Alice had been strapped in it looked like they'd taken the seat along with her.

I walked round and lifted the boot. Empty. I slammed it closed and walked back to the road. Looked up and down. Looked at Shaughnessy. He nodded. Same conclusion.

'They wanted us to find it,' he said.

The car could have been driven right into the lay-by where a line of trees would have hidden it for a few days. But Kim's abductor had backed the car onto the grass right by the road. Nothing illegal to raise eyebrows in a passing patrol car. But a position guaranteed to catch the eye of anyone out looking.

'Do we know where they intercepted her?'

'Three miles back. There's a long bend, trees one side and a wide verge on the other. They passed her and pushed her onto it. The glass is in the road. It would have been over in thirty seconds.'

I looked that way. Thought about it. Cars flashed by. I went to the

Fortwo and checked the glove compartment. It's where people once kept maps. The compartment was empty. I reverted to my phone. Downloaded the area map. Not as easy to read but what I was looking for was there. I crossed back to Shaughnessy.

'You hit the main road up ahead,' I said, 'then drive a couple of miles and turn off.'

Shaughnessy got it.

'The Covault estate,' he said.

'They could have ditched the car twenty miles away. It's on display here for a reason. And this is the last convenient spot before you turn off for the estate.'

'You think she's there?'

'That's where they're pointing.'

'So they're inviting you in.'

'They want me there and under control. But this is bad timing. Covault has a wedding on. He's a house full of aristocracy, an army of catering people, the vicar waiting in the wings. This is a bad day to have me poking around.'

'Lad saw no choice,' Shaughnessy said. 'He's realised how fast we're moving. Needed to get you off the street. Take control of the situation.'

'And he's played his threat card. Snatched Kim.'

Shaughnessy thought about it.

'Lad's tied to the estate today. That's where all his people are. So he'd no choice but to go with the risk of bringing you in and hoping he can contain the situation until the guests have left.'

'And Kim might *be* there. It's a big estate. He could stash her out of sight for the day.'

'The problem is you. How does he keep things quiet if you turn up?'

'He'll watch and wait,' I said. 'Act fast when I show.'

An engine roared and Bernie's Land Rover angled onto the grass. Bernie killed the engine and jumped out.

'What's up?' he said.

~~~~~

'Here's what Lad is thinking,' I said.

We'd talked it through. If we were guessing right then we were ahead of the game and our plan might just work. If we were wrong things were going to get messy.

'He's posted a neon arrow pointing to the Chester Wood estate. He wants me to believe that Kim is there. He wants me to come for her.'

'She's there,' Bernie said. 'Lad wouldn't have the spare bods to cart her off somewhere else and watch over her.'

'So he's luring me in, which is a dicey game with the place full of Covault's guests. But he's betting on my making things easier for him.'

'He's betting on spotting you coming in,' Shaughnessy said.

'He assumes I'll go over the wall. The estate is six or seven hundred acres. That's a lot of ground to cover if I get loose. But Lad is watching the perimeter. He'll have people ready to go the moment I'm spotted. They take me down and bundle me off somewhere safe until the party's over. Maybe the same place he's holding Kim and Alice.'

Bernie grinned. 'The guy likes to live dangerously,' he said. 'You think Peter Covault knows about this?'

'No,' I said. 'Lad wouldn't want Covault sweating in his tux.'

'So that's Lad's plan,' Shaughnessy said.

'Then there's ours,' Bernie said.

I watched two cars pass.

'Yeah,' I said. I looked at them. 'There's ours.'

CHAPTER FORTY-THREE
He wasn't in such good shape

I eased the Fortwo through Chester Wood's main street and followed the estate wall out. Passed the stables yard, which was jammed with catering and service vehicles. Reached the main gates. They were wide open. Two guys in black suits and ear buds were controlling access but I spun the wheel without slowing and skidded the Fortwo between them before they could step out to block me. The Fortwo yawed and rocked and considered rolling over but I fought it straight. Stamped on the pedal and shrapnelled the guys as they ran out behind me. They ducked and yelled and vanished in my rear-view.

The driveway swung round the stable buildings then reversed into a slow "S" that climbed through an avenue of flowering limes backed by woodland. I hit the crest and the trees opened to a view of a house three hundred yards away across an ornamental garden. The rear of a Jacobean monstrosity, lined with arches and windows, dwarfed by massive wings projecting out to cupola-topped corner towers. An overwhelming projection of wealth to greet visitors, even if this was only the back view.

It was the archetypal English country house, inhabited by the same family for four hundred years until the money dried up and forced a sale to the National Trust with a rental retained on a domestic wing for the final generation to live out its fading memories.

But the National Trust didn't own this place. In a world of globe-spanning new wealth, palaces like this were just as likely to take the fancy of a tech billionaire or oil prince who'll have it off your hands in a flash minus the option to rent a wing. When you sign the completion forms you're out.

In this case the buyer had been Peter Covault. A house to fit his world view. Built for show, its purpose was fulfilled as completely today as it had ever been: look at the rows of windows, the brooding wings, the towers, and you knew that Covault's global interests were doing okay. It was like driving towards a fortress.

The driveway split to circle the gardens. I chose left and raced alongside a decorative stone wall. Greenery and sparkling fountains flashed through the balustrades but there was no-one strolling amongst them. The party was round the front. I hit the top end and rolled onto a gravel area serving a grand rear entrance. The area was jammed with expensive cars with expensive chauffeurs sitting inside reading the paper or out smoking fags. None of Johnny Lad's people about, though that wouldn't last. The goons on the gate would have phoned through and the troops would be scrambling. I'd sixty seconds before they caught up with the change of plan and switched their attention from the wall cameras.

Chamber music floated over the roof. The party in full swing out on the park. I ditched the Smart and jogged across to the trees. Took a path into them.

I'd put a three hundred yard swathe of woodland between me and the stables. I worked by memory and dead reckoning to get back down to them.

My map and Google had shown three estate outbuildings. The first of these was the stables block. The second had been a small pavilion set in a woodland clearing out on the park beyond the house. The third was a row of cottages or storage buildings by the wall on the far side of the estate, a mile away.

Lad wanted me to believe that Kim was here, and I was giving it a seventy-five percent chance that she actually was. Which meant she was either stashed in the main house or one of the outbuildings.

But my first objective was Lad's command and control centre. Lad had an army in today, but an army is only as good as its eyes. The estate had a security room somewhere where Lad's people were watching camera feeds on live screens. Security would normally be two guys. One checking-in visitors at the gate, one watching the periphery. The gatehouse would have a screen for the gate but the periphery cams and proximity sensors and house alarms were probably in the stables. That was Lad's control centre.

A Sussex garden wedding isn't a max security event even with all the Bentleys and Rollers and Italian aristocracy about, but when you need to show who's top dog amongst the top dogs an army of men in black are a nice touch. Covault would have a platoon in here today. And who was Johnny Lad to argue? He was taking fifty K to have his guys standing around looking mean.

Only the game had been upped.

Lad had decided on a real security exercise. He'd warned his crew that they'd be getting visitors, which raised a few cheers for sure back at the office. Who wants to stand around watching the toffs for eight hours?

But their ear buds had just crackled the news that the game had changed, that the caller had come in the front door and their line was breached. They were on the defensive.

The path branched and branched again. I kept moving downhill and the ground eventually levelled and then the stables wall was there in front of me.

An internal wall. Camera-free.

I shinned over and dropped eight feet onto cobbles behind the buildings. Crossed to the nearest door. It opened into an area still used for stabling. Just two horses in. I jogged down the stalls and found a bolted door. Backtracked and went back out and along the rear of the building. Tried a locked door. Tried a third. It opened and let me into a workshop and garage jammed with ten million quid's worth of luxury vehicles. Some new, some older than the Frogeye. I spotted stairs and went to check the upper floor.

A dark corridor along the back of the building. An open door part way down. Light and voices.

I took a gander and found Mission Control. It was a large room running across to the front of the building with desks and cabinets and a bank of twelve screens on the wall. The screens were multi. Forty or fifty views of the estate, mostly covering the periphery wall with a few of the house entrances and parking area. The parking view featured an orange and black Smart Fortwo with suits milling round it. None of them was looking in the direction I'd taken, and neither of the two guys watching the screens was looking over his shoulders.

Sloppy and slow. For fifty K.

'How's it going, fellas?' I said.

The screen guys jumped a mile and scrambled to face me. One of them was six-three and somewhere north of twenty stone and turned slowly but the nearer guy turned faster, which earned him a rendezvous with my fist. He dropped. Then the big guy accelerated and caught up. Clocked me with a belt on my ear that greyed my vision. I twisted and hit him hard. Kneed him in the groin and pulled him down over my thigh as I stepped back. Dropped a double-fist pile-driver on the back of his neck as he folded. I left him kneeling and turned to kick the first guy who was half up. He dropped. Out for the count.

Both down for the moment.

But my ear was stinging and bells were chiming. I grabbed the desk for support.

Sloppy tactics on my part.

If I'd kept quiet I could have taken them both without damage. Sometimes you have to chose between smart comments and safety. If I ever write a book on private investigation I'll advise my students to ditch the comments. Though I still wouldn't be practising what I preached. Call it a character flaw. A lifetime of unnecessary cuts and bruises. I took a moment and let my vision clear then got to work, pulling out electrical leads. Computers and printers and screens went dead. I moved fast and secured the men temporarily then trotted down to the workshop and brought back wire and duct tape and some cloth. Plus a claw hammer. I finished binding the two goons then used the hammer on the screens. They were blank without their cables but better they stay that way.

I checked my watch. Twelve minutes since I'd driven through the gate. I'd allowed half an hour to put their security hub out of action. Ahead of schedule.

I opened my tac.

'Eyes blind,' I reported.

Lad had lost his surveillance.

Next objective: find Kim and Alice.

Simple.

If I was lucky they'd be in this building. If not I'd have the house and estate buildings to search. If I was really down on my luck they weren't here at all, but I didn't want to think about that one.

I crossed to the window and looked out at the yard. No-one moving this way. By the time Lad realised he wasn't getting his intel. I'd be gone.

I searched the stables' upper floor.

Just old junk. No sign of Kim.

It would have been too easy.

I decided to skip the gatehouse. It was right next door but Lad's gate crew would be holding station, tense after their screw-up, watching for anything that moved. And the house was small and lived-in. Curtains said that the building was used for security sleep-overs. Not a place to hide Kim.

So the next stop: the main house.

A thorough search would take a day. There had to be two hundred rooms in the building, sculleries and broom closets included. But I didn't have a day. Didn't need it. All I needed was a sprint through, looking for a door guarded by Lad's people.

And if I excluded the working rooms and living rooms and broom closets, if I excluded the ground floor altogether, I was looking at seventy or eighty rooms. Maybe twenty corridors. Doable.

I shinned over the stables wall and jogged back up through the woods. My ear was aching like hell but my dizzy spell had settled and adrenaline sustained me.

I came out of the trees up by the house. Lad's people had abandoned the Fortwo. Searching elsewhere. The chauffeurs were still reading and smoking. I walked across to the building.

CHAPTER FORTY-FOUR
Things just happen

Halfway across to the nearer wing, four of Lad's people appeared from the building. I stepped behind a corner. The men walked out onto the parking area, heads down, listening. When their buds had finished squawking they split up to talk to the chauffeurs. I turned and walked along the wing and went in through an open door near the front of the house.

A corridor took me past a scullery and kitchen to a makeshift food preparation room busy with staff in and out. I grabbed a waiter's checked waistcoat from a line of pegs as I went in. Left my jacket hanging. I could kiss that goodbye. The chances of me coming back through here in one piece were slim. I'd no time to find a dickey bow to match the other waiters but my dark slacks and light grey shirt under the waistcoat were good enough for first glance. No-one was looking for impersonators.

I crossed the room and grabbed a silver tray. A couple of glasses of champagne would have completed the look but the empty tray held up front would do. People see what they expect to see. I left the stream of waiters and opened a door. Came into a massive drawing gallery and library running on the back of the main building. A hundred feet of parquet floor. Shelves to the roof, stacked with old tomes. Deserted. I backed out and tried again. Found stairs ascending the wing. Jogged up to the top floor and found a narrow corridor serving a line of closed doors. Silence. No suits guarding any of them.

I went down a floor and checked a similar, wider, corridor. Heard movement and scraping behind one of the doors. No suits outside it but why was someone in there with the party in full swing? I turned the handle but the door didn't budge. I walked to the adjacent room. Its door opened and let me into a deserted bedroom with beautifully preserved oak panelling and a made-up bed but no clutter or luggage. Unused. A connecting door was set into the panelling. I stepped across. Got lucky. Unlocked. I pushed it slowly open and walked into the locked room. An identical bedroom but this one had luggage and

214

clutter and a bed in use. A half-naked woman atop a wholly-naked guy. The woman turned and shrieked but the significance of her agitation was lost on the guy. It took a few more swear words and her twisting roll as she abandoned ship to get his eyes open. When they did it was his turn to scramble for cover.

I held up the tray and asked if champagne would be in order but the guy was swearing too loudly to hear as he scrabbled for his clothes. The scrabbling is always the giveaway. I'd seen it a thousand times. One or other or both of these two shouldn't be in the room, and even if it was only staff barging in their instinct was to run for cover. The woman did what she was supposed to. Pulled the duvet around herself. He did his bit. Grabbed for his pants.

I took their confusion as a negative and apologised. Stepped back through the connecting door.

The room had told me something at least: the floor was being used by guests, though there were a couple of spouses out in the garden who'd be surprised at just *how* used one of the rooms was. But Lad hadn't brought Kim to an occupied part of the house. I abandoned the wing and found a dogleg that let me onto an impressively wide corridor taking me across the back of the main building.

Two hundred feet of carpet and museum-grade ornaments but only three doors each side. The bedrooms behind them would really be something. But none were guarded. No sounds came out. I eased a door open anyway and took a shufty. I don't know what the rules are on preserving old interiors but this room had been modernised to impress royalty. Marble, gilt, mirrors everywhere. A bed the size of a tennis court with satin and silk shining in the light. Stuff lying around. A lived-in room. For Covault family. Exclusive. If the Queen turned up for a sleep-over she'd not get in here.

I stepped over to the massive windows and looked out over the parking area. Lad's people had vanished. Maybe the chauffeurs had pointed them towards the stables.

I went back out and continued across to the far wing.

Same result as the first wing, minus the flying bedsheets. I tried a few doors and found hit and miss signs of occupancy but no-one home. I finished and went up to check the top floor of the main house which held the servants' old attic rooms. Found nothing but empty corridors and bare rooms.

I'd covered five percent of the house but ninety-five percent of the likely places. Total search time: fifteen minutes. Better than a day.

So not the house.

I went back down and followed the line of waiters out through the front entrance onto a stone-balustraded terrace overlooking the front gardens and park.

Life, finally.

Tops, tails and glam everywhere.

Immediately below the terrace was a lawn decked with tables and chairs, groups of guests. Beyond that another flight of steps down to an impressive garden that ran a hundred yards across to the wilderness of the park. The garden was beautifully mown grass, small trees, ornamental shrubs and flower beds, all the way out to the low hedge that bordered the parkland. Half way across a small orchestra sawed away on a stage alongside a monster marquee, their music diminished by the open expanse. And big as it was the garden was crowded. Groups of three, five, ten, milling with drinks and canapés. Laughing and chatting. Barely space between the groups for the waiting-on staff to get through. Some of the waiters proffered drinks. Most were humping food to the marquee. Seemed we were in the lull between the nuptials and reception. An hour out in the sun. I made a quick count. Estimated a couple of thousand guests. When a billionaire drops you an RSVP you don't think twice. The line of honour was going to be impressive when the couple went in.

I stood at the terrace balustrade and looked across to the park. I needed to get over there, into the woods. The pavilion I'd seen in the satellite photos was sitting in a clearing two hundred yards in.

I focused back on the gardens. Spotted three of Lad's guys in the crowd, lone suits listening to ear buds that weren't telling them much. Their heads turned this way and that as they searched for the gatecrasher. I looked more closely and saw that one of them was sporting tinted aviators and his mouth was moving. Johnny Lad, co-ordinating. Two more of his people came into sight beyond the marquee, walking the park periphery, picking up a path that ran out towards distant trees. Maybe reinforcements for the pavilion. My interest pricked up.

I took a moment, keeping well back under the portico as Lad and his soldiers continued the same slow movement of their heads, discreetly scanning. But they were too low and their vision was too limited. The crowd was against them. A waiter standing patiently was invisible.

A group rounded the marquee, bigger and noisier than the rest and when the bodies parted I spotted Peter Covault in a dinner jacket with the bride on his arm. He wasn't the groom and he wasn't the father but he was the money and the bride was the centre of attention which meant that his place was right there. Etiquette tells you to give up the centre ground occasionally but I guess you don't build a global empire on etiquette. A gaunt woman in a five thousand quid hat walked at Covault's other side with a look on her face. Jane Covault, his wife. A fair bit younger and a hell of a lot better looking than Peter even with the strain on her face.

Then I spotted Barclay Brent and his girlfriend following the group. Barclay was relaxed, charming, looking almost respectable in his tux. The whole mob looked almost respectable, though I'd need my rose-tinted specs to get the full picture. What you saw, when you looked at these people, when I looked at Barclay grinning at the groom who looked about as Italian as Fred Trueman, was the power of wealth. But power's never a single flavour. It's a mix, like concrete. And it can break you like concrete. It can throw you down airshafts and roll you into lakes. I zoomed out again to check back in with Lad's people, cheap waiters in black suits, invisible to the party guests. Another of power's flavours: invisibility. Things just happen the way you need them to. You don't need to know how. If you don't know you don't care.

I spotted my way out to the pavilion.

The garden to the right would give me wedding guest cover for most of the way across to an orchard wall. I'd have just thirty yards of open ground before I'd be camouflaged by the stonework and heading towards the trees. If Lad's people spotted me the chase would be on but I'd be in the woods before they got close. And if there was a welcome party at the pavilion the big unknown would be settled. We'd have located Kim. We'd fire up the next stage.

I moved onto the steps to descend to the lawn. Stepped aside half way down to let a line of guests pass by. Then the guy on the end of the line caught my eye and smiled before he knew what he was smiling at.

James Coleridge Devonshire, Peter Covault's legal guy, all starched up in his shirt and tux.

Then his brain caught up. He stopped dead, which stopped his wife and the rest of the line. His reflexive smile evaporated. He clamped his lips to wait for an explanation while his friends threw funny looks at the inferior waiter who'd snagged his attention.

I held my smile, hoping Devonshire had the sense to play this cool. This wasn't his party. Who the hell knew whom Covault had invited? Or maybe I had a day job.

'Nice to see you, James,' I said. Sometimes inane is best. Removes the need to develop a real conversation which I didn't want. I didn't want to provoke questions and I didn't want Devonshire's pals to stay standing on the steps for five more seconds where someone was going to notice us.

'Mr Flynn,' Devonshire said. His computations had crunched the numbers and pinged the conclusion that his standing in the present company wouldn't be boosted by a scene; that what was needed was a quick getaway. Only curiosity held him back.

'I'm puzzled,' he said. 'What am I missing?'

I held the smile. Held the tray. 'You don't want to know, James.'

His eyebrows went up. Understanding. Seeing the potential scene.

'Got it,' he said. 'Most interesting. I must have a word with Peter.'

But getting away was his priority. I didn't stop him.

He turned and coaxed his wife onwards and the line of revellers took their cue and moved away up the steps. Devonshire didn't look back. He'd have his word with Peter all right – he'd enjoy prodding the bastard with this little firecracker – but only from a safe distance.

I turned to continue down.

Then another group caught my eye. Four men and five women drinking and laughing on the lawn just twenty yards away.

One of them was Kim.

CHAPTER FORTY-FIVE
Change of plan

I stopped as if I'd run into a wall. Stared at the hallucination.

But the hallucination didn't fade. Held solid until the world flipped and a new version of reality locked in.

Kim hadn't seen me. She was leaning in to talk to a guy her age across the group's animated chatter, wearing an off-the-shoulder blue dress and blue heels. And she didn't look like a kidnap victim at all.

Same lovely face. Different world.

I fought shock. Beat it.

The best weapon is surprise, and when it's used against you the best defence is speed. You accept the new situation. Don't waste time with what-ifs and how-comes. Accept the new reality.

The new reality was that I'd been taken for an idiot. That Kim had been playing me. That everything I'd thought I'd known was wrong.

The new reality was that no-one needed rescuing.

I opened the tac channel.

'Abort,' I said. 'Job cancelled.'

A brand new plan: get out. Ask questions later.

Then Kim turned and spotted me and her chin came up in shock. She stepped back from the group and her eyes tried to deliver a message, but out in the garden one of Lad's goons had raised his own head and was watching me and his mouth was moving. I saw Lad and another of his people turn their heads. Then all three were moving.

Kim stepped clear of the group but I didn't wait. I hopped back up the steps and pushed through the flow of waiters back into the house.

I strode across a grand entrance hall running two hundred feet back under a glass dome. Figures from another era stared from the panelled walls. Old family portraits retained by Covault as decoration. His own ancestry weren't up in oils.

My destination was the Smart, out by the back steps. But halfway across the hall two men appeared to block me. I diverted left. Pulled at a door and came through to a tennis court sized lounge. Broke into a jog. If I could get out into the park they'd have lost me.

A door in the far side of the room got me into a corridor running past a small stairway. If there was any symmetry to the house the corridor would dog-leg beyond the stairs and I'd be out.

Then a door opened ahead and a big guy bundled out swinging a cosh. I hit him hard in the solar plexus. Follow-up with a right hander to his nose and a left to his temple which stopped him. The cosh splintered woodwork and he went down. I hopped free and round the staircase and would have made it if the door up ahead wasn't locked. By the time I'd backtracked another guy had come running from the lounge room and a third was walking down the stairs. The cosh guy was almost back on his feet.

Two guys on your level or one above you.

My level.

I charged to gain the advantage and Cosh went down again but the guy behind him stepped away from me. The guy was Lad. Lad's tactics were smarter. He lifted a gun.

I stopped.

'Is that legal?' I said.

Lad held the gun steady. I half turned to assess my chances with the stair guy. But he'd stopped five steps up. I wouldn't get to him fast enough to dodge Lad's bullet. I turned back.

'That will make a hell of a bang,' I said.

Lad smiled. 'A big one. But no-one will notice. Just a single bullet in your thigh to stop your antics. Your choice, Flynn.'

He waited.

I chose. Deferred offensive action.

Lad stepped forward and kicked the cosh guy. Gestured to the man on the stairs.

'Take him up,' he said. He stepped across and brought the gun closer. Raised it. The distance was irrelevant but the psychological kick was impressive. The gun's barrel looked a mile wide and it looked like it might go off at any second and Lad looked like he didn't care if it did. The music played on outside.

The guy came down the stairs and raised a nasty looking Taser pistol. No more legal than Lad's gun but quieter. Lad stepped over and pulled my mike and ear bud free and threw them down. Then he stepped away and Taser came out and motioned me up the stairs. I went. Lad followed, talking to his people.

We climbed to the top floor where Taser pointed me down a short corridor to an attic room filled with junk and a table and a few kitchen chairs. Lad followed us in, still talking into his mike, and Cosh eventually rolled up behind him and parked himself beside the door. He gave me a look filled with promises.

'Sit down,' Lad said. His gun had disappeared and Taser re-holstered his weapon.

I remained standing.

'C'mon. Sit!' Lad said. 'We need to wait.'

'Standing is fine,' I said.

'Have it your way,' Lad said.

He pulled one of the chairs out and sat down himself, leaning forward, arms on his thighs.

'What are we waiting for?'

'Mr Covault wants a word.'

'He's already had a word. I thought our chat was over.'

Lad looked at me. His aviator's glasses obscured his eyes but his mouth slanted. 'You and me both,' he said. 'But Mr Covault is the boss.'

I unfastened the waistcoat and threw it onto the table.

'What does Covault want to talk about that we couldn't have covered over canapés and bubbly?'

'He'll explain,' Lad said. 'Meantime I'd like to know how many friends you've brought with you.'

'You pay people to find that out,' I said. 'Get them out on the park. It must be dull standing round watching the knobs getting drunk.'

'It is. But this is urgent. I'm not comfortable with the idea of your people in here.'

'Correct me if I'm wrong,' I said. 'But wasn't this your game?'

'Yes. I wanted you here. Necessity. And I was hoping you'd come alone, maybe two of you. I'd still like to think that's the case.'

'Let's see what your guys find.'

'There are two of you at least,' Lad said. 'You've a guy in the stables neutralising our surveillance.'

I didn't correct him. The less accurate Lad's information the better. And now that the adrenaline rush was over I was back at the picture of Kim partying out there. I was sifting the new realities. First reality: Kim had set me up. Lured me to this phoney rescue so Lad could get his hands on me. And I'd fallen for it on the back of the phoney feelings we'd shared. I've been turned down by a few women but never turned over. I thought about the flame that had sprung from nothing. But someone as beautiful as Kim can light a fire whenever they want and the sucker they're burning won't know a thing until the water's thrown on to souse the thing into a smoking mess. I'd have kicked myself for not being smarter but it would be pointless. If you're smart that way you'll spend your whole life hiding. Still, it felt as if I'd been kicked by *someone*.

I pushed the thought aside. Immediate priority was finding why Covault had brought me here. Why it needed the charade. Maybe when we had our chat it would all make sense. Maybe it wouldn't. Nothing had up to now.

We waited five minutes. Then Covault arrived.

~~~~~

His carnation was still fresh but he was breathing heavily and his big, wide, ugly face was flustered.

I'd have put his discomfort down to his sudden teleportation from the arm of the bride but since this was his show I guess it was just the climb up the stairs.

Johnny Lad jumped up and pushed his guys out and Covault slammed the door on them then rounded on Lad.

'You've got to be kidding,' he said. 'Here? Today?'

So maybe not Covault's show.

'He's an enterprising guy,' Lad said. 'I did warn you not to underestimate him.'

'I didn't underestimate him,' Covault said. 'Specifically, I said he was a bloody dangerous bastard. And I told you to fix it, John.'

'That's what I'm doing.'

'No: private investigators running round the park on my niece's wedding day is not fixing things. We're going to talk about this.'

'It's almost over,' Lad repeated. 'Here. Today. We can sort this out.'

'Yes.' Covault finally turned to look at me but he was still speaking to Lad. 'We *are* going to sort it. Here and now. Mr Flynn...,' he cracked a smile: 'You're a damn persistent guy. You're causing all kinds of problems.' He threw up his hands and laughed. 'Okay,' he said, 'you win.'

I didn't feel like a winner. What I felt was that I'd just lost the world. What I felt was that I knew less now than I did when I crashed the gate. If there was a winner's prize it was well wrapped. I was probably beginning to look a little flustered myself but it was all anger.

'Tell me why I'm here,' I said.

'It's the same as yesterday,' Covault said. 'I want you to stop chasing after documents and looking for murderers.'

'And the answer's not changed.'

Covault pushed himself up onto the table beside me which blocked Johnny Lad from my view. A psychological thing. My world was Covault, a tux, a carnation. Schemes and emotions and power smouldering in his eyes.

'Think about it,' he repeated. 'What have you got?'

'We've got a document that's going to blow your floatation sky high,' I said. 'We've got evidence that says you or your people – specifically Mr Lad over there – killed a private investigator in an attempt to reach whoever was blackmailing your company about the document. And we've got evidence that your step-son was involved in the extortion with an accomplice called Coates. You remember Mr Coates? Well the funny thing is that he's suddenly dead too, and that one's on Barclay.'

Now Covault seemed perplexed. But he X-rayed me. Held back a moment whilst he searched for the right levers. Finally started pulling.

'You're deluded, my friend,' he said. 'You haven't got the document and you haven't got anything on the P.I.'s death because it was an accident. And rehashed accusations about my step-son don't add up to anything. Barclay's just a little prick. He hasn't the gumption to extort my company, much less murder anyone. We checked him out. You've got the wrong man.'

'Tell that to the police. They'll be checking Barclay themselves this evening. Barclay was involved in the extortion along with Jeremy Coates. Until they had some kind of falling out. Now Coates is dead. Stick your head in the sand all you like, Peter, it won't change a thing.'

Covault took another moment. Stared at me. Eventually spoke.

'You're right about Jeremy Coates. He has taken us for a small fortune. But let's quit this "dead" nonsense. The man has run off to spend his winnings.'

I looked towards Johnny Lad. A reflexive reaction. Lad was still hidden behind Covault, but I'd have liked to see his face. Maybe Covault believed what he said but Johnny Lad knew for sure that Sam Barker hadn't driven himself into that pond and I was suddenly wondering how much he knew about Barclay Brent and Jeremy Coates. Because something wasn't fitting.

'Now you know it all,' Covault said. 'Coates was extorting us over the document and we paid him off. That's the end of it. All the other stuff is make believe.'

'You're forgetting that there's a copy of the document still out there,' I said. 'It was Coates' insurance policy. Which is about to pay off. When the document sees light of day your floatation will be history.'

Covault's eyes slitted up. It was like looking at a reptile.

'The document will never see light of day,' he said. 'We recovered it this morning from Mr Langlois.'

I grinned. Should have guessed.

'Your hired help tipped you off,' I said. 'She's good, by the way. Fed you everything whilst she had me tied up in a Mills and Boon. Is Kim her real name or did she prefer to be phoney through and through?'

Covault looked at me.

'Her real name is Avril,' he said. 'Avril Covault. My daughter. And for the record I don't approve of that kind of subterfuge.'

'I'll bet you don't. But that's the point: you don't need to approve of anything as long as the job gets done.'

Covault didn't rise to the bait.

'Avril may be a little wilful but she's smart,' he said. 'Smart enough to get what she wanted from Langlois.'

I'll bet.

'Is Langlois still in one piece?' I said.

'Of course. He didn't want to hand over the report but Avril explained that she was with you so he obliged with a view of the document – to take the photographs you'd suggested. Then Avril got rid of him for thirty seconds and swapped the document with a dummy she'd taken along for the purpose. A copy of the Tatler, I don't doubt. She's fond of the magazine. Your Mr Langlois isn't such a bright spark.'

Which made a few of us. I held the grin. It was making my face ache more than the thumps but I kept it there.

Covault's daughter.

I needed to keep up with the social scene. You never know whom you'll be dating next. My grin turned real for a moment as I pictured Lucy's face if I'd actually turned up with Kim. Lucy would have recognised her in a flash. That would have been a scene worth witnessing. But Avril Covault was never going to turn up. The one risk she'd taken was approaching me the first time. But once she was through the door without being recognised she was safe. If Lucy had been in the office her scheme of leeching onto me would have died. And if Lucy had recognised her from the Foxglove street photo it would have died. But a face in a telephoto street shot isn't the same as a technicolour in the Tatler. Without context and quality Foxglove's subject could have been any woman. If anyone should have smelled a rat it was me when I walked into that Mayfair mansion. A successful businesswoman might work up to a cosy pad in town but just how cosy? Because Mayfair is as cosy as it comes.

Covault broke into my thoughts.

'Things are not the same as yesterday,' he said. 'Yesterday you were tilting at windmills but there was the risk you'd dig out something that would embarrass us. Today you've nothing. The extortion is over. There's no more document out there. And no proof that anything untoward ever happened – neither the extortion nor your imaginary murders.'

He pushed himself off the table. He was a big guy. He still spoke from four inches advantage.

'Flynn,' he said. 'You're a bright guy. Come and work for me sometime. But let's drop this wild goose chase. This is a plea from me. And to show my appreciation I'm happy to propose a more apposite remuneration. Yesterday's offer was paltry in the light of all the tricks we've played on you. Agree to end this now and I'll have a cheque for one million pounds in your hand tomorrow morning.'

He looked at me. His eyes gilded the offer.

'A million pounds,' he repeated. 'That's how important it is to me to keep the boat steady. A bargain price to protect my company. What do you say, Flynn? Have we got a deal?'

The furnace glowed. I felt the heat, the power of a guy who can throw a million quid at you on a whim. A guy who always gets his way.

'No,' I said. 'We've no deal.'

He stared back. The furnace burned. His cheeks were actually red. Didn't look healthy.

'Whether or not the document gets out and torpedoes your floatation is fine by me,' I said. 'But my concern is the two dead men – one of them a result of your actions, Peter – and a million pounds doesn't start to cover it. So we're going to get the evidence that ties you and Lad and Barclay to the bodies and you can float your company from a jail cell.'

Covault remained motionless. Watched me without reaction. Finally his lips moved.

'A million pounds, Flynn. Walk away with a million pounds or walk away with nothing but hunches and rumours and a wild goose chase. Take a breath, Flynn. Think about it.'

I was taking all the breaths I could with the hulking bastard looming over me. And I'd had enough of the stink.

'No deal, Peter. Keep your money.'

Covault stood back. Embellished his theme.

'Persist with this,' he said, 'and we'll stamp on you with everything we've got. Just put one toe over the line and your firm is out of business. We've people to do that.'

I didn't ask whether he was referring to the people who worked through lawsuits or the ones with coshes. I kept quiet until he got my point and the two of us shared the nice little exemplar: when you've got the power details don't matter. Things just get done.

'I think we're through,' I said. I made to step round Covault but he blocked me.

'Take twenty-four hours,' he said. 'Come and talk to me.'

He turned and walked out.

I grinned at Lad.

'I don't know how much he knows,' I said, 'but I guess it's as much as you want him to. But you know it all, Johnny. And you're right in the crosshairs.'

Lad said nothing. Put his head out to call his people back in.

I'd had enough of the party. I walked to the door.

'Flynn,' Lad said.

I waited.

'You know too much.'

'I guess I do,' I said.

That's when the crack sounded from the corridor and wire darts pierced my shirt and put me down on my back with fifty thousand volts contracting my muscles. The pain was off the scale. I didn't go out but my vision dimmed and when I tried to roll over my muscles didn't cooperate. Then the pain stopped and Lad was pulling me up, arms behind me, clipping my wrists with a plastic tie. Then they walked me to a chair. My limbs were working again but the barbs were still in and Lad's guy still had his finger on the trigger. I sat down.

Lad produced more ties and got my arms and legs secured to the chair.

'You think you can talk me round to that million?' I said.

'There is no million,' Lad said. 'The offer's withdrawn. All Peter needs to know is that you won't be bothering him again.'

See?

Things get done.

Another tidying up operation was about to start.

CHAPTER FORTY-SIX
He's had you bite off more than he can chew

Lad sent his men out. I tested the bindings. They were pretty good. I wasn't going anywhere without the chair.

'What's the plan?' I said. 'Have you found another lake?'

Lad came over. Squatted.

'Who is working with you on this?' he asked.

'I'll check the records,' I told him. 'Let you know.'

'Is there another copy of the report?'

'That's my secret,' I said.

'Of course,' Lad said. He stood. Twisted from the middle and smashed a backhand fist across my cheek. I went down sideways with a crash. The blow was to my right side. Balanced the clout I'd taken in the stables. I'd have two rosy cheeks tomorrow, taking the optimistic view.

Lad levered the chair back up and got me back on four legs.

'That's my plan,' he said. 'To get those answers.'

'Sounds risky,' I said. 'I've got a hell of a scream.'

Lad smiled. 'And I've got a hell of a quiet cellar on the other side of the estate.'

'Attacking fire with gasoline doesn't work,' I said. 'Conscripting my firm when we said no; killing Sam Barker. Bad ideas, both of them.'

'Granted I'd have been better off not dragging you into this,' Lad said. 'But I learn from mistakes. I cancel them.'

'This one isn't cancellable.'

'We'll see.'

'So you squeeze the information out of me and have me disappear, then... Well: then you have to make other people disappear.'

'I'm assuming that the only ones who really know anything are you and the P.I.'s sister. One or two others at the most.'

'Does Covault know what you're planning? Will he have to dredge up a denial about me?'

'He'll have nothing to deny.'

'Which is what makes him such a slimy bastard. He didn't know about Sam Barker, did he? He just knew that his problem went away.'

'A necessity of business. There are always things that need sorting out without exposing a company every reality.'

'Like I say: slimy. But Covault's had you bite off more than he can chew this time.'

'Of necessity. He had a potential disaster brewing.'

'And you're his clean-up guy.'

Lad stood and leaned back against the table. Studied me, calculating how far this clean-up was going to stretch him.

Then he turned.

Avril Covault – aka Kim Waters – had just walked in. She still looked stunning in her off-the-shoulder dress but her face said she was no longer in a party mood. It dropped further when she saw me, something like pain in her eyes, but I'd seen a few things in her face over the last week, none of them real.

'What are you doing?' She asked Lad.

'We're discussing how to bring this to an end,' Lad said. 'Your father had the idea of a handsome payment but it's not going to work. Things are a little beyond that.'

'How?'

'Scraps from the table aren't going to divert our friend here.'

I grinned at Avril, looking for any sign that Lad's sub-text had registered. Lad was happy to kill on the company's behalf but he would never sit at the table. He'd be sitting below it like a dog, observing the millions they threw around as lubrication. Lad's voice said it all. The company would be paying him a nice retainer but the cash was always tainted by the knowledge that it was all pin money for people like the woman in front of him.

Avril was still watching me. She took in the plastic ties and the blood on my cheek and looked like she was about to say something then pulled herself straight. Turned to Lad.

'Give us a moment,' she said.

Lad smiled and walked out. Avril pushed the door closed then came across and squatted to my level.

'Eddie,' she said. 'I'm so sorry. For everything. This shouldn't have happened. We just need you to give us a break on this.'

'Or what? I go the same way as Sam Barker?' I gave her a leer that would have been impossible yesterday.

'Please,' she said. 'We've been put into an intolerable situation. The survival of the company is at stake. Just one rumour, one false story, and our whole future is in jeopardy.'

'Got it. And you need to kill anyone who might leak that rumour.'

Avril's eyes widened. She stood up and shook her head like she was shaking off fleas or a nightmare.

'It was all a terrible mistake,' she said. 'Johnny picked up the wrong signals and overstepped his remit. My father was furious when he heard what happened to Sam Barker.'

'Your father told me ten minutes ago that he didn't believe Sam was murdered. How does that tie in with furious? And did *I* pick up the wrong signal when you walked into my office?'

'I'm sorry, Eddie. That was unforgivable. We were panicking. We needed you to help us find Sam. Then later when Johnny realised that you weren't walking away he convinced me that I needed to stay in contact, somehow push you back.'

'Stay in contact? Is that what we were doing?' I grinned. 'You played me for a fool with that romance routine. But I won't deny it: you were good. Lying and acting are naturals for you.'

'There was no act, Eddie. There is none now. My feelings are genuine.'

My grin stretched. 'So are mine. Remorse and disappointment. But mostly embarrassment. They're all genuine.'

'I've betrayed you,' she said. 'I know how you feel.'

'Spoken by a true repentant. What do you want?'

'However this all started it's brought us together, Eddie. I don't want that to change.'

My grin held solid. Lucky I was tied. I'd have collapsed in a swoon. Avril eyed the bindings.

'Let's get you loose,' she said. 'Johnny's gone too far again. If he's hurt you...' She was looking at my cheek, which must have looked impressive. And there was no *if* about it.

'It's nothing,' I said. Ever the tough guy.

'I'd give anything to have had this not happen,' Avril said. 'All except meeting you, Eddie. That has felt so right. Please believe me.'

'I do believe you,' I said. 'And maybe you believe it yourself. But I need to be up front here: I don't date women who think they're above normal conventions, who play power games that get people killed. So get me free then we'll talk about things.'

Then the door opened and Johnny Lad came back in.

'Our ride's ready,' he said. 'You lovebirds patch things up?'

'Cut him free,' Avril said. 'What the hell are you thinking?'

'I'm thinking that we need to take this guy somewhere for a little talk.'

'By "talk" you mean beat him half to death? My father has made him an offer. He wants him to consider that offer. Let him go.'

'No can do, ma'am. Not until we've talked.'

'That wasn't a request.'

Lad lifted a lip. 'I work for your father, remember?'

'If you work for one of us you work for all of us,' Avril said. 'And if you ever want to work for this company again you'll do as I say.'

'Sorry,' Lad said. 'If your father wants to let this guy go he can tell me himself.'

'You know he wouldn't condone harming Eddie.'

'He wouldn't want to know. Not the same thing.'

'Damnit! Free Eddie now or I *will* bring my father back. And his patience will have worn thin. We've had enough of your games, Johnny.'

'Not going to happen. Go and talk to your father. Flynn is taking a ride with us, meantime.'

Avril looked at him. Clamped her lips. Anger smouldered across her face.

'I'll talk to him,' she said. 'Then we're going to find another way to run our security affairs. I won't cover for any more of your criminal acts, Johnny.'

Lad smiled. Cold but full of the humour of the thing. 'You don't need to cover for me, Avril,' he said. 'You can just turn a blind eye, the same as you've always done.'

Avril looked at me.

'Leave this with me, Eddie,' she said. 'I'll sort it out. This isn't how it's meant to be.'

'Well,' I said, 'I suspect it is. I agree with Johnny here. Your father won't want to know.'

Avril's look broadcast fear. She made a decision. Turned and left.

Lad watched the doorway for a few seconds then came over.

'Truly and honestly,' he said, 'I never know when it's an act. Does she really want to save your skin or just convince herself that she's done her best?' He stooped and smiled. 'What do you think, Flynn?'

'Fuck you,' I said.

CHAPTER FORTY-SEVEN
An accident waiting to happen

Lad cut me free but left my wrists tied. Cosh and Taser came back in and grabbed an arm each and marched me down the stairs and out through a side door to a boxy little Suzuki four by four. They folded the front seat and pushed me into the back. Cosh squeezed in next to me. Leaned to stare me out. The blood from his busted nose enhanced his stare. If he'd been wearing a Rambo headband I'd have been scared. Then his stare creased into a smile. He was thinking ahead to guard duty.

Lad jumped into the passenger seat and Taser took the wheel and we rolled out along a path that ran alongside the gardens. A hedgerow blocked the party from view but the music came through nicely. I pictured Avril over there, talking to her father.

The back of the Suzuki was a sardine can. I didn't know whether Cosh was trying to crush me to death or asphyxiate me with his body odour but one of them was going to finish me if this was a long trip. He was still watching me.

'Later,' he said.

Then the hedge dropped away and the party burst out in full colour. Guests, waiters, marquee and orchestra. The thing was continuing as if nothing was happening, the guests oblivious of the Suzuki crawling down the path away from the house. Another little allegory for the workings of Covault's businesses.

Johnny Lad turned his head to watch. I wondered what he was seeing.

Then hell broke loose.

The Suzuki braked, throwing me and Cosh against the front seats, which is uncomfortable with your hands tied, and dangerous with sixteen stones bouncing around. I strained clear and saw what had planted Taser's foot on the brake. Fifty yards away a John Deere tractor with a lowered front loader was steaming through the party. It angled between the orchestra stage and the marquee in a flurry of leaping guests and spilled drinks. Almost got through but then its rear tyre took out the corner of the stage which went down. The

233

music squealed to a stop. The Deere continued, cornered the marquee but misjudged that too. Tension ropes were ripped free and the tent sagged and sank as the tractor ploughed on.

Towards us.

Guests were running all ways and the security guys were holding their buds and yelling and Johnny Lad's ear bud was squawking alarm.

The tractor accelerated.

Up in the cab a big black guy was riding the controls like an F-16 in a power dive. His eyes were on us and his hands held the wheel on target.

Fifty yards had become thirty then twenty before Lad saw where this was going. He screamed a Go-Go-Go! at the driver but Taser's foot slipped and the Suzuki kangarooed and stalled and it was over. We were dead meat. Tractor incoming at range zero.

The crash was cataclysmic and painful as the loading forks slid under the 4x4 and pushed us half off the ground. But then the Deere stopped in a roar of diesel and things would have been okay if the forks hadn't lifted and rolled us right over.

I took Cosh's full weight, which would have been deadly if we hadn't kept rolling, first onto the roof then onto the vehicle's smashed side. We came to a stop with the driver's door up and me atop Cosh.

Lucky break.

Pandemonium ruled inside the Suzuki.

Lad was yelling at Taser who'd fallen on top of him and Taser was trying to twist free to get his hands on the driver's door but was mostly just landing kicks in Lad's face and neither was getting anywhere. Then the door popped and Taser accelerated upwards like an alien abduction and was gone. Lad unwound himself and grabbed for the door frame with his gun in his hand but then he took off too. Disappeared into a din of smacks and curses. The din stopped and the Suzuki was peaceful for five seconds. Then it rocked and rolled and Bernie Locke's ugly face came grinning into the cabin and his beefsteak arms were folding the driver's seat to pull me out. I could have got myself out but that's Bernie: Action Man. Maybe the Suzuki was about to explode or something. I didn't know. I was hauled out as forcibly as Lad and Taser except that Bernie set me onto my feet instead of planting a fist, which had been the other guys' landing experience. Lad was crawling towards his gun but Bernie stepped across and grabbed it, then leaned back into the car and flipped the driver's seat back to keep Cosh inside.

I stepped back, winded, hurting like hell where my tied arms had been crushed beneath me and Cosh. I was in one piece but that was about it. I looked at Bernie.

'Jesus Christ,' I said.

Bernie checked the safety and pushed the gun into his waistband. Grinned.

'Sorry pal,' he said. 'Blame John Deere. Why the hell they put the loader lever right next to the gears I can't imagine. You've got an accident right there waiting to happen.'

'He's got a knife,' I said. I gestured at Lad who was kneeling to take the air. It wasn't a warning. I wanted the ties off before any more accidents happened. Bernie helped Lad upright. Lad tensed, working out angles and timings, but Bernie said '*Don't*, matey' and something got through. Lad was bleeding but he still had sense. He pulled his knife out and reversed it. A good sign. No concussion.

Bernie took the knife and freed my wrists and I massaged my arms. The left one was hurting like crazy. I suspected a pulled muscle. Bernie spotted my face and grinned, the way he used to after he'd accidentally bounced a cricket ball off my head. I'd been hospitalised twice because of this guy. How his leadership seminar execs ever escaped alive I'd never figured.

We turned to watch the wedding party drifting towards us like stragglers from a plane crash. Three of Lad's men held the vanguard, unaware of Shaughnessy and Harry closing fast behind them. Lad's people came round the tractor looking for trouble but Johnny saw how it was and told them to stand down. He didn't recognise Shaughnessy or Harry but he knew they weren't on the guest list. Saw enemy in strength. Got the picture that the intruders were comfortable whichever way things went. And his choices, without his gun and with Bernie Locke standing at his shoulder and with Peter Covault storming across the grass, were limited.

Covault came up and looked at Johnny with his mouth wide. No words came out. Lad's firm had a single job today which was to make sure that everything went off smoothly, and Covault's look said they'd be talking money-back arrangements. He looked fit to explode. It took a moment to pull things together then he turned with a mask smile to urge the party-goers to return to the main lawn. Everything was fine. Everything was under control. The crowd didn't look convinced but they started drifting back.

Covault watched them go. Turned back. His voice was controlled but his face was pale. Apparently the tractor and marquee weren't his only worry.

'We're wanted inside,' he told me. 'You too, Johnny.'

He turned and walked away.

Lad watched him for a moment then stepped round Bernie and followed across the lawn.

I grinned at the crew. My arm was hurting like hell.

'Looks like the real party's about to start,' I said.

~~~~~

Some party.

We were in a panelled drawing room hung with riding and hunting portraits. Out beyond the windows the orchestra had started up again. The Titanic was re-floating. The guests were disappearing into the stabilised marquee with something to chat about over their wedding breakfast.

There were seven of us in the room.

Me, Peter Covault, Johnny Lad and Barclay Brent.

Plus DS Keith Prior and another plain clothes guy.

And Yvonne Barker.

Johnny Lad looked tense. Barclay looked scared. Covault looked like he was about to tear the place down. God knew what I looked like.

Prior talked and we got updated.

Yvonne had taken him to Jeremy Coates' body whilst we were planning our assault on Covault's party. He'd hiked in to the airshaft and seen what was there and called his people in. Once the scene was secure he'd come straight here. His shoes were a mess.

Intro over, first things first. Prior arrested Johnny Lad on suspicion of the murder of Sam Barker. Lad's face was expressionless as the notion sank in that he'd walked into a trap, but he went along with the formalities, computing the odds on Prior having anything that would stick.

After the formalities Prior's pal escorted Lad out and Prior came over to me. Looked at me. Took in the bruises and a cut on my temple that I'd just discovered.

'I ought to arrest you too,' he said, but he said it quietly. Here wasn't the time. 'You were sitting on that body for two days.'

The claim was figurative but his eyes conveyed meaning: 'You need to come back right now and go through it,' he told me. 'Are we clear?' The DS had the face of a bank manager but a mask of steel.

I said I was clear.

But neither Johnny Lad nor I were the main reason for the little gathering.

The main reason was the guy staring Prior down when he turned away from me. Prior started to speak but Peter Covault struck first.

'There'll be consequences, Sergeant' he said. 'Mr Lad has no idea what you're accusing him of and you couldn't have picked a worse day for this bungled intrusion.'

Prior stayed placid.

'We don't investigate crime on an appointments basis,' he said. 'We've a dead body in the woods near here that looks like foul play. And I've reason to connect the death with the murder of an investigator called Sam Barker. I'll be talking to Mr Lad about that this afternoon. But I'd like to know what you and Mr Brent here know about both of the victims.'

'Absolutely nothing,' Covault said. 'This is folly. You've just wrecked a wedding, detective. And you've embarrassed me and my family. So be very careful what you do or say.'

'I will, sir,' Prior said. 'And I apologise for the intrusion. But I need statements from you and Mr Brent. Do I have your cooperation?'

'Certainly,' Covault said. 'Will tomorrow suffice?'

'It won't,' Prior said. 'We need to go in to Bromley now. With luck we'll only detain you for a few hours.'

'And if we *don't* like?'

'Then I have sufficient suspicion to take Mr Brent in under arrest. And yourself too, if you obstruct the investigation.'

'Arrest me,' Covault said, 'and you'll have a chief constable breathing down your neck before we get to the station.'

'As you wish. But save your threats, sir. We're going to get this done however we play it.'

He tilted his head, first in my direction then at the window.

'What kind of a wedding party is this? It looks more like a war out there.'

'Mr Flynn has committed a gross trespass,' Covault said. 'We were trying to smooth that over without involving the police.'

'Mr Flynn is already involved with us. And his information suggests that your company is involved in misdemeanours linked to two murders. Is he correct?'

'No.'

'Good,' Prior said. 'I'd like you to explain that to me back at Bromley.'

But Covault wasn't cooperating. 'Arrest me if you've got cause,' he said. 'Otherwise I'm not available this afternoon.'

Prior thought about it. Pulled back.

'Okay, Mr Covault,' he said. 'I'll talk to you later.' He looked at Barclay. 'But I need to talk to you right now. Can I expect your cooperation? Or must we take the formal route?'

Barclay said nothing. Cooperation, I guess.

'We've a warrant to seize your vehicle,' Prior continued. 'Do you have alternative transport?'

Barclay didn't answer.

'Good,' Prior said. 'So: I'd like to see Messrs Brent and Flynn at Bromley police station in one hour. You too, Ms Barker. Mr Covault: I may be back later.'

'Pray you aren't,' Covault said.

'I do,' Prior said. He turned and walked out. Yvonne followed.

Covault and Barclay looked at each other then looked at me. I grinned.

If I'd been Prior I'd have arrested the lot of them. Made sure they turned up at Bromley. Barclay was still stunned and trying to catch up, wondering if it was time to run. With me in the room he and Covault weren't going to discuss it but once I'd gone they'd agree their story which would be basically be that no-one knew anything. Mouths would be zipped.

It wouldn't be enough.

CHAPTER FORTY-EIGHT
Tower of Terror

In the event, I was the one who didn't show, which had to be blowing up a shitstorm of bad karma at Bromley and maybe a coronary for Prior. But Prior had Barclay Brent tied up for a few hours and it was an opportunity I couldn't ignore.

I wanted hard evidence to link Brent to Coates' death, and his apartment might be the place to find it. If I dug something up it would give Prior ammunition for his investigation, and the fact that I'd gone in uninvited wouldn't be his problem.

Harry followed me back into town. Traffic was heavy but it was moving the other way. We were walking down Jermyn Street barely seventy minutes after we left Covault's estate. We stopped and looked up. Harry shook his head.

'I'm living the life inside one of the planet's richest families,' he said, 'I'm living up *there,* I'm not going to feel the need to rip people off.'

But Barclay *had* felt the need. Maybe we'd find out why. Or maybe the explanation would stay inside the family. What wasn't going to stay inside was Barclay throwing Jeremy Coates down that airshaft.

And the other thing that was going come out was the Singapore document. It would only take rumours and there'd be subpoenas out for the report. If the liabilities were not in the company books as they flogged their shares then we were looking at major fraud. The whole nest would be turned over. And the investors would be running for the hills. Peter Covault was in for a rough ride.

But Harry was right. The real puzzle was why Barclay had been ripping off the company. And why he'd killed Coates. I could dream up answers to explain the murder – someone getting greedy or scared, someone changing their minds and threatening the scheme so that Barclay had no choice but to have Coates disappear. I could dream of a dozen explanations. But the guy living up in this penthouse wasn't a ruthless killer. And Brent had been ringing Coates' Bexhill doorbell *after* he'd supposedly killed him. So maybe he didn't. And maybe something in this building would explain it all.

We walked underground and took the lift to the floor below Barclay's penthouse. Harry could have beaten the key panel and taken us on up but it would have taken half an hour. We opted for the faster route. The lift stopped and Harry gave me a leg up and I pushed the roof panel open. The panels provide emergency egress when lifts get stuck between floors and the fire brigade has to shimmy down the shaft. Unlike in the movies, lifting the panel cuts the power and clamps the brakes. You're not going to take a Tower of Terror ride whilst you're up on the roof.

I heaved myself up and crouched in the dark atop the lift. Keyed my phone torch and illuminated the lower step of the penthouse floor at chest height. I planted the phone and grabbed the door supports and pulled myself up to stand tip-toe against the metal where I could reach up to the release latch. Ten seconds later I slid the door open and retrieved my phone. Leaned over and looked into the lift. Empty. Harry had already headed for the stairs. I dropped the escape hatch back into place and climbed out into the penthouse and slid the door closed. The lift's power came back. Ready to go.

I checked my shirt and slacks. They were history. The grease and dirt smudges weren't going to come out. At least I wasn't wearing my good jacket, which was hanging safely on its peg in Covault's mansion. Maybe one of the staff would find it a good fit.

I was in a foyer of marble and bright wood panelling mottled with sunlight from an impressive floor-to-ceiling window. The window gave a partial view of the city between the neighbouring buildings. If the penthouse had been two floors higher the view would have been truly impressive.

I walked round and unlatched the stair door to let Harry in. Pointed him at the alarm panel. He carried his bag across. Came straight back.

'Not set,' he said. 'The guy must have good insurance.'

We walked into a lounge walled on three sides with glass. Took a moment to admire the view. The view of the city was still restricted but the roof garden was a blaze of spring flowers. Seemed Barclay had a good gardener flown in.

Harry shook his head again.

'I still don't see it,' he said.

We went through the apartment wearing latex gloves, careful to keep things tidy, unsure what we were looking for. Maybe a phone or computer or a dodgy bank account or threatening letter from Coates. Concentration took effort with all those picture windows. We weren't high enough to see the river but you could stand there all day watching the London rooftops. And Barclay hadn't skimped on internal decoration. Glossy wooden floors everywhere, parquet and patterned tiles, wood panelling and carpet-grade wallpapers, gilded mirrors.

It took nearly two hours but we got three things.

The first was a printed ticket receipt and itinerary for Jeremy Coates' trip to Singapore. It was nothing we didn't know but the purchaser had been Barclay. He was linked solidly to the trip.

The second was paperwork from four overseas bank accounts. Two in Switzerland, one in the Caymans, one in Bahrain. No statements or balances but the accounts would interest the tax man. And if Barclay had just extorted the company then the cash was in one or more of those accounts. The company floatation had been targeted at one point two billion. And Covault had tried to throw a million at me like confetti. So an extortion payoff might be anywhere between a million and, say, one or two percent of the one point two. That's a range of one to twenty-four million. And my guess said that Barclay would have aimed high. Say twenty million. Those overseas accounts would be bulging.

The third discovery was Barclay's laptop.

Harry couldn't get into the emails without a lot of work but he did find a downloaded document that detailed a six month rental on a villa in Barbados that had just been taken out. Harry went online and brought the property up. It was located just outside Bridgetown. A bungalow just off the main road with a small lawned garden and kidney pool shaded by palm trees. Harry smiled, thinking of his next holiday with the missus. The place looked damn nice. Problem was, it didn't look *billionaire* nice.

I looked at the promo pics for a while and then I got it. Closed up the computer and stood gazing out of the window, seeing a picture that finally made sense.

And we'd got the links that would let the police put it all together.

They'd be talking to Barclay at length over the next week and they'd come in here and tear the place apart. And if the paperwork was missing, which it would be, they'd fall back on the phone snaps we'd taken as we went through. And Qantas would back them up on the Singapore flight purchase.

Barclay Brent wasn't going to sanitise his link to Jeremy Coates.

Which meant he was linked solidly to the extortion.

My phone rang.

Lucy.

She'd been trawling through public info and talking to a contact of hers who was married to a guy who worked at Diamond Covault. She'd also had a call back from our society contact Philippa Scott who was the sales director of a firm that ran a few south-east regional newspapers and society magazines. We'd once helped Philippa with a family problem and her gratitude ran to the offer of occasional help with research.

'Barclay *did* extort the company,' Lucy said.

I'd known it.

Lucy explained and things locked into place. Barclay's conspiracy with Jeremy Coates made sense. And Peter Covault's assurances that Barclay was *not* the extorter made sense. And the six month Barbados rental made sense. And Jeremy Coates' dive down that tunnel airshaft made most sense of all.

When I talked to Prior – before or after he broke my door down – he'd have the whole picture. He'd have all the evidence and direction he needed to snag the guilty parties with a net that would hold up in court.

I told Lucy I'd see her tomorrow – assuming I wasn't holidaying in Bromley nick – and killed the call.

That's when a chime out in the hallway told us that the lift had arrived. Harry looked at me. Barclay Brent was back.

'Time for a chat,' I said.

The lift door opened and Barclay and his girlfriend came through and jumped a mile.

Barclay looked a little less dapper than he had at the estate. He was still wearing the dinner jacket and bow tie but his lapel had lost its carnation and his face had lost most of its colour and all of its assurance. He'd aged. The shell-shock that lined his face was there even before he spotted us.

He froze for two seconds then backed towards the lift.

'What the fuck,' he said.

'Barclay...' I said. I walked over. He kept backing. Pulled the girl with him. But the lift doors had already closed.

'Get the hell away,' he said. 'I'm calling the police.'

'Why bother?' I said. 'They'll be calling you tomorrow. I'm sure Prior told you that after your lawyer showed up.'

Barclay pulled out his phone. Looked at me.

'What are you doing in here?'

'You know who I am, at least,' I said.

'Of course, I know! You wrecked the damn wedding. You were at the club the other day.'

'So you noticed! Well if you'd paid closer attention, Barclay, you'd have known who I was right then.'

'What the hell do you want?'

The tremor in his voice was panic and fear. I grinned.

'I want to save your life,' I said.

CHAPTER FORTY-NINE
He's still going with Plan A

We told Brent's girlfriend to stay put and took him out into the garden. He still didn't know why we were here but he knew that more bad stuff was incoming. He was having a rough day.

Not as rough as me: no-one had driven a tractor at him. I sensed PTSD circling on that one. Maybe not tonight or tomorrow but the nightmares would come. I'd have a word with Bernie when we settled his fee but the bastard would just laugh and remind me that what doesn't kill you... etc etc., which is a fine adage unless the thing that doesn't kill you keeps coming back to try. By my count I was on my seventh near death experience with Bernie Locke in close proximity.

But I wasn't the only one thinking of death.

Barclay Brent had picked up on my "life saving" comment. Looked scared for the first time, though the fear had at least calmed him. I introduced Harry and we stood at the railings. I turned and leaned back against them and looked along the line of the building, up and down. A dizzying montage of clouds and ants. Must be good, living your life in the stratosphere, watching the suckers down in the street. Not so good when the building started to sway.

'What did you tell Prior?' I said.

'Nothing. If he wants to talk to me he'll go through my lawyer.'

'Prior knows most of it,' I said. 'You know that from his questions. And he'll tie things together pretty quickly. But Prior isn't your main concern.'

Barclay was watching the cityscape with his hands in his pockets, trying to claw back a little confidence. But he wasn't seeing the view. 'What do you mean?' he asked.

'If Johnny Lad squirms out of this he'll go back to Plan A. Which means he'll come for you.'

Barclay shook his head.

'Why would he come after me?'

I folded my arms. Looked sideways.

'Time to stop pretending,' I said. 'You know what I'm talking about. You just haven't appreciated the true peril of your situation.'

Brent looked at me. Gave me perplexed.

'You're a terrific actor, Barclay,' I said. 'And you've got nerve. Scamming the company from right in the centre. But if I'm right the centre hasn't been a comfortable place for the last couple of weeks. Did you think they'd not come after their money?'

Barclay continued his confused act. I gave up. Grinned at Harry.

'Why don't we just throw him off the roof,' Harry said. 'The idiot wants to commit suicide.'

I turned back to Barclay.

'Look at what we have, Barclay. Then you can decide whether you want to keep your neck on the chopping block, which is where it is right now.'

I took him through it. A mixture of hard evidence and speculation. But the speculation was solid.

'When your mother married Peter Covault you thought you'd hit the jackpot,' I said. 'What does a spoiled rich kid ever want other than to be more spoiled and more rich. When that ring went on your mother's finger you were floated from a world of public schools and night-clubs and bad-boy flashy pickups into the stratosphere of corporate jets and country clubs, yachts and penthouse apartments.'

Harry was watching the street, gripping the railings and thinking what the missus would say if *they* ever floated up here.

'But you never really belonged to Covault's world,' I said. 'Peter saw through you the moment he met you. You came with the package when he married your mother but he knew you'd never fit. Flashy cars and worsted suits don't fool sharks like Covault. He turns away ten like you every time he interviews for a tea boy.

'So you came with the package but you stayed peripheral. A notional company job where you couldn't do much harm and a token half mill. salary plus half the rental on this place as a company write-off. And access to a the special places where Covault's name is gold. I guess you don't feel so peripheral at the golf club, but that's because you never spot Covault's pals lifting their lips when you turn your back.

'And what's this place costing you? I'm guessing, after the company contribution, a quarter mill. a year with service charges.'

Barclay didn't enlighten me. I doubted if he knew the figure but his accountant was probably having a few sleepless nights.

'Then there's your running fees. All those club memberships and holidays in the sun and sports cars. Can't be leaving much from your net salary with Diamond Covault. And that's before we add in the gambling habit we just heard about. Life in the pressure cooker. As much stress as fun. And to top it all you get to see Peter Covault's dirty looks every time you open your mouth at one of his HQ management bashes. The guy's got no time for you. And stepson or not, he's waiting for the excuse to pull the rug from under you.'

I turned. Leaned to peer down from the parapet.

'Life on the edge, Barclay, wouldn't you say?'

I looked back.

Barclay pushed out his cheeks and shook his head. Said nothing. But you saw the pressure stretching his lily-white privileged skin tight.

'In summary you're not quite the company man the world believes. You show up at work and you show up for family shindigs and shoots but you're hanging by your fingers and you know it. Scraping around to make half a million a year stretch in a family that spends that much on a wedding party. And wondering when the rug is going to be pulled.

'Then there's the other company man, Jeremy Coates.'

An ambulance siren wailed down below. I watched blue lights ease pedestrians aside. The buildings channelled the din. A reminder that Barclay's pad was not, after all, in the clouds.

'You'd never heard of Coates before the Singapore problem,' I said.

I pushed myself away from the parapet. Barclay stayed put. Lacking animation. A shape moved behind the door glass across the garden. The girl, watching three silhouettes discussing more bad business to top the day's bad business, watching her dreams crumbling. She knew that Barclay had slid onto a steep slope today.

'Coates was one of Peter Covault's archetypal worker ants,' I said. 'The little guy who oils the company wheels. And Covault knew Jeremy's name even if he *was* a little guy working for an even smaller guy, because Peter makes it his business to know who the real talent is. Real talent doesn't sit in his boardroom. He doesn't want them anywhere they might get the full view. He needs them down in the basement where they can live with the contradiction between their value to the company and their own position of chasing crumbs from the table. Coates was one of Covault's key players, overseeing his projects, keeping the contractors in line, but he lived in a ground floor cage. Got around the contradiction by inflating his status with his pals, projecting himself as a big shot guiding Diamond Covault's global expansion. But reality was different. As different as it could be. Because Coates really was a key player whose expertise mattered when they were hiring and firing contractors, watching for tricks and short cuts, but at the same time he knew he'd never be let out of his cage, never earn a decent salary or gain a seat on the board where he could at least fire his own incompetent boss. Kind of sad: Jeremy could puff himself up with his pals but he never had the confidence to make waves inside the company. So Peter Covault knew him and nodded to him in corridors but Jeremy sensed that the day he stepped out of line he'd be on the dole.

'And finally it happened.'

'A contractor screwed up in Singapore,' Harry said. He was leaning over the drop.

'Ten years back,' I said. 'When Covault's Far East HQ, went up. The architect's design analysis for some kind of bracing system was flawed, and then dodgy materials got into the construction and Coates or his boss didn't spot any of it until two months ago when cracks and shifts told them that things weren't right. When Coates commissioned their Singapore consultants to take a look he probably still thought it was a routine check. Nothing to alarm Covault. But then the report came in and suddenly they had a disaster on their hands. The building had critical defects which were getting worse every day. All it would take would be the failure of a damper system – whatever that is – and the thing would topple in a storm. And even first-estimate repair costs were upwards of a billion. And that's when Coates found out his worth.'

I walked back to the railing. Faced Barclay.

He shrugged.

'Coates couldn't keep his mouth shut,' he said.

'Let me guess: Covault ordered the report pushed under the carpet until he'd run his floatation and grabbed the investors' cash but Coates wouldn't play along. Professional ethics. Maybe pride. Maybe part of it was that the order came from his boss who was toeing the company line without any concern for safety issues and stock market legality. Perhaps if Covault had buttered Coates up personally, bribed him with promotions and bonuses, he'd have gone along with the deception. We'll never know. Coates had never been corrupted by the concept of a real stake in the company.'

'Peter tried to talk to him,' Barclay said.

'But too late. He only collared Coates after the guy had dug his heels in and wrapped himself tight in his professional pride. He wouldn't go along with a cover-up, and Covault's response was a threat to shut up or pack his bags.'

Barclay smiled.

'I was there. Peter was usually smarter than that but Coates had already been sounding off, threatening to go public with the report. Peter didn't like the attitude. Lectured Coates about company loyalty and when Coates argued he lost patience and fired him. Peter's a piece of shit but he's usually a better judge of people.'

I jabbed my hands into my pockets. A breeze flicked at us through the buildings.

'Well that judgement was as bad as it gets,' I said. 'Self-proclaimed company guru Jeremy Coates says the wrong thing to the big guy and suddenly he's sitting shell-shocked in his Caterham lounge wondering where the local Job Centre is located. And that's when you spotted an opportunity.'

Brent turned to watch the view again. I waited until he looked at me.

'Here's how I see it: you contacted Jeremy. Persuaded him that the report had to see light of day. Safety and company ethics and all that.'

Barclay had something like a smile on his face. Regret, maybe. I looked across at Harry. He shook his head.

'Look at if from Coates' point of view,' Harry said. 'All those years thinking you're it and suddenly there you are, sitting at home in shock, seeing your real worth. Then your doorbell rings and it's one of the big guys, come to tell you that he's on your side, that you and he need to stop the caper and protect the company. Better to take the financial hit for the Singapore problem and hold on to integrity than go through the courts later as they try to dig out who knew what. The bigwig is sitting right there on your sofa explaining that you need to get your hands on a copy of the report, fast. The

Singapore consultants won't know that you've been sacked yet so all you have to do is fly over and ask for a copy. And they're not going to refuse the guy who commissioned the inspection in the first place. You already had the air tickets when you rang Coates' doorbell, is my guess.'

'Only you never intended that the report see light of day,' I said. 'What you intended was that Diamond Covault would pay a fortune to get it back and that if they came after the extorter all the evidence would point to Jeremy Coates as the sole player. And you'd make sure that Coates never told his side of the story.'

'Speculation,' Barclay said.

I looked at Harry. Turned to watch the view again.

'Reality, Barclay. We've evidence – circumstantial and material – for everything. And the police have most of it. They're just missing the paper trail we found here, and they'll soon have that. You'll be up for embezzlement as well as the fraud against company investors. But the police are not your problem.'

I watched the puzzlement that had come back into Barclay's face. He couldn't imagine a problem worse than the mess he was in, the fact that whether the company survived or not, whether they buried his extortion racket or not, that he was out of the life. By the time this was over he'd be looking for a bed-sit in Barking unless he could hang on to the twenty million he'd stashed in his overseas accounts. But he wasn't seeing the real trouble.

That stash was going to kill him.

'Johnny Lad wants the money,' I said.

Barclay looked at me.

'He knows you have it,' I said. 'When I told Peter Covault that you were the guy extorting his company he was confident I was wrong, because he'd checked you out and you were squeaky clean. But you weren't squeaky clean. So the question was: who'd done the checking out? Only one possibility: Johnny Lad had given you the clean bill of health. Now why would he do that?'

Harry grinned. Fastened his jacket against the breeze.

'Lad confirmed that you were the guy,' he said. 'And there's only one reason he'd hide it from Covault.'

'He wanted the thing to blow over,' I said. 'He wanted the company go through with its floatation and write off the extortion payoff as loose change. Then he was going to come after you and squeeze you until you handed over the cash. He'd choose a time and place where he'd have your attention for as long as it took. And he *would* persuade you, Barclay. And he'd make it an unpleasant enough experience that you'd never talk about it afterwards.'

Barclay's face was as tight as a drum.

'But now we've a change of plan,' I said. 'Johnny Lad has got himself into the firing line. So he's got to run. Go for bail and disappear before he gets to court on the Sam Barker murder charge. But he'll come after you for the cash as he originally intended, only with higher stakes. Because if they ever catch up with him and do drag him to court you'd be a key witness. So now he needs you to disappear. For good.'

Barclay looked at his feet. The logic had finally sunk in. He seemed to collapse inside. He turned and walked to a seat and took the weight off his legs whilst he fought a losing battle to persuade himself that he still had a life.

'You need to give us everything now,' I said. 'You need the police to have enough on Johnny Lad to ensure that bail is refused whilst they progress their enquiry. Hit him now and Johnny will never get loose to come looking for you. Clam up and you'll find yourself somewhere alone with him one day.'

Barclay sat forward. Stared at his clasped hands. Sought solutions that weren't there. Pictured himself with Johnny Lad.

'Of course I scammed the company,' he said. 'But I didn't kill Jeremy Coates.'

'I know,' I said.

The ambulance siren started up again down below. The racket stopped Barclay as he started to speak, and he shrank into the din, flinched from the harsh intrusion of a new world. He waited until the noise died before he opened his mouth again.

'Shit,' he said.

CHAPTER FIFTY
Blind eye

The river walk was teeming with people out grabbing the sun. Herbie and I moved slowly up towards Tower Bridge, watching faces. Backpackers, courting couples, weekend trippers. The pace was dictated by Herbie's explorations. Back in his old life, wandering the streets with a homeless guy called William, he'd probably covered a good percentage of the twenty-five thousand streets that gets you the Knowledge. His lifestyle was different now but his mission was the same.

Canines have it good. They keep their nose to the ground and concentrate on the here and now. If it's not threatening it's not there. People aren't that smart.

But the sun on your head, voices and colour, the river glittering – what's not to feel good about?

'Hey?' I asked Herbie. 'What's not?'

Herbie looked up. His grin answered.

We arrived at a waterside bistro with multi-level decking. Twenty outside tables with cloths and folded umbrellas. We went up and found Avril Covault watching the world from behind a pair of sunglasses. When she saw us she pulled them off with a speed that conveyed a desire to reconnect. She signalled to a passing waiter. Raised her eyebrows to me. I shook my head. I'd had coffee. Herbie snuffled across and she bent to pat him.

I sat. Watched Avril's brilliant smile across the table. Could see that the smile took effort.

'I'm glad you came,' she said.

My phone had rung ten times yesterday evening. I'd resisted picking up until I'd got things straight.

'I'm going to keep saying this,' Avril said. She leaned in. The smile had gone. 'I'm sorry, Eddie. More than you could imagine. What I did was unforgivable.'

I watched her, trying to work out how Avril's face was different from Kim's. There was something I couldn't pin down.

'Why our firm?' I said.

'Johnny had a bee in his bonnet. He'd heard you were the best and we needed the best. We'd slipped up and the extorter had got clean away.'

'You didn't have to find the extorter. Why not just write off the loss?'

Avril paused.

'It's not my father's character,' she said. 'He's never been beaten at anything in his life. The cash was small change but the knowledge that he'd been ripped off wasn't. He had to come out on top. And there was the risk that there were copies of the document out there. Johnny convinced him that the extorter would have an insurance scheme, that the report would surface down the line. The Singapore liabilities were going to come out, of course. That wasn't the problem. The problem was a report that pre-dated the floatation.'

'Which would be fraud,' I said.

'Fraud is a strong word. We'd costed-in the liabilities. The share price would have taken a hit when we revealed the problems but the investors were still getting a great deal. In ten years we'd be paying our shareholders fifteen percent and their stock would have doubled in price. But we needed the floatation cash to enable our plans. Which now included the Singapore rebuilding.'

Which still sounded like fraud to me. When the bad news came out the punters would take a hit and rhetoric about a rosy future just wouldn't cover it.

I looked down the river. The face of the Covault Complex was a blinding beacon three miles away beyond the Canary Wharf buildings. I watched it as I spoke.

'When we turned down Lad's dirty work someone should have educated him that the refusal meant we weren't the right people for the job. Coercing us was stupid.'

'I tried to convince Johnny to go elsewhere.'

'Was that before or after you posed for his threat photos?'

I looked back at her. She took a moment to find the words.

'Before,' she said.

I went back to watching the river. Grinned. She broke the silence.

'Johnny was convinced you just needed a prod, and better to fake a threat against me than use a real one. He didn't know the other women. They were bluff. There was no real threat. We just went out and I walked over to talk to a child and make it look like she was mine and Johnny snapped away. The child's mother was right there, just out of the frame. But I thought that coercing you was a bad idea.'

'And when we turned Lad down a second time? I guess that's when he went for the personal touch, the face-to-face. And again, after we'd located Sam and were looking for Lad he told you to get closer still. I guess that was a bad idea too.'

Avril watched me. She hadn't touched her drink since I'd arrived.

'I'm sorry, Eddie. I should have stopped it. But Johnny convinced us that you were a threat. That things might get out of hand very quickly.'

'Did he tell you exactly *how* close to get?'

She leaned across. Touched my hand. 'What happened between you and me was genuine, Eddie. You're angry and shocked, but you know it was real. For me it was a revelation. I've been cocooned in my father's world my whole life. Meeting you gave me a glimpse into an alternative. One where ethics and people matter. There was nothing fake about me falling for you.'

She sat back again. 'Shit!' she said. 'I cried myself to sleep last night wondering how I could make this right.'

'You can't. You still inhabit your father's world. The company is still your life. I hear you're the biggest player in their overseas expansion nowadays. Have an office the size of a tennis court over there. Word is that you're slated to take over the whole thing. That's going to be tricky with ethics and people tying you up.'

Avril followed my gaze down river. Maybe she could see her office. Or maybe she just saw the blinding reflection.

'You're right,' she said. 'The company is a monster, fuelled by ambition and power. Misguided sometimes. Sometimes ruthless. It's easy to lose touch. But I love that world, so I'm not about to act the innocent damsel. But neither am I the woman I was two weeks ago. For the first time I've wondered whether I might do without that world, or at least take a different approach. You opened my eyes, Eddie.' She looked back at me.

'True love,' I said. I tapped the table with my fingers and grinned at her, though I wasn't feeling too merry. 'Romance makes fools of us all.'

'I need you to know that this is real for me, Eddie. Too real to abandon.'

I held the grin.

'Tell me,' I said, 'how did you think it would go when you had to spill the beans that I couldn't meet little Alice, that Kim Waters didn't exist?'

'Kim Waters still does exist!'

'Humour me.'

She thought about it.

'In truth: I was scared to death,' she said. 'I just had to convince myself that you'd forgive me. That we'd both pick ourselves up and find a way forward. But I don't know whether I really believed it was possible.'

I dropped the grin and leaned across.

'The real trouble was that once the dust settled you were going to have more on your mind than romance. Finding a way forward together would need to start with me keeping quiet about everything I knew, which was not going to happen. And your real focus would be dealing with the fall-out if the report did hit the streets, which it's now about to do. Those were always going to be your real issues.'

'We're releasing a statement on Monday. The floatation is postponed. But the company will survive.'

'What about Sam Barker and Jeremy Coates? They didn't survive. Are they just collateral in your corporate games?'

I watched her but she'd broken eye contact. Turned back to the river. The glint in her eyes might have been tears.

'I can't deny anything,' she said. 'My father neither. He's depended on Johnny Lad for too long. They've been associates since our first Singapore development. And we knew Johnny was ruthless. We just turned a blind eye.'

'Not so blind. You were still playing Lad's game after Sam Barker's body was found. You knew who'd killed him. And when Jeremy Coates disappeared you must have had your suspicions.'

'Johnny was a lone wolf. We knew only what he wanted us to know. But he was losing control on this one. So there was a...' she thought about it '...lapse of judgement. We should have stopped him. Let everything fall as it would. But my father kept hoping against hope that things would clear up, that we'd never need to know the detail. Johnny was history, though. Once the affair blew over we were going to say goodbye. He'd never work for the company again.'

'Did you know it was Barclay extorting you?'

She shook her head.

'We should have listened when you told us that. But Johnny checked him out and said you were wrong. He put Barclay in the clear. Now we know different I can't say I'm surprised. Barclay's a spoilt, lazy brat. He came with the package when my father married Jane. We all knew he'd do something stupid sooner or later.'

'He probably believed the same himself. And then he saw his opportunity when Coates was fired, persuaded him to cooperate in ripping the company off. Though I guess you'd never have credited him with being ruthless enough to kill Coates to keep all the cash for himself.'

Avril's mouth opened.

'Did he do that?'

'Would you believe it?'

She thought about it. Nodded her head. Sadness in her face.

'Yes,' she said. 'Now I do.'

I watched her for a moment then pulled a print from inside my jacket and slid it across the table.

She looked at it. Grasped what she was seeing. When she looked up this time there was the shine of fear in her eyes.

'Barclay didn't kill Coates,' I said. 'The day of the murder Barclay was at his golf club. That's the club's parking area in the snap. And that's Johnny Lad climbing into the Isuzu. He borrowed it for four or five hours to go and pick Jeremy up in Bexhill. He lured him out somehow – probably just parked the Isuzu outside the apartment and rang the doorbell – and by the time Jeremy realised that the driver wasn't Barclay, Lad's people had pounced and bundled him into the vehicle. Using the Isuzu was a plus all round. The first plus was that Jeremy dropped his guard when he saw it. Assumed it was Barclay come to talk to him. The second was that the high bed and cab roof facilitated Lad's task of lifting Barclay over into the tunnel airshaft once he'd interrogated him. And the third plus was that if Coates' body was ever found and anything traced back to the vehicle then Barclay would be the perfect suspect for the killing.'

Avril was watching me.

'We picked up the CCTV from the club. It's timed a few hours before Jeremy Coates' estimated time of death. But here's the thing: when you look at the video you see Lad simply walk up to the vehicle and drive away. He's either the world's best car thief or he had keys.'

I smiled. Avril didn't.

'Barclay told us everything yesterday. But he didn't know anything about Coates' death. And he quoted his day at the club as his alibi. But then we talked to his girlfriend and she remembered something.

'Apparently after Barclay had gone out that day she had a visitor. One who had the key to the penthouse floor and was surprised to find anyone home. But the visitor gave an excuse for calling and stopped for a quick chat and almost certainly, during that time, picked up the spare keys for the Isuzu.'

Avril shook her head. Just once. Barely perceptible. She saw it all.

'Not so much a blind eye,' I said, 'as a helping hand. You knew exactly what would happen to Jeremy Coates once Lad picked him up. But Johnny had persuaded you that Coates was a risk. He needed to find out from him whether there was anyone else involved and whether there was another copy of the document out there. Lad told you that Coates wouldn't be hurt but you knew that was a lie. And acquiring the pickup keys for him makes you an accomplice to murder.'

Avril's eyes glittered. Searched for something that wasn't there.

'That's why I came here this morning,' I said. 'I wanted you to know before the police come to see you. Call it a courtesy.'

I stood and whistled for Herbie.

'Jesus, Eddie,' Avril said. She spoke softly. 'The whole thing just blew up in our faces. Is there no way we can work this out?'

She looked up at me but saw emptiness.

I whistled again. Herbie came out and moved towards the steps. I nodded at Avril.

'Take care,' I said.

I turned and left.

CHAPTER FIFTY-ONE
The fundamental rule

I stopped off at Connie's for two takeaway coffees and took them into the building.

The light was on behind the glass and the sign was turned, and Shaughnessy and Harry were in my office with Yvonne Barker. She was sitting uncomfortably in one of my visitors' chairs. Harry was perched on the arm of the other. Shaughnessy was tapping the barometer glass.

I handed Yvonne a coffee. Checked with the others. Shaughnessy was fine. Harry had tea brewing.

I planted my own brew and brought milk and sugar. Yvonne was smiling for the first time since I'd met her. Not exactly joy. Just the reaction to being in a comfortable place even if the club chair wasn't contributing. She stirred her drink with purpose.

'I thought I'd be in there a week,' she said.

I sat and racked the Miller back to a comfortable drinking angle. I'd spent half the weekend in Bromley myself answering Keith Prior's questions. Forwards, backwards, sideways. He didn't tell me everything *he* had but I sensed it was solid enough to quash any notion Lad might have about bail.

The outer door opened and Lucy came in. She was carrying newspapers.

'They've already got the story,' she announced.

She held the papers up. Two of the serious dailies. The story wasn't the main headline in either but it was front page. A police investigation was ongoing into shenanigans related to Diamond Covault. Rumours of criminal activities. An unexplained death. The police were being cagey, leaving the journalists to embellish with their own findings. Rumours of bad financial news that the company had been hiding. Rumours of infighting. Rumours of an upcoming investor statement.

'Their floatation's a dead duck,' Lucy said. She perched herself on my desk. If Lucy wrote front pages they'd save ink. 'But we got the guy who killed Sam.' She was looking at Yvonne.

Shaughnessy gave the barometer a final tap. He'd dropped the needle a full half inch. He adjusted the marker and turned.

'Yvonne tells us they've charged Lad with both killings,' he said.

'Prior updated me last night,' she confirmed. 'They've got traces from Sam's car and jacket that link Lad to his death. Enough to hold him in custody whilst they gather forensics for Coates. Add in the circumstantial evidence and the redacted version of events the Covaults' lawyers will script and they'll have motive and opportunity, all pointing to Lad.'

She gripped her cup.

'So this one's a plus,' Shaughnessy said. He walked over to lean an elbow on my mantelpiece beneath the Bogart poster. 'We got our man. Hardly touched his cash.'

I grinned. We'd bank most of Lad's fee even after Bernie Locke's bill came in. Not that we'd be keeping it. Yvonne Barker could decide where the money went that helped kill her brother. Though whichever way Yvonne spent it she wasn't looking at a plus. Sam's office in Streatham would already be up for rent and Yvonne would be riding a hearse later in the week. But we'd got the guy responsible, and maybe the people behind him, unless the lawyers worked a miracle. Yvonne caught my eye. Still smiling but it was a sad smile. She shrugged her shoulders.

'He screwed up,' she said.

Sam.

Shaughnessy agreed. 'Dead drops,' he said. 'They should be foolproof.'

And that was the bottom line: the harsh truth that Sam was dead because he screwed up.

Harry went out to fetch his tea and a digestive. Sat back down. Dunked.

'It was a good scheme,' he said. 'Barclay knew Covault wouldn't stump up the cash before he had his document back so they did it in instalments. Four deliveries, four payments. Each quarter payment got a quarter of the document. Four cash transfers to Barclay's offshore accounts followed by four deliveries. And Sam's job was to run the exchange.'

'Sam found four hotels with room safes,' Yvonne said. 'Then rented them under a false name and put the document parts in the safes. Once Barclay confirmed each payment Sam gave him the location of a dead drop where the receiving party could pick up the associated hotel address and room key along with where to find the safe code. Sam didn't give me details but we know he left the last code in the Gideon Bible.'

'All watertight,' Harry said. 'The guy leaving the documents is long gone before the recipient is given the dead drop location where he can pick up the hotel details and key. Watertight. As long as you stick to the fundamental rule.'

'Never go back,' I said.

Yvonne's face showed regret. 'Sam knew better,' she said.

'Sure,' I said. 'When Lad tried to lure him back to the BestBreak he sensed a trap. But Barclay insisted he go.'

Shaughnessy walked across to watch the sky. An endless grey blanket. Springtime on hold. He turned.

'My guess,' he said: 'Lad contacted Barclay during the last instalment and told him that the safe code didn't work.'

I planted my coffee.

'Barclay was waiting for confirmation that the last delivery had been received and that the thing was over,' I said. 'But then Lad messaged him to say that the safe code didn't work. And Barclay couldn't take the risk that Covault really *hadn't* received his delivery because he knew that it would mean the thing wasn't over. Covault would have no choice but to come looking for him. So he told Sam to go back. Check he'd not entered a bad code when he left the document. Sam must have smelled a rat. Instinct told him to trust his own competence, but Barclay was insistent, threatened to release Sam's name to the extorted party. He pressured Sam and Sam gave in.'

'Mistake,' Harry said.

'He'd be looking over his shoulder the whole time,' Shaughnessy said. 'Planned on a quick in-out. Sixty seconds in the room then gone. But Lad had set things up to slow him down. He'd taken the document and then reset the safe code to keep Sam busy for a couple of minutes.'

'That's why the Gideon code didn't open the safe,' I said. 'It took me thirty seconds to realise that the code was useless then another sixty to get the safe open without it. Same for Sam. Except that time ran out and he heard Lad coming in. Opted for that dive out of the window.'

Harry reached to grip Yvonne's shoulder. 'Sam knew it. If you go back you're walking into a trap. Because the only reason you're tempted back is that the enemy has set it up that way.'

We thought about it for a moment.

'The only consolation is that Lad will be off the streets,' I said.

'What happened with Coates?' Yvonne asked. 'Why was he hiding?'

'Because Barclay was scamming him. He'd convinced Coates that they were obtaining the document to make it public, to stop the floatation fraud. But once Coates arrived back in London with the document Barclay spun some bad news – about the company reacting badly, about lawyers and bailiffs out in Singapore. He persuaded Coates that he needed to stay out of sight until the document had become public and the company were tied up with their Singapore problem and the floatation fraud and lost interest in him. So Coates disappeared to Bexhill. But Barclay's plan was always the extortion, for which he needed to keep Coates out of sight until the exchange was over, then have him disappear permanently and take the blame. His plan was to spin Coates a story that the company was playing hard but offering a carrot – a buy-off if the report was buried. Coates could either face a legal fight, maybe end up in a Singapore jail, or disappear with a million quid. Barclay had a Barbados rental ready to go and a million pounds to transfer. But when he tried to contact Coates to kick off the final part of his scam he couldn't. Because Lad had already found him. He'd probably followed Barclay on one of his trips to Bexhill.'

'How did he know that Barclay was involved?' Lucy asked.

I grinned. That one was not Avril. She'd given Lad everything I'd given her but Lad had already uncovered Barclay. Barclay's own theory, during our penthouse chat, was that he'd been caught answering the phone Sam had given him for the exchange scheme. Lad had kept Sam's own phone after he killed him and called the extorter for no other reason than to apply pressure. Got lucky when he spotted Barclay picking up. They were already assuming that Coates was in on the extortion but now Lad knew that Barclay was behind it.

'But Sam had discovered Coates too,' Lucy said. 'That note in his office said he was looking at him.'

Something we'd puzzled over. What put Sam on to Coates? We got that answer too from my chat with Barclay. He'd been in shock on Friday, which meant he talked too much. Maybe things felt easier once everything was off his chest.

'Barclay gave Coates away,' I said. 'It was part of his plan to point to Coates as the extorter. Coates was already the obvious suspect since he was the one who'd brought the document back from Singapore, but Barclay needed Covault to be sure, so that he'd not be searching elsewhere once Coates had disappeared. So Barclay left a pointer in the last delivery. He left a phoney return slip for an online purchase in the package, as if it had got in by accident. The slip had Coates' name and address. Pretty crude, but the ploy might have fooled them – Lad included – if Barclay hadn't picked up the phone when Lad called the extorter's number.'

'And then there was Avril Covault right at the centre,' Lucy said. 'Feeding everything back to Covault.'

'Back to Johnny Lad, to be more accurate,' I said. 'The bunch of them were in panic mode once the fire started to spread. So she was assigned to keep an eye on me and perhaps dissuade me from searching for Sam's killer. And she was good. Played the Damsel in Distress to a tee. Showed that Foxglove was right behind her. That graffiti in her house was effective. But her main job was to report everything I found so that Lad knew every step we took. Only I didn't tell Avril everything. And what I didn't tell her turned out to be crucial.'

'You told us she was a nice girl,' Lucy said.

I grinned.

'A bad call.'

'Maybe just the circumstances... You liked her, Eddie.'

'I liked her a lot. But circumstances aren't an excuse. You don't work with the bad guys by chance. When you know that problems are being solved that shouldn't be solved then you're complicit. "See no evil" doesn't cut it.'

'So she's not such a good guy,' Lucy said. 'Can't make it any easier for you, seeing her thrown to the wolves.'

I grinned. Planted my empty cup.

It wasn't easy. But then Sam Barker and Jeremy Coates hadn't found it easy at the end.

See no evil.

One of the privileges of power.

I wondered what Avril would be seeing today as she stared from her window up on the thirty-fifth floor of the Covault Complex, waiting for Prior. I looked past Shaughnessy, out through my own window.

Endless grey.

There'd be the same view at Bow Creek.

I flicked the lever. Brought the chair upright and stood. Everyone followed suit. Yvonne shook hands and thanked us for everything, which wasn't much, and said she'd see us. She walked out and the party broke up.

I sat back down in the empty room and swivelled the chair and stretched towards my Post-it stack.

Call-backs waiting.

THE END

ACKNOWLEDGEMENTS

Thanks to the home team here in Cumbria for their assistance in catching up after a delayed start.

My wife, Odette, checked the early draft and found a few weaknesses that threatened to give the game away to the astute reader. I've corrected these wherever I could but almost all mystery stories that don't cheat via a contrived *deus ex machina* or unexpected intervention by little green men will be guessable by the smartest. And I don't claim to be a Robert Goddard or Gregg Hurwitz: my stories are primarily private investigator action, not mystery. I just like to put in enough of the latter to keep the reader intrigued and, crucially, to ensure that the detective is caught flat-footed sooner or later, which, of course, we're all waiting for.

Support from behind the study sofa has been provided by our rescue collie-cross, Tim, who acts much as those factory whistles to announce tea breaks, whilst general security has been covered by our younger and more energetic collie rescue Lola, who's main job is to scare away any postman bringing royalty cheques.

We do our proofreading in-house, and it's only via the direct experience of trying to spot every typo in a read-through of 100,000 words that an appreciation can be gained of just how difficult the task is. That's why mainstream publishers pay professional proofreaders. That's why mainstream publishers have typos in their books. So, as always, please ignore the odd error. If books were perfect there would be fewer of them.

Michael Donovan.

Cumbria, December 2019

BEHIND CLOSED DOORS
Michael Donovan

Family feuds, booze and bad company. Teenager Rebecca Slater's walk on the wild side has taken a downward spiral. And now she's disappeared.

But her family don't seem to have noticed. Wealthy, private, dysfunctional, the Slaters deny that their daughter is missing – even as they block all attempts by Rebecca's friends to contact her.

So the friends contact a private investigator.

Eddie Flynn is good at finding people. And he's good at spotting lies. It doesn't take him long to see through the Slaters' denials. So he digs around, and isn't too surprised when some unpleasant people come scuttling out of the cracks in the Slaters' perfect world.

But for these people the teenager's disappearance is part of a plan. One that's too important to be threatened by an investigator with more persistence than sense. So it's time for the investigator to disappear...

Winner of the **Northern Crime 2012** award, *Behind Closed Doors* has been acclaimed for its departure from the norm for British crime fiction...

'Donovan refreshingly breaks [the tradition] with remarkable success'
Cuckoo Review

'Eddie Flynn is part Philip Marlowe, part Eddie Gumshoe, a likeable wisecracking guy but with a temper when roused ... humour ... violent confrontations ... well recommended.'
eurocrime

www.michaeldonovancrime.com

THE DEVIL'S SNARE
Michael Donovan

They call them the "Killer Couple". Accused of killing their daughter the Barbers have been on the run from public opinion for two years.

But the Barbers are still fighting. And if their high profile campaign to clear their name and get their baby back has made them rich that was never their intention.

Meanwhile a failed prosecution hasn't dampened the media's hunger for revelations. Their investigators are on the job, moving towards an exposure that will spotlight the Barbers as the killers they are. And now a dangerous vigilante has joined the fray: if the system can't bring justice he'll mete out his own.

P.I. Eddie Flynn doesn't read the tabloids. Shuns limelight. Trusts only in facts. But can't resist challenges. When the Barbers come to him for help he pushes judgement aside and signs up. His mission: keep them safe and find their child.

Sounds like nice, solid detective work. Until Flynn realises that his clients are hiding something...

'A slick, dynamic mystery.'
Kirkus Reviews

'Escapism at its best'
Postcard Reviews

'... complicated ... wonderful ... brilliant. I recommend anyone ... to try this book. [It] will haunt your days and nights.'
Georgia Cuthbertson, Cuckoo Review

www.michaeldonovancrime.com

COLD CALL
Michael Donovan

In the black of night the intruder breaks into the victim's house armed with a knife and garrotte. Her body is found thirty hours later, a mass of stab wounds, a deadly laceration round her neck.

Is this the Diceman, killing again after seven years lying low? Or does London have a copycat killer?

P.I. Eddie Flynn has been out of that world since his failed hunt for the Diceman let the killer go free and cost him his job in the Metropolitan Police.

Now, with the new killer on the rampage a bizarre phone call from his dead victim drags Flynn right back to centre stage and a new hunt. But this killer – copycat or not – takes a P.I.'s interference personally.

So now he has a new focus for his madness.

"Chilling ... crafted with style...
wild nightmarish scenes."
Bookpleasures

"Masterful... If you haven't been
introduced to Eddie Flynn yet, be prepared"
Red City Review

www.michaeldonovancrime.com

SLOW LIGHT
Michael Donovan

Waiting waiting waiting waiting waiting waiting waiting waiting waiting waiting waiting waiting waiting.

Waiting waiting waiting waiting waiting waiting waiting waiting waiting waiting waiting waiting waiting.

Waiting waiting waiting waiting waiting waiting waiting waiting waiting waiting waiting waiting waiting.

Waiting waiting waiting waiting waiting waiting waiting waiting waiting waiting waiting waiting waiting.

Waiting waiting waiting waiting waiting waiting waiting waiting waiting waiting waiting waiting waiting.

"Waiting waiting"
Review Source

"Waiting waiting"
Review Source

www.michaeldonovancrime.com

Printed in Great Britain
by Amazon